Soul in Passage

Shadows and Whispers from a Sane and
Insane Boyhood

A NOVEL BY
John W Spencer

"Soul in Passage," by John Spencer. ISBN 978-1-949756-03-6 (softcover); 978-1-949756-04-3 (eBook).

Published 2018 by Virtualbookworm.com Publishing Inc., P.O. Box 9949, College Station, TX 77842, US. ©2018, John Spencer.

Acknowledgements

I wish to recognize Cynthia Hayes, Celeste Kampe, Susan Keehn, Pat-Yee Spencer, and Deborah Young, who read and gave useful comments to earlier versions of this manuscript. A special thanks to Dr. John Huer, who first encouraged me to begin writing years ago.

Foreword

THE REMEMBRANCES OF A BOYHOOD were always in his head, given permanent residence and allowed to stay for so many untold reasons. They swirled around in a mind catapulting through numerous layers and boundaries of a reality hoped for, where dreams danced and told tantalizing stories, some quite exciting and relevant, others just plain stupid.

Life journeys were "peeled back" and a growing cycle exposed where events happened; sometimes for the better, sometimes for the worse, but never willfully discarded as irrelevant. Sane or insane voices resonated from far-away places where a gang of friends of long ago had much to discuss about their successes, failures, chaos, and other things too terrible to imagine. A human spirit appeared at the edges of sensibility and sought to reconcile and imbalance guilt within a maturing conscience, a conscience that needed and demanded such delicate workmanship.

And God, must not HE also be available in some dimension—protecting, supporting, but also never completely understood, a distant friend on uncertain terms where there was a searching but no complete discovery, no connection? Angels smiled, or at times frowned, and then became frustrated with one boy's immaturity and confusion about God. But was he really to blame? The kid never said he fully understood life, its fairness or lack thereof, and certainly not its unpredictability. How can anyone understand all or any part of the elements of elan vital? He was certain of a potential to be loved and cared for, a purpose for existence—God and circumstances dictated that, didn't they? His church taught these truths, so they must be self-evident!

It was the 1950s and Elm City, Indiana, was Zachary Stevens' home town. Businessmen, farmers, professionals, students, and many others lived there and made up its core, its very being. The two private colleges and the schools for the deaf and blind, a large hospital for the insane, a factory that made Ferris wheels and another one that stitched jeans and suit coats, all exemplified a proud diversity. And of course, God was never to be ignored! There was a church on each of the four corners of a city block. Town folk, stand up and take bragging rights! No other place on earth had such a "religious" configuration, an honor to God, as delivered by the residents of Elm City, Indiana.

The buildings on the city square, all planted so firmly, included one with lookout and protection vantage from its seven stories! The town's people felt safe and were able to conduct serious business as they called out for attention with their own attitudes and their own special and persuasive innocence. They saw so much, experienced deep feelings, and said so little.

But now it is time to tell a story about many things and many people. In one theatre of life, a partially tattered curtain goes up, and scene one begins. There is an air of excitement. Slowly, ever so slowly, and with the slightest of ease, without much noise or fanfare, drapes shuffle, move, and reveal more stage, more of a breathless surround. Lights are dimmed, characters come into view, and they ready themselves for movement and action. Consciences and minds are to be opened, dissected and examined. Words of joy and sorrow, which have escaped from yesterday, are now on front-center stage. They are ready to be spoken once again. Zachary Stevens anxiously waits.

Contents

"*My dear girl, we can't turn back the days that have gone. We can't turn back to the hours when our lungs were sound, our blood hot, our bodies young. We are a flash of fire–a brain, a heart, a spirit. And we are three-cents-worth of lime and iron–which we cannot get back.*"

—Thomas Wolfe, *Look Homeward Angel*

"*Don't you wish you could take a single childhood memory and blow it up into a bubble and live inside it forever?*"

— Sarah Addison Allen, *Lost Lake*

One:
The Robbery of Fred Duncan

A vicious attack on an old crippled man,
An unwitting bystander, A partially failed plan,
A robbery disrupts long-held friendships and sanity,
A boy's conscience appears with indecision and no clarity

THE PARTIALLY LEADEN CLOUDS refused to stop circling but increased in speed, moved as a constant vortex, and produced a noise that was shrill and unconscionable. Layers of some type of membrane(s) displayed ill-conceived objects, heads or skulls and other partially discombobulated bodies that were arranged in a circular pew-like order. They appeared more than willing or able to greet a most sly but naïve "visitor," judging by their roar of approval and the shaking of their mutilated and torn hands and fingers. "Go ahead and become successful," the voices shouted out. "You have our permission, you have been selected to represent us; do so, well!" There was much tumultuousness, screaming, and putrid smells; most unusual was an all-consuming, never-ending disruption of any semblance of gravity or balance by an unseen force that moved everything up, then down, and around and around—a roller coaster ride with no opportunity for exit. Then, and quite suddenly, another static force moved a body through dimensions not demarcated or locked into any time constraint. Dazed, Carl Stewart awoke in bed, wet in sweat, dry in mouth, exhausted but excited from execrable dreams that gave phony purpose and resolve.

For reasons unclear at the time, an initial clattering noise, perhaps a partially stuck valve in the Elm City bus's engine, was not heard by gabbing passengers. Later, a more piercing sound developed, as if some part of the motor had become incapacitated, slightly smashed or even split open. This racket was now made available to everyone including the driver, who suddenly realized his bus, now disengaged and dead, was completely unable to respond to any commands, no matter seniority or intensity of yelling!

Inside the bus, it became apparent there was an air of tension and spurious angst. One thoughtful lady shouted out, "Thank God at least we didn't turn over," and in resounding unison the rest of the frightened passengers collectively yelled back, "Amen."

The driver, Bob Avery, turned cautiously in his seat while he attempted to keep white hair out of his face and very small spectacles on a bulbous nose. This day the ruddiness of his entire face seemed even more noticeable—blood vessels and arteries in his neck became pronounced, and a strong, pounding pulse appeared ready to explode.

A fat belly with generous overhang at the waist did little to disguise terrible eating habits and futile exercise. Sweat poured from his face and neck, and a grey shirt reflected circular spots of wetness under his arms and back. Large nicotine-stained fingers shook and temporarily appeared unable to function, to grab or to hold anything. He sat precipitously, almost out of his seat, knees bent, body partially twisted; an accurate and fair analysis of this preposterous scene would be that of a man in partial shock, a complete wreck, just as the bus.

For a group of innocent bus passengers, frustration, anger, and just plain naiveté rose and became a mix and part of a frustrating journey. One rider, a scrawny kid with orthodontic work, was to soon face a testing of life-changing proportions. He would see and learn about the darker side of human nature. The way he responded charted and played a role in the development of his conscience and added to the many twists and turns of a journey toward adulthood.

In another part of town, a skinny guy by the name of Carl Stewart, one who bore a face heavily endowed with acne scars, went over a very secret but organized plan for the commissioning of a robbery. It was not very complicated. A grocery store had previously been "cased" several times and accurate mental notes made of surroundings and potential customers. The owner of the store, a fragile man, would never put up a fight or cause problems because if he did, there would be serious consequences, physical action taken.

And today was the best shot at hitting the jackpot because, in preparation for the weekend, there was money in the cash register. More questions now needed to be asked: Did he have a good cover for his face? Yes. Was the car gassed up and the license plate covered up? Yes. Was he confident? Yes. There were to be no slip-ups or mistakes. His heart beat fast, but that was okay—the exhilaration felt from head to toe was rewarding enough while the adventurous spirit inside his mind stood at attention, ready for further commands.

A personal conversation with his bladder had been made. Often, when he became excited, there was an urge to pee. Control of bodily functions must be maintained and strict orders given to an organ that needed to listen, and then stay quiet.

The trip to town this day would be nothing more than a ruse. He had easily deceived his family, because they thought he was to go to Elm City to replace a broken carburetor for the farm tractor and expected him back no later than noon.

But really! What a house of fools! There was a depressed mother who drank Jim Beam whiskey after breakfast; a mean, useless stepfather who was an alcoholic and did as little work as possible. He was generally passed out in another world by lunchtime. And then there was a sister who was never at home, always out with men, single or married, which led her mother to declare, "Her boyfriends outnumbered the stars in the sky."

She was a problem for Carl. A well-shaped body never covered by much dress and an attractive, scintillating face allowed for pernicious thoughts to percolate and hang around in a scurrilous mind—ones not to be shared with others. He had never sexually "been with a girl," but his own sister? Lately, he had to exercise even stronger self-control without much cooperation on her part. *Orders to self: Stay focused and think only about the money soon to be yours, and then a jettison out of a hell-hole. A family of losers would then see one of their own become a fully consecrated winner.*

The bright sun, a strong breeze, a sundry of smells from fields of corn and alfalfa, along with an inner voice that said, with a supportive tone, *'relax and take your time, you are cool and in control'* helped to ease tension. Duncan's Market came into sight, and several people could be seen entering or leaving. The kid drove around the block twice, produced a belch and recovered the taste of cereal eaten hours before, quickly reminding him of his noxious habit of not chewing food. The car, now parked and hidden behind some trees, sat unnoticed but ready to be driven away when so commanded. He waited and

4

thought, farted, and then had a quick drink of his mother's whiskey. It would not be long now; showtime was rapidly approaching. Who was he kidding? Defeatist thoughts permeated his brain and reminded him of the consequences of screwing everything up. *'Deep breath, Carl, now relax!'* Of no use, the kid was scared shitless.

The broken-down bus sat as if it was dead, no discernible movement. Bob Avery was pissed! He cussed as he pulled a black toggle switch with his left forefinger, which opened a rather lame front door. Whoosh went the air pressure as the sections of the door sandwiched open. The steering wheel then received furious beatings with no mercy while the passengers were told to get out and wait under a grove of trees. A comical scene continued to unfold, with more than just a hint of incredulousness.

A well-worn and somewhat defeated bus driver limped or retreated out of the bus to a large white-frame house with a wrap-around porch which needed a re-paint job. His plan was to make a phone call to the bus company for help. It might be suggested that for Bob's sanity, his wife might show up in the family car and rescue him from an embarrassing circumstance, a total failure of man and machine. Hardly likely!

A forehead was wiped and a curious thought given: *maybe it would be better served if the bus was just blown up.* He briefly had a fleeting fantasy about flying high and far beyond elm trees, now bending to and fro in a strong breeze. A quick and permanent disappearance from everything was truly needed. Cars went by and people waved and laughed. No one stopped. Why should they? Everything was under control.

Four very disgruntled, angry, lost adult souls, plus a younger boy with curly blond hair, stumbled from the vehicle. First up, a rather large lady with a big black hat cocked half-heartedly on a large, cylindrical-looking head. "I've ridden this bus for five years and have never had anything like this happen," she recounted. Her heavily made-up face, full of sweat and certainly not peaceful, was placated with blanched rouge in need of a massive tune-up. The fat around her arms, legs, and ankles proudly expressed itself as mashed skin, wrinkled and hardly captivating. She was overweight, no obese, likely from eating too much candy and sweets. Her dress was chartreuse in color with a nondescript design of circles and lines. It fit tight and appeared at times to stretch, begging for freedom from a hulking frame. Uneven and slightly discolored teeth, uncomfortably perched in a very small mouth, consistently ground in unison when she became tense and nervous. They were sharp as knives and always readied themselves to attack the nearest prey when called upon. The large cane in her hand, used to aid in walking, was no doubt another useful and potential weapon. People who might stare at her face would swear that one of her eyes was fake, a "glass eye," but of course they also refrained from making any opinions known. As she waddled through the open doors with some difficulty, the bus breathed a huge sigh of relief.

The woman was simply obnoxious! Her complaints had flown around the inside of the bus, and then become stuck somewhere, indefinitely suspended in time. "They should take better care of these buses and check them out to make sure they run properly. This could not have happened at a worse time; it is hot as hell, and I can't seem to stop sweating," she remorsefully replied. No one listened. No one much cared what she said.

After leaving the bus, she took small steps followed by brief rests. More steps, and then she sat down on the grassy yard with a loud groan. A look of hopelessness was tattooed on her face for at least the remaining day. "I just know we are going to be here forever. I was to travel to Cambridge City tonight to see my niece. She is ill, and I had planned to stay with her for a few days. The president of the Elm City bus lines is going to get a stern letter from me that will reveal the complete failure of his worthless bus line. I'll put him in his place!"

Known throughout town, she had information about everybody's business, and she loved to tell it to anyone who was foolish enough to spend the time to listen to such nonsense. If there was an administrative board or some community effort in town, she was generally the chairman. She had opinions about everything and knew nothing. She was truly a nowhere individual, bound on a bus likewise going in the same direction as she—nowhere.

A second passenger, a man of middle age, popped up and said, "We are all going to have to remain calm until a new bus arrives." His well-pressed brown suit, tie, and shined black shoes made him look rich and important, and his slicked-down hair, very white straight teeth, and slightly oily skin added to the guise of professionalism. Maybe he was a banker on his way home from work. These phonies had easy jobs because they only worked until two o'clock in the afternoon. They handled other people's money and could be counted on to carefully watch who was spending and who was wasting.

Advice was always given on how to handle finances and, of course, bankers were the best examples. Morals were beyond reproach, or at least that was the guise presented. Any kept secrets were deep, very private, and the town depended upon strict confidentially all the time—well perhaps most of the time.

"How long do you think we are going to have to wait?" someone asked. The man replied, "I don't know, but it may be more than an hour." He reached into his pocket, and he took out a watch, stared at it, and then hoped that time might slow down.

Perspiration dripped from his face. It was 3:10 p.m. by his watch.

With some exasperation, he took off a suit coat, and as with the bus driver, huge amounts of stained areas over the front and underarms of a slightly discolored white shirt were obvious. A wily smile crossed his face. He gave a report that the whole day had been a disaster from the early morning, when his car broke down on the way to work. It was required to be towed to German's Garage for "evaluation." His wife had said to be home no later than 4:00 p.m. because she had a hair appointment. "Now," he so meekly said, "everything has been thrown off kilter." Still, he assured himself, it was nobody's fault, and getting upset did no good.

He was a fast talker and a denier of reality, adept at social interactions by the way he communicated. Perhaps he was not a banker, but instead a salesman; there were plenty of those types up on the town square. Some sold clothes, or shoes, or pretty rings and watches. Others managed dime stores, dispensed medicines, or "called the shots" at credit unions. All these folks shaved daily and smelled of Mennen lotion, which also helped to reveal bright, shiny faces.

Another passenger, perhaps a high school student, played with her long dark hair and then removed some very thick glasses from her face. She appeared tense and anxious. Her clothes consisted of a pair of jeans neatly washed and pressed, a blouse, and some cheap-looking tennis shoes. Her face, covered with acne, seemed to change expressions by the second as tears came unannounced, quickly and unabatedly. Between heavy breathing and sobs, she related that her job at one of the restaurants in south Elm City might be in jeopardy. The boss was not a compassionate man, and he would be upset about her tardiness. The young girl had applied for work at many of the restaurants throughout town and spent many months filling out applications, only to receive zero offers. This job was important because it helped to pay bills. Her father had become ill and was not able to work. "I don't know what I would do if I lost my job," she babbled.

All the passengers tried to reassure her that maybe if she explained to her boss what had happened, things would be okay. She countered, "He is an ass . . ." and then briefly stopped crying. She smiled and got up, walked to another area of the front yard, and started to cry again. Her grief would remain private, just like her.

A fat kid with red hair, who lived several blocks east on Clay Avenue, added his two cents by throwing small rocks and cussing at speeding cars. He was recognized by everyone on the bus because of a story recently reported about him in the *Elm City Courier*. The stupid twit had stood up in his school's cafeteria and announced to amazed teachers and frightened students that the junior high school was full of buttholes and queers. His solution was to torch and blow the whole place up. Police were called, and he disappeared for a few days; things eventually returned to normal. Mental problems were obvious and, of course, nothing was done—an accident waiting to happen. His commentary about today's events: "I am angry about this *&#$ shit. If I could find the guy who was head of this bus line, I would do more than write a letter to him! I don't like that fat-ass bus driver." Then, a strange, weird type of laugh was generated from deep within a rotund belly and aided with a smirk on a sickly-looking face; he then ran off and disappeared into a grove of trees which surrounded and arched over a small alley. The kid was different, no doubt. Everyone agreed they were glad he had permanently taken a leave of absence from the group!

And then there was Zachary Stevens. He was a twelve-year-old kid who had just begun junior high school; not very tall, shy but adventurous, one who blushed a lot. He was impatient, irritable, but only at rare times, and had lots of thoughts competing for his attention. But he tried to love life, not always successfully, and often said that "joyful spirits" jumped up and down inside his heart and mind with much enthusiasm and pride. Who knew how or why? He certainly didn't. Life was taken one day at a time, with no expectation of much of anything happening. But he felt free and full of living.

A few minutes earlier he had, for no reason, laughed, felt joy from somewhere, just as the bus passed by the large clock in the window of Baker's Furniture store, located one block south of the square. Time: 2:58 p.m. Did he not feel the summer heat inside and outside the coach, which was beyond any discussion? Slivers of wind-gusted air, filled with dust and a sundry of other things, passed through small windows. Zachary, though, was impervious to everything except the thoughts and voices bouncing around inside a partially vacant brain. The "commentary" by his closest friend, Buddy Logan, continued to persuade, cajole, and attempt to manipulate him into joining a gang of neighborhood boys who lived on a major street in Elm City called South Main. They called themselves the South Main Gang (SMG), and the boys were all invincible, or so they thought! Zachary disagreed and viewed them as just a bunch of strange weirdos.

The gang was made up of two brothers, one of whom joked all the time and acted weird, while the other seemed to fight, or at least was highly touted for fast swings of fists which rarely missed their target—the mouth, nose, or eye of some unfortunate victim. Other gang members played sports and were much more athletic than Zachary, and some were quiet and reserved. Zachary had many questions regarding any reason(s) why he should become involved in this cabal. Buddy's voice needed to shut up; Zachary would remain an "outsider," it was safer that way.

Then, a diversion from thoughts, reality back, and a quick look at the comical bus parked adjacent to the curb, back-end hood opened. He yelled out to no one in particular, "What a shit mess! What am I to do? Walk home? I need to get out of here." Had he known of the events which were soon to transpire a few blocks away, he might not have been in such a hurry to leave a pathetic but also humorous situation.

He went over and sat down under a huge elm tree and felt a slight breeze whip across his face as he gazed off into the distance. Leaves from a tall maple tree shimmered and deflected sunlight, and provided a brief respite from the heat. Slowly, ever so restfully, he stared off into space and hypnotically slipped into a slumber. Soothing remembrances of past weekends of fun and innocence began to invade an incomplete consciousness.

It was the summer of 1952, and Elm City, Indiana, was under what seemed like an endless, sweltering heat spell. Zachary had been at the air-conditioned Times Theatre located two blocks east of the city square. He had watched Gene Autry in the movie *Cow Town* and relished the scenes of good guys chasing bad guys on horses, which eventually led to the shooting and killing of all evil in the world. Of course, there was a bonus of musical interludes, which included "Down in the Valley" and "Bury Me Not on the Lone Prairie."

The songs were always funny because Gene Autry never sang, just moved his mouth—at least some of the time. His sidekick, Gabby Hayes, blabbed a lot, and it was impossible to understand anything he said. He told lots of jokes, acted nervously, and danced around—one of the good guys and friend of the hero cowboys. In addition to the major feature, there was a short news film about a place called Korea and military fighting; a cartoon might then flash on, maybe to dispel some "paired-off lovers" from too much kissing and other unmentionables.

Zachary and his friends spent time in the theatre lobby and closely eyed anybody, especially the girls, who visited the concessionary where candy was sold; wayward glances were exchanged, some partially hidden, and others less so. Of course, lust and fantasies never counted and could never have been measured, felt, or understood!

The boys looked at each other and said stupid things, none of which were of much significance, while the girls giggled and parlayed with much anxiety and insecurities. And those "tempters," the ones with the big eyes, smiles, and questionable reputations—they stayed around and listened for offers from young hipsters making inviting pleas to disappear into seats and become lost in dark corners of the theatre where romance and love might be found, if only momentarily.

Another movie theatre, the Majestic, was located up the street in an old run-down building where the window to the ticket booth was dirty, partially broken, at least cracked. Tickets were sold by an old guy who had a mouth full of black teeth and eye spectacles around his nose. He rarely smiled and often just squinted. Zachary's friends said that the guy lived by himself but kept a couple of dogs and a pet raccoon for company.

Of course, there was nothing majestic about this movie theatre. It was a place where mice lived under the seats. Some of these creatures were big and fat, most likely a result of popcorn eaten from the floor, carelessly discarded by a pair of "kissers" more intent on satisfying adolescent desires than watching a boring movie. Kids told Zachary that the mice sat in your lap if you gave them enough popcorn. Of course, these stories were nothing but bullshit. Lying was well tolerated in Elm City—it had its own existence, understood by all.

This day, after watching the movie at the Times Theatre, Zachary had taken the bus marked "South Main" from the town square. Bob Avery was always the driver and a good friend. They discussed baseball and, of course, the pretty girls who carefully walked on narrow sidewalks and were waved at while summers, which were always hot as hell, were ignored. The breeze that came through the bus's small windows was never much protection against the heat from an unforgiving sun. Bob was lucky, because there was a small electric fan mounted on a pole and positioned to the left of the large steering wheel. The passengers, though, suffered the worst indignation, since the air was quiet, stale, and hot, unforgivingly hot. The seats, made from some kind of an amorphous plastic, held the passengers in place. When the bus began jerking, coughing, and panting for air, after the "engine demons" arrived, the seats became partial "belts," sticking and locking human butts, preventing falls, preventing further injuries.

The words at first were faint and distant, but then they woke him. "We are going to be okay; we are going to be okay." Zachary jumped up, his heart pounding. "Another bus will pick us up in thirty minutes," Bob yelled. He appeared to have calmed down somewhat, but the embarrassment on his face was difficult to disguise. Now, for at least one passenger, the wait was over. Zachary decided that Bob and his passengers would have to deal with their frustrations by themselves. The kid would exit this craziness and walk home alone, heat and all.

Obediently, a hot sun tagged along and riveted down on him, trying its best to redistribute every part of his body into a mass of scrambled skin and bones. Zachary took one step and then another as the concrete appeared to melt around his shoes. If he stepped too hard, he guessed, the sidewalk might give up, and he would sink in and disappear to unknown places. He carefully skipped and dodged all the uneven cracks and bumps to avoid an early trip to perdition. His skinny legs and knees felt the tensions and complained loudly, but were ignored. They quietly swore that all this nonsensical work was unnecessary, and at least one threatened to simply quit, or at least go on strike

Misplaced curly hair blew everywhere and gave the appearance of a lost shaggy dog without an owner; however, the kid was happy again. For one brief moment, he forgot the heat and felt a sense of relief that a broken-down city bus was not going to spoil and sully any misplaced attitudes; things were going to work out okay . . . but life is always full of surprises, even for a kid who had way too many fantasies.

Ten blocks straight down South Main Street, Fred Duncan went into the freezer of his small grocery store. His leg hurt—it always did after he stood for a few hours, but today the limp was even more obvious. It was cold inside the freezer, and he was in a hurry to grab a slab of meat. Small sections of pork ribs were cut up and carefully wrapped into pieces of cellophane, and then weighed, priced, and displayed as his most prized product for inspection by hungry customers. He worked hard and believed that every day was going to be better than yesterday.

The grocer was a short and balding man with a pleasant smile and lots of silver and gold in his teeth. He was the first and only proprietor of the market and was always friendly to everyone, including a kid who asked too many questions and had a lot of braces on his teeth. He carefully listened and paid attention to anything said to him. Zachary had always felt he was sincere and interested in his thoughts and commentaries about life, but there was a downside; the old grocer's health was never good. When he walked, he had a limp. A shiny light-brown cane made of hickory wood was his tag-along friend. It was used when walking became difficult. As a child, he had fallen out of a barn and broken his leg. Healing had not come properly or completely. Pleurisy was another health ailment. The coughing was inevitable and often painful.

His family, a wife and daughter, lived in a small house behind the grocery. The teenage girl had polio, and for unknown reasons remained at home and sat on the porch all day and waved to anyone who looked her way. There was a look of betrayal and loneliness which punctuated a face, and no doubt a spirit. Maybe the gestures were her way of connecting with somebody, anybody. Zachary felt a tinge of sadness when he saw her on that porch. A tinge or welling up of tears sometimes occurred. Why? Did he feel sorry for her plight in life and frustrated for not being able to "do something" to help her? She was an enigma, a puzzle piece that refused to fit into any picture. Or, maybe a more honest appraisal was that he felt some guilt for simply not going up and talking with her, and becoming a friend—something he never did.

The store was, in all honesty, a large shack. It consisted of a grey front and an enclosed metal awning which captured sun rays and threw them like a perfect strike onto a billboard that proudly advertised Camel cigarettes. The light, at this moment, specifically reflected onto and highlighted a picture of a package of smokes; a possible hidden suggestion: *"Buy me now."* A large screen door with a bright orange handle was the entry point into the grocery. Written in fancy letters were the words "Lucky Kid Bread." Directly inside were shelves lined with canned goods. A small aisle went to the back of the store and intersected with the small meat counter. Smells emanated from many different places, including the wood shavings scattered around the back of the meat counter, meats laid out on a small chopping block, and spices in tightly enclosed bottles, neatly placed on shelves near the entrance of the store.

The floor was wood, and parts of it had worn glued-down linoleum; other sections of the floor were simply unpainted and partially rotted out. When walked on, there were creaking noises and the uncomfortable feeling of a buckling, shifting, and a total collapse being seconds away.

In the front window were bananas, strawberries, and other things not describable; and most likely not edible because of beginning mold. Selling fruit had to be a risky business. Potatoes in numerous five-pound bags were neatly lined up on the floor. They waited patiently and proudly for selection, to then be carried home for the ultimate disgrace of becoming baked and consumed.

The meat selection, found in the rear of the store, was mostly hamburger and a few sickly-looking steaks or pork ribs. A machine used for grinding beef into hamburger sat in the corner and looked bored and alone. The most popular of all meats, baloney, was elegantly displayed in the front case. It was the cheapest and sold out early in the day.

Next to the meat counter, candy and soda were sold. A small refrigerator-freezer that displayed eggs, milk, butter, and ice cream was nearby. A cash register sat in the center aisle on top of a counter.

A small chair was perched by the side of the meat counter, and it was here that intense and serious conversations about life—its unfairness, difficulty, and complexities—were shared. Fred did most of the talking, while Zachary just kept his mouth shut and listened. The grocer always looked uncomfortable, noticeably in pain, gritting his teeth. "It lessens my hurt," he would say. Sometimes, though, he laughed and commented, "Don't grow old, Zachary; stay and think young." Fred was clearly unhappy and depressed with life. He needed someone to visit and cheer him up. Zachary had been that person for the past year. One important discussion was Zachary's incessant description of his dreams to play in the major leagues, ultimately with the St. Louis

Cardinals. It would take a lot of practice, but his work would eventually be rewarded. A huge contract was to be written, and later a big car purchased and driven around town during the off-season. People would be in awe of a local boy in professional sports, and everywhere he went, there would be demands for autographs.

* * *

The bell by the side of the front door, used to alert Mr. Duncan of people arriving, rang but went unnoticed. A young man who wore a dirty brown sweatshirt and jeans moved quickly through the door. He was about six feet tall and had a scar on his face that was partially covered by a bandana. Black motorcycle boots moved in forced unison and made a thud on the floor. The cash register was easy to find—he had been in the store before, several times. Keys were hit in no order, but the bell, which would signal the opening of the drawer, did not sound. The money inside breathed a huge sigh of relief, safe for now.

Fred came out of the freezer, saw the man, and asked, "What kind of meat do you need today?" The guy replied, "Do you have any fresh watermelons?" Mr. Duncan answered, "Sure, take your pick, they are on the floor by the milk case. They just came in late yesterday."

The grocer put the meat cleaver down, rang the register, and waited to make change for an expected purchase. Suddenly he felt a strong push that came quickly, without warning. He staggered as he grabbed the wall for support. His neck became arched in an awkward position, but it helped him get a better look. It was then he noticed the meat cleaver in the guy's right hand while a left hand moved toward the till of the cash register, preparing and guiding greedy fingers to their assignments.

Raw anger seethed into every cavity of Fred's body, his arms temporarily weak and useless in defense. Blood drained into his chest and legs as he moved into an attack mode; fists were readied for quick, direct, and strong hits. Breathing became intense and short. Then a quick thought: *Who does this guy think he is, coming into my store, pushing me around? Is he going to take money out of my cash register? That will not happen. I will warn him once, and then a butcher knife will be used to stab him while I kick him in his balls.*

The robber, however, read Fred's thoughts perfectly. He turned and sneered. The old grocer came over and attempted to swing the knife at Carl. He missed and made only slight contact by nicking his shirt. The guy lunged forward before Fred could swing the knife again, grabbing the old guy's wrist. Mr. Duncan fought back. He was well-built and strong, a result of lifting bales of hay and other heavy objects throughout his youth. Very quickly, the young man swung and hit Fred on the side of the face with a force that knocked him back against the meat counter.

Without delay, the robber brought the meat cleaver down hard on the top of Fred's head. Blood gushed all over as the grocer fell to the floor, gasped, and fought to stay conscious. While he was down, the robber kicked him in the stomach and felt much satisfaction. The contact with soft unprotected tissue was exhilarating, and for a split second he wanted to keep kicking, venting more of his anger and frustration at Mr. Duncan's refusal to stay on the floor, as well as the kid's own exasperation about a useless life spent with a worthless family. The administration of brute force, which fractured ribs, face, and teeth, was of no consequence; remorse was not evident, never considered. Fred began to experience wooziness as he attempted to hold onto the guy's boots and twist his leg. The robber, however, was resolute as he again swung the meat cleaver, cutting Fred's arm. This time the old grocer released his grip. He simply had never been prepared for the kicking his body received by a wild, out-of-control thief, and a distressed stomach told him so.

The bell by the grocery door again rang as a woman came into the store. She was dressed in jeans and had a scarf over her head. Immediately, it was apparent to her what was happening, and she screamed out, "Stop hitting that old man." A bloody cleaver was sent flying over the back of the meat counter, and a voice yelled out, "Get the hell out of the store," as the dark shadow of someone unknown to this witness darted out the front door. The woman's mouth remained open while her emotions appeared frozen in time. That was when she noticed a limp body on the floor with no movement, not talking, and quite possibly without life. A terrible smell from someplace had to be ignored as the woman, visibly upset, again began screaming, "a robbery, a robbery." She then made a quick exit out the front door and ran down the street toward a gas station with a large "Phillips 66" emblem staring down over three gas pumps.

In the mix of all the chaos, a crowd of people at the gas station had started to congregate and view what was going on with some degree of amazement and interest. A couple of gas station attendants stopped for a moment and called out, "What is happening?" The woman kept screaming and crying, "There is blood all over the place." Finally, Ed Owens, the manager, realized he needed to do something fast, so he got on the phone and called the sheriff's office.

Movement did not come easy. Fred tried to twist and change positions but had difficulty. Blood was everywhere. His head ached, and any purposeful movement from his left hip, knee, and leg appeared impossible—his body simply refused to obey commands. He felt a sharp pain in his legs from a fall onto the hard floor. He thought: *if I roll over and get next to the soda machine, I might be able to push myself to a standing position.* Blood dripped down his face, into his eyes, and caused difficulty seeing. There was a metallic smell that was nauseous. His stomach had initially started to ache, but now it wanted to rebel and throw up everything inside. Slowly, ever so slowly, he began to feel all his senses start to slip away. There was a ringing in his head, faint at first, and then it increased in loudness while his fingers began to tingle. Varying intensities of light appeared, and then everything just disappeared and gave way to total darkness, unconsciousness now complete.

So far, so good; the robbery plan had worked, but the thief was also worried. *Had someone seen his face when that bandana slipped during the fight with the grocer? Move quickly! Get away! Get the # *^+, out of here!* He had run the short distance from the store and had not been seen; now he was to start the car and drive north toward the Elm City Square. Both car windows were down, and the cross wind had helped to dry some of the perspiration from his face. The mask and hat were off — time to breathe and live again.

This was his first "job. "He felt total stimulation and excitement. Money had been stolen, lots of it, and he was not going to get caught. Unfortunately, it had not been his plan to become involved in an altercation with the grocery store owner. He mused: *What could I do? Just let the old guy get his money back? I certainly had to protect myself. The woman was just a nervous idiot; I have no worries about her. I believe I am in the clear; life is good.*

Yes, Carl Stewart had successfully robbed a grocery store and escaped. He was temporarily happy. The winds of fate, however, were beginning to circle, with other more fearful consequences.

The Elm City bus remained in its disabled state. Zachary, long gone, had now passed some large homes fronting South Main Street with signs out in front which read "Rooms for Rent." The residences sat back from the street, and three or four concrete steps provided boundaries required to be traversed to reach the front yards. Circular porches with large back chairs and cushions invited all to sit and watch automobiles ignore speed limits as they raced to or from the busy local square. The kid's only focus and goal was to reach Duncan's Market, where he would stop and get a soda, and visit a safe and favorite place to rest and spend time with a good friend, who was the owner. This day there was much to tell him about a disappointing bus ride.

Zachary looked afar and saw the Pontiac dealership across the street from Duncan's store. Loud voices could be heard: *was that a woman screaming?* A figure, perhaps a man, ran out of the store and quickly jumped into a car and accelerated in Zachary's direction. The sedan made a very sharp right-hand turn, zoomed right past the kid, and then accelerated past an old red brick church, where a good portion of the Negro community worshipped on Sunday morning. Zachary had jumped back to avoid colliding with such an unstoppable object. Two different and anxious souls briefly exchanged glances. No words were exchanged, time dimensions shrunk, private thoughts secretly guarded.

In full display and sticking out of the car's window was a tattooed arm embroidered with a design of a snake. An immediate thought flashed quickly through Zachary's mind: *This is not the first time I have seen this guy and his tattoo; but where?* As the tan car drove past, a decal of a motorcycle was visible on the rear of the car. The license plate was covered with mud, and a chain hung from the car trunk. A vague and nondescript nervousness enveloped Zachary. Something was very wrong.

Carl's mind and thoughts raced out of control! *Make this turn! Watch out! That kid just stepped out in front of me. Jesus! What the hell was that shit thinking? He must be off in some other land or time. His red face, skinny legs and arms, and sissy clothes make him look like a mama's boy. Oh well, he is a nothing. Ignore him and go on. Carefully steer the car away and don't hit the punk— no need for any more witnesses; however, he had better look out, or I am going to take him down.*

Whoops, it looks like he fell back. Is he okay? Yep. He is looking at the rear of the car. He won't see anything of importance. I must get out of this area quickly.

The best place will be home. I can count the loot, and then decide how to spend my well-deserved earnings.

Wait a minute. That kid looked familiar—someone I have seen before. Should I stay around and watch what he might do?

The robber was in conflict. If he waited, the police would be in the area looking, snooping, and asking questions. But that kid? *Where had he seen him, his curly hair and bony knees? Try to remember, stupid. Keep thinking. Where? Where?*

The police sirens blasted loudly and furiously. Breathable air seemed partially sucked up somewhere and not reclaimed. Further up the street, several people ran in and out of Duncan's Market and yelled, but the words were indistinguishable. What was going on? Police cars flashed by in a hurry and parked up on the grass. Zachary was puzzled. Was the guy and the tan car that raced by seconds ago involved with all this excitement?

People stood around the store and said very little; a few looked either scared or were crying when Zachary eventually arrived. The front door was bent and partially off its hinges. One large man with a very round stomach, which stuck over his belt, said that there had been a robbery inside the store. A woman was more detailed: "Mr. Duncan has been hit in the head with a meat cleaver, and we must stay outside. Two police officers are now in the area."

Zachary walked around to the side of the store and looked in through a small window. It appeared a bomb had exploded inside. Cans of vegetables and bottles were all over the floor. Several shelves had collapsed. Police officers, initially outside writing things down on pieces of paper, went inside and just mumbled to themselves as they stood close to a limp body on the floor.

The kid needed to find out more about what had happened; most importantly about his friend, Fred Duncan. There was another screen door at the rear of the store that opened into an area filled with crates and boxes. It would be a safe and excellent place to hide. Often, Zachary helped clean this area and never expected pay, but sometimes he received a free bottle of soda for his hard labor. He quietly slipped in and found a place to hide behind some boxes.

The police officers spoke in hushed tones. Fred was on the floor, and blood covered most of his face and head. He lay in an awkward position, one hand stuck under his hip, and he appeared to be staring up at the ceiling with no movement. Zachary wondered if the old guy might be dead.

Several officers examined Fred's hands rather closely, while another man with some black rubber tubes listened to the grocer's chest. A white shirt was completely covered in blood, some of which had dripped down onto the wood floor. Next to the counter on the floor, a meat cleaver remained alone and ignored. The officers needed to evaluate it carefully, but they delayed. The meat case and the soda machine were spotted in what appeared to be bloodstains. An old chair, now broken apart, was thrown up against the wall. It had a partial resemblance to what appeared to be the current state of Fred Duncan.

Someone popped off and said, "A white guy ran into the store, hit Mr. Duncan, and then ran out after taking money from the cash register." Another officer reported that someone, a woman, had witnessed the robbery.

At that point, one of the officers came in with a person nervous and crying. She told them the man had thrown a meat cleaver, and that she had been frightened he was going to hit her. She asked the police if Mr. Duncan was dead, and they said nothing, but continued to write things down in a small book. The lady replied, "The robber ran past me, left, and then seconds later a car zoomed out from the back of the store. I don't recall anything about the vehicle. I was so scared, I shook all over. I am proud of myself for not passing out." All reassured her that she was going to be okay, and then asked if she had seen the guy's face. "No, he had a mask that covered most of his eyes and mouth. I would never be able to identify him, I am sure."

A policeman announced that he was going to smoke a cigarette and check the back of the store. Zachary heard the pronouncement and realized he needed to move quickly, so he repositioned himself and squeezed into a tight space and breathed quietly. The officer came back and paced up and down. His shined black shoes were visible between the cracks in the stacked boxes. The kid tightened up his legs and held his breath. Pain radiated all over his body, and a heart appeared ready to bounce out of his chest. A mouth became dry, and nervousness competed with pain. Then, some rustling noise and an unannounced and unplanned visitor showed up.

At first the feeling of movement just below his right leg might have been attributable to a foggy, anxious imagination. Then, without warning, a large grey mouse moved ever so slowly across Zachary's leg. It was much bigger than any of the mice at the Majestic Theater. Zachary watched the beast very carefully as it sniffed around, ambled across his leg, crawled over his foot, and looked up as if to say, "We are not going to have a conversation—you look too boring." The feckless animal then disappeared behind a large wastebasket, most likely to investigate things of greater importance.

Body positions were carefully and quietly changed. Legs stretched as new and welcomed blood flow went to carefully monitored limbs, which refused to knock anything over and make noise. The policeman looked directly at the area of boxes where the kid had hidden and saw nothing. A cigarette was then finished, and a brief trip back to the main part of the grocery to stoutly report, "All clear."

New sirens were audible from far away. Two men began to move Mr. Duncan, now awake, onto a bed with wheels. He tried to speak but appeared to just mumble; words came out of his mouth and then reluctantly disappeared into space while some new characters arrived at the store. They took "center stage," as if to now demonstrate their importance. A man who said he was from the courthouse asked questions about how much money was taken, and if anybody might be able to provide details of the appearance of the robber. The witness replied, "The guy was of medium build and had a large hat and a type of mask over his face." Zachary's stomach churned. Thoughts abounded: *Was this a partial description of the guy he had seen a few minutes ago, driving uncontrollably past him?*

Suddenly, Mr. Duncan tried to speak but made little sense—just a lot of mumbles. Chief of Police Runyon walked through the door as if he had much authority, but a lot of frustration too. "Every witness has their own version of what happened. They can't all be correct," he bellowed out with a powerful voice.

Mixed messages flew everywhere. Someone had told the Chief of Police that the robber was bald, got into a truck and then made a U-turn and disappeared down Main Street. Others, from across the street at the car dealership, thought the robber went out the front door and ran around in back and moved quickly through the brush and trees. One man told the police the guy left in a large convertible with other people in the car who talked and laughed. The car zoomed north and disappeared. No one admitted they had seen the guy up close or could report what he looked like—no one except the lady who had directly encountered the robber in the store. *How could so many people see so many different things? How could so many people be so wrong?* For a very brief moment, Zachary felt a strong urge to laugh at all of these idiotic descriptions.

Then a group of two men and a woman came into the store with a small rack of brushes. They discussed among themselves the evaluation of the robber's fingerprints by a technique called "dusting" that involved collecting very slight details of skin impressions, and matching them with other fingerprint impressions on file at the police station. Zachary listened intently, tried to understand, and then became "thoughtfully incompetent" to any of their gibberish.

Dr. A.G. Ferris showed up for medical assistance, examined Fred closely, and then applied some bandages to his head. The wounds were deep, and he commented that Fred might have brain damage. "I will need to take him to the hospital for further and more detailed examinations." Other hospital people wheeled Mr. Duncan outside on what was called a "gurney"—a stretcher or cot with wheels. Fred looked bloody, his face pale, and he appeared asleep again. Maybe he was just resting; or for all Zachary knew, maybe he was permanently gone from this world. Several men loaded Fred into an ambulance and took off for the hospital.

The police then came out, put a big lock on the front door, and told everybody to leave. Someone from the local paper took a picture of the store, and Zachary left unnoticed. Traveling with him was a confused, baffled, and troubled conscience. Other people had stories they told the police. Zachary had stories too, but chose to keep quiet. *What was he afraid of?* A lazy, somewhat fragile brain and mind were thoroughly surveyed. No response, just a lot of silence. And then came the whispers . . . *you had better keep your mouth quiet; what you know and what you saw have no importance, and if you start blabbing about some guy in a tan car driving away, the police will only laugh at you; the guy you tell them about will learn about your story and your stupid imaginations, and he will come back looking for you. Want that?*

Tony Scott had just finished pumping gas into a sleek black 1949 Ford sedan. He walked back to the office, a tan-brick building, worried about the excitement next door.

An anxious and obnoxious salesman from Indianapolis waited for change from a five-dollar bill used for the purchase of gas. Many salesmen stopped at Ed's station because it was located close to the highway, motels, and restaurants. These sellers of all types of wares congregated at the station to talk, argue, and to show off items they peddled to ambitious store owners. They had their own egos, their own sales pitches, and their own unique ability to lie well with no perceivable attempt to ever tell the truth, at least most of the time. Their consciences were what some described as always absent without leave from static minds.

One fool blared out, "What's all of this talk about a robbery? The woman who just ran into the gas station office acted like she was crazy. Does anyone know what happened? I must get on down the road, but I don't want to miss witnessing a real robbery. My clients can wait. I haven't seen such excitement since a car accident near Lafayette a few years ago." The man was strange, nosy and fat, with a horrible body odor. His eyes bulged out, his face was partially unshaven, and his worn clothes had long ago given up any hope of still looking presentable. He was ignored, and rightly so!

"Have you heard about the robbery at Fred's store?" Zachary ruefully asked upon arrival at the gas station. Tony replied that a few minutes before the police arrived, someone had run into the station and reported that a robbery had occurred at the grocery down the street. A woman, very upset, had told them what the robber had done to Fred. A call was made to the Elm City police department. Tony thought he had seen a 1948 red Plymouth coupe drive very fast down Main Street and make a right turn on Highway 63, heading west.

Zachary said nothing while Tony went on with conversation. "Fred was a very quiet and private person who never bothered anybody and really did not deserve any of this," he said as he continued repairing a tire with a large nail in it. He gave Zachary his best counsel: "Get on home, there is nothing more for you to do around here."

The afternoon sun had slowly disappeared in the west and was now barely visible beyond the tops of trees firmly planted around the state hospital grounds, located across the street and further south of the filling station. Zachary agreed with Tony's advice that a safer and much happier place was at 1132 South Main—his home, where he lived with a mother, a grandmother, and a lot of dreams, unspoken fantasies, but hurts too.

As he walked home, there were noises and incessant questions that percolated inside his head. *Why didn't he tell the police what he had seen? What was he afraid of?* A conscience came to chat and determine recognition, but Zachary put it back down in its place. Of more immediate need was to figure out how to make the guy and his tan car and the whole afternoon disappear into space and never return! The walk slowed to just a dribble as he tried to calm himself. He thought he heard some of those reoccurring whispers from earlier, then an idea. If he ran very quickly, the "shakes" inside a heart, mind, and body might be replaced with more safe and comforting dialogues. But then a small problem developed. Out of the corner of his eye, he saw a car following him. It must be somebody slowing down to turn into a driveway; however, the car stayed behind and went very slowly. This was odd, since South Main Street was a major highway that eventually went to Indianapolis. Cars traveled fast and were always in a hurry to get out of town, in anticipation of reaching the major city in Indiana as quickly as possible.

Zachary turned his head ever so slightly for a further peek. To his amazement, he realized it was the same guy and the same car he'd witnessed earlier driving away from Fred's store! The person did not look at him, but just stared straight ahead. The car then sped up, a brief glance given to Zachary, and then it was gone. Zachary thought: *Could it be possible that the guy may have figured out I might be able to identify him? The same decal and chain are hanging out of the trunk.*

Inside his car and partially hidden, Carl mused: *That kid must not see my face. If I sit high enough in the seat, I will probably be okay. This damn heat has caused sweat to drip all over my face and into my eyes. It stings. I need to eat, but I can't—my stomach feels like it is full of something terrible that needs to come up. I am going to watch that kid and get a better look at his face. I know him. He is looking at my car. Did he see me? No, I don't think so. He is singing to himself. The kid is weird. I should not be worried about him. He would be easy to give a good ass-kicking to if necessary.*

The traffic is too heavy for me to park the car on South Main. I am going to Superior Avenue and watch and see what house he goes into. Then I will at least know where he lives. Maybe I should just pull in the alley, get out of the car, and talk to him right now, check him out. If he knows me, I am going to have to

29

do something. Why did he have to cross that street and see me earlier today? Now I've got problems I don't need. The punk is going to have to keep his mouth shut, or else. Carl drove to Superior Avenue. He wanted to get out and walk around a bit, but there were people across the street who stared at him.

Carl looked out the car window and exclaimed out loud to himself, "Where in the hell did that kid disappear to? He was just walking on the sidewalk, and now he is gone. I'd better get out of here and go home. If my family find out I got a lot of extra money, I will tell them I won it in a game of craps." He then continued slowly down South Main Street. The car turned left onto Superior Avenue, and it immediately stopped. A car window opened, and an arm and head stuck out.

Zachary noticed and thought: *Why did he park the car? Is he planning to meet and talk with me? That is not going to happen.*

Do something to fool this guy. Instead of continuing down South Main, quickly turn left and run down the alley past several houses, and cut through a couple of back yards.

Zachary then moved past some women neighbors, who waved and asked, "How are you doing?" They told him about police sirens and asked if he had seen or heard anything. He fabricated and said, "No." All of them began to gossip about a new neighbor who had just moved in. Zachary quickly darted around an old red barn, over several fences, and arrived at a familiar and safe back yard.

The large bushes, which surrounded part of his house, provided good cover to hide behind. Very slowly, he peered out to see if the robber's car was still parked on Superior Avenue. It was not. Carl had driven off to places unknown. A very brief sense of relief welled up inside, but at a deeper level, he somehow guessed their paths would cross again.

Emotions began to spill over and bounce between reality and imagination. Nothing felt very reassuring. Now, though, safe at home, Zachary's room would become his place of solace, or so he hoped; however, Mr. Duncan's face and vacant stare and a lot of blood kept coming back into his troubled, frightened mind. He was sure that someone must have seen him slip around to the back of the store. People talk, and they can never be trusted.

Jean Stevens, Zachary's mother, was a popular first-grade schoolteacher, liked by many students for her supportive smiles and positive attitude. She watched her diet, had a trim figure and a good sense of humor, but not today. She was tired and depressed about her failed marriage, the heat of the day, and maybe a lot of boredom from not teaching during the summer months.

"You look upset," she commented to Zachary as he began to tell her about the bus and its engine problems. "That is to be expected. The Elm City bus line never runs very well," she replied. Nothing was said about Mr. Duncan. If she were to find out he withheld information about a robbery, frustration and anger might mount up quickly, and punishment would likely follow. Instead there was silence, a common occurrence in the Stevens household, and Zachary excused himself and went to his room for more thoughts and inner conversations.

It would be impossible to deny the events of the day. It was also true that Zachary was scared, but also angry as to why he had to be the one picked to see things he wished he had not. Of course, it was always possible that the guy he saw had nothing to do with the robbery, but the chain of events witnessed by Zachary argued against that view. There were two separate risks in divulging his knowledge about the robbery. The first was that he would not be believed. One criticism of Zachary, by people who knew him, was that he asked too many questions, talked too much, and that he lived in a dream world. He was very good at spewing "big bunches of shit." Many folks would no doubt believe and say, "Zachary, someday you are going to be a good salesman because you fabricate so well, and you certainly have a great imagination. But never forget Pinocchio and what happened to him!"

But a deeper emotion resonated and caused more pain. He could not bring himself to admit that the person he saw, and just knew he had seen the guy before now, was a permanent integration into Zachary's life—and only in a bad and dangerous way. If Zachary were to give information to the police about what he saw after the robbery was committed, the whole town would read about it in the paper, including at some point the robber, and Zachary's identity would then be compromised and become fair game for retribution. In no way did Zachary want to be the one to come forward and put himself in the limelight. One thing was for sure; the face he saw tracking his every movement from inside that old car was believable, even if his fantasies often were not.

Zachary pushed his mind to remember, think, think, as he smacked his head a few times. No luck! Zachary's eyes and brain had seen too much this day; things inside his whole being appeared to be on fire, and rapid unrelenting anxiety, for the sake of sanity, needed to be repressed and buried, not to be found. Also, uneasiness tinged with sadness whirled around mind and brain. Was Fred Duncan, Zachary's secret confidant and one of his earliest and best friends, in jeopardy of leaving this earth permanently?

A confused kid, to quench a dry mouth, got a drink of water and looked out his bedroom window at a very dark night. The maple tree and a lonely sandpile could barely be seen in outline against a moonless night sky. There were discernible noises of the rattling kind, varying in crescendo, refusing to remain still.

Later, as he lay in bed and looked at the ceiling, it appeared to slowly move in one direction, and then reverse itself and move in the opposite direction. Suddenly there was a shift as the walls appeared to move toward him, and then, ever so quickly, retreat back to their boring normalcy. Zachary had a brilliant idea: *Might the room just open up and allow him to fly away to another place, perhaps freedom? Or . . . what if instead, it tightly closed in, suffocating an insignificant life?*

Heaviness invaded his legs and arms; his throat again became dry and parched, as if he had been without water for at least a year. His heart beat rapidly and begged and pleaded to come out of his chest, to disappear, never again to be remembered. A perilous thought: *Was he going to see someone following him in a tan car for the rest of his life?*

Restless sleep came forth and danced and faded, giving way to strange dreams. Elm City buses, painted in bright colors, drove carelessly, ran off the road, and people laughed, moved around, talked, and yelled to each other. Some folks appeared to be doing some kind of strange jig and singing. The drivers had masks on their faces, odd masks with smiling, up-turned mouths, frightening-looking eyes. Who were these people? Voices cried out, "Come on and join the 'fun buses.' You can go many places and see many things and people. You will not be disappointed; it will be the ride of a lifetime you should not miss!" Then another dream came, a dream more disturbing: He saw faces which darted around, faces of friends, some of whom smiled, including a few unknown to him. Shallow faces laughed, while other faces appeared attached in some bizarre way to dead bodies. Fred Duncan flew in and for a moment seemed to be calling out to him. Zachary did not understand the words—they appeared distant. Then out of nowhere, still another face, a face he had seen within a tan car —the robber's face—and it again sneered at him and said,

"Stay away! You will be hurt, and you are not ready."
Behind the face was a sign with a picture of a
motorcycle shop. Zachary woke in a sweat and panic.
He suddenly remembered more about the guy in the
tan car and how he knew him.

⎯⎯⎯◦━◦⎯⎯⎯

And in some faraway place . . .

*A good and proper angel has been observing Zachary's
behavior unfold and regretfully says: "The kid has done
something stupid and unexpected—become fearful and
cowardly in attempting to meet a life challenge sent to him.
He will need to regain some balance and develop more
positive self-confidence in both his mind and soul. In future
months and years, many people are going to come into his
life and give support and direction, and some will even give
much-needed spiritual advice and energy that will help him
assuage and right a wounded conscience. Our prediction is
that he will surprise many and learn to come to grips with
the evil forces in the world, and eventually win the battle of
wills."*

*Not to be ignored were the skeptics. Another angel from
a devilish group laughs and says: "Just watch how events
following his complete meltdown at Duncan's Store will
take shape and allow for this total loser to continue to
screw up and self-destruct. He doesn't have now—and we
will do our best to ensure that in the future he won't ever
have—the will, the maturity, or really anything to survive
life's testing.*

*The power and temptations we send will overwhelm
him—it is always the weakest ones, those with the most
doubts, little family, and few friends' support, that are our
best candidates. He will be made to see how useless
religion and spirituality really are for developing the phony
things in life called 'character', 'witness' and 'faith.' It will
be our joy to watch him fail, knowing that the battle and
subsequent winning of his soul, we bet, is a foregone
conclusion!"*

Two:
A Bus Ride to Confusion and Doubt

A boy rode a bus to find solace and hope,
Fear and guilt came along and allowed little chance to cope,
A friend heard a story of violence and cowardliness too,
Could any help be given, could anything be made anew?

THE THORTON MOTOR SHOP was located two blocks directly in back of Duncan's Market. Zachary, as a sixth grader, often went there to watch some of the older boys work on motorbikes.

James Haney, a tall kid with red hair, taught him how to work on engines using various types of tools. Bigger kids hung around, smoking and talking about girls. There was a guy who had a scar on his face, who rarely smiled and looked angry all the time. He was dirty and had some type of tattoo on his arm of a lady and a snake. Once, someone asked him what the tattoo meant, and he told them it was none of their business and to piss off. He worked on an old Wizard motorbike, perhaps his own, never talked to anyone, and smoked cigarettes which constantly hung outside of his mouth, stuck to dry and thick lips.

The owner of the shop had once told Zachary that the guy's name was Carl Stewart. "Stay away from him. He has a temper and does not like to talk to anybody, a pain in the ass, a real strange hombre." Someone else mentioned that Carl had been in prison in southern Indiana and had moved to a small farm outside of Elm City after his release from jail. Last summer it had been reported that several kids, including Carl, were involved in an altercation. The police had been called and a strong warning issued to behave less aggressively! Little was known about the family, except they were poor and lived off a tiny plot of land, farming crops of beans and corn. Their residence outside of town was just beyond the city dump, where on Tuesdays and Thursdays city workers burned garbage. Smoke from this mess arose on the tails of an Elm City wind, which blew across the city with no thought to direction and caused putrid smells for all to enjoy.

—————◦—————

Ah! The wonders of a night's sleep, even one filled with so much comedy, but also much oddness laced with scares. Zachary, still partially numb from that sleep, stretched and reflected that he was now sure this was the same guy who had attacked his friend Fred Duncan. Things seemed to fit together including a haunting face that refused to leave the dark corners of Zachary's mind. But what could he do? The experience of a witnessed robbery, just twelve hours before, had caused much anxiety. There were simply too many dreams, too many remembrances of violence, as well as just plain cowardliness.

Now, as a new day dawned, he again had to face a robbery adventure with doubts and a conscience that was scrambled. The future was anything but certain, but it was time to deal with a man who might possibly be on a hunt for him. A plan of action needed to be forged, and a good one, he surmised, might be taking another ride on the Elm City buses. It was a cheap way of relaxing, and for just a nickel and transfers, he could spend hours revisiting his hometown and friends. The witnessed robbery experience had an exhausting effect on him; it was a time for reshuffling, a coming together again of mind and body.

The weather had broken with overcast skies and a very light mist, while the temperature dropped to a cool seventy-five degrees. The sun had become frustrated with all of Elm City and its complaints about the heat, so showing mercy, it refused to blast out direct rays and pester humanity, at least for today. And for sure, the bus would never break down two days in a row! Most importantly, a more welcoming face had presented itself into Zachary's mind—a savvy seventh-grade friend who might be of help and come to his rescue, help repair a partially fractured mind.

This guy, Bob Rawlings, had wavy black hair, thick glasses, skinny arms and hands, and a big brain. He and Zachary had known each other since the first grade, although Bob had long ago forgotten how and under what conditions they had first met. Zachary's friend had an older sister who was smart, and because she went to college, Zachary guessed she might have helpful advice to give. He understood he had created a mess for not being honest and telling facts to the police. It would be imperative for a journey to start with plain and open honesty, no fibs. A strong belief had to be held that optimism would fight nonstop against doubts, depression, defeatism and guilt. As Zachary ran across the street to catch the bus, he thought the noises he heard in his head were cheers of encouragement from someplace; maybe innocent bystanders. Impossible! Must have been only a strong wind blowing amongst the tops of elm trees.

An anxious kid stood alone and waited for a bus to take him somewhere, anywhere. He peered down

South Main Street and saw there was little traffic. Off
in the distance, the square grey front of the Elm City
bus chugged straight ahead, directly toward him. As
it departed Morton Avenue, transmission gears
shifted, and very slight black smoke arose from its
exhaust pipe. The "South Mainer" came straight
toward him; it was upright, did not list in any
direction, and moved in a straight, direct line in total
anticipation and belief of never again destroying an
engine. Each wheel of the bus turned in a forward
direction. Zachary felt a sense of exhilaration and
promise as the bus slowed down and stopped.
Between the two large headlights, he thought he saw
a faint smile from the front of the vehicle.

Doors opened, Zachary climbed aboard. Ahead of
him was a ride that this time would be uneventful—
no loss of engine control, and more of a response
from a conscience that had been shoved around,
moved in many directions, and opened and infused
with repeated stabs of guilt. Somewhere in this
confusion, there had to be a faint glimmer of victory.
Suddenly, he recognized that something was very
wrong. His friend Bob Avery wasn't in the driver's
seat.

"Fred Duncan didn't deserve that type of
whipping and punishment! I hope he is going to be
okay. What kind of a stupid idiot would hit an old
man over the head with a meat cleaver? The guy who
did that senseless robbery needs someone to kick
him hard between the legs and beat his face with
fists. Bob Avery was so upset about the trouble he
had with his bus yesterday, that he took some sick
leave. His wife told me she was concerned he might
have to go to the hospital because of chest pains. He
got a good night's sleep and will be back to work in a
few days."

The new bus driver failed to stop his verbal
babble. He moved, twitched, and sat behind a large

black steering wheel. His short legs and small frame, plus a large black mustache, reminded Zachary of a popular comedian, Groucho Marx. Words echoed and bounced around the walls and seats of the bus, just like the pieces of food stuck to the driver's mustache, which moved in synchrony every time his lips went into overdrive.

Zachary paid his fare, looked around, and noticed the bus was empty except for a large man who smoked a cigar and sat in a front row next to the driver. The kid tried to think of something to say, but nothing came from only blank spaces, so he went to the back of the bus and took a seat in the last row. Here, he would be free from hearing and seeing craziness from the driver. No such luck!

More conversation from the intractable driver: "Do you think they will catch the guy who robbed Duncan's Market? I heard that he wore a female wig and ran out of the store, took it off and put it in his back pocket. Some guy told me this morning that there were two women who waited in a large car parked outside. After the robbery, they drove down South Main Street toward Indianapolis. I bet they had a ball with the money they stole. The newspaper reported they took almost a thousand dollars. Just think of all the fun you can have with that much money!"

The emotions, which churned and rumbled inside Zachary, voted for a loud, boisterous response: *Why can't you shut your mouth, you idiot? You have no idea what you just said. Ignore the weird-ass, he is hopelessly in space; look out the window and pretend you are not here!*

Then, the driver tried to change the atmosphere by asking a ridiculous question. "What do you think of the St. Louis Cardinals baseball team?"

Question ignored! Absolute silence! The speed of the bus increased, and large portions of the Elm City State Mental Hospital whizzed by. Mental patients walked its grounds, and some even claimed to see

God, or at the very least hear voices, ones which emanated from inside their heads. At least, as far as Zachary knew, he and his friends were never able to replicate these "gifts" of extra-sensory perception.

During the fifties, Elm City was a bustling town, many things happening. There were several state institutions that provided for the blind, the deaf, and the mentally ill. The many staff of these facilities reaped a benefit—steady employment. There were two well-known and respected colleges providing important educational training. Industry hired, paid, and kept many workers busy with their manufacture of plastic bags, men's suits, salad dressing, and most importantly Ferris wheel rides for carnivals and late summer state fairs. Cornfields became partial natural fences, setting the town off from the country, while the downtown square provided a major hub of activity.

The city worked hard to have a sense of pride, a caring place—one with a big heart that tried its best, sometimes succeeding, sometimes not, to help and provide for others. It seemed so incredulous that anyone would use a meat cleaver to assault and then rob an innocent man, whose only intent was to sell groceries to people in need of food.

The bus continued through parts of South Elm City, and as it made its way back to the city square, it passed Zachary's old grade school where memories, both good and bad, resided and readied themselves to move front and center when called upon. This place of learning, Franklin Grade School, tried hard to educate both motivated and non-motivated kids, some who looked forward every day to attending, others who never wanted to learn but instead create havoc. Zachary had a brief interaction with one of those kids yesterday. The principal had a good heart and good intentions, but also possessed a hard and well-used paddle for the disobedient. The student body consisted of smart kids, dumb kids, and strange kids; there were boys who had girlish behaviors, and for this sin they were mercilessly beaten, bullied, and forced into hiding; and then there were girls with pretty faces, the ones who stole Zachary's heart and gave it back all too quickly.

There were two girls who had strong feelings for each other, but not for boys. They were taunted and made fun of as their own sense of identity slowly became marginalized and shaped for life. But why were they this way? Did God know about all of this? A coach, a gym teacher, listened and tried to care for developing physical prowess. Act out and be a shit, and you could be guaranteed to get your ear shaken up as portions of you body were lifted!

Maybe Zachary's most important and crowning achievement was a track race that he and a friend named Jeremiah, along with two other kids, participated in. It was a first-time competition against kids his same age from other grade schools in Elm City. They ran and won a 440-yard relay and were awarded blue ribbons. The accomplishment and "emotional high" felt after that race from the clapping of hands of friends and family, plus a picture taken for the local paper, needed to be bottled up and kept for an eternity.

There was, however, a more awkward issue. The fastest runner at Franklin School, Jeremiah, was Negro. To Zachary, this racial difference was of no relevance; but to others there was an accomplished job of hiding racial prejudice. While the town did not openly declare Elm City as segregated, the loss of equal access to jobs, or use of the local swimming pool by all skin colors, or choice of any seat in a movie theatre, directly pointed toward discrimination, even if some thought it was just barely audible in tone.

Jeremiah once told Zachary that he could "feel" a sense of superiority in certain people. These emotions and attitudes were never openly discussed, but rather were deceitfully hidden, especially when Elm City townsfolk, partially guided by the Negro kids who excelled in athletic contests, celebrated sports victories over other high schools. *But why would people hate, dislike, nor trust individuals based on their skin color, gender, marriage situation, or really any belief? It seemed so petty and wrong.*

But this was the decade of the '50s, the decade of many "beginning challenges" worldwide as well as at home, where there was a very open and loud mutual distrust by some people about the United States government and its true intentions. Civil rights were on the minds and consciences of more than just a few citizens. Arguments made in court, and some eventually won, gave the right to everybody to attend public schools of their choice, and to occupy any seat on a bus or at a lunch counter. It was more than just a right, but now the law of the land; but that never stopped a "festering discourse" among parts of society. Zachary would eventually see a small ray of hope, pride, and honest self-evaluation of his prized city when the town integrated the pool and the movie theatre. But racial discrimination remained hidden in the hearts of certain people and became a very personal matter, which lasted way too long. Did people spend too much time reflecting on the discourse of racial discrimination? Many guesses, no consistent answers! This was truly "the silent generation."

These memories conveyed thoughts that cried out for forgiveness and self-honesty; but none were heard. Instead, they were bound in a collective consciousness as a kid peered out at a city from a bus window and puzzled at the complexities of life— of people— and most importantly himself. But life must move forward, and so too did a city bus, past a grade school, past many memories and toward forthcoming new challenges.

Just beyond Zachary's grade school was Wolcott College. There were a lot of students, only women, who seemed to talk and smile a lot. Some might wave if a glance was given, and for Zachary, thoughts and fantasies were kept very quiet and secret. With all of those women available, Zachary knew that someday he would meet one, and she would become his wife; they would have lots of children and live in a big house with many bathrooms and no coal-burning furnaces. Zachary searched through many young Wolcott College women's' faces during his years in Elm City, looking for the perfect wife. He found many, although fortunately for all, courting never occurred!

Upon arrival at the square, the driver shouted out, "End of the line, everyone off!" Zachary came out of his slumbers and recollections and quickly exited, and then he boarded a new bus. He was now on his way to Bob Rawling's house and much-needed time with a friend who was to hear an unbelievable story.

———◇———

The West State Street bus was the first of four buses lined up on the Elm City square. During the fifties, its route took passengers out to the wealthiest part of town, where large homes, important people, and inflated egos all intersected and lived as one happy family. A sense of pride and financial stability collided with resplendent envy held by the rest of the town.

After turning off the square, the bus passed by the tallest structure in White County, the seven-story National Bank of Elm City. Just beyond, a bakery came into view; across the street was a drug store with a floor made from very small black and white tiles. Wooden booths covered with carved initials from "lost or found" loves provided decoration, and if one listened carefully enough, giggling might be episodically heard from dark corners. The menu: hamburgers, cokes, malted milk shakes, and french fries.

The Union Pool Hall was just down State Street, and kids congregated here and some sold local newspapers. Other sluggards hung around a pinball machine that graciously received deposited nickels, which were quickly lost because of terrible eye-hand coordination. In a large room, adjacent to the food counter, were six or seven pool tables. High school kids congregated and talked about the basketball or football teams, or gossiped about their latest girlfriends and how lucky they were to be in love.

More recently, though, people began to speak in more hushed tones. A hint of anxiety was discerned concerning a military draft into the United States Army. Many boys were on orders to go fight a "police action" across the world in a place called Korea. The look on people's faces signaled continued worry, especially by those who had no plans for a college deferment.

Carefully hidden was the fear of the unknown, of what might happen when machine guns and live ammunitions were involved and possible death or maiming of body and mind occurred. Baling hay, cutting corn out of beans, harvesting corn fields, selling life insurance, and socializing at the Elks Club would be put on hold until the world could be saved from evil forces afar.

The large White County Courthouse, built over 100 years ago, was across the street from the pool hall. Its bright red roof highlighted a yellow limestone building. A large clock, one that had not worked for years and was always in need of repair, much to the chagrin of many residents, hung over the center of an arch which covered the first-floor entrance. An American flag flew from the highest point of the roof. A black-iron picket fence partially circled each side of the building, affording protection or most likely privacy, protecting it from the "common areas" of town buildings and a few homeless individuals looking for a place to sleep.

Once, Zachary had slipped into the courthouse and looked at the large thick wood banisters polished to a bright shine, ones that people could hold onto as they ventured to the second and third floors. He listened carefully to the judges who yakked in the courtrooms, and he watched the lawyers scurry around with briefcases and looks of seriousness on their subdued faces. No doubt, somebody's life hung in the balance, and just the right words had to be spoken to a judge who wore a black robe and rarely smiled.

Today, as the bus passed by, one man ran very quickly toward the courthouse with a face of pain and distress. He was the same guy Zachary had seen yesterday outside of Fred's store—a strange fellow who had asked questions and wrote answers down in a small booklet. He was called an "assistant district attorney." Zachary wondered if he might have some special news or information about the robbery. Perhaps the man in the tan car had been caught, and they were going to bring him over to the courthouse for judgment and hanging. Then, Zachary remembered the men's restroom had an outside entrance. The man disappeared inside with hands close to a belt buckle, prepared for a quick execution of well-practiced movements for taking a nature break.

As Zachary sat on the bus, some people talked about the robbery, and one of them read out loud from the local paper: "Our police have tried hard to catch the guy who robbed Duncan's Market, but no one has given much useful information. Everybody has claimed to have seen many cars going off in several directions. What a mess."

Another person wondered if Mr. Duncan was going to live or die. "The paper said he was in 'a serious condition, but that he should survive.' I bet there are people who may have seen something and just don't want to come forward and get involved." At that point, Zachary quietly changed seats and opened a window. The fresh air felt invigorating and much needed. He looked out and began to feel anger throughout his entire body as a heart beat faster, chest tightened, and a parched mouth developed. The complete fickleness of fate took over a mind.

Why did he have to witness certain events yesterday? Why didn't he take another route home, which might have been shorter? Or, why did the bus have to break down at the time it did, just before reaching Zachary's house? And maybe most importantly, why was he just a complete and fully documented coward?

———————◇———————

"Carl, pass the beans and meat. I don't remember when your mom cooked a better meal; I don't want any comments about how beans just make you fart," Mr. Stewart commented.

"There has been a lot of talk about a robbery of some kind yesterday at Duncan's Grocery. Does anybody know if they caught the person?" the mother asked. Everybody became quiet, and then Carl's sister spoke. "I was cleaning the house today, and I saw Carl's bag partially opened with a lot of money inside."

The sudden silence in the room was deafening. Everybody stared at Carl, and he replied, "I won that money yesterday gambling."

His father looked at him sternly and asked what he was talking about. He didn't recollect that his son ever gambled. He did know that Carl lied a lot. Carl thought to himself and knew he could not give a believable answer. He was trapped and knew his old man would see through his lies. He mustered up some little-used courage, and then spoke: "I need to tell all of you about . . ."

"You did what?" his mother replied. "What were you thinking? You have broken the law. There is jail time in your future. That kid will tell the police. You must have #$*@^ for a brain."

Carl tried to pass that comment off by laughing a bit, and said the kid was no problem. He was too weird to make any sense out of what he saw.

The sister cried and screamed out, "You #*&@ idiot! Now the whole family is going to look like a bunch of fools. If that guy you butchered dies, it will be big trouble for you, maybe an execution. I am

46

going to have to leave town to get away from all of this stuff."

Mr. Stewart then assumed command and spoke with authority. "We have to come together as a family. Protect our own. When I work out the details with my sister who lives in Briggs City, I am going to send Carl there to stay with her until this mess blows over. In fact, Carl may stay there permanently and work. No one is to say anything about what we have just learned. We will dispose of the money, sell the car, and go on about our business like nothing has happened. Everybody must keep their mouths shut. Carl, you are to stay at home for a while, and then eventually find out where this kid lives. You are not to touch him in any way. We are going to have to figure out if he knows anything."

Carl felt angry—no, really pissed off—and his heart beat fast with a shade of anxiety and tension thrown in for good measure. He wanted to hit something or somebody. "I need my money," he replied.

His dad looked at him for a moment, and then said, "Do you want me to call the police?"

The State Street bus continued past more downtown areas before residential homes came into view. The inlaid red brick in the road's middle section eventually gave way to an entire covering of asphalt. Years before, trolley cars roared by on steel tracks and carried people home from work; that partially bricked path was a reminder of yesterday and all the people who moved so quickly through an active and vibrant city. A Trailways bus station, a funeral home, and a fancy hotel which served delicious meals at expensive prices, especially on Sunday, then the four-corner churches, and finally a real treat—some of the most beautiful and expensive homes in Elm City.

These "mansions," all built around the turn of the century, had large yards and were set back a considerable distance from the street curb. One house stood out. It was named the Claimet House and was three stories in height with a roof cupola, all red brick, and built in the 1800s by a man who was the president of the bank. The house was over 7,000 square feet in size and had always been the "prize of Elm City." Rumors abounded that, when he was campaigning for president, Abraham Lincoln had attended a "get-together party" and danced away the night on the second floor. Current fabrications include that if you looked hard enough at night, during a full moon, you might be lucky enough to see a rather tall man with a beard moving around to the beat of music. Zachary believed it all to be nonsense, with the only thing moving white curtains blowing in the wind.

During the early '50s, television had come to Elm City, mostly to the wealthy residents of the west side of town. The ownership of "TVs" was always a topic of interest and envy by many of the locals, especially those who were without these "magical boxes." Most of the screens, measured diagonally, were thirteen to fourteen inches with hazy reception; however, if a mountable and flexible antenna was moved around, luck might prevail and a clear image would appear, but not for very long.

The sets cost 150 to 250 dollars and were often the subject of bragging rights for the rich kids who came to school and described all the shows and sporting events viewed. Sometimes, when the stories became too embellished with just plain bull, it was not uncommon for one of the tough guys from the north side of Elm City to explode with anger and plant a fist upside some smart-ass braggart's face. Eventually, with the progression of the decade, more people in town purchased sets and a new civility reigned.

As Zachary stared out of the window, he suddenly saw a kid, Ramon Hughes, he knew from junior high school. He jumped up with anticipation and pulled the exit cord, and got off the bus to greet a sports friend. It would be useful to try and get his mind off unsettling events for a short while. Nothing would be mentioned about the robbery—too risky, and the source where gossipy stories were spun.

Ramon was a good athlete, the starting guard on the seventh grade basketball team. He was a little taller than Zachary and perhaps a bit skinner. A blond flattop haircut adorned a strong-looking face which rarely smiled. Dress was always simple: a white tee shirt and a pair of faded jeans, and atrocious-looking tennis shoes, torn and filthy dirty. Most of the kids thought Ramon was a complete jerk because he had a smart-ass mouth and liked to bully and make fun of people, often using language peppered with obscenities and put-downs.

He had one enduring positive characteristic: Ramon had nominated Zachary to the junior-high school basketball coach to play one game against a small-town rival so tiny in size that it had no restaurants, no gas stations, and took less that a few nanoseconds to drive through. Zachary played a few minutes, scored no points, but did get to wear the school's junior-high jersey; and he discovered the school's athletic dressing area, where half-time strategy talks took place within the esteemed boiler room. Here, viewing included watching a rather large rat run underneath some dirty rags indiscriminately thrown into one corner. "Stardom" in other sports such as baseball would come later, but not basketball—Zachary was too short, missed too many shots, and never passed the ball, a mortal sin never forgiven by the school coaches!

Zachary called out, "Hey, Hughes, what are you doing today?"

"Not much. Have you read the paper about the robbery out by where you live?"

Feelings resonated inside, and Zachary said very little.

"Yeah, I read something in the paper about it," Ramon replied with a wiley smile. "Bet I know who did it."

"Get out of here, how would you know who did it? You were not there."

Ramon explained, "Some of the older kids around where I live told me that a mental patient from the hospital jumped over the fence and went in the store, and hit the old grocer over the head. I have played on the grounds of the Elm City State Hospital, and there are a lot of crazy people out there. Once, when I played tackle football, a patient began laughing and yelled a bunch of cuss words at a tree."

Zachary reflected: *Ramon doesn't know the whole story, but I am not going to share anything with him. He has too big of a mouth and a confused brain, and by the time I finished telling him my account, he would mistakenly tell others that I, no doubt, helped rob the store!*

"Want to go over and see Dixie White?" Ramon asked.

Dixie was a cheerleader at the junior high school. She was well known for her friendliness to everyone. The two of them, Zachary and Dixie, had met while they served on Student Council. Somehow, Zachary had been told she "liked him," whatever that might mean, but he had his doubts.

"I have no interest in her. I am on my way to see Bob Rawlings."

"Bob Rawlings? That odd guy nobody likes?" exclaimed an astonished Ramon.

"I am going over there because I need help with some math problems, plus I may talk to him about attending his church." This, of course, was all nonsense and lies, but Zachary knew he had to conceal his true reasons for the trip.

A long silence, then Ramon spoke: "I sometimes think about God and that stuff, but I start getting a headache, so I just go out and practice my jump shot. I must make the high school varsity basketball team. I want to go to State and help win the title for Elm City High School."

Another thought then popped in to Zachary's brain, a story only Ramon could tell, maybe embellish. But it truly was unbelievable, made so real because of the history of Elm City and slavery.

A lot of old homes surrounded the area where the two boys had been gabbing. One of these residences had been a place where Ramon often visited. An elderly woman lived there, and she had told him of its interesting history, of visitors who temporarily visited, and how love, kindness, and bravery had been shown.

"Hey Ramon, tell me about Mrs. Carter again," Zachary retorted. Ramon gave a slightly embarrassed smile and related that this woman, when a very young child, remembered her mother telling her about how their house had been used as a "drop-off" point for Negro slaves from the South, now on their way to either Chicago or Detroit to find new lives, permanent jobs, and most importantly freedom from cruel Southern plantation holders. They arrived with not much more than the clothes on their backs and a few dollars. Emotions were always evident, but the families were determined to forget the past and make a better life for themselves.

Many of the slaves, including the children, bore scars and marks over their bodies from where thick bullwhips had been used to make them obey. The families would huddle together at night and sing prayers to God, thanking for their freedom and hoping for a new life. Once, it became so loud that the neighbors complained, and the police were called; some person came by and demanded to search the house. Luckily, the family went into a coal bin and nobody thought to check it. Another time, a family was hidden in a haystack. Mrs. Carter, Ramon's friend, said that as many as 100 families spent time at different houses and at least one church before leaving very quietly in the night and traveling in wagons, on their way to the bigger cities and deserved opportunities.

Then, Ramon became a little excited and said, "She showed me some old material that look like men's pants, and a coin a little girl had left, her way of saying 'thanks.' I wonder if she ever made it to freedom."

Zachary looked at Ramon and wondered, *was that a tear I saw in his eye?* No, never! Not tough Ramon, for he never showed feelings. But the noticeable crack in Ramon's voice and a far-away look could not be ignored. Zachary wondered not only about Ramon, but how well many people hid emotions, maybe too perfectly. Was it really bullshit Ramon told to make himself feel important? Maybe there were personal things inside him that were simply too deep to understand or uncover, at least for now. Later, in Zachary's journey through high school, he would hook up with Ramon again. Feelings experienced by Ramon would come out again, real tears, copious in amount, and words of sadness and loss about a girlfriend who was soon to leave him, never to return.

At the end of West State Street, where Zachary eventually re-boarded the bus, the Indiana State School for the Deaf came into view. Several hundred deaf students from all over the state were provided an education, kindergarten through the twelfth grade. Elm City was proud to have the school, and many kids, including Zachary, learned some aspects of sign language to communicate with the deaf population in town.

The school's main building was red brick, three stories high, with long porches attached to the second and third floors. In the back was the administrative wing where there were smaller classroom buildings, a dining hall, and student dormitories.

Students were not warehoused or isolated from the community. During the weekends, they walked downtown, free to look and touch life, and to use their hands and fingers to communicate with each other. Sometimes words were mouthed with great difficulty and lots of patience. It was amazing to watch the speed with which they displayed emotions and conversations. Many of these kids were shy and often would not look anyone in the eye; others verbalized and made sounds in the hope they would be understood. They smiled big, toothy grins and produced sign language both manual and visual; the shapes and movements of the hands were important. Letters and words were represented by positioning the fingers in certain positions, curved or extended. While it took time to recognize and assimilate these hand positions, the communication and understanding of thoughts and feelings was nothing short of priceless, the best example of the strength of the human spirit.

After the bus passed the deaf school, it made a U-turn onto College Avenue and whizzed by Indiana College. The school was founded in the early 1800s by a group of people from some fancy university back east. The college library and administrative buildings were covered by a faded red-brick façade. One building, located next to the library, was partially round, with a very old wooden grey porch in front. A sign in front described it as a place where students were taught physics or math upstairs, and psychology on the first floor.

A second building to the south had a brick tower with a bell on top that rang, signaling the time for class to either begin or end. There were a few small classrooms inside, worn wooden floors painted a flat black, while a large chemistry lab adorned the back of the first floor. Upstairs, there was a room with a strong smell of some chemical, which permeated the entire area. Across the hall there was a classroom in which rows of seats were mounted on an angular raised floor that extended up one side of a wall, almost to the ceiling.

The college had a prominent history. Many politicians and debaters had frequented its campus. Today, it was still very much involved with the community because so many local high school students, upon graduation, then became "IC" students. It was much less expensive than Wolcott College across town. Zachary dreamed this might be the place where he someday might also sit in old wooden seats while he learned about chemical letters and equations and remained carefully balanced, not tumbling down rows of seats and landing unceremoniously at the professor's feet!

The bus then approached Diamond Street, Zachary's stop. He got off and as he glanced at the sky, he watched the tops of large maple trees fan together in the wind. The leaves shimmered in the sunlight as they reflected vibrant green colors. If he listened carefully enough, whistling sounds might be heard, followed by other faint noises from branches fighting a brief stir of wind. There was a sweet smell of something in the air, perhaps jasmine. An air of excitement readied him to bravely approach his destination and be a risk-taker.

Bob's house was in the middle of the second block of Diamond Avenue, just past Grove Street. It was a two-story wooden frame structure, painted white and partially bound by a small porch in front. As Zachary climbed three steps and pushed the black doorbell, a slight feeling of anxiety came over him.

Events from yesterday resurrected themselves and for a second, a tinge of nausea lapped around his innards as quick visual memories of a bloody cleaver, ghastly sights and smells from a limp body on a floor, plus a snake from a tattoo flashed by, and then disappeared. Whispers from other places: *You idiot! Why are you here? What do you expect to accomplish? Your story will not be believed. When you tell your lies to Bob, he will see you as nothing more than a coward, someone the police might now want to put in jail for failure to cooperate as a witness. How are you going to explain why you were hiding in the back of the store while your friend was on the floor with a butchered head, close to death? Plan to ever tell your mother? She would be so proud of your bravery!* Suddenly, reality fought its way back into a disheveled mind, clearing itself of evil demons, which exited on cue. The front door opened, and Bob's sister gave the invitation to enter.

.

Bob's laugh was deep and guttural when he was told about the bus and its mechanical problems. "Really," he replied, "a bunch of helpless, angry people, who I can imagine were quite troubled. I bet if I saw the faces of some of those people I would know them. This town is full of many varied and strange people!" The humorous conversation would lay the groundwork for what was to come next, the contents of which would be anything but funny.

Zachary described his walk to Duncan's store and his observation of a man leaving the store, although he could not see the person's face; then a description of a specific car that drove by and almost hit him was given, including suspicions he held about the driver and the way he acted—excited maybe, as if he had just done something. But nothing more was said about the robber or what Zachary really knew—that they had been previous acquaintances.

"You were lucky nobody caught you hiding in the back room," his sister commented, and then she added, "don't you think that is the worst place you could have picked to hide?" Zachary felt his face flush in response to that negative comment, and for just one moment he wanted to say something angry back to her, but then he realized she was correct. In agreement with that remark, Bob's face turned serious. "Did you tell the police about the man who almost ran you over?"

Zachary replied, "No." He recounted that he wanted to say something, but was scared no one would believe him, that the papers would print his name, and the guy would find him and maybe take a meat cleaver to his head.

"Think hard, Zachary. Are you sure the guy who ran out of the store was the same one who almost drove over you a minute later?" his sister asked. Zachary answered, "I think so. He must have hidden his car along the side of the store in a small grove of trees, where no one would see it; then after the robbery, he jumped in and roared off and almost hit me. Things happened so fast, I am not absolutely sure."

Bob asked an even more difficult question: "Zachary, have you seen this guy before?" to which Zachary replied, "I don't think so." That of course was a lie, but for some reason he did not want anyone else to know he knew this guy and his name. Then the sister interrupted, "If you can visually identify a person you saw acting suspiciously around a crime scene, you need to immediately go to the police and tell them. The police will then be responsible for sending out a bulletin informing the public there is someone they want to talk to regarding this crime. If he is later arrested and found guilty, he would be sent to prison, and that would be the end of it."

The conversations were making Zachary feel more unsettled, pissed off, and nauseously guilty. He had to mount a defense. "What might happen to me after the robber got out of prison, or what if he escapes from jail, or worse yet, what if he is not found guilty and simply released? If I reported to the police what I saw, and it then got in the newspapers, the guy might come after me. I certainly don't want to deal with all of that crap."

Bob's sister, though, became resolute and stern in her response. "That would never happen. The police would protect you. You must go to the police now and tell them everything you know about the robbery. Just explain you were scared and now have become brave and want the police to make an arrest. You are trying and wanting to be a good citizen. I am sure they will understand about your concerns and hesitation. You are a valuable witness. How can you keep all of this in your mind? Don't you have a conscience as to what is 'right' and what is 'wrong'?"

In reaction, Zachary remained silent and thought: *I know they are trying to be helpful; that last question from Bob's sister stings, but I don't want the police and the rest of the town to find out what a chicken-shit I really am. They would never believe me anyway. It's easy for Bob and his sister to give me advice, but I am the one in the middle of all this trouble. Advice is easy to give, but for me, at least, much harder to take and use. Is there ever going to be a way out of this mess?*

Nothing was said for a long time. Zachary knew they were perplexed, just like he was. Bob agreed with his sister. "Yes, it is normal to feel cared and worried about the guy coming back at you, but you must tell the police what you saw, because it might help catch the guy and keep others from getting hurt." Adding on, the sister then suggested, "How about this plan? You might write a note about what you observed and mail or sneak it in some way to the police department. You could write something like: 'a man was seen driving a tan car very fast away from Duncan's store after it was robbed.' Then include other information, and be as thorough as possible."

Zachary thought for a minute. One phony excuse might be that he had atrocious handwriting. Maybe he should tell Bob and his sister about how the guy followed him home after the robbery. *Too late now! Too confusing! Just keep silent!* He remembered things his dad had told him a few years before about

57

keeping his mouth shut concerning certain "secret things" that needed to be kept from Zachary's mother, mostly involvements with other women. Further thoughts bounced within a head. It did seem of extreme importance that police authorities learn of the information he possessed; yes, the sister was on to something. The problem was Zachary imagined the law would blame him for withholding evidence, and the penalty offered up would be some type of reform school. Quite honesty, he was less interested in whether the guy was caught by the police than in saving his own skin. He was a coward, and he knew it.

Total quiet permeated the house for a seemingly long time, and then Bob asked if Zachary wanted a glass of water or a soda. "Have you told anyone else what happened?" Bob asked. "No"

"It should stay that way for now."

Bob then came up with a new and startling idea. "Maybe you need to talk to God and let him advise you."

Zachary was not sure what to do about that idea, laugh or become depressed. He viewed religion as something people did on Sunday out of some misplaced guilt or "too goodie" behavior. Bob said that he would offer up a little prayer. Zachary felt his face become warm. *What was Bob talking about?* While it was true Zachary had gone to church a few times with his neighbor, Buddy, the fondest stories he remembered were those about how easy it was to steal candy from the YMCA before attending services.

Then, out of nowhere, Bob commented, "How about praying right now to God?" Zachary said nothing, but thought: *Why should I involve God? What a stupid idea! When I have prayed for things, nothing ever happened; the angels were always far away, maybe AWOL, much too busy with other, more important things.*

A short prayer was given, and then some soulful reflections that Zachary's decision to keep his mouth shut was a huge mistake. The sister likewise seemed to understand (without directly commenting) that despite Herculean attempts to offer suggestions, Zachary had simply seemed too scared and too immature to acknowledge much responsibility. She knew the problem would not go away, and Zachary would be left with doubts and a conscience to deal with. Against this disconcerting backdrop, Zachary's visit with Bob was over. Spiritual advice had been given and considered, but other things concerning a robbery were not agreed upon—a neutral point with no direction forward.

After he left Bob's house, Zachary boarded the State Street bus and continued back to the town square. More homes with large porches and lots of elm and maple trees in the yards whizzed by, as did the public library with its dark stone front and pillars which supported a high, arching roof.

The library was a safe place he often visited to get books to read, especially during the summer. Once, while in grade school, he had enrolled in a summer program at the library and won some useless prize for reading the largest number of books. He and some other kids got their pictures in the paper, and Zachary met a redheaded girl who, one Saturday morning after they had disappeared into a semi-dark corner of the library stacks, taught him the art of kissing on the lips. She reminded him that he had much to learn about love! That summer went by too soon, just as she did—to other places and presumably other boys—never to be seen again.

The bus turned north and arrived at the square, where its number one position was assumed, directly in front of the Rexall drug store. Zachary left the bus and stood facing a surly summer wind that seemed as misdirected as his own thoughts. It would be a few minutes before the bus to take him home would return to the center of town, so he just stared at nothing in particular and thought about his prize: Elm City, Indiana.

The square was the city's heart and soul. This was where people came together on Friday nights after the local school football games to celebrate victories; to trade gossip about which farm had the biggest corn crop yield; and who had his barn filled with hay earliest after Labor Day; and most importantly, where the best sale prices could be found for back-to-school clothes that featured "real specials" like boy's denim overalls by Lee at the grand price of $2.50. Bib overalls were purchased by the many farmers who came to town to shop and see a movie, or to have a drink at one of several bars prominently located on the east and west sides of the square.

There were about thirty shops located in the heart of the city. Some were department stores, including a Woolworths, a Kresge, a JC Penney, Montgomery Wards, and a Sears Roebuck, where Coldspot refrigerators went for about $150 to $175; there was a furniture store that sold a two-piece living room suites for around $200 and a hardware store, a couple of jewelry stores, a shoe store, and a Piggly Wiggly grocery with its trademark black and white tile boundaries on the front facade. There was also an aging hotel called the Douglas, as well as a movie theatre and two banks.

Many doctors and dentists had their offices in a tall bank building. An elevator took worried and frightened kids to their feared destiny, located on one of the seven floors. After appointments, though, everybody went up to the top floor to view Elm City and the surrounding rich farmland. If one stared long enough, the ground and the trees merged together and disappeared off into the horizon.

The bustling traffic included cars, farm trucks, and huge cattle trucks that weaved in and out of position and continued round and round, then exiting on their way to deposit cargo in some faraway place. At four-thirty every afternoon, except Sunday, kids screamed out, "Courieeeeeeeeeeeerrr, five cents." Heavily weighed-down bags took their places over slumping shoulders as these mighty "paper warriors" sold the local newspaper in front of stores, bars, and bus stops on the square. When the wind cooperated, the smell of popcorn and hot dogs invaded and conquered everyone's desires and tastes.

As Zachary stood alone and continued his wait, he realized what he needed was something difficult to find— peace and complete suppression of a robbery, of a robber in a tan car, and most importantly, a guilty conscience that stayed around and annoyed. Elm City was his town, and its people were here for his support. He needed memories, happy memories, to assuage a frightened and troubled mind and spirit. He must refocus and jump-start a life again. He sat down on a hard, uncomfortable bench to do more soul searching.

The trip to Bob's had been the start of a long journey to find some help. But the sojourn had not yielded the results for which he had hoped. Maybe it had become a bus ride that really went nowhere. A lot of words had been thrown around, while self-awareness and emotions were ignored. He discovered, however, something about himself: That open confession and the revealing of secrets seemed impossible for him to do. He needed to find help for so many things, but where? A small thought permeated Zachary's mind. *There may be people in your town who want to help you if you ask. But can you learn to trust them?*

Bob had offered to take Zachary to meet and be part of a Sunday school class. If God was so big and helpful, maybe ideas garnered at a local church might provide Zachary an opportunity to act upon and give some needed defense from a dangerous man in a tan car. Bob had told him on several occasions that he prayed a lot and believed God answered prayer. And that "evil people" could be helped by really knowing and trusting God.

But just how evil was Zachary Stevens? He needed to grow up and take some responsibility; maybe he should have some faith that things would work out okay, if he just trusted older and wiser people like Bob's sister. Her good advice would no doubt be ignored, because it allowed for a rich and defeatist imagination to take over and convince him of things that simply were not true. The fear of the unknown was rampant, but it was his decision to make: *either seek a change, take a risk, try honesty, or remain silent and continue to carry guilt around in a heavy backpack.* Thoughts continued, and then were interrupted by the noise of cars, people in a hurry to board buses, and kids selling newspapers. That may have been why he did not see a tan car slowly drive by, speed up, and then disappear into an evening darkness destined to win its fight against a fledging sun failing miserably to hold onto its power of light.

Inside a filthy auto, Carl Stewart both reflected and talked out loud quietly: *"There is that kid who is going to be a problem for me. I want to stop this car and fix him for good. It is because of him that I don't have my money, and I must leave town. If I could just find a place to park the car, I might be able to catch him before he boards the bus and take him behind one of the buildings and scare the crap out of him. Then if he still is not able to assure me that he will keep his mouth shut, I will use a knife on him; or maybe not. I now remember he is the kid that hung around Thornton's shop. What if he tells others my name? I could give him ten dollars, maybe even fifteen, and then warn him that if he ever tells anyone about what he saw, I would have to hurt him. He is not a big kid, so there is a lot I could do to his body; break a leg or mess his face up. There is a rush of anger inside me that I feel right now; calm down. I guess I will go over to Steve's Tavern and have a shot of whiskey."*

At that point a semi-trailer truck sounded its horn and a driver yelled out a series of words not fit for print or human ears, but the message was clear: "Move on, buddy, I have to get off this square and down to Indianapolis."

The time had come for a worried and scared kid to take some action. He would reluctantly take Bob's advice, roll the dice, and check out this God stuff, even if it involved church and religion, plus much phony baloney. Who was the ideal person to help? Best answer: the minister of the First Methodist Church of Elm City, Indiana, a guy who had a broad smile, a caring heart, and a slight lisp in his speech.

Three:
"Onward Christian Soldiers Marching"

I'm told I must believe in Jesus and learn the Nicene Creed,
Can I remember all those words, I frightfully ask and plead?
Do I want to be a Christian soldier marching as to war?
Saying things I may not mean, becoming just another bore.

DARRELL WATKINS SWEATED BULLETS of perspiration behind his shirt collar when he taught about God and the Bible; there was no other apt description. His lips trembled with the very faint hint of a smile. One of his hands held the Sunday school lesson, the other supported his chin. He was poised on the edge of his chair and looked more than slightly nervous. A class of junior high school kids asked a bunch of pesky questions, including, "Did Jesus really come back to life? Why was his ministry so short? Was Eve tricked into failing and blame?" The kids sat in a very small room upstairs at First Methodist Church. A window was cracked open to let in fresh air, but it was ungodly sticky and hot during the summer. Everybody melted into an indescribable mass of protoplasm and smelled terrible. Darrell mused, "Why am I doing this?"

Eddie Watkins, a kid who made lots of stupid queries and had an annoying way of talking too much, wondered if Jesus had really come down from the cross and back to life. Bob Jacobs commented that was what they had discussed and previously agreed upon—well, not entirely. A couple of the other kids asked, "Why do portraits of Jesus show him mounted on the cross?" Bill Grant, a kid who never wore clean clothes and dispelled nameless odors, said that the crosses he had seen were empty, just like the tomb where Jesus had originally been buried. Then Sarah Myers, one of a plurality of girls in the class, asked if Jesus was the only person who claimed to be the son of God. Darrell looked at her and only responded with a slight smile that suggested *I am not sure.* Bob Rawlings then smiled, "Jesus is the only one mentioned in the Bible who is the son of God." But Sarah would not give up. She was persistent. "Our neighbors, who are Mormons, believe in the existence of many Gods, but I don't know which one they worship." Darrell moved around in his seat, as if it had become too hot for comfort.

Two other boys, Steve Jackson and Joe Gruneau, said little and appeared to have a difficult time staying awake.

All agreed, though, that the events in the Bible had occurred so long ago, it was difficult to believe in them—the stories seemed "lost in time," with no real proof they ever occurred. Larry Taylor, an odd duck who always seemed to ask negative questions, reflected, "Why didn't Jesus give his disciples more opportunities to raise both men and women from the dead, and to heal more sick individuals? By the way, where is Jesus today? He left, and we are here to fend for ourselves."

Darrell then said, "Don't forget the Holy Spirit as a perfect helpmate."

Several joined in and commented, "Who amongst us has ever seen a Holy Spirit?" The quiet was absolutely penetrating. Everybody waited, and then waited some more. Darrell said nothing, and suddenly the bell rang. It was time to get robes on and get over to the Y for a brief choir practice, and most importantly to socialize, exercise vocal cords, and eat candy and chew gum taken—actually stolen—from the snack bar before singing at the "big church." Parents and a congregation, especially Pastor Harris, waited with a bit more than just bated breath.

On each corner of a city block, west of the square, there were four different church denominations. First Methodist was the largest place of worship in Elm City. Its large stained glass windows and concrete walls were firmly implanted on the southwest corner of State Street and Church Avenue. It was "Sunday home" to the many Wolcott College students from across town. But more than just one group attended; it was a heterogenous congregation.

Zachary's friend, Bob Rawlings, had first encouraged him to attend First Methodist Sunday school, and later consider becoming a member of the church by taking a confirmation class. Zachary began to reason that if he became more religious, God would intervene and make the man in the tan car disappear. How or why this might happen was not exactly clear. The Methodist church sponsored the largest Boy Scout troop in Elm City. Zachary fantasized that if he joined what was called "Joe Hassle's Army," he would assimilate with a group of kids and receive protection that would collectively chase away a guy with facial acne and arm tattoos.

The other places of worship included an Episcopal church located on the southeast corner. Christmas Eve services always produced a large turnout of people eager to hear special holiday music, chat, and become holy—at least temporarily.

The Baptist church was on the northeast corner and held summer Bible school and revivals to "save souls." Converts would go outside the church on the sidewalks and encourage individuals to have their sins washed away. Things often become temporarily nuts when kids ran up and down the street handing out "salvation tracts." These small pamphlets showed pictures of people going up to a glorious walled garden called "Heaven," or down to burning flames and mean-looking creatures residing in a place labeled "Hell." Below these pictures was the question:

WHERE DO YOU PLAN TO SPEND ETERNITY?

On the northwest corner was a Presbyterian Church where nothing much happened. What an architectural splendor! Four churches, so close physically, but so different in many other ways.

On the Sunday morning after the robbery and Zachary's visit to Bob Rawling's house, Pearl Logan and her thirteen-year-old son, Buddy, picked up Zachary for a trial attendance at First Methodist Church. Buddy, a big kid and a friend, was already a member of the SMG and had often encouraged Zachary to join the group. Buddy described the gang as the one place where Zachary could find acceptance and happiness. But Zachary had deferred for many reasons, including shyness, insecurity, and doubts about the pompous and full-of-shit ways some of the kids acted.

Pearl honked the car horn several times, and then she peered out from under the large brim of her hat to see if Zachary was coming. Her big smile revealed large gold-capped teeth, a heavily made-up face of rouge and lipstick and a colorful dress. As he approached the car, she commented, "Hello Zachary, are you ready for a visit to Sunday school?" Buddy sheepishly smiled, slid down in his seat, and told his mother to shut up. The black, four-door 1949 Buick moseyed on down South Main Street, and Pearl felt important for her role of transporting children to learn about God, Heaven, Jesus, and other things she would never know about; probably a good thing.

The outside of First Methodist was a grey and white façade made up of cement blocks and limestone. The front faced east, and steps went up to four large doors that allowed a main entrance for spiritually needy people; alternatively, these doors also provided a quick exit when the sermons became too boring and a need existed to beat the crowd to an early Sunday lunch.

A few hundred feet beyond, a set of stairs went to the pastor's office. This partially hidden entrance could be used for both arrival and departure without being seen, something most parishioners thought he relished!

On this and subsequent visits, Buddy and Zachary would enter the back of the church to attend Sunday school. Some very old wooden stairs went up to the second floor, which connected to a narrow walkway and a series of doors with numbers on them. Their classroom number was four, and it was here they listened to stories about God and Jesus. No one was ever asked to take tests, no grades were given out, and everybody tried their best to behave. It was God's house, so order and reverence prevailed most of the time. Occasionally, however, some were to wonder if the devil had not become an uninvited onlooker for the sole purpose of provoking disorder. These thoughts were never shared—how could they? This was the house that belonged to and was owned by God, and He alone was the sole Director in charge!

The church's floor plan provided a second-floor loft-balcony area, which afforded a good view of the main sanctuary. It was a convenient place for kids to hide and throw spitballs and paper airplanes down upon people while they were engaged in varying degrees of prayer or simple idle gossip.

On the first floor in the back of the sanctuary was a large "overflow room" where temporary chairs provided additional seating for large events such as

Easter and Christmas. Many non-church folks showed up to receive "holy" support on these holidays. Downstairs was a large kitchen and recreational room for parties. In the far back were rooms where Boy Scout Troop 109 met.

All adults and many older kids who regularly attended church were eventually "nudged" into working, either in the nursery, teaching Sunday school, or singing in the choir. The church choir was a peculiar mix of members, including adults, teenagers in high school, and a few college students. The result was an occasional complement of musical harmony which had the potential for either sounding melodious, or cacophonous, or somewhere in between.

Buddy talked Zachary into "auditioning" for the choir, although it was apparent the kid's education had never included the exercising of rather dormant vocal cords. Certainly, this part of his anatomy was not well tuned and was unpredictable in terms of quality and quantity of any sensible noise.

Early one Sunday morning, about a month after the robbery, a bunch of confused and frightened kids went down to the front of the church, where the organ was located. They listened while Mrs. Grant played some notes, and then were asked to respond by singing "la, la, la" in tune with the piano chord. All voices sounded terrible, but Mrs. Grant just smiled and instructed, "Keep listening to the piano chord and match your la, la, la to it." Everybody tried, and recognizing they were failing, laughed much too loudly.

Afterward, invitations were given to all to join the choir, maybe an early sanctification of and for spiritual blessings, but that must be only a guess and perhaps a dream.

Choir practice was at the Elm City YMCA, a large building directly west of the Methodist church. It was open on Sundays after 8:30 a.m. Additional practices might be held during the week when special musicals were presented. Buddy and Zachary were always the earliest ones every Sunday for choir practice, and it was here that the fine art of thievery was first formed. They would first "scout out" the area well before Mrs. Grant, the choir director, eventually arrived to quickly review the music to be used in church service for that day. A deserted piano in the back, in need of a good dusting, temporarily came alive with its music produced by Mrs. Grant's nimble fingers, and while the choir was not the greatest sounding, all believed that a good God, always patient, gave much-needed forgiveness and grace!

On one side of the practice room was a large snack bar and kitchen. Temptation reigned, and was given into quickly and effortlessly. There were many possibilities for the satisfaction of culinary lusts. Wieners could be purloined from the refrigerator, and then hot dogs made, candy and chips taken from a counter, and soda from a dispenser.

Once, a hot dog had been cooked with disastrous consequences. Zachary had never used the meat steamer and was not familiar with the controls. A piece of meat had been taken from the refrigerator and boiled. The bottom of the steamer had a crack on its undersurface.

As the water became hot and the meat simmered, sticky water came out of the bottom and dripped all over packages of candy.

Zachary then became angry and inadvertently touched the cooker and burned his hands. Buddy came over, and together they wiped up the mess and were sure they heard voices of laughter from somewhere in another room exclaim, "Good job."

The hot dog with mustard, onions, and catsup heavily applied was quickly gobbled down, just as several choir members came in the front door and announced, "Hi everyone! Are we all ready for worship today?" Zachary wasn't, and a stomach agreed!

Alice Tinkham was a tall, middle-aged lady who wore very small glasses that were used for the reading of sheet music during choir practice on Sunday mornings. Her hair was brown and cut short; a small mouth only partially covered an attractive face. She was always alone, rarely smiled, looked depressed with life and most likely with herself as well. Her job at Wolf's department store involved selling expensive cosmetics and perfumes, none of which she ever used or could even afford. Her private thoughts about the attitudes of the rich customers who populated the store she kept mostly to herself, although Zachary might have guessed there was little "church love or forgiveness" for any of them.

She and Zachary sometimes chatted during choir rehearsals, and he was surprised to learn that her biggest fear of singing solo was that she either would forget the words of the song, or she would not be able to hit the high notes; the worries, though, were never realized because she was too much of a perfectionist.

But there were other issues in her life, not so holy, not so easy to talk about, which demonstrated what a mess her journey had been and how close she was to coming apart. She had initially joined the choir because she felt the need to get back in church and be around "Christian people." Her marriage of eight years had come to an end after her husband ran off with a waitress who worked at some beer joint east of town.

This unplanned disruption had caused Alice to search for God, redemption, and turn from "a wasted life of sin and degradation." She had made many attempts to pray, and pray a lot. A Bible was read and studied, although she readily admitted there were large parts that defied full understanding. Certain sections of the Old Testament called "Proverbs" and "Psalms" reassured her and lifted spirit and soul when she became sad and depressed. Then, a new day would break, and old dark thoughts slipped back into her life, including emotions of every nature that at times refused to take even a short break from inundating body and soul. Stability in her life seemed impossible: many questions, few answers.

The result became feelings of emptiness and a lot of body aches with pains in the stomach and gut. There was often little desire to eat, and she rarely slept well. But she also readily admitted that it was too easy to sit and feel sorry for herself, and simply think about her many problems and past mistakes.

The church, according to Alice, had not been very helpful or supportive. She wondered if there was not a tinge of judgment when information got out that her husband had run off with another woman. She recounted to Zachary, "It was like they thought it might have been my fault that he just up and left."

One of her major complaints, and there seemed to be many, was that church services were "too set" with no change or difference in what went on from week to week. The music and the hymns described things about Jesus, but it was difficult for her to make any connection with what the pastor taught. Zachary told her that he, likewise, never fully understood what was happening during the service. It seemed to him that many people looked bored, not really involved, maybe wanting to be anywhere but in church.

At one of the practices, Alice sang an angelic-sounding solo that was unbelievable. The words were clear, and the high notes easily reached and held, and then held even longer. After she finished, the entire choir applauded. She appeared somewhat embarrassed by the attention.

Later, when she sang the piece before the congregation, the congregation became still with awe. Zachary thought to himself: *How can this woman be so unhappy, and at the same time sing like she is filled with what people call the Holy Spirit, whatever that might be?* He looked at the faces of people in front of him, the congregation, and they, quite uncharacteristically, appeared to be crying—experiencing their own personal "God moments." It was obvious that when Alice sang, beauty, happiness, hope and forgiveness, and maybe something beyond any capacity to explain, were experienced by the church; a belief the Holy Spirit was at work

Zachary felt a need to compliment her on the solo. From somewhere in his confused head, he asked if she was happy and hopeful that things might get better for her. She became quiet, and a tear appeared on the side of her face. She paused for a minute and then said, "Zachary, you see a lot in other people, and that is a real gift God may have given you. Don't ever lose it." He paused, and then he wondered whatever caused him to ask her such a question. Zachary wished that Alice Tinkham, a lady who had a life of so little transparency, might likewise be comforted. The sad fact: She never was!

<hr/>

Her eyes were gigantic, green, and bright as emeralds, with a perfect face free of any imperfections, acne, wrinkles, or other such things. Teeth a flashing white. She was a favorite of everybody in the choir. Laura Simpson, a student at Westcott College, had a great personality but deep secrets, too. One day before choir practice, she and Zachary visited alone. After a long pause, she said, "I want to tell you a secret I have carried around much of my life. Promise to tell no one."

The answer: "Sure."

When Laura was fourteen, an uncle she trusted came over and asked if she might help him move some items in his house. He told her that his wife and others were going to help. When she arrived at the house, he requested that she hold a heavy box, and she agreed. But then things became crazy because he reached over, touched her face and attempted to kiss her. She freaked out and immediately dropped the box while fear and anxiety took over as she bolted for the door. The relative grabbed her and quickly placed her on the floor. He proceeded to hold her down with one hand and push her dress up. As he moved to lower his pants, she kicked him between his legs, then jumped up and ran out the front door.

Upon hearing this unbelievable account of a sexual assault, Zachary was dumbfounded and didn't know what to say, so he wisely kept his mouth shut. Laura's voice trembled and reported that this relative was an important man in the community—a trusted banker. Laura had fears that no one would believe her story, and that quite possibly the whole family might be damaged, humiliated, and tense; angry feelings might be an outgrowth because of such an unbelievable story.

"I just decided to live in denial, but never accept this terrible experience,"

Her best response, she reasoned, was to stay completely away from the guy. But fears and scars remained. When she was alone, memories flooded her consciousness. In her sleep, she relived her uncle's attack. Voices and whispers told her, "You are to keep your mouth quiet because if you tell anyone, you will be found out." Then she would awake trembling, exhausted, and confused. More than once, she thought her uncle was standing behind her; she would take a quick look, see nothing, but was sure she had heard movements and saw shadows of a body.

The uncle had to be no good, and Zachary reported that he wanted to knock his teeth out. He told her so. She smiled and then pleaded, "Please don't tell even your closest friends."

Zachary wondered, *why did she tell me something so personal?* A weak memory came back into a curious mind from boring times in Sunday school when the concept of "evil" had been presented. It was proposed in the Bible to be personified by a being called the devil, a real person who roamed the earth destroying people. Most of the kids thought this "force" was simply imaginary; not real, but kind of funny, maybe even a joke. "Do you think your uncle is part devil?" Zachary asked, realizing he had no idea what he was asking! Laura looked at a confused kid for a long time and then, without flinching, answered, "Yes."

Laura eventually stopped coming to church and the choir, maybe for many reasons. Zachary thought about her often and wondered if her bad dreams ever went away. Was she ever able to forgive or forget an insane uncle who must have been totally evil? The kid would never know what happened to her, nor see firsthand the resilience of the human spirit. Years later, he would have been impressed to find out that she received a graduate degree in psychology and counseling, and eventually directed a center for sexually abused women.

There was one man in the choir, Peter Owens, who Zachary became close friends with. He was tall, maybe over six feet; glasses sat precariously over a very small nose, all blending in with a plain, nondescript face. He worked as a manager of a shoe store on the square. His family was large and included four children, all of whom were still too young to attend school. They had little money, but the marriage was strong, and it was evident that much love prevailed in the family. They were always together laughing, holding hands, and often hugged each other warmly with emotion.

Peter often showed up early for choir practice, and he and Zachary talked about many things, including spiritual topics. One day, after a particularly difficult Sunday school lesson that had dealt with the blessings of a strong and loving heavenly father that earthly fathers should emulate, Zachary felt like he wanted to punch the wall. Anger swelled up inside and there was the strong inclination to scream words, words most unholy. He was about to stick a rather large number of candy bars in his pocket when Peter showed up and immediately commented on how upset Zachary appeared.

"What's going on with you? You have a mean look on your face." The kid wanted to say that he had to leave because he was not ready to sing for God today. Then a small voice inside his head said: *Be patient and tell him about your dad.*

So, Zachary took a deep breath and started in on a long and lonely story about a dad, his abuse of alcohol, and the women with whom he enjoyed company. The kid recounted the painful memories well and accurately, because they were etched into his mind; they refused to go away and remain silent.

Zachary remembered a night he could not sleep, so he went to the front porch and witnessed an unbelievable scene—his father, parked in an old jalopy, embracing some unknown woman. Later, upon reaching the porch and finding Zachary still there, his dad realized what Zachary had seen and said, "Maybe it's better to not say anything and upset your mother. Sometimes there is a need to keep quiet and not cause a lot of trouble within the family."

As Zachary's narrative became re-focused in front of Peter, there were feelings of sadness and loss. Words and feelings collided. A fear of how foolish but also vulnerable he had become to a stranger.

After much silence, Peter looked straight into Zachary's face and said, "I had a similar experience with my dad. He drank all his life and eventually died of a problem with his liver. I got my strength and hope from God and the people at this church. Pastor Harris has always been a help. He is a very spiritual man and has always explained things about how much God loved me and only wants the best for my life. A new confirmation class will be starting soon, and I would like to recommend you to the pastor as a good candidate. Is that okay, Zachary?"

Zachary thought for a while and wondered how someone as great and large as a God might reach down and help him. It sounded too good to be true. Maybe he should trust Peter and tell him other things—about robberies, about violence, about cowardliness, and maybe also about a very dangerous man, perhaps a friend of the devil. Certainly, he could go to this confirmation class even if it was boring and fake his way through learning about a bunch of religious stuff. Some memorizing parts of the Bible and a creed were involved. Zachary could easily do that, while any real interest or commitment toward developing spiritually would be missing, but that was okay. Who knows! God might even fool him and not turn out to be so distant. But could he be sure? Personal thoughts: *I guess I will not appear too ungodly. I will fake this one and tell him 'yes' even though I have my doubts. Enlist in the Lord's Army? What is happening to me?*

Then, a lot of noise and choir members bolted in for some strong attempts at singing at the top of their voices for the entire church, and maybe with some luck, God too. Conversation was over, but traces of varied emotions remained in Zachary's brain, slowly percolating, seeking friendly shadows to befriend.

The First Methodist congregation, as with the choir, had a mix of people with many different life histories and issues. The students from Wolcott College, and there were many, sat on the right side of the sanctuary in rows four through nine. Very starchy clean faces and smiles revealed a readiness for a spiritual message from the pastor.

Their walk around the square and down West State Street every Sunday morning was an event observed and welcomed by the entire town. Maybe the laughter and talk were too loud and boisterous at times, but who cared? Zachary's friends often left the sanctity of church to watch all those pretty college girls on their way to spiritual enlightenment. Many fantasies also had to be present, but certainly never mentioned or discussed by a bunch of boys, including one kid who sang for God and tried to remain focused on hitting all the high and low musical notes.

Directly in the center of the church, the loyal and long-standing congregation of church members of many years could be found. This group consisted of older women with large hats of all sorts and colors; gigantic necklaces or elaborate broaches on multicolored dresses; and much too much facial make-up, with mouths buttressed by dentures which clattered incessantly. Hushed whispers and conversational topics were always a matter of great speculation, but generally not spiritually uplifting. In contrast, the men sat quietly as if in some other world and likely wished they were apart from the gabbing.

The Lewis and Wilkinson families were always located near the center of the church. These helpful folks provided the hand fans used to circulate a small breath of fresh air during the hot summer months. Advertised on the fans was information about eternal peace, burials, and appropriate addresses and phone numbers.

Church bulletins were handed out to worshipers after they slowly lumbered into the sanctuary and sat down. Latecomers were always directed to the balcony on the second floor. Ushers had great difficulty containing their irritation with those who failed punctuality. Attendance was good, and God must have been minimally satisfied. Sometimes, Zachary's mother came and sat by herself. She smiled, and Zachary guessed she was proud he was singing in the choir, although this was only a guess.

She never made much commentary about his church involvements.

The service began with a song of praise that provided a theme for subsequent hymns sung during the offering and prior to Dr. Harris's sermon that always lasted twenty-five minutes. Zachary rarely understood what the pastor talked about, likely true for the rest of the choir and large portions of the congregation.

A sermon came with anticipation and interest, attention readied, but all appeared to fade away as time dribbled by—too much preaching about God, sin, and jumping around within the pages of the Bible, first in the Old Testament and then the New Testament. When it was especially hot, some individuals, generally the men, slipped off into a light slumber.

An example: one Sunday a large man who sat near the back of the church began to snore quite loudly. Then, to everyone's amazement, he fell out of the end of the pew into the aisle. Eddie Lewis, a kid who always laughed too much, started to giggle. Mr. Jones admonished, "Quiet in the choir!" Dr. Harris looked around, smiled, and kept on with his sermon as if nothing had happened. Someone helped the man back to his seat, where he remained alert but also embarrassed for the rest of the church service.

The offering was a special time at First Methodist. Certain select and trustworthy men, who possibly took themselves too seriously, performed the task of collecting money. They came to the front of the church, stood and carried plates lined with a cloth material, passing them row by row throughout the entire congregation. These ushers seemed to have a "better than thou" attitude and watched very carefully who was contributing. The collection plates went throughout the choir, and Ralph Jones and Jeff Lake made sure everyone was given an opportunity to contribute. Zachary rarely made attempts, except when Ralph Jones held the plate in front of him, perhaps a little too long.

On one occasion, several children served as "guest" ushers. After they had taken the collections, they started back down to the front. One rather fat kid tripped and caused money to fly everywhere. Zachary wanted to laugh, but for self-control, pinched himself. The pastor came down and helped pick up the cash and envelopes. As he bent over, the unthinkable happened! One black and one brown sock could be clearly observed. Zachary and others felt relieved that even ministers of God had some disparity in their selection of clothes. Later, Ralph Jones mentioned that the choir members should be respectful in church. Things like the color of the pastor's socks, despite their mismatch, must be simply ignored. Larry Taylor then made a good comment: "At least the pastor did not have holes in them." Everyone agreed, and support for the pastor strengthened.

One day after church following a long-winded sermon, the pastor stopped Zachary and said, "You look sad and not particularly interested in what we are learning about in our preparatory church membership and confirmation class. Might we have a little conversation?"

Zachary told him there was a lot on his mind, things he had difficulty sharing with others. Past turmoil, always kept secret, included a mom and dad with a failed marriage, or more recently a grocery store saga filled with a lot of blood and deceit, made him feel sad and like a big failure. Awkwardly, he mentioned that once he went out into the backyard and wished he was brave enough to climb high up in a tree, jump down, and maybe break his neck. Perhaps there would be no more pain. Fortunately for him, he guessed, those kinds of feelings never came back, at least not as strongly. "I am glad for that," the pastor said. Then Zachary asked the pastor to read his poem.

"I stand so much alone, few friends, few hopes, few
dreams. I notice myself so frightened, so dishonest, and
confused by others' tricky schemes,
I have so many questions about myself and why I refuse
to grow up, be more whole,
All I ever wanted from life was some understanding and
to better know a slightly curious soul."

"That is an interesting and curious poem. You
have some writing talent. Zachary, I wonder if some
of those feelings and questions have any solutions to
them?" the pastor commented. Zachary could not
think of anything to say and remained quiet. He then
asked, "Do you think that God really cares about me
or any of us kids? Maybe when we get older, he might
like us better."

"I know without a doubt that God loves you at
this very moment. He knows your name and knows
every hair on your head. He has always wanted the
best for you. That was true from the time you were
born. He has a plan for you; don't ever forget that."

"What plan was there for my dad, or for my
mother?" Zachary asked. "They are both divorced. He
left home and has become a bum in Chicago. I
remember once he called home and said, 'Zachary,
this is your dad.' Then he started crying, and at first
I thought I was going to cry too. But I didn't and
instead just felt defeated, sad, perhaps fearful and
angry."

Then the pastor interjected: "I know, Zachary,
your mother came to see me after your father left
home. She was a very brave woman, and I know she
has and will try to do the best to raise you. Your dad
had a sickness of the mind, and he was never able to
get some of the demons out of his soul. They had a
good hold on him. Your mother will guide and give
comfort and advice during the next few years."

The silence that followed was penetrable to mind
and soul, and it caused Zachary to take a chance
and try to dig down and get some more heavy
garbage out of a reclusive conscience.

"There is something else I need to talk about, maybe confess. My conscience pains. You will keep this information just between the two of us?"

"Of course."

Zachary then recounted the story of his friendship with Fred Duncan and the surreal events of the robbery, as well as what he had witnessed. He described his fears about Carl Stewart, especially if they were to ever meet face to face. As he spoke, he watched and felt support from the pastor, whose eyes did not once deviate from directly focusing on Zachary's face. "That is quite a story, Zachary. I am surprised that even with not telling anyone about it, the police were never able to apprehend the guy. I know you must have felt great fear, but did you also feel guilty for not helping the police with information?" asked the pastor.

Zachary stammered, "Yes."

The pastor seemed in control and suggested, "Let's pray for forgiveness and let God speak to your heart."

Zachary agreed, but he found his mind wandering as the pastor talked to God in only the way that "religious" people can and do. The office ceiling didn't open up with celestial creatures, and Zachary worried more that the pastor would not keep his mouth shut about what he had just heard, especially to a church that seemed to be a wide theatre of gossipy talk. Much doubt remained that any prayers heard "upstairs" might be responded to by a God so far away, so unknown to him.

The pastor continued: "All of us find ourselves in various situations throughout life, some of our own making and others not. God watches over us and protects us daily. It is my firm belief that as Christians we have 'help-mates' that are all around and close to us; perhaps in other dimensions we don't see or understand. These personages are from God and represent His total Holiness. The Bible calls them 'Angels' or 'Holy Spirits.' We must believe that heavenly bodies not only watch over us, but also talk to and support us in time of need.

"As to how to handle your current dilemma, I can't tell you that you must go immediately to the police and tell the authorities what you know about the robbery. Keep asking God for advice, and listen as hard as you can for the slightest of whispers from inside your mind."

That directive from the Pastor would be a difficult task for Zachary. He had never really understood much about God or how to "personally" talk to Him beyond rote prayers. The kid hoped, without asking, the pastor would be his spokesperson to God.

But how would that work? He wondered if the pastor would even agree. Suddenly, as a slight change of subject, Zachary was asked if there wasn't a time when he had taken a risk, put effort out, and became proud of his accomplishment. Something from a summer past came into his mind.

A bunch of restless kids had been discharged from school for a three-month break. Boredom was everywhere as Zachary sat on the front steps of his house and gazed over at the state hospital grounds.

Suddenly, a guy by the name of Earl Little, who lived down the street, came by with some other men, and he asked Zachary if he would like to go with Ed Franklin's State Hospital softball team, the Elm City Red Sox, to Culver City and be part of the team for an important game.

"We should be back by midnight," Earl reported.

Zachary knew his mother would resist the plan, especially since it was out of town. Perhaps if he begged and bribed her by offering to cut the yard and not ask for payment, she might agree. She consented with the stipulation that all homework was to be completed by the next night. A team of grown men and a kid then left to briefly live a sport fairy tale played out on a softball field.

In the car, in addition to Ed Franklin and Earl, were two other guys, Randy White and a pitcher, "Lefty" Thomas. Lefty pitched every game for the state hospital. When Zachary climbed in, all said, "Hello, Rookie," except Randy, who looked the other way. He must have objected to taking a kid along to play in a men's softball game. His response was not all that unusual, Randy always appeared discontented. When he played softball, he complained his teammates were too slow and failed to put out enough effort.

"Come on," he would say, "start playing ball, quit making mistakes and play with more determination and spirit!" Without a doubt, he would be Zachary's least likely supporter.

Despite a cross breeze, which swept through open car windows, perspiration dripped nonstop from everyone's face and neck while a radio blasted an old hillbilly tune about cheating hearts and good-looking people doing cooking. It was hard to hear what Manager Franklin said, but it must have included reviewing signs for stealing, taking pitches, and other stuff Zachary knew nothing about. Lefty took out some chewing tobacco and asked Zachary if he wanted some. "No thanks," was the answer, and then Earl bragged about the St. Louis Cardinals and how they were going to win a pennant this year.

A discussion of married life then ensued, and Lefty mentioned he wished he was single again, and with no hint of common sense, began to describe things he wanted his wife to do with him in bed. "Shut up," Ed yelled out, "There is a kid in the car."

Everyone laughed, including Zachary, although he had no idea what anyone was talking about. That was probably a good thing.

The trip proceeded through small towns with their one movie theatres called "Strand," "Indiana," and "Paramount." The little towns had small town squares, at least one gas station, and a school building built with light colored bricks of Indiana limestone.

They arrived in Culver City, and Ed produced a uniform. Zachary made a quick exit into a grove of trees and changed clothes. Ed told him that he would be a substitute on the team and might get to play, or be a "base-on-ball runner" for one of the slower players. One thing known about Zachary—he ran very fast, short distances only.

The ballpark was bigger than the one in Elm City. People paid to get in, and the field had dugouts for the team players to sit and feel anxious. There were bleachers on either side of first and third base. Behind home plate in a cavernous area under the spectator seats, sodas and hot dogs could be purchased. Huge trees sheltered behind the curvature of the outfield fence, which was painted an off-grey color. A hundred people or more came out to see the game. At the Elm City field on the hospital ground, there were rarely more than twenty people who bothered to show up and watch a bunch of grown men become kids again, albeit briefly.

Zachary sat quietly on the bench and eagerly watched the game. The opposing pitcher was a tall guy with a thin mustache and skinny arms. At first it appeared he was not throwing very hard, and Zachary imagined that he might have a chance to compete if he got into the game. Suddenly, as the warm-ups continued, the pitcher threw harder, and the ball traveled faster than even Lefty's best offering; this was not an encouraging sign.

Ed came over and reassured Zachary. His counsel: "Don't worry. When you are at bat, I am sure he will pitch slower." Zachary, of course, believed this bullshit because he always lived such fantasies during his childhood, a form of protection which helped protect fragile self-confidence and deny any fearful reality; this had to be one of those times.

The game started at exactly 7:30 p.m. Zachary's team hit first. After the first two batters were retired on strike-outs, Earl smashed one down third base for a double. The next hitter walked, and then Randy came to bat. He appeared relaxed, and on the second pitch he hit the ball over the left field fence for a home run. Randy came back to the dugout to the cheers of the team, walked over to Zachary and said, "That is how it's done, sport."

Jitters exploded inside Zachary's stomach and bounced from cavity to cavity as Ed looked down at Zachary and winked. Lefty continued to pitch and was impressive. He either struck out, or got the hitters to ground out or fly out. The game proceeded with the Elm City team ahead by five runs. Ed kept looking Zachary.

Then, big-time fear showed up. Zachary was told that he would bat next. The pitcher smiled as Zachary walked to the plate, and for a moment, Zachary thought that maybe pitching speed would be adjusted. Was he mistaken! He never saw the first pitch. It was in the pitcher's right hand, and then a ball smacked into the catcher's glove. "Striiiiiiiiiiiiiiii . . . ke!" yelled the umpire. The only thing Zachary saw coming toward him appeared to be a white blur. The next two pitches missed the strike zone. The rest of the team shouted encouragement, although some may have laughed as they prodded him to hit a home run.

The pitcher threw a change-up and the ball started for Zachary's hands. He did not back off, unusual for him, for he was secretly always afraid of being hit by any pitched ball. This time, though, he kept both of his legs together and timed the swing to when the pitcher's throwing hand came around and released the ball. He stepped forward and connected. The ball went straight up in the air just beyond the pitcher. The second baseman, positioned perfectly, made a simple catch.

The cheering from the Redlegs dugout was loud and boisterous. Zachary felt he had hit a home run as he returned to the dugout. Randy came over and said, "Welcome to the majors, rookie." Earl and Ed laughed and commented that Randy had paid Zachary a compliment.

Lefty went on to pitch a no-hitter, his third of the season. Zachary played right field for two innings and made two catches and no flub-ups.

After the game, they stopped at an A & W Root Beer stand and celebrated the win. Zachary suspected that had he not been with the team, they might have had drinks a bit stronger in alcohol content at places close to the highway, where juke boxes lit up dark walls and women laughed loudly into the night.

The ride back to Elm City was joyous. It most likely was not the game as much as it was the confirmation that Zachary realized he had some athletic talents and was able to use them with a degree of confidence. Character, strength, and belief in self all came together, if only for a short moment. Ed told him that he might want to think about playing for the team on a regular basis when he grew older. Randy smiled and winked, and that sent a message of acceptance not soon to be forgotten.

As they sped through towns and farmland, the smell of honeysuckle drifted into the car. It had become cooler outside, and Zachary thought that life was maybe too good. He wished his dad could have seen him play. What advice or comment might he have given or shown? Zachary felt a brief bit of sadness, and then the emotion was gone, just like his old man.

The pastor listened attentively. He told Zachary that acceptance by anybody was very important, and observed that because of the softball game, Zachary had grown in confidence. Zachary agreed with ever so slight a smile.

"Zachary, you should not allow yourself to only think about all of your failures, because if you do, that is the best way to continue to feel depressed and unhappy."

A confused boy thought: *Singing in the choir and meeting people in church is okay, but I don't feel like I have any closeness to God. It was helpful, I guess, for the pastor to listen to my confession and reassure me that God cares, but I still can't experience much "religious happiness" or freedom from a guilty conscience. It seems easier to sprout words than to really touch and feel God and heaven.*

Zachary left the meeting and started home, facing a cold, bitter wind. The tears came too easily and seemed to freeze on his face. Just the mention of his parents brought back feelings. The emotions needed to be tucked away and forgotten, maybe stay lost. But he admired their persistence. He, though, had found a new friend in Pastor Harris, even though little was understood about conversations masked with a "spiritual vocabulary."

As Zachary's walk continued, the wind picked up, and darkness descended and totally wrapped around and enveloped a confused kid. A car passed slowly by, and although Zackary did not recognize the automobile, he knew the face that peered out belonged to Carl Stewart.

A faint smile was produced, and then the car's brake lights came on and movement stopped. The driver got out and called, "Hey kid, come here!" Zachary had quickly ducked behind and burrowed into a thick bush while a heart beat fast. It was apparent Carl Stewart was still in town. Absolute silence and good cover produced invisibility; and then a one-way conversation began.

"Zachary, I know you are out there. Listen to me. I know a lot more about you than you might think. Let's talk. I might let you take a ride on my motorbike. But we have some things to chew over, you and me."

A scared kid refused to move, or even breathe; silence must be maintained. Finally, a car's motor revved up, and Carl Stewart disappeared into darkness.

Carl reflected: *That was the kid I saw at Duncan's store, I am sure of it. I need to keep after him, be persistent. Yet he really saw nothing, so how would he know that I robbed that store? My dad may want me to not bother him, but I can't risk having that piss-ant out there on the loose with an open mouth that could be dangerous. I don't have much time . . . here in Elm City for just a few days. Shit, I wish I did not have to go back to Briggs City. It's such a boring place to live, and I need more money. There are ways for me to get some cash. I have been successful, and I can be again. Zachary and me need to settle some things. I wish my mind would stop racing like a stock car. These damn thoughts keep bouncing around in my head and seem out of control. Somehow, I must figure out how to make Zachary just go away, disappear . . .*

A frightened kid remained in the bushes for at least another twenty minutes, then darted out and ran home. He had thoughts too, but ones not worth repeating. It was more important to focus on getting to safety, and then retreat to a pretend world where things like Carl, a guilty conscience, and maybe life itself could disappear, at least for the night.

———◆———

The next time Pastor Harris met alone with Zachary, he surprisingly asked a very specific question. "Zachary, how well do you really know God?" The kid's reply was that he didn't think he and God were such good friends, and often when it came to "religious things," his mind went blank. He simply could not come up with any words of clarity about God, Jesus, or anything related to religion.

The pastor smiled and asked Zachary to listen carefully. A discourse was then started about God and man. "I believe you and I were created by a vastly more intelligent being than we can truly understand, but we also should remain confident in our belief that He has always existed.

Can we ever fully realize what God's son really did for all mankind and specifically for you, Zachary? You have read about it in Sunday school class, and you proclaimed it every time the Nicene Creed was recited in confirmation class. Christ, son of God, went to places no one else ever went, especially to the poor and outcast. He touched and healed sick people, loved and forgave women who sold their bodies for money. He had meals with robbers and other failures in society. Why? He wanted to show His Father's love. He wasn't for some, He was for all, and He was personally for you, Zachary.

"Can Jesus be believed? Of course, he can. Change occurs for all who seek after God, but people need to abandon an old life in favor of a new life, a new beginning. Keep these facts deep in your mind, Zachary, and don't ever forget what I just said. Carefully read John 3:16 about God's love for you and how much He has always wanted to save you for His very own."

Zachary was quiet and thought to himself: *I don't understand a lot of this, but it sounds too good to be true. Who doesn't want to be loved and recognized by God? But according to what is taught in Sunday school, God seems just too far away. Since we can't see him up close or ever know that he hears anything we say to him, how do we really know that he truly ever forgives us? One thing I know for sure is that I don't forgive that robber and all the stuff he dumped on me! My mother has never forgiven my father, and I doubt she ever will. What I want is my conscience to stop reminding me of what I did after the robbery. What do I have to do to get guilt far away from me? Confess? Tell the truth? How do I ever know FOR SURE if I am forgiven?*

After meeting with the Pastor, Zachary shared some spiritual concerns with Buddy, Steve, and Joe as the gang members spent useless time walking around the square, peering into shop windows. The kid spoke of his conversations with the Pastor, but all of the kids immediately replied, "Stevens, shut up! We don't want to hear any more talk about religion. We get enough of it on Sunday mornings." Zachary, embarrassed by the comments, did a good thing; he shut his mouth and began talking about some of the girls in the class. All felt relieved! He was back on a safe turf once again.

⸺⚬⸺

It was certainly true that all people eventually die. Chester Rice—a man who weighed at least three hundred pounds, was well liked by all, sang in the Methodist choir, and often did solos during offerings—departed planet Earth for places unknown on the following Tuesday morning. Some said he had a heart attack and collapsed at home. His wife found him on the floor, gasping for breath and praying to God to take a sinful soul, or at least that was what she reported!

Dr. Harris notified the group that the next confirmation class was to be postponed for a week, because the church needed to prepare for a funeral. The pastor seemed to be as surprised as everyone else at the suddenness of the moment, and yet he recounted that, "God had 'called' Chester home because there were better things for him to do on the other side of eternity." Zachary wondered what those things might be; Eddie and Buddy likewise mused aloud about eternity and if Chester Rice was now truly "singing with the saints."

Since the funeral was on Saturday, choir members were told to meet at the church on Friday night for a rehearsal. Sadness was rampant. Many in the choir and congregation mourned his passing. Someone said that Chester was a good and faithful Christian and had now gone to a better place. Zachary guessed they were talking about heaven.

"Does anyone know for sure that Chester Rice is in heaven?" Eddie asked. Ralph Jones just looked around without smiling and replied, "Focus on your

91

tenor part and concentrate on smiling while singing, and less on where Chester Rice might be."

Zachary wondered to himself if Chester, presumably now in heaven, heard prayers from the church and talked to God about all of his earthly friends. Most likely, Zachary would never repeat Eddie's question to Ralph because he either didn't know, or more likely, didn't care.

The funeral started at exactly ten o'clock with a completely full church. The atmosphere dripped of heaviness and sorrow. Various people spoke and said nice things about Chester. Some of the women in the front pews dabbed their faces with small handkerchiefs. The temperature was unusually cold for fall, but somehow the inside of the church was hot, and everybody had a fan with the words "Wilkinson Funeral Home."

Dr. Harris spoke about how important it was to remain strong during difficult times. There was a large casket with flowers at the front of the church. A few hymns were sung, and then the service concluded. The family was escorted to the outer doors, where they were greeted by the congregation, followed by more crying and more hugs. Even Dr. Harris appeared sad. Tears were obvious in his eyes as he shook hands. Those who sang in the choir were complimented on how great they did. Zachary acted like he was thankful for the praise, and then he walked home alone with his own private thoughts.

One nagging question Zachary always had was: *did God really know everything, and did He really care about everybody on the planet?* Zachary continued to view God as distant, far away, with at times a very angry temper. In one story from the first part of the Bible, Zachary remembered, God had caused the destruction of most of the human race through a torrential rain. Only a few people were spared and allowed to live. The lesson was that the entire world was wicked, and God needed to make re-adjustments and start mankind all over again.

But Zachary wondered, *was this an admission of a mistake by God? Maybe He wasn't so perfect after all!*

At the next and last confirmation class, Dr. Harris announced that during the presentation of the candidates to the church, he was going to ask some questions concerning everyone's belief in Jesus. He gave examples: "Did Jesus come into this world to save man from sin?" The answer: "Yes." Then he would ask other questions like, "Do you believe in Jesus Christ as your personal savior?" The answer: "Yes."

According to Zachary's calculations, there would be ten different questions that would all be answered "Yes" in unison. This was the easiest part, and everyone looked forward to it, since it would signal the end of the confirmation examination. The more difficult part was remembering and appearing to correctly say in order the Nicene Creed and the Twenty-Third Psalm, both of which had been studied diligently during the classes.

It was obvious to all that Dr. Harris had been a good teacher, very patient, and at the last meeting said, "I know that each one of you will do your best. Are there any questions?"

Someone asked if Jesus was in any pain during the time he hung on the cross. Eddie wondered if Dr. Harris knew when Jesus would come back for everybody, and how this would happen if we were already dead. Someone else asked if Jesus was born of a virgin, how did the husband feel and was he mad at God?

Dr. Harris replied that Jesus was in tremendous pain when he hung on the cross, because all the sins of mankind had been placed onto him. Also, he said that after we die physically, our soul leaves our body, and we become alive again with God in another place and with another type of body. Mary's husband was helped to understand her predicament through the working of the Holy Spirit, who acted to change Joseph's heart.

One of the girls in the class asked if Eve's disobedience in persuading Adam to not do what God commanded meant that women were to be thought of as the "first" sinners.

Dr. Harris said that God allowed the devil to use Eve, but that both she and Adam were responsible, and then subsequently all of mankind was likewise judged guilty because their "sinful nature" prevented them from living a perfect life.

Someone else commented, "Was Eve set up to fail?" Dr. Harris said that God had given the commandment to both Adam and Eve, and they had a free choice to obey or not obey. He appeared a little more uncomfortable staying on this topic for very long. Papers were arranged and re-arranged and fidgeted with. Everybody became quiet, and there was an air of relief.

While all liked the pastor, doubt still existed about some "religious" things. Eddie replied that some of Dr. Harris's answers were difficult to believe. How could one man, Jesus, endure all that pain? How could he arise again from the dead? He was dead, period, and without life. Buddy said that he felt some of the things were too difficult to understand, and that maybe everyone would just have to trust what Dr. Harris said because it was written in the Bible.

Eddie said he didn't understand any of it, but that maybe the plan should be they first learn the creed, and then they could be accepted as members in the First Methodist Church. Maybe someday in the future, all of them might believe more about God.

Zachary continued to wonder about believing in something without fully understanding what it meant. Bob had once told him that sometimes we had to believe in things, even when we failed to always understand or see them clearly. He used the word "faith," but both of the boys had a hard time understanding what they were supposed to do with this "faith thing."

Bob and John had struggles understanding what to do when they messed up. Pastor Harris had said that life was about "messing up," but God has always been in the "forgiveness business." They both knew that they would ask for a lot of forgiveness, many times.

Then Zachary remembered the girls who lived behind him on South East Street. They told him that they always received "instant" forgiveness when they confessed their sins to their priest in the Catholic Church. They were "cleansed." The priest was appointed by God to help forgive all the sinners, but only if they were Catholic. He envied those girls and their shortcuts to God. Once he had asked Pastor Harris about priests in the Catholic Church, and the subject was changed rather abruptly.

Confirmation examination day finally arrived. It was a Sunday. They had finished with choir duties and now were ready for the dreaded testing. Everyone was scared and nervous. After the choir members picked up their robes, Mrs. Grant said, "We should all pray together," and so everyone knelt on the hard floor and asked God to keep their minds "open and fresh." Zachary was proud of himself because he had been extra good that morning. He stole no candy and did not look at a rather attractive girl in his confirmation class, who often stared at him for no reason while sitting in provocative positions.

All the kids went into the church from the pastor's office. The first part of the program involved reciting the creed in front of the congregation. The words came quickly and easily. Buddy messed up a couple of times, but Eddie, Bob, and John were perfect. Everyone got a round of applause after they finished. Then the Twenty-third Psalm was recited, and Dr. Harris asked some questions about Jesus: "Do you believe in the Lord Jesus Christ as your personal savior?" The kids screamed out, "Yes!" Several of the older members of the church, who were nodding off, suddenly jumped in their seats.

The pastor then announced that everybody was now a full member in the church, and that certificates of membership were to be mailed out. Ralph Jones came down with a big smile on his face, offered his congratulations and said, "What a great job all of you children did. You now can officially sing for the Lord." The kids felt relief.

Later, back at the Y, Eddie said they should take some candy as a reward for their hard work. Zachary looked around and didn't see anybody. Would it be okay to put several packages of gum in his pocket to chew for a baseball game to be played later that night?

Zachary wondered: *was God looking over his shoulder, since he now was an authentic church member?* Eddie waited and became impatient with a cuss word when suddenly Ralph Jones appeared again and said that he had a treat for all of them.

He reached in his pocket and gave each one of the kids a brand-new dollar bill!

Somehow evil and temptation slipped away, out the back door, and three kids wondered how they would spend their fortune. God must have been proud of them, at least that day, and maybe even smiled upon a bunch of boys and girls who had no idea what they had just done . . . or not done.

Before they left, the pastor spoke with Zachary for a few minutes. He was very eager to introduce him to the scoutmaster, Joe Hassle, the director of the Boy Scout troop that the church sponsored. "He is a wonderful Christian man who will teach you a lot. You will have very good and memorable times with scouting."

Zachary felt excited, but nervous too. Another kind of journey was to begin, and there were to be attempts to find maturity within a very different atmosphere than what he had been accustomed to. More importantly, the things he had learned from Dr. Harris, such as "forgiveness," were to be tested in ways he had never dreamed. A military lifestyle was on the horizon. A man would come who honestly believed that Boy Scouts were really miniature Army recruits in platoons run with toughness, unfair discipline, and idiotic instructions on standing at attention, keeping a mouth shut, and marching with a backpack. The journey, a passage, had to continue, and Zachary would soon discover more about life in the raw—the good, and the less than the good. Forward, march!

Four:
An Army of Boy Scouts

Attention everybody, Sergeant Hassle's in the room,
Scout Troop 109 is now in session, silence like a tomb,
Show no feeling show no cares, smiles not allowed,
You're in the Army, you are somebody, be completely proud.

THE ROOM HAD A SLIGHTLY STALE, musty, and unhealthy smell. Ceiling lights provided illumination, which allowed visibility, though barely. The walls were painted an off-white with a few pictures of landscapes hanging in no particular order.

Zachary's position "at attention," had not changed for at least fifteen minutes. The feelings he experienced included a stinging in his back that started just above his butt. Legs felt stiff with pain. He had to take a pee, but there was no way for him to leave his platoon formation. His bladder and heart were both beating in unison, and fast. Was that a very faint tinkle of something moving down one leg? In frustration and physical torment, Zachary was ready to yell out a deep, guttural scream of unsacred words not fit to be heard in any part of a church building. Troop 109 was preparing for its Wednesday night Boy Scouts meeting.

When Zachary Stevens was in the sixth grade, Bob Cope, his gym teacher, had first encouraged him to join Boy Scout Troop 109. He recounted, "This will be a good place for you to learn new things and mature." He was partially correct. Zachary would learn about discipline, but he also would discover where hate and forgiveness intersected, both of which were not always contained in equal portions or occurred at the same time.

The scoutmaster, Joe Hassle, was a manager of a sports store on the square. He had been in the Army during the latter part of World War II. Upon meeting Zachary, he had initially asked, "Do you think that you really want to be in Scout Troop 109, Zachary Stevens?" Zachary said nothing, but smiled and nodded his head. He didn't know that earlier, Bob Cope had told Joe, "Don't be too rough on Zachary— at least, not for the first week." Everybody laughed except "Sergeant" Hassle, a man who rarely smiled and had an attitude that exuded toughness and absolutely no compromise.

The leader of Troop 109 was of average size and build, with a slightly receding hairline and a stern face. One of his fingers was partially missing, the result of a "war injury." His voice was deep and loud. The stare, if you ever received it when he was angry, was more than enough to strike fear in the heart and possibly displace bodily fluids and other unmentionables in some degree of quantity. He had a particularly interesting habit of walking up to and placing his face three inches directly in front of a frightened "recruit" and shouting, "Listen to what I am saying to you, I don't want to hear you even breathe." The guy was loved by all.

The troop met in the church basement behind the dining hall. Jack Duff, assistant scoutmaster, persuaded Zachary to arrive early at church his first night so he could explain "expectations." Much uneasiness was felt, including anxiety and insecurity, regarding not only Joe Hassle but the troop, and most likely boy scouting. But a scared kid went down stairs, through the back door, into a dark, dank, and very quiet basement. Lights were turned on, and as Jack approached him from the stairs, Zachary noticed how young he looked with his perfectly combed hair, tan face, a starch-cleaned Boy Scout uniform, and perfectly shined black shoes.

The first order of business was to learn the correct way to stand at military attention, which meant to stand straight as an arrow and say nothing. Foot angles were at forty-five degrees, and from this position, right or left turns were then made. Under no circumstances were any emotions to be shown. Eyes must remain focused and never stray.

Then, more difficult things were discussed—the use of swats—a direct form of physical punishment for tardiness, talking after being called to attention, not moving quickly enough during drills, arguing, and other things described as "unpredictable possibilities." Swats were given in front of the entire scout troop, although sometimes the offender might be called into a room, jokingly referred to as "the torture room," but it was really an office. Troop meetings started promptly at seven o'clock with the calling of "attention in the ranks," and Scoutmaster Hassle marching in. He would walk up and down the "ranks," examine each of his four platoons of scouts and say nothing, just glare.

During Zachary's first night, as he stood at attention, there was a single muted sound, then a sharp crack, followed by a bad smell. Jim Eller laughed, as did others. Scoutmaster Hassle's face became red, and he shouted, "Who did that?" No one said anything, and Joe yelled out that if the person did not "own up to this evil deed," everyone would stand at attention for thirty minutes. A hand from one scout was raised, and a sigh of relief was felt by all who were thankful to God for the reprieve. Sergeant Hassle told the kid to get in the back room. Everyone anticipated the whack of a paddle; to their surprise, all was quiet.

A frightened warrior came back and appeared upset but said nothing. Later, he told Zachary and the rest of the troop that if he got into any further trouble, he would not be allowed to go on the much-anticipated two-week camping outing to Colorado later in the year.

Suddenly, a call out: "Stevens, front and center." It was time for Zachary to practice military moves. To make sure he knew right from left, he made a circle by connecting thumb and forefinger on the right hand. A straight move out and a turn to the left was executed, but not impressively. The command "about face" was given, and a right foot was placed behind a left and an attempt made at swinging the body around. It was not a clean pivot, and Zachary began to stumble. There was some snickering in the ranks, nothing said. Joe went ahead and introduced him to the troop as a new member, and later came by and told him to work on his marching drill movements.

At the end of the night, all pent-up frustrations within the troop culminated in a wrestling match within a drawn circle in the center of the meeting room. Everyone jumped in and attempted to eject each other out. The last man standing in the circle was the winner. Zachary's first night in the circle resulted in an extremely quick and unceremonious exit. The winner was a husky kid who was older and liked to brag about his strength. He told Zachary he needed to get tougher, maybe lift some weights; otherwise, he would always be a loser. Scoutmaster Hassle had a good laugh, and Zachary realized the kid was correct, as well as being an asshole. That did not lessen the thought of seeking revenge, maybe a kick in a more sacred part of the stupid jerk's body during group wrestling when bodies were positioned chaotically, and fair, responsible competition waned or was non-existent.

On the way home, Zachary felt a sense of relief. He had survived a Boy Scout meeting without swats, although he knew his time was coming. Scoutmaster Hassle was a man who seemed to relish the role of a commander. But what kind of a guy was he with family, work, or relaxation? Un-answerable questions!

The passage here was to move on with and become curious about a new world just around the corner. The Elm City winds came from all directions, and as they kicked up dust, imaginary whispers conversed to Zachary as he ran the last leg of the trip to his house on South Main Street. The kid was sure he heard voices say something, maybe a laugh, or a sigh, but the words were indecipherable. No doubt, just a faulty imagination, but then again . . .

Scout Troop 109 was divided into four platoons. Zachary was placed in the Bears Platoon with six other boys, several of whom had attended his grade school, and one who had played on a basketball team named the *Chevrolet Fighters* with Zachary.

Two of the boys in the Bears Platoon, Bobbie Metcalf and Tony Russell, said little when Zachary tried to socialize with them. Each time he tried to initiate a conversation, they just looked at him as if he was crazy, and then they disappeared. Another kid, Buck Davis, was both strange and almost blind. He wore thick glasses and seemed to have an odd sense of humor. Younger kids felt terrorized by him because he arm-locked necks, bent fingers back until there was pain, and then smiled when yelling occurred. Zachary realized he would need to get along with Buck by developing some degree of forgiveness, patience, and most importantly, keeping a mouth shut and opinions to himself.

The scout uniform included a brown khaki shirt and pants, a red neckerchief, and a "garrison flat cap" which could be folded and placed in the belt when standing at attention. Following washing, the shirt and pants required much ironing to get the wrinkles out. Mother faithfully taught the skill, and

Zachary eventually learned with a few accidental burning of fingers, followed by well-executed cuss words yelled out. (Soap in mouth, less than ten seconds, a standard practice if the language became too vulgar.) Black military shoes were shined before each meeting, and the challenge was to remove residual paste from fingernails. The kid, though, became an expert in uniform care!

Scoutmaster Hassle conducted careful inspections and disciplined those who failed to wear the uniform properly. It was to Zachary's credit that he was one of the few in the troop never given a swat for a failed uniform presentation. The same could not be said of other forthcoming misdeeds.

A part of every scout meeting involved mastering the requirements for reaching various levels of rank in the troop. It was necessary to learn how to tie various knots, wear the uniform correctly, and to memorize the scout oath and law. The annual trip to Colorado utilized skills learned from the scout manual, including how to pitch a tent, to swim, to cook food, to clean gear, and to learn the essentials of first aid. Most of the requirements for "tender foot" and "second class" were fairly easy to meet, but after "first class," when merit badges could be earned, expectations steeped quickly. Only a very small number of scouts made the coveted rank of "Eagle Scout."

One Wednesday night, about four weeks after Zachary was first initiated into Troop 109, the testing of a "recruit" and his scoutmaster's tolerance occurred. The entire evening had been uneasy and unpredictable, with wet weather, thunder and cold outside, and deviousness, misplaced attitudes, and manipulation. Zachary had passed the platoon inspection, and everyone was working on merit badges. Most of the scouts had been sitting at a large table, learning how to pack equipment into small bags and fit them in a snug manner into backpacks. Buck Davis decided to play pranks and act weird.

The fearful new Boy Scout had taken a nature break, and when he returned, he discovered a group of pictures of nude women in his packing gear. Suddenly and unexpectedly, Scoutmaster Hassle walked by and asked, "Where did these come from?" Zachary stammered and said he had no idea how they got into his pack. Buck blurted out that he had seen Zachary look at them earlier in the evening. Zachary erupted with total anger at the lie Buck had just told, and he planned a very swift execution of a right hook to a nose. Joe interceded before any punches landed, and he told Zachary to go to the back room and wait.

As Zachary sat alone in the "torture room," he thought of ways to explain his innocence. Anger bubbled around in a brain and mind concerning further retributions to a f#@*&$ ass%*&# who was blind and couldn't see.

The intensity of emotions was so high that little thought was given to any forthcoming punishment. In fact, Zachary worried that he might attack Scoutmaster Hassle when and if he came through the door and pronounced the penalty of a swat or two. Then more rational thinking prevailed, and he convinced himself that any swat he might receive would not hurt. How could it? He was just too angry to care and leave any part of his body available for feeling pain. Heart and soul became permeated with rage and cried out. Zachary told both to shut up. They, of course, refused to listen.

Joe came in and said, "I am disappointed in you, Zachary. This type of material is not to be part of any boy scout's equipment. Throw the pictures in the trash can, and your punishment is one swat."

The position was assumed, the sting came quickly. Zachary then asked the veritable scoutmaster what he should do the next time someone "planted" things on him. Joe was quiet for a long time. Then he replied, "Leave Buck alone, and if I hear any more reports of fighting, you will get another swat." Zachary guessed Joe didn't believe him, and that was most disappointing. Was this to be how Zachary would be remembered as a Boy Scout—a pervert who took pleasure in looking at vulgar nonsense?

The shamed kid was told to return to his worktable and finish his scout assignments for the night. He looked forward to meeting Buck in "the circle." Unfortunately, the weather did not cooperate. It was storming outside and parents were in a hurry to leave. The troop was dismissed early, and revenge took a leave of absence for the night. Zachary worried how he might be perceived by the other kids. He should not have. Most of them wanted to know where the "one shots" (pictures) came from. "Ask Buck," was all he said. Suddenly, Buck was the most popular kid in Troop 109!

On the way home, Zachary debated whether he should say anything to his mother, but he finally relented. She understandably became angry, but then said that this might be a good lesson to remember. "A lot of people can and will, for many different reasons, disappoint you in life. Fighting or trying to get back at people is not how to settle your differences. You need to forgive, Zachary." No doubt she thought of what had happened to her regarding an attempted purchase of their rented house; and of the bank official who had told her that schoolteachers did not make enough money to pay a mortgage, especially a single parent raising a small boy.

A review of the whole incident honestly revealed that Buck and his stupid jokes were irrelevant. The bigger disappointment was Scoutmaster Hassle. How could he not have figured out that Zachary had been set up, and then choose to do nothing about it? There had been a noticeable smirk on his face when Zachary questioned him about what he should do if it were to happen again; clearly Joe was not going to change his mind, because admitting a mistake was not in his personality.

The rain and wind blew in periodic gusts and tossed leaves and debris all over the car and street as mother and son drove down South Main Street. They passed Duncan's Market, now closed for the night. Zachary looked at the locked front door and the dark, unhappy windows. He wondered if Fred felt as helpless as he had at Boy Scouts that night—angry, unforgiving, and confused. Zachary knew he must eventually move on from this moment, but it would take time. He needed to sulk for a while, and maybe fantasize about getting even with Joe and Buck. There was no idea and no plan, just a lot of random and blurry emotions that flew in every direction, just like the rain and leaves.

Fred Duncan eventually survived the robbery and assault, but remained more than just a little angry about his predicament. He experienced much confusion and loss of memory, and a limp was more noticeable and more painful. The store was closed, and he moved on to a small rental farmhouse to live out a remaining fractured life. He and Zachary never again met nor communicated, and the old grocer failed to learn useful information from a young kid, his friend, who saw so much that fateful day of the robbery and kept quiet because of shame and cowardliness.

One important skill in Boy Scouts was to read and follow directions from a map. Joe had once said, "You must at all times know your location in the wild, because your life might depend upon it one day." Zachary and others had their doubts. Joe was known to overstate many objectives, but Zachary was to find out later that this "overkill of survival" would have some maturing and relevant consequences.

On an early Saturday morning in the spring of Zachary's first year in Scouts, armed with drawn and written directions, each platoon was sent out to find certain objects throughout Elm City, and to then make notes of the time and what was found. The honor code was to be followed, and a reward given to the platoon able to find the largest number of items in the quickest time.

Zachary's platoon was directed to go to a store on the square and locate a black belt with the initials "KC" on the side. The most likely place was a women's department store. Groups of two each were formed and went to every store. Just before noon, Zachary found the belt at King's Department Store. A note was made of the details where the store was located, the belt, its use, cost, and the time it was discovered.

The next point required them to travel east on State Street. Danny drew the route to take, and it was determined that the location was straight out to the Elm City School for the Blind. The directions and map detailed that there would be a tree located in the back of a building with a partial tin roof. The building was easy to find, but then a slight problem arose, as there were many different trees. How were they going to locate which tree held the next clue? A tree, standing approximately twelve feet in height, with a prominent rounded top became a possibility. The directions instructed to take a piece of twine and make a straight line from the tip of the tree's longest root and measure fifteen yards in length. At that point, they would be at the base of a bush.

A hole was then to be dug, six to eight inches in depth below the surface—task accomplished—but nothing found. The string was rechecked, including its attachment point to the root and the distance. A larger hole was dug. No luck. What had gone wrong? Next plan: Stop! Rest! Have lunch!

Jimmy thought the string needed to again be rechecked. Zachary suggested there might be more than one tree of a similar description with roots going in a northwesterly direction. They looked again and saw one tree that was set off from the others, one they had missed on an initial pass. Its area at the base had been well covered by dead leaves.

When they cleared the debris, they found three large roots going out from the base of the tree that directly pointed to a small bush and a maple tree in a clearing on the other side of the fence that enclosed the School for the Blind. The string was redirected, another hole was dug, and wow, a new set of directions found!

They were now instructed to go to the spillway at the Elm City Lake, where they would encounter a new challenge. The comments instructed them to "bike out past the Vesco Plant, go under the railroad trestle by the water plant, walk past an area where lots of kids swam during the summer, and arrive at the spillway." There, a new set of directions would be found in a coffee can located within "visual distance" of the top of the spillway.

The kids arrived, and their faces quickly exuded a look of surprise, disbelief, and a quick observation: "Oh no!" The coffee can was set in a rock-weighted box in the middle of the concrete embankment. One of the scouts had to carefully walk out to the middle of the spillway and retrieve the can without falling and sliding to the bottom. A plan was quickly developed involving the use of a rope to be stretched across the top of the spillway, and then some brave individual would grasp it and slowly traverse out to retrieve the can. Zachary was the smallest, so he was chosen for the dangerous assignment.

The next problem: where could a rope be found? Zachary remembered one hanging on a wall at his next-door neighbor's garage. It had been used to help haul containers to the turkey farm. He offered to pedal home and retrieve the rope, and be back in ten minutes. When he arrived, Mrs. Scott listened and said, "Go ahead and take the rope; we never use it."

He quickly pulled it down from the wall and started back on his bike. Just as he turned the corner on Superior Avenue, a familiar tan car whizzed by. Old memories flooded back, a stomach and heart sickened.

On the back bumper was the same decal visible the day Fred Duncan's store was robbed. Zachary got off the bike and noted that the driver, a woman, apparently did not see him as she and the car disappeared around the corner. Something was odd and different. The person who drove the car was certainly not the guy he had seen the day of the robbery. Had the car been sold? Who was the driver? A lot of questions and fears were suddenly resurrected.

Of course, Zachary did not know that the Stewart family had sold the car, and that he was safe from a grocery store robber ensconced far away in another town. But would Zachary remain free of this menace? Things are never what they seem.

The bike ride back out to the lake was quick, and everybody was relieved that he had a rope and now a possible way to fetch the next prize. They went down to the bottom of the spillway, and Jimmy waded over to the far side of the embankment with one end of the rope. There was plenty of length, and several kids held the other end and carefully walked up the opposite side of the embankment, stretching the rope tight.

Zachary carefully held onto the rope and slowly maneuvered to the center of the spillway without slipping. One arm was used for leverage, the other to reach down and get the small can out of the box. He cautiously turned around and slowly worked his way back. Suddenly, with one hand on the rope and the other holding the can, his feet went out from underneath him. He worked his way up to a standing position again and threw the can to a nervous fellow scout who waited at the edge of the embankment.

The directions inside the can said to go straight out Hardin Avenue and proceed to where it intersected with Vandala Road, and then turn left, and proceed out to the Community Park and "find a picnic table by a trash can." Another box with the instructions "do not open" would be located inside. These items were easily found after a search of three trash bins.

The scouts then continued to another part of the lake, where they pitched a tent and fixed dinner. Jack Duff showed up, recorded everything, and told them to open the container. Inside was a piece of paper, which said the following: "Go out and catch six snipes."

Each person was directed to a separate specific point to wait, watch, and catch the animal in a net attached to long pole. Snipes were described as small creatures, about the size of a rat. They did not run fast and would not bite. The whole thing sounded suspicious and a little crazy, but Zachary blindly obeyed and waited, then waited some more. He thought he heard noises and went to investigate, and found the rest of the platoon eating s'mores over a camp fire. They asked if he had caught any snipes, and Zachary said frustratingly, "No." They reported that Scoutmaster Hassle was on his way to the campsite and would not be happy. A slight smile emanated from a platoon member's face, but he said nothing.

Finally, Scoutmaster Hassle arrived with a stern look and no smile. He told them they had placed second out of four platoons and should be proud of themselves. He asked Zachary, "How many snipes do you have for me?"

"None," was the answer.

"Did you see any?"

"No," Zachary replied.

Joe then said that was understandable, because there were none to be found; they were just imaginary. It was, in fact, an initiation into this part of the troop. The laughter seemed too loud.

Later, Zachary asked if Buck had been initiated into the snipe hunt. The response: "No." A plan began to develop in the darker recesses of Zachary's mind, a place where both glee and wickedness sometimes could be found. They co-existed, and most likely enjoyed each other's company.

The Elm City High School football team played its home games on Friday evenings. One night in October, when Zachary was a freshman, he and fellow Boy Scouts from Troop 109 performed during half-time with the school band. All were excited to show off their marching skills in front of the hometown. Zachary and his friends, Buddy and Jimmy, walked next to each other, whispering way too much.

"Hey Stevens, remember your right from your left when commands are given. Otherwise you will be marching by yourself and going in the wrong direction," shouted Jimmy.

"I will use my right hand and make a circle with my thumb and forefinger to keep me focused," Zachary retorted.

"The noise from these band instruments is too loud," Buddy said. "I would like to kick the guy banging that drum."

Some of the other kids tried to trip the person in front of them as they walked, but that behavior abruptly stopped when Joe Hassle yelled out, "Cut the crap, order in the ranks."

The high school fans clapped as the troop neatly crossed the fifty-yard line, did an about and right face, and then stopped. The announcer made some comments while Zachary allowed himself the pleasure of looking at the faces in the crowd. There were a lot of pretty girls, men dressed in coveralls, women wearing strange-looking hats, and one face that stood out—Carl Stewart.

Two pairs of eyes riveted on each other, and Zachary thought that Carl smiled, but he couldn't be sure. What Zachary felt was a fear of what might happen next.

Half-time ended and show time over. The scouts stopped to get a soda at the refreshment stand. Carl came over to Zachary and said, "Hey kid, how are you doing? Know me?" A frightened response, "Just fine, finished marching, planning to go home." *A heart raced as if it was going to bounce out of a chest. A mouth became parched, and troublesome thoughts became resurrected. What did Carl want? Question rightfully ignored.*

Jimmy and Buddy came up and asked Zachary who he was talking to. Zachary shrugged, and the three Boy Scouts then piled into one of the scout leader's automobiles for a welcomed exit.

Carl lingered and thought: *I need more time alone with that kid. I think I can do some big-time persuading, but if not, other measures will be taken.*

The encounter with Carl for this night was over. Displaced feelings were left at the football field. Zachary peered out of the car window and watched houses and verdant front yards dusted by leaves sweep by, while he wondered how much longer this situation with Carl was going to last. *Is that guy going to continue to keep watching me and interrupting my life forever? What does he want from me? What is his problem?* Help seemed so far away.

John Goff's camera shop was tucked away in a corner of the square next to the Indiana Theatre. Every summer Scoutmaster Hassle sought his help when the troop went to Colorado. Movies were taken of all the scouts in action for the two-week period by Mr. Goff, who was eager to get out of a boring town and enjoy a brief respite and some peace and calm from a nagging wife.

The parents enjoyed watching the film, but they were never told of the large amount of editing before final showing. Mr. Goff used a large piece of glass that was held in a vertical position with the words written on one side, "Boy Scout Troop 109, Elm City, Indiana," while simultaneously filming through the glass a bunch of Boy Scouts marching out of the Methodist Church and boarding automobiles. Scoutmaster Hassle was always prominently featured with a serious face, and it appeared that all were on a journey into some type of war or conflict. The townsfolk, especially the parents, thought the troop outings were a good preparation for the boys to learn discipline and responsibility. The boys gleefully focused more on briefly getting away from controlled insanity and meeting some new girls.

The first day out, the caravan of eager scouts including Zachary Stevens headed toward Kansas. The scenery changed very little, except when crossing over the Mississippi River. Hills and valleys eventually gave way to fields and fields of corn, hay, and more corn, and more hay. The heat inside the car was impenetrable and unforgiving. Sweat and smells were everywhere.

The first night, tents were pitched somewhere outside of Clarksville, Kansas.

"All issued tents must be perfectly squared, with no creases," was the written command strictly enforced by Scoutmaster Hassle. "Inspection" resulted in the evaluation of how well each troop member had accomplished this task. Secondly, but equally important, was the storing of equipment on the inside of a tent (e.g., clothes, cooking utensils, blankets, sleeping bags); thirdly, the general outside appearance around the tent—it had to be free of any litter or trash.

When Joe came by and evaluated Zachary's camp, he found several tent stakes incompletely driven and some wrinkles in one side of the tent. Punishment: one swat. Fred, Zachary's tent partner, was more willing to get the whole inspection thing over, take the swat and make the adjustments. Zachary felt no remorse, but did feel a lot of other things.

Later, Zachary and a pair of buttocks that were still reeling from a swat, Jimmy Eller, and tent mate Fred Harris slipped down an isolated path to clear their heads and ventilate.

"Do you think we will be able to get through this trip without any more swats?" Zachary asked.

Jimmy replied, "Scoutmaster Hassle is okay. He is a tough guy, but he will prepare us for a rough junior-varsity football coach next year when we start high school."

Fred chimed in, "I don't like the swats, but I am sure it will make me more careful about obeying orders."

Zachary thought to himself: *Bull-$%&@. I think the scoutmaster is too strict. What is the point of getting a whipping for some stupid wrinkle in a tent?* Fortunately, no one else was to hear this commentary and a kid was to never experience the consequence of what an answer might feel like!

In the evening, a small campfire was built in front of the tents and small pieces of iron rods, fashioned like a rack, were laid on two large, flat rocks placed on either side of the fire. Tinfoil-wrapped potatoes and vegetables were then placed on top for cooking. Culinary adventures were experimental—some better than others. But the scent of food on the grill was priceless. Food cooked outdoors over fire and smoke had a personality all its own and made other unpleasantries just disappear, at least for a minute or so!

Jack Duff had previously bought a large amount of hamburger meat, buns, beans, veggies and some fruit. A fantastic meal with s'mores was prepared, and everyone appeared more relaxed, although the beans eventually got their revenge. All the scouts, Zachary included, learned to pretend and ignore well, and not act stupid or joke around about physiological actions in or out of the presence of a military man on a mission.

The anticipated Pony Express station was the next "educational stop." It turned out to be a broken-down building just outside of some small town in Kansas. A boring lecture was given about the movement of mail on horseback between Joplin, Missouri, and Clarksville, Kansas. The building had been used to route the mail further out west. Some of the scouts roamed around the grounds and seemed to revel in the coolness of a bunch of shade trees, which partially boarded a small creek meandering off to nowhere. Hope was strong that this stop would end quickly, and Colorado would be in sight. It did, and Troop 109 arrived early evening in eastern Colorado, as planned.

Later that night, it was announced that in the morning a "snipe" hunt was to be conducted. Zachary's arch enemy, Buck, became excited and interested when a senior-rank scout, most likely a Star or Life grade, gave a description of snipes as small, creepy animals with tan dotted backs.

Precise locations were given where the snipes most likely might be found. Nets were to be passed out to aid in their capture, an award given to the scout who caught the largest number. Buck proudly announced that with his nets and other bags, he would catch the most. He looked at Zachary and announced that he was going to "make Zachary appear foolish because he had not previously been able to catch any snipes." Buck predicted his large catch would force the entire troop to realize his keen and sharp abilities as a Boy Scout; all would salute and call him "Master Snipe Catcher."

The next morning, Buck was taken by several "decoy scouts" into the woods and told to look for the creatures. He appeared excited and began collecting his materials, adjusting his glasses, and making sure he had plenty of water. He boasted, "I expect to fill my nets within two hours!" The rest of the scouts snuck back to camp and waited with eager anticipation.

Less than an hour later, Buck returned filthy, dirty, and wet. He had lost his glasses and had trouble seeing. Apparently, he had fallen into the creek and almost drowned. He said that he had seen a lot of snipes but was unable to catch any. When told they never existed, he got angry and pugnaciously disagreed; everybody laughed, and he then settled down.

The entire troop then went back into the woods and found his glasses close to the creek bed. After the "snipe incident," Buck never played tricks on any of the scouts again. Maybe he felt somewhat embarrassed by the whole incident. How could anyone now doubt that obnoxious and mean-spirited behavior might be changed for the good by a small and nonexistent animal with the name 'snipe'?

Somewhere in the affairs of mankind, a book must have been written devoted to the "Highest Knowledge of Human Behavior," stating that when mistakes in life are made, there are always opportunities for learning different courses of action, so that further bad choices are avoided. And more importantly, the best teachers are adults who can and will demonstrate ideal role models, especially for children.

But what happens when stupid grown-ups misbehave, are completely drunk, and are holding loaded guns and bows and arrows? Perhaps, under those circumstances, learning goes in a reverse direction, and children become the instructors and provide a more honest reality, including focused sanity for "disadvantaged elders."

Zachary and a few other scouts needed to meet a requirement of hiking and taking pictures of various fauna and flora indigenous to the area in which they were currently camping. Bags were packed, and all set out on an adventure for which none was prepared—certainly one they would not forget. While wind whipped at their faces, the scouts viewed the huge, slightly snow-capped mountains surrounded by rich landscaping of barley, wheat, and various other fields of unknown vegetation, large lakes, small lakes, and rushing rivers.

The boys had been out for about two hours, and feet plus backs were tired. A rest was called, and all paused for a snack break. That was when they first heard noises, calls from somewhere.

"Help! We are stuck down here! Can you see us?" was the pitiful, urgent cry. The scouts rounded a small curve and positioned themselves on the side of a steep hill. Down below, the pleas continued, "We need help! Someone is hurt!"

Zachary looked down and gasped, "Oh my God, I can't believe what I am seeing."

About thirty feet below were two men in what appeared to be a very unusual situation. One of them was on his back, and from his facial contortions, he appeared to be in great pain. A leg was extended at an odd angle, and blood covered part of his shirt. The other man was sitting down trying to adjust some kind of a makeshift device, most likely a splint. But how ridiculous! The branch that was fashioned to be used to hold a damaged leg in place was ill-conceived, totally useless, much too small, and much too flexible.

The injured adult produced a quizzical smile that betrayed a lost awareness of reality, while the numerous empty cans of beer thrown around the campsite and the strong smell of both alcohol and urine indicated a more complete and accurate picture of total chaos.

One by one, the scouts carefully climbed down the steep cliff and told the men they would help. The uninjured man replied, "We have been down here for two days with no food and little water. We came here to hunt and have not bagged a damn thing."

He tried to get up, and then fell back down again. The other guy with the injured leg began to moan and recounted drinking a lot of beer, and then tripping and falling about thirty feet, subsequently landing in an awkward position on his leg. He crawled back to camp using both his hands and legs, one of which was in great pain. He seemed quite proud of his accomplishment despite the fact it had taken him an hour. His companion gave no help, for he had completely passed out, totally inebriated! The mishap must have happened recently, judging by the appearance of fresh blood. A quick scan of the camping area revealed a couple of guns and a large bow and arrow next to a small hut made from tree limbs and brush.

Zachary and Danny Winters gave the men their own lunches and water from their canteens. Fred was appointed to go back to the scout's base camp and bring additional help.

Jimmy Elder went out in the woods and used an ax to secure several large pieces of wood to be crafted into a splint. A creek provided water for cleaning wounds and dirty skin, and a first aid kit was used to apply bandages. Next, the campsite was straightened up and conversation was aided and improved by the eventual sobering up of the two rather sickly-looking individuals.

Zachary was curious about the bow and arrows and was told they had planned to use these "weapons" to hunt deer if they ran out of ammunition. The only problem with this idea was they were so drunk, how could they accurately shoot anything? Both laughed in very peculiar and strange ways. Zachary wondered, quietly to himself, if these guys were "mentally okay."

Perhaps they needed an evaluation and some help. He knew of such a place across the street from where he lived in Elm City. The two men were both lucky they had not shot and killed each other; then another very silent and personal thought: *maybe, they should have.* One thing was very apparent, the hunters were only interested in themselves and their predicament and had absolutely no desire or interest in anyone else, including some rather astonished Boy Scouts. Oh well, what did it matter . . . two very separate parcels of humanity on two very different journeys!

Fred eventually came back with help. The injured hunter was loaded onto a stretcher, and with great care, the men were taken to Jack Duff's vehicle. They both were eventually driven into the nearest town to get further aid.

On the way back to their campsite, the boys laughed and had long conversations about the two hunters. They wondered what their thoughts were when they drank and handled loaded guns. What if the scouts had not come by? Did they save lives? Were they real heroes? They thought they were, and that was all the mattered.

Upon their return two boys, Joe Gruneau and Buddy Logan, congratulated Zachary on his part in helping the campers. They had many questions and comments about the rescue mission.

"You guys showed real care and concern for a couple of drunks," Buddy replied. "I don't know if I could have done as well as you did."

Joe Gruneau commented, "Where did you learn to give a shit about others, especially a couple of losers? I bet at church. God must be proud of you!" The scouts knew about Zachary and his "religious struggles," and laughter was loud, boisterous, perhaps too much so!

Joe Hassle was likewise impressed with what Zachary and his fellow scouts had done. He told them they would be recognized later in the year at a scouting banquet. Everyone thought that now disagreements and fighting would be a thing of the past. Heroes and only good "Scout behavior" were now ensconced within Troop 109. They could not have been more mistaken.

* * *

Zachary's tent mate, Fred, had always been a good and dependable friend. He was someone with whom Zachary socialized and shared secrets. They bonded and trusted each other. That was why it was not surprising for Zachary to go to his defense in a time of need.

Several kids from another platoon had come over and started an argument with Fred. Strong words and feelings were exchanged. There was a lot of pushing, shoving, and swinging of fists. Retribution filled the air. Zachary intervened, and one of the kids told him, "mind your own business." There had been a recent disagreement over assignments of a work detail from several previous evenings. All were upset and angry. Zachary needed to get out of the way. He didn't.

One of the kids pushed Fred, and the other kid threatened to hit him in the mouth. Fred smiled. When the kid swung, he ducked and a fist with little force hit Zachary on the side of the face. "Get out of here, Stevens!" someone shouted. Zachary grabbed the kid, they went to the ground, and spit flew into Zachary's face while blows were landed to faces and chins. Jack arrived and separated the combatants.

Joe Hassle's face was not a happy one. He demanded to know how the fight started. Fred told him that there had been some disagreement about a work detail.

A frown deepened and overtook the entire body and personality of the frustrated scoutmaster, who dismissed all of them and said that he would speak to each individually. For reasons unclear, Zachary was first on his list. It was clear that Joe was way beyond being totally flabbergasted. How, in just a few hours, had a hero Boy Scout gone to being a "disobedient soldier?" How could that occur?

Zachary explained that he became involved in someone else's problems, and a fight broke out. The scoutmaster then wondered why he fought over a disagreement about garbage details. Zachary thought for a long minute, and said that Fred was his best friend, and he was going to stand up for him. A fight then ensued, and Zachary needed to defend himself.

The look from Sergeant Hassle was long, steady, and betrayed total fury. "Stevens, you have grown in many ways since coming into this troop. I have watched you with some pride and noted how well you have fit in. You could go very far in the ranks, but you need to control your behavior better, especially when you are in or around groups of people. You can't settle problems with your fists, but rather, you must learn to talk things out. Think before you act, and ask yourself this question: Am I going to do something I might regret later? You do agree with me, don't you?"

Zachary thought for a minute and said, "Yes." He was then dismissed, and Fred was called in.

Later, Fred said that he and Joe had a talk, but that it was private. Zachary did not ask if he got a swat or not. They went back to their tents, and Jack Duff came around to see if they were okay; he then proceeded to get all the kids to apologize. Fred told Zachary he "appreciated the support." Zachary had other thoughts and comments not worth mentioning.

The call came out to Zachary and the other two scouts involved in the fracas to assemble in front of Scoutmaster Hassle's tent. The rest of Troop 109 watched in silence. The order was given after the three boys had been standing at attention for what seemed like hours.

"Go get your backpacks, fill them with your clothes and eating utensils and march around the campgrounds until sunset." A few snickers were heard, and then the scoutmaster yelled out that at the next noise, the entire troop would march with Zachary and his friends. Dead silence.

The walking was hard enough, but the weight on the back became more uncomfortable after a couple of times around the campgrounds. Zachary sweated profusely and felt angry with no remorse.

Yes, he had apologized to all concerned, but now he thought this punishment unfair. What is wrong with expressing different opinions and, when necessary, standing up for what you believe is right and fair, and if attacked, being prepared to defend yourself? What was this marching going to prove? The sun was slowly disappearing into the west, and so too was Zachary's interest in remaining a member of Troop 109. He began thinking about Carl Stewart and wishing he was bigger and had more muscles; maybe some junior-varsity football training in the fall?

Central City, Colorado, was next on the agenda. Its history was both fascinating and mysterious. The famous "face on the barroom floor" of some hotel had been painted by an anonymous person. It turned out to be the face of a rather pretty lady, perhaps the wife of the owner of the hotel. Again, mischievousness was in the air. Several kids began acting out, as if they were just a little drunk and were on their way to the bar to request a beer. Scoutmaster Hassle immediately ordered everyone out of the building. His face looked emotionally drained, and no doubt there were thoughts about the short amount of time left on this trip

Zachary had once been told by his grandmother that each person receives assistance from a "guardian angel"—an invisible person who protects. She may have been correct.

The troop had stopped at a gift shop to get some postcards to send home. Upon return to the car, Zachary took the front seat next to the steering wheel.

The kids in the backseat began slapping his head. He turned to respond when his right arm accidently hit, mounted on the steering wheel, a gearshift leaver not fully in the "parked" position. The car went into neutral, and it rolled down and hit the side of the building. Much glassware on the many shelves inside the building was a prime target for destruction. Then something unbelievable happened. No glassware fell! No damage! When the driver came back, he never knew or appreciated the effort of a bunch of frightened scouts who pushed a car back up the hill to its original position, while Zachary then eased the gearshift back to the "parked" position. No trace of any evil deeds! The scouts and Zachary sat very quietly, perhaps reverently, as if they might have just been visited by an extra-terrestrial guest.

The Royal Gorge was the last place to visit before heading home. A suspension bridge had been constructed between parts of the Rocky Mountains, and it spanned the Arkansas River. Everybody walked on the bridge, and several kids remarked how much fun it would be to jump off with a parachute and float down to the riverbank.

Zachary suspected that Scoutmaster Hassle wished some might just do that, and maybe without a parachute! They had been together for ten days, and all were ready for a return to Elm City. A re-appraisal of Scoutmaster Hassle's face confirmed this guess.

In Kansas, the scouts camped close to a large federal prison called Creavenworth. There were multiple old, decrepit red brick buildings surrounded by maple and oak trees, and a very large chain-link fence with rolls of barbed wire on the top.

Dangerous criminals were housed inside. The scouts listened to several of the volunteer drivers in the car caravan, and Scoutmaster Hassle lectured about what a life of crime might get you: "ten to twenty years or more in Creavenworth."

As the scoutmaster talked, Zachary remembered something—the robbery at Mr. Duncan's grocery and the way Fred Duncan looked after being hit over the head with a meat cleaver. A mental flashback, and Zachary once again saw the guy who committed the robbery, an image of a large tan car, and an arm strangely tattooed. The wind picked up, and Zachary looked at a barred window and saw someone who peered out —maybe at him— very intently, very personal. The man's face was mean, scarred, and must have had a history, a violent history.

As Zachary went to sleep that night, for just a moment, he pretended the man staring from behind those prison bars was the robber from Elm City, now safe in captivity and never again to cause harm. Wishful thinking! What Zachary feared the most was more stalking by the robber when he got back to Elm City . . . more waiting and watching, so closely.

Where was that kid? His thoughts were fixated on one person. Carl Stewart had been working various part-time jobs throughout Indiana and was unhappy, unfulfilled, and angry. There was still no money from his well-planned robbery. His father had seen to that! Carl's mind held much resentment: the unfairness of hard work, much risk and no reward. He realized, however, that something had developed: a conscience.

He had heard that Mr. Duncan was not dead, but just slower in movements and memory. Of course, it was the grocer's own fault! The idiot should have never tried to take back the cleaver or attack Carl. Stupid behavior resulted in great harm, greater punishment.

There also was the issue of the rest of his family. They had supported him in a small way by not telling anyone, and this must have been most difficult for a sister who always had a hard time keeping her mouth shut. But it was apparent they did not want him around, and that his sojourns to visit, work, and sometimes relax at his aunt's house in another city were appreciated by all. And the one thing his father had done, which was helpful, was to gather information about Zachary: name and address. Now when Carl was in town, he could drive by and check out Zachary's house, which was done probably too much.

A decision was in the making that Carl tried to ignore, but could not. Zachary had to keep his mouth shut and tell no one. But how was Carl to ensure that he could always believe that Zachary would do this? Then some other thoughts percolated that were more frightening, but maybe reality-based. Was a more *permanent* solution to the problem of an uninvited witness, Zachary Stevens, in the making? It would take guts and involve a huge risk, but Carl felt some tinge of excitement and resolve.

It was good to get back to Elm City—the hunter's home from the hill. They unpacked gear and staggered out of the church into welcomed parents' arms and cars that took them home. Old friends could be told stories—some true, some only slightly true, and others just lies. There were secrets not to be shared, but kept private, including tales of sore buttocks and painful chins. The hero stories were the best ones, all without much effort and with a slight bravado injected for good measure. There would be memories of many things and people, some good and some not so good.

In the fall, Zachary would reassess his life and journeys for clarity and better direction. He decided to leave the Troop. It had been fun, but new things needed to be tried and tested. It had been difficult getting used to the military way the Troop operated. But he also recognized a little respect for Joe Hassle. He was a difficult man to like, much less to understand. But it was good, even useful, that this "Army Sergeant" paid a visit into a boy's life, albeit only briefly. Joe and the Scout Troop allowed Zachary to learn patience, obedience to authority, and forgiveness. It would come in handy later in life when Zachary was confronted with strong-willed people, friends, and certainly a lot of, for want of a better term, assholes.

He had sought to find a way to become free of guilt. Religion had been tried and failed. The problem: lack of faith, or immaturity, or maybe both. "Religious messages" were not on the menu at present. What he did not know was that spiritual notations were in fact becoming "registered" within his unawakened brain. They would sit quietly, unannounced, "resurrected" later in life. God was not done with him. But neither was Carl Stewart.

Five:
Fifty Dollars' Worth of Soap

I need a little money to go to summer camp,
So buy a box of soap and become an instant champ,
Your contribution will help beyond what words can say,
And I will have keepsake memories for many a day.

PAUL CUSTER, THE DIRECTOR OF THE YMCA in Elm City, shaved once a week and rarely brushed his teeth. But he was a happy, balding man, slightly bulged at the waist, pants worn too loose. His white shirt was never ironed and seemed slightly soiled, a tie never visible. His big, toothy smile and friendly "Hello" were honest and energetic. He told Zachary how he could have a summer adventure at Camp Silver Creek, located across the Indiana border, south of Cincinnati in the grand state of Kentucky. Paul was a good salesman, ever encouraging and directing in a friendly way.

"This is a place you should go and visit for two weeks, Zachary."

"How would I get there? Why would I want to go?"

"You take a train from Lafayette to Indianapolis, and then on to Cincinnati, and from there you take a bus. It is a strong Christian camp where you will meet a lot of other boys who love God and love the outdoors."

"How do I pay for it?"

"By selling soap. Lots and lots of soap."

The boxes of soap were rectangular and made of white cardboard. Each box contained four small bars and cost forty cents. The outside of the box was emblazoned in red: "HELP THIS BOY GO TO CAMP." Paul reported that if fifty dollars of soap was sold, the camp fees would be covered. Last year, several kids had even tallied more than that amount, so part of their transportation costs had also been paid.

Paul gave Zachary a booklet that described the camp with its own lake, cabins, and a large dining hall, all located just outside a small national park. It seemed interesting, but the kid had concerns. The goal for the camp was to develop the hearts and minds of young men within an "enclave for the lost and wounded." *Most doubtful, with a tinge of phoniness and a lot of self-aggrandizement and judgement*, Zachary mused. Secondly, everybody at the camp would be a stranger, and it was over 300 miles from home. Homesickness would be obvious. And what if the kids were not friendly? What if he didn't want to stay at the camp? Perhaps the food might be terrible! *"Oh, shit, take a chance and be a risktaker,"* a voice from somewhere said. Decision made: Go!

A small truck was used to load the saleable soap merchandise and transport it to Zachary's house. He suggested potential customers from Zachary's paper route might be good starting points. The plan was to collect the money first, keep a record of addresses, and then later deliver the soap. In addition to the paper route, the suggestion was made to sell to customers around the neighborhood where he lived, and later badger people on the town square.

The kid's first customer was an older lady who subscribed to the *Chicago Sun-Times*. She arrived at the front door in her bathrobe with misplaced rouge and lipstick, smelling of distilled spirits taken way too early in the morning. He showed her the words printed on the front of the box and told her of his plans for the summer. Jitters and a lot of stammering ensued, and he suddenly felt ridiculous, while a whisper complimented him on such a terrible presentation. He was sure a black shadow of some kind flew away with a faint laugh just at the completion of his sale pitch. The comment from the lady was encouraging. She would be more than happy to buy a box of soap. The problem was, she only had a twenty-dollar bill. That was okay. An order was taken, and she was assured he would come back for payment. Would all sales, though, be this easy? Much uneasiness and doubt!

The next customer proved more difficult. A Mr. Wells questioned why anyone would want to go to camp. Zachary replied, "To learn about a new part of the United States I have never been to." Mr. Wells grumbled, "What a waste of time and money."

Zachary reminded him, "But you will be getting four bars of soap to keep yourself clean." What a fantastic sales line, he thought! The door was suddenly slammed in his face. The windows and house seemed to shake and go into permanent shock. A re-assessment of soap retail sales might be needed.

Another elderly lady, Miss Lilia, was also well known from Zachary's paper route. She came to the door in a cotton dress with large flowers, and when she saw Zachary, she broke out into a big smile, revealing a lot of gold in her mouth. She had difficulty standing up to listen to a sales pitch. Eyes blinked and blinked some more. There was a smell Zachary could not accurately decipher. After he finished, she said nothing, then burped, and with an unforgettable blank stare asked him to come back tomorrow. He reasoned she was drunk and would never be a good prospect.

Families who lived in a trailer park on the outskirts of town had been suggested by Paul as potential customers. Most of them worked on the construction of a new plant being built on the east side of town. Wouldn't a lot of these folks need to clean up after a hard day's work? They were solicited, and a grand total of three boxes sold. Disappointment became ever rampant as Zachary wondered if he would sell even ten boxes. Another eight homes were tried, all with the same result: A big zero! A strong wind spiked his face, and rain in big drops splintered him on a quick bike ride home.

With each pedal initiation faster than the previous, he thought of the need to go and talk again to Paul . . . there had to be an answer for his "sales woes." Summer camp was becoming an unlikelihood. A rest and a nap appeared to be the best thing to do.

At first, a very unsettled mind stirred and resisted any level of somnolence. But complete relaxation finally prevailed and slumbers, a deeper sleep, and a dream state jolted Zachary's consciousness from his bedroom bed to a gravel road where legs felt tired, and there was very little scenery, just a few small hills. He guessed it looked like places where cowboys roamed many years ago—places with lots sage brush, but not much else.

Suddenly, as he walked around a curve, he encountered Carl Stewart sitting alongside the road. He appeared to have been injured, because his leg was bleeding. The two of them looked at each other and for some strange reason, Zachary was not afraid. When Zachary spoke, Carl initially gave a vacuous response, appeared scared, and asked, "Will you help me?"

Zachary had no bandages to stop the bleeding, but thought he might be able to apply pressure on his leg—that was what he had been taught in Boy

Scouts. As he moved toward Carl, Zachary suddenly discovered that some force was holding him back and preventing any movement. He tried to use his legs, but they appeared frozen. He shouted to Carl, "Say something!" but there was no response. More blood came from Carl's leg, and he appeared to lose consciousness. Then without any warning, Carl disappeared, and Zachary miraculously moved again. What had happened? Where had Carl gone?

A slightly confused kid woke with tired eyes. He got a drink of water and stared out his bedroom's back window at a maple tree, its high branches blowing and arching over from strong winds. His face felt some relief from the breeze, and as the wind picked up, a shrill noise could be heard and then eventually faded away. Was it human forced? What was the meaning of a dream about encountering such vivid components of blood, violence, and pain, all present in his most feared adversary? He must permanently rid himself of this menace, but how and when would be the best time?

<hr>

"Find new pockets in Elm City to sell your product that may seem unconventional to others," Paul advised a few days later. "Why not try to sell on the Elm City square to all of merchants; then go out to the west side of town and sell to the rich people. They should recognize a need and help. Also, go to the truck stops and try to sell to the drivers of those eighteen-wheelers."

Zachary smiled, but inwardly he was battling demons, those unhelpful creatures that convinced him that his task was an impossible one. *"Give up; you are not going to sell any more soap. You are a loser"*

Determined, he realized it was a time to recalibrate and take Paul's advice, see if his luck might change. This was not a time to fail. And as Zachary became re-motivated to sell soap with a new passion, a 1950 Plymouth sedan began moving around the Elm City square unnoticed, circling and circling. An arm with a decipherable tattoo hung out the car window. Eyes stared straight ahead, a purpose in mind.

Questions popped up for direction of a narrative in the making: *Can the presence of "evil" ever be felt? Are there boundaries where it might hover and reveal purpose . . . delicately tapping on a shoulder, whispering ever so quietly in a wind which slowly blows in many directions, subtly disturbing, but not directly confronting before running away, laughing boisterously? Do you ignore or try to initiate?*

It was July, and the heat beyond just hot. Zachary's day was finished. He had good sales on the square and was buoyed by the positive comments received from some of the owners of the stores. Yet he still had uneasy feelings inside both stomach and mind, feelings which had been with him for most of the day. Something was wrong, out of place, unsettled.

As he rode his bike down Fleet Street, out of the corner of his eye and slightly adjacent to him, he saw a car slowly turn off the square. He took a second look and realized that he did not recognize the automobile, but the driver looked familiar. He started peddling faster, while the car picked up speed and drove around him. The driver focused on Zachary for the longest time, and then he looked away. A noticeable scar on his face was clearly visible, as was the long, oily hair.

The pit of Zachary's stomach felt tight and upset; a heart pounded in a chest cavity that did not deserve such physical tension, pressure, and direct slams. The face of the stranger became recognizable as Carl Stewart, the guy he had seen driving away from Fred Duncan's store the day of an assault and robbery.

Zachary peddled faster to make an escape, when suddenly the sedan stopped less than a block away.

The driver got out of the car and he opened his hand, exposing something not clearly visible. He shouted, but Zachary was too far away to hear clearly discernible words. Then, distracted, Zachary collided with a telephone pole. The bike and basket took the brunt of the collision, while boxes of soap spilled all over the street. A block away, a group of men sitting outside the House of Johnson Bar laughed at the entire scene that unfolded in front of them. None were aware of the potential seriousness of what would happen next.

Carl slowly walked toward Zachary, and he revealed what he had been holding in his hand—a pearl-handled switchblade knife. His eyes became riveted to Zachary's face. Shaken and scared, Zachary was not able to find a voice. Then Carl broke the silence: "I know you! Answer me, kid! Do you know me? We have met before!"

Zachary garbled out, "No, I don't think so." Then he offered, "Maybe you are the guy who worked on bikes at Thornton's Cycle Shop a long time ago."

"Yeah, that is where we saw each other."

Then an important question from Zachary: "Why do you have a knife in your hand?

Carl replied, "I carry it around to protect myself and to use it on people who try to fight with me."

"I have no argument with you. I am on my way home from selling soap and had an accident," Zachary stammered.

Carl responded, "You had better get your stuff picked up. Why are those guys from the House of Johnson walking down here? What do they want?"

Zachary spoke nervously. "I don't know. Maybe they want to see if I am okay."

Carl thought for a moment. Then he gave Zachary a pissed-off look, followed by a slight smile. "I think we have seen each other somewhere else beside the cycle shop, but I am not sure. Did I see you around Duncan's Market on South Main Street more than a year ago? I know I was driving fast and turned the corner, and thought I was going to hit you. I guess we were both lucky that I didn't."

Zachary looked straight ahead and had plenty of thoughts and things he wanted to say, but didn't. Carl was testing to see if Zachary showed any response, and then continued. "It does not matter. I have a job now in Evansville, My dad and I had an argument over some money I made, and he forced me to leave town."

The perspiration was heavy and drippy. Zachary shook all over but did a good job of disguising his fears. "I don't know who you saw. It wasn't me. Some of my friends say I look like a lot of people in Elm City. I guess you will enjoy your new place."

Nothing else was said, but Carl showed Zachary the knife again, blade open. He stared at Zachary, commenting, "The blade is very sharp. I have a stone cutter at home that keeps it like a razor. You look like a kid I saw the day Fred Duncan's market got robbed. I was driving toward town and saw some guy run out of the store and jump in an old truck. I didn't want to be involved because the police know me, and I didn't want any hassle from them. That is why I drove as fast as I could to get away and almost hit you. If I were you, I would never admit to anyone that you saw me that day, or even know me. Do you understand?"

Zachary looked at him and replied, "I understand."

The communication was clear, and as Carl went back to his car, he laughed quietly to himself and appeared to think he had scared the shit out of Zachary and at the same time sent a strong message: *Keep your mouth shut!*

Zachary guessed the guy was just stupid, a real loser; that knife he held was real, though, and certainly could never be considered a loser or stupid! The oxygen around him felt vanquished, drawn out, and the quiet penetrated all parts of his body and mind. Air appeared to be moving in slow motion, or maybe no motion, like an indescribable tilt of reality, a feeling that all form was sliding off edges of ground into space, a moving from light to grey to darkness.

Carl reflects: *That guy is bigger now, but he still seems like a kid. His arms are more muscular, and he is a little taller. He was afraid, all right; I saw him shaking. He must have thought I might use that knife on him. He will keep his mouth shut, even though I am not going to be in town anymore. It has been a while and nothing much has been said about the robbery, so I am safe from him and safe from snooping police.*

The look in his eyes when I told him to forget about me forever showed he was plenty scared, and I think he believes that if he tells anyone, I will be back with my knife.

Life is good. Dad must now give me that money I so rightly earned. Elm City and this whole mess will continue to be a distant memory, including a cowardly and lying witness. He won't be a problem for me.

Carl Stewart would again leave Elm City in just two days; his story and bigger things to happen were in the mix for him.

Several men from the House of Johnson Bar came over and gathered the boxes and put them back into the bicycle basket. Zachary had a slight cut on his leg, and they asked if he needed help. "No. I'm fine."

Somebody spoke and said the guy with whom Zachary had just interacted with was a well-known troublemaker, and that he should have nothing to do with him. While amazingly the police had never identified the person responsible for an assault and robbery of a grocery store, one of the men from the bar commented, "I wouldn't be surprised if that Stewart fellow wasn't the one who robbed Duncan's market." A response from another: "He is too stupid to pull off such a heist!"

Zachary rode his bike nonstop down South Main Street. He looked back and saw nothing, but he still peddled fast. Arriving home, he ran up to his room, tore off his jeans and bandaged the cut on his leg before heading downstairs for dinner.

As Zachary prepared to go to sleep, he thought back about his unplanned meeting with Carl. The best news—the guy was leaving town. And Zachary now might focus on those dreams of going to a camp in Kentucky, free of any fears from discombobulated tattoos, an open pearl-handed knife, and an acne-scarred face.

Two days later, Paul called with another idea. He suggested that Zachary go with him to the Elm City Country Club, where he was to give a pitch for community involvement for some project. While there, Paul said he would mention to all the "fat cats" that Zachary was having a final push for selling soap to pay for camp, and they should help a local kid close out an ambitious project.

Zachary heeded Paul's advice and, to his surprise, he sold the rest of his soap and met his goal. He now had enough money to pay for two weeks of summer camp in Kentucky.

One of the people who bought several boxes was the banker who had rejected Zachary's mother's application for a home loan. Zachary had not forgotten nor forgiven this guy, and found it hard to smile when the two faced each other.

"I am sure this money will be used wisely, and you will enjoy camp," the banker said. "Be careful and not let the bugs bite you too much." Zachary said nothing, but he still had to admit to, at times, thoughts concerning vengeance and retribution. Then reality: *No! Ignore and do not act on such thoughts from such a stilted mind! There are more important things to attend to.*

On the day everyone was to leave, Paul drove the camp attendees to Lafayette and put them on a train, *The Hoosier Special,* which travelled between

Washington, D.C., and Chicago with intermediate stops throughout the Midwest, including Indianapolis. There were seven Pullman cars, a dining car, and a club car rounded at its end. On the front of the diesel locomotive were the words "New York Central System."

After boarding the train, a stern-looking conductor in a blue suit and cap yelled, "Tickets, please!" Zachary guessed this man must have seen many interesting people ride this train—the rich, the famous, and the poor—maybe even a few criminals.

Fields of corn and alfalfa flashed by the window and blended together to make vibrant colors of gold and green. Young shirtless boys, protected from the sun by wide-brimmed straw hats, strenuously worked stacking hay. Their movements appeared robotic, in step, non-stop. A cool breeze was directed on his face from a small fan located above his seat. As the train crossed the muddy Wabash River, the side-to-side rocking motion lulled him to sleep. He later awoke and saw ponds and kids swimming and diving from dead tree logs. He remembered a poem from school about a "Swimmin' Hole," but the words to the poem and the author's name eluded him.

Then, a feeling of hunger lazily worked its way to Zachary's brain. A dining car was located, where he found white tablecloths, silverware, and waiters dressed in black pants and white starched coats briskly moving around, serving food and liquor. After viewing the menu, Zachary wrote his selection: "hamburger, fries, and a Coke," on a white piece of paper and placed it on a silver tray. Food orders were sent down a little elevator called a "dumb waiter." Later, the desired fare returned in like manner from the kitchen below. Everything was expertly done, and Zachary felt like a "big-shot" eating with such high-class service in palatial surroundings. Payment of the bill included tipping the waiter; something his mother had taught him how to do. When the train arrived at the Indianapolis station, the conductor announced that the stop would be forty-five minutes.

John Spencer

Back from lunch, Zachary suddenly heard a voice from behind him say, "My name is Don Errands, is this seat taken?" A skinny kid who appeared to be a little older than Zachary quickly sat down. His hair was brown, flat-top cut, jeans well worn, a soiled black tee shirt, and a face slightly bathed in sweat. He was hot and out of breath, as if he had been running. But it was his eyes that Zachary noticed; they moved quickly to one side and then the other, especially when he talked.

"I live outside Indianapolis. My parents sell racehorses and often travel between Indianapolis and Louisville. I have been riding horses since I was seven. I get my kicks racing them around the track, feeling the wind in my face, always working hard to improve race time. I used to fall off a lot, but now I don't. I learned to never be afraid of riding fast." Zachary marveled that he spoke all those words in just one breath!

Don went on to describe the house he lived in as "huge," two stories including a wrap-around porch on the first floor. Each bedroom had its own attached bathroom. The floors were made of wood imported from South America, and the grounds were large, with lots of trees and bushes. A staff was assigned to keep the grass cut and perform other outside duties. While he was talking, Zachary noticed Don clutched a large brown bag tightly. "Don't you want me to put that on the overhead shelf?" Zachary asked.

The mysterious kid appeared uneasy. His eyes darted back and forth, and he responded, "No," and was then quiet for a few minutes.

Soon, he was chatty again. He told Zachary that he was fifteen and a sophomore in high school. He was a good student and played drums in the school band. He also played basketball. In one game, he scored twenty-one points before some type of injury forced him to quit the team. The kid's eyes began darting around again, and Zachary wondered if something else might have happened.

"I am on my way to see my brother, who races horses and lives in Louisville. He drives an Italian sports car and has many girlfriends, lots of money, and a house with servants. Someday I am going to have a lot of money," Don said, and then the subject was changed quickly.

"You can't believe all of the movie stars I saw at last year's Kentucky Derby. I got autographs from Gene Collins and Randolph Owen. They signed my horse blanket. Gene talked to me for a while, and he asked how I liked taking care of horses. He may have been a little drunk, though, because he had difficulty mounting his horse. I don't care about that. I've seen a lot of people who drink and get stupid. I was just so happy I got a chance to talk to a real movie star."

Zachary told him about his town, a small place in Indiana where he played baseball, enlisted in the Boy Scouts, and tried to be very "religious" but without much success.

Don listened intently and asked, "What is it like to be 'religious'?" A reply from Zachary: "To live a good life and believe in God and Jesus. But I don't know what I believe." He then looked away for a minute and softly said, "I understand what that might be like."

For a moment his face changed, and he looked different, as if something had shaken slumbering feelings inside. Then an obvious change; he focused directly on Zachary's face and said, "Life is not always what it seems. It is a game. To survive, you must be selfish and grab things when you can, and not look back. My parents were quite religious and talked about God all the time. Believing in God for me is always a waste of time. The only way to get ahead in life is to be at the right place at the right time. Take charge of your life when you are young, and don't let anybody take advantage of you. I am in the business of selling merchandise, and I trust no one."

The train arrived at the Cincinnati terminal at about five-thirty in the afternoon. When Don stood up, Zachary noticed a large scar and small marks on his forearm. Outside the train car window, there was some confusion. People tried to get off the train at the same time a group of policemen elbowed their way through a door to one of the passenger cars. Zachary wanted Don to leave his name and address, but when he looked around, the kid with the marks on his arm was gone.

Who was that guy named Don Errands, and what was in his bag? Did it have anything to do with the police and the law? Some fat, sweaty man arrived at the platform and asked questions; he showed a photograph to a group of people, and one woman pointed to the train car where Zachary and Don had been sitting. The officer asked all the passengers, including Zachary, if they recognized a rather fuzzy picture of someone. Zachary wasn't sure if it was Don or not, and gave no reply.

Don Errands disappeared and was never seen or heard from again. He was an interesting but puzzling guy who must have had a lot of hidden stories, and no doubt told "big fibs." For unclear reasons, Zachary liked Don and wished he could have learned more about him. There was something mature-like and cool that Zachary recognized, maybe a kinship sought after but never found. Certainly, there were things which Zachary had also experienced and knew about; things not told to others. Secrets remained just that, deeply hidden. But what could be recorded was that on a train bound for summer camp, Don Errands became a short-time, special friend—a guy maybe involved in illegal activities. But Zachary could only guess.

The next challenge was finding the bus that would meet and deliver four hungry and tired kids to summer camp. The boys looked for a vehicle with the anticipated "Camp Silver Trout" signage; none was in view.

The kids walked around , and then with no grand announcement, a medium-sized van with the words "Camp Silver Trout Lake" painted on the side pulled to the curb. The driver got out and asked, "Are you kids from Elm City?" Everyone yelled, "Yes!" He reported that the drive would be about two hours south and east from Cincinnati. Most importantly, dinner would be waiting for them.

The bus initially stayed on a major highway for about an hour, and then it veered off onto a small dirt road full of twists and turns. Many small bridges were traversed, and off to the side were fields of hay or thick brush. Creeks meandered over the countryside and eventually gave way to heavy forests, so dense that little sunlight appeared to reach the ground. The road later became asphalt and gravel. Finally, the main gate to the camp became visible. Logs, painted a rust color, were strung out as a fence that went off in both directions from the gate. The road wove around to the main administrative building about a quarter of a mile beyond. Upon arrival, a scrumptious dinner was immediately served in a large dining hall, and then equipment that included blankets and a pillow were handed out, and Zachary took a bus to cabin #5, Bear Claw Village.

His cabin residence for the next two weeks had a screen door, which led into a musty room with six bunk beds. He claimed a lower one. In the back of the cabin was a large table used for making crafts and playing board games. Later, other kids joined him, and he learned they came from all over the Midwest. Very little was said for the first couple of hours; nonverbal learning and testing was in play, with subsequent friendships then to be decided. Off to one side of his abode was the latrine, or "pee-piss" house. It smelled strongly of cleaning solution. In the center of all the villages were benches and an open pavilion, where an adjacent large pit could be used to light bonfires in the evening, or planned group activities were made for a busy schedule during the day.

This was Zachary's first time away from Elm City with no close friends. Jimmie Eller had told him about homesickness. He described it as a feeling in the pit of the stomach, which hurt and produced a lot of sad feelings. It could be counted on to stay for a day, maybe longer.

The cure was to make friends quickly and not think about home.

As if on cue, the next day Zachary received a letter from a thoughtful mother and grandmother. They both must have understood about a teenage boy who faced his first camp experiences completely alone with potential fear and loneliness. The letter, in part, said, "Zachary, this will be your first big test surviving in a new and strange place. I know you will make it, and although we both miss you, we also know you are going to enjoy yourself and come back a different person." He wondered what she meant by "a different person" and was puzzled a bit. Then he laughed, went down to the lake, and watched some kids swim. Later, it became time to go back to the cabin and find out about his bunkmates.

Five other kids had been assigned to Zachary's cabin. Joe Baron appeared to be the same age and size, with two very skinny legs and arms complemented by a flattop haircut and big ears. His hometown was Cincinnati.

He looked unhappy as he sat on his bunk. Zachary wondered if his red eyes might be a clue he had been crying, so he asked, "Do you miss home?"

"Only Sunday visits to Coney Island with a few friends," Joe replied. Zachary suggested the two of them take a walk on a trail leading to another village.

Joe had serious, sobering stories to tell. They were not lies, but descriptions about a life that contained more than just mysteries about the human spirit, its goodness, its deprivations, or its biggest failures.

A horrible incident had occurred a year ago. His stepfather had come home drunk and began beating his mother. She tried to call the police, but the guy became violent and hit her over the head. Blood was everywhere; furniture became broken and displaced, screams filled the air. Joe had previously tried to get his mother to leave a hopeless and disastrous marriage, but she said, "Things will get better, just wait and see." They had not, and this time his mother was unconscious on the floor.

A scared kid quietly hid in the closet. The stepfather went around the house looking for him. When the guy came to the closet, Joe heard heavy breathing and clumsy attempts to open a closet door. He was in a panic state, frozen and static. He had positioned himself behind some long coats that provided partial cover. His breathing became more self-contained, a racing heart beat loud, tearing at a chest for escape, at least to Joe's sensitive ears. The out-of-control stepfather grabbed coats and threw them around, but as if by a miracle, the ones Joe hid behind were left alone.

An extremely angry, frustrated man slammed the closet door shut and cursed loudly. All was quiet. Joe waited for almost an hour, slipped out of the house, and then he ran to the neighbors. Police were notified.

Joe's mother never regained consciousness from the head wounds and eventually died. The stepfather was arrested but admitted to nothing. The police threatened that if he did not confess, they would bring forward an eyewitness. He eventually pled guilty to assault and was given a long prison sentence. Joe was permanently removed from the home and sent to another address, a farm outside Cincinnati. One of the social agencies enrolled him in a YMCA program that subsequently sent him to camp.

Zachary was quiet for a few moments, and then finally said, "What a scary story! I feel bad your mother died. You must still miss her." Joe replied that he continued to think about his mom a lot but also knew he must move on with his life. He admitted to being sensitive about so many things, including anger toward his stepfather, who he wished would just die. Zachary understood that thought well.

"Tell me about your life, Zachary.,"

A narrative began— known only too well—a broken home, a neat town, crime and violence, and recognition from a scout master who was like a drill sergeant, but also in some way was oddly admired; a church pastor who talked about a God who seemed so far away and impersonal that Zachary admitted quite awkwardly that he had become "partially immune" to religion.

The scene was set. Two boys, from less than ideal homes, ensconced in the mountains of Kentucky toting very different but very real "heavy baggage"; they truly were kindred spirits in certain ways. It may not have been an "accident" that they were placed in such a planned environment. Would respect and understanding about the unpredictability and unfairness of life be represented and felt? Would they learn from each other? Time is always patient.

The "plan-of the-day" began each morning with the playing of reverie. Bunks were made so that the sheets had forty-five-degree angular corners, tucked in without wrinkles. The cabins were cleaned, and then cleaned some more. The latrine was washed every day, and then a camp counselor inspected the entire village. If the cabins and latrine passed inspection, chow hall was open and hungry campers attacked the dining hall with no mercy. If not, and this happened too often, more cleaning, more sore muscles, and much more non-Christian comments and feelings were offered up, with no need for further elaboration or clarification.

Since the camp was ostensibly Christian, time was spent daily reading parts of the Bible. There was a leader who reviewed a passage, and then each group discussed and made comments about parceling out the "meaning to everyday life." Questions were prepared for the leader to ask, but most of the time, sensible answers were not forthcoming from the "congregation." Welcomed endings included a prayer and much-desired dismissal. Zachary was able, because of his previous training at his church, to say a few things when it was his turn to lead. Many of the others had no understanding of the Bible and spent their devotional time in light or heavy slumber. Zachary's comments were of little relevance or impact, primarily because of his own doubts about spiritual things. His present "religious" maturity and state of mind was easily communicated to all campers attending, either consciously or unconsciously; however, pictures of a group of boys, one holding a bible, made for good pictorial inserts into the camp's advertising materials.

The food was mediocre at best, although many got tired of what was called "shit on the shingle," a type of gravy and corned beef served on toast at breakfast. Lunch and dinner consisted of cooked meat and vegetables. The song sung by so many campers, "Here we sit like birds in the wilderness, birds in the wilderness, birds in the wilderness, here we sit like birds in the wilderness, waiting for dessert," never seemed to hasten its arrival. Like a bad habit, though, the song stayed in their brains the entire camp time, and maybe even beyond.

A DAY IN THE LIFE OF A CAMPER: After breakfast and the raising of the flag, hiking or sports such as softball was on the agenda. In the afternoon there was swimming in the lake or a pool near the center of camp. Wrist bracelets were made using "boondoggle," plastic strips woven and knotted. Mail call was held in the early afternoon, and then classes of many persuasions offered, including types of landscape fauna, artwork, and woodwork, followed by dinner, and then back to cabins where letters were written or senseless conversations occurred. Finally, a campfire was lit and, to prevent fire danger, a trench dug around the outer perimeter. Selected campers manned dirt and water pails. More songs and silly phrases were sung, and s'mores roasted. Socialization was to be the ideal among and for varied types of personalities, lending itself to learning and appreciating differences in people and hopefully lessening the development of prejudice. The goals for all campers were that they would leave Camp Silverlake changed for the better, ready to go out into society and become useful Christian workers, always for the "Kingdom of God."

To accelerate this goal, Sunday church was held in the dining room. A pastor from a local church came over and preached about sin and hell. It was sometimes hard to hear what was said, because many of the kids held their own "private" sermons amongst themselves. Others took naps or told jokes. Zachary tried hard to listen, but he eventually gave up because of distraction, boredom, and lack of any spiritual motivation.

As the sermon became more intense, the preacher likewise became angrier, and his face turned beet red as he railed about sinners and the need for redemption. The story was familiar, and Zachary certainly continued to have doubts about God. He wished for a "Savior" who might help him deal with homesickness. After listening to the preacher, however, Zachary wasn't so sure that the people in heaven had much interest in a kid with any malady, especially one as benign as nostomania.

Cloudless mornings were common in the summer, and on one of them, a group of campers departed on a fishing expedition designed to learn about nature and competition. Prizes were awarded for the largest number of fish to be caught, irrespective of size. All the boys were on an "honor system" which, broadly translated, was meaningless. The camp counselors' station wagons arrived, and everyone piled in. A hitched trailer was loaded with small boats.

Zachary's partner was a kid who lived somewhere in Ohio. His name was Dave, and he had recently complained of severe homesickness for a girl with whom he claimed to be in love with. Today, he felt better and proudly announced, "I am ready to catch fish." Promises were made to loan Zachary fishing lures which Dave's father, an expert fisherman, had made.

The two boys got into their boat missing an important commodity—life jackets. The counselors had unwittingly and unbelievably left them behind. None of the campers should have been allowed in the boats, but couldn't rules be circumvented?

Everybody knew how to swim because they had previously passed and received an "intermediate" swimmer's card. But one camper, who hid in his barracks when the test was given, had no swimming abilities, told no one, and today was Zachary's boat partner. David had never lost his fear of swimming, despite many attempts by his father to teach him. Water was fine to sit on when protected by a boat, but its touch to skin, when buoyancy was required—out of the question!

The rule was simple. All "boating" campers were required to stay around the edge of the lake. Under no circumstances were any of them allowed to go beyond forty to fifty yards of the shoreline. The bottom of the lake had to remain visible. David and Zachary rowed slowly toward its most southern part, and then used a rock as an anchor so they would not float off toward deeper, more dangerous areas.

Lines were thrown into the water, and it was now boredom time. The most likely fish captives were blue gill and crappie. Neither Zachary nor Dave got any catches or bites during the first hour and a half; however, the time was not totally wasted. Conversations were started without any pretense or sensitivity toward privacy. Two boys alone allowed for words and concepts to fly loose, without censor, and certainly with even less understanding of meaning.

David spoke of a girlfriend with brilliant red hair and a pretty face. The two of them often snuck out behind her house and kissed. Then more descriptions were given of touching parts of her body, and how excited she made him feel. Zachary sat and acted as if he understood what David was talking, about even though he did not have a clue.

The father was described as a preacher, a man of God. He viewed women as the weaker sex, ones who needed a lot of attention and care. The history of women was as follows: Eve, described from the Bible as a helpmate, had initially persuaded a man named Adam into disobeying God. They were both disciplined, and because of their failure to obey, everyone else in the entire human race was held accountable and blamed. David said that now everybody had "bad genes" first passed on to us from our parents, and then later by us to our children. Women needed to be watched closely When Zachary asked what kind of "watching" David was referring to, the subject was changed, and a suggestion made to use a new lure.

Zachary reflected for a moment after hearing this discourse and remembered that somewhere he had heard the Bible described as "good news." What David portrayed hardly seemed to be in that category. He remembered Dr. Harris had been questioned by a girl in his confirmation class about women, specifically Adam and Eve. The pastor had appeared uneasy and not willing to say much. Zachary's conclusion was that Dave's father did not like women.

Then, a continuation with a startling question. "Zachary, do you know anything about sexual intercourse?" Zachary initially said nothing but thought: *why is he asking a question about sex? This conversation is going in a strange way. I will bullshit him and try to change the subject.*

"Yes, sure, I know all about that stuff from things I read in health class, and even some drawings on bathroom walls . . . my friends have done an excellent job of teaching me about sex. Let's move to another part of the lake to fish."

Of course, Zachary lied, but he was not ready to hear such information from a teenage "sex expert," even though it was true he had always been puzzled about the mechanics of sexual intercourse. He did remember about two girls in his grade school caught kissing each other. Perhaps by the time these two girls reached high school, they would start dating boys. Or maybe life had a way of ensuring that some are just different. Unlike some of his friends, he never felt hatred toward either of these girls. How could he? They were always and forever his grade-school friends. There had to be something wrong about judging others harshly, so unfair and presumptuous.

At that point, David became serious, and he asked Zachary if he could keep a deep secret. Zachary cautiously replied, "Sure, you can trust me."

Dave described that at times he disliked his father and viewed him as too judgmental. His dad viewed the entire church congregation as "spiritually immature," full of sin, and even his own family as "partially imperfect." His prescription: Read more of the Bible and become spiritually mature like him.

He admitted that he had tried to do what his father had suggested, but without much success. "At least he taught me how to tie lures well." For a minute, the kid from Ohio turned away and a very perceivable voice inflection was noticed; composure was then regained, throat cleared and emotions back in check.

Zachary listened and reasoned that something was missing. Somewhere he had heard things like love and forgiveness discussed, and wished he could only put all of this "religious" information together so that it not only made sense to him, but he could talk about it. The only thing Zachary knew for sure was that he was a sinner with no hope of ever attaining the perfection of David's father!

"My dad was not like your dad at all," Zachary revealed. "He drank all the time. There were always a lot of women who called on the phone to talk to my dad. I guess he was a permanent sinner." Absolute penetrating silence. Nothing said for a long time. Then David commented, "I bet your mom was unhappy."

Zachary felt some sadness and took a few deep breaths, then turned so that David could not see the tearing in his eyes and witness a full emoting of anger for the loss of something he never could express, much less understand.

Did both boys have imperfect dads? They agreed that somewhere there had to be another place where dads were good and forgiving, where peace and harmony was found twenty-four hours a day.

Then Zachary remembered that Pastor Harris, in one of their conversations, spoke of such a place. It was called heaven, and here a perfect Father could be found. He asked Dave if he knew of such a place, and the reply was, "Only too well. My dad constantly reminds me of how often I may miss going to this place if I am not perfect in everything I do."

Zachary said nothing but thought: *Have I already missed getting to heaven? Maybe it is a land of promise I will never be able to find.*

Suddenly, his limp fish line pulled out and away from the boat; maybe he had his first bite. He tried to relax and use all his strength to slowly move the fish around to the side of the boat. Dave helped, but as Zachary tried to pull and bring the fish up out of the water, the hook broke and the fish escaped.

Zachary temporarily forgot about church, sin, and heaven, and instead spewed out some strong cuss words that had "God and Jesus" identified, but not in complimentary ways. Dave felt awkward as he witnessed anger and disappointment surface from Zachary following a messed-up first catch.

The day moved in what seemed like slow motion—the heat of the sun gained strength, and there was a wish for another chance to catch a fish. Finally, a slight pull, ever so lightly on Zachary's line. He pulled back, and out of the water came the smallest fish known to mankind. He pulled it in, and David shouted, "Throw it back!" Zachary wanted so much to keep that fish, his first, but he dutifully obeyed.

Dave had better luck— he caught a good-sized blue gill. It was much larger, but he likewise decided to throw it back, maybe to make Zachary feel better. It really didn't matter; none of them had fishing licenses, and they had been told they could not keep any fish they caught.

With time, the sun slowly moved to the crescent of a hill, then disappeared as a red ball delighting in finding new places to impress with its great heat and light. Two very junior fishermen admired the scenery, although no commentary was ever made concerning the upward angling of thick green trees extending to various heights in the hills and forming an almost perfect surround of the lake. A very light wind produced columns of flying leaves, shimmers, and audible ripples over the water lightly touching and rocking the boat. The drying of perspiration and subsequent cooling of two red, sunburnt faces could neither be ignored nor appreciated enough.

David subsequently moved around in the boat and reached down to get another lure. As he turned, he suddenly lost his balance and fell out of the boat. The water was about five feet in depth, and Zachary told him to hold onto the side, so he could pull him back inside. He extended his hand, and as Dave pulled, Zachary quickly departed the boat into the water, face first! Dave fought to get into the boat, and through awkwardness and poor timing plus weight distribution problems, the boat flipped. Upset with himself, he began screaming and hitting the bottom of the boat with his hand.

A small amount of blood appeared on Dave's forehead where he had struck the oar lock. It was only a scratch, but he became frightened and continued kicking and flailing his arms and legs. Zachary yelled to him to swim to shore, but Dave countered, "I can't swim, and I don't want to drown! I don't want to die!" Zachary's heart pounded as he treaded water and pondered his next move.

Zachary knew he must swim over to Dave, grab him, and reassure him that he was not going to drown. "Dave, take one hand and grab the side of the boat, and I will support you; we will then move toward the shore." He grabbed the anchor rope and pulled it up, and began to push the boat to land. David was told to continue to hold onto the side. They progressed slowly, but in a straight line, and eventually reached the safety of a muddy bank.

An exhausted and frightened fisherman collapsed into some grass and appeared to have difficulty breathing. Zachary considered applying artificial respiration, a technique he had learned in Boy Scouts. But he then changed his mind and had David sit down, place his head between his legs, and simulate coughing, producing small amounts of water from his mouth. A band-aid was used to fix the head wound. David believed that Zachary had just saved his life, while Zachary said it would be best to say nothing to anybody about what had just happened. There would be too much risk in exposing a host of sins, not the least of which would be the acknowledgement that David had not been truthful about his fear of water and inability to swim even one stroke. Silence for two campers became more than just golden.

After their return from fishing, sex talk, and a near-drowning expedition in the mountains, Zachary was wet, confused, and disappointed in the day. The sun was gone, and he knew he had to get a shower and warm up.

Both he and Dave remained frightened concerning what had happened at the lake. Dave knew that he would be in a lot of trouble if it was discovered he did not have a swimmer's card; Zachary would have to address why he waited to report the accident. But then, what about the esteemed group of counselors who forgot life jackets? Mistakes were made all around; it was just debatable who the greatest screw-ups were. But Zachary was to never forget the way David's pale face looked when he first came out of the water. He thought back to Boy Scouts and life-saving lessons learned.

Joe Hassle might have been proud of what he did. Then again, who knows? The scoutmaster would have been upset with David for lying about his swimming ability, and with Zachary for covering up certain things. Both would have been good candidates for swats. Then, Zachary had a few soul-searching thoughts . . .

The scoutmaster was tough, but I think he understood me better than I realized. His discipline was maybe unfair at times, but I learned survival; things that have come in handy. Maybe the troop experience was not such a bad thing. I wonder now if I could have told him about today's events. Maybe I am working toward finding more of a conscience and trying do the "right thing," to be honest and face up to certain consequences. I still, though, have a long way to go toward being more responsible and mature. I need help, but from who? Oh, self-evaluation can be so difficult! Memories of Boy Scouts and other particularly thorny issues, including a bloody axe, were soon replaced by sleep. It was always easier that way.

Bonfires were times to socialize and tell stories—some true, some lies, and others just scary. One of the counselors, Jack Black, recounted his version of the history of Arrowhead Lake. He asked if anyone had ever seen a ghost. Most answered, "No." Jack said that over a hundred years ago, there had been large tribes of Chickasaw Indians living around the lake. There had been two different groups that had argued over land and fishing rights. The disagreements became heated, and the tribes decided to select the most beautiful woman from each group to individually take a canoe to the middle of the lake and engage in a battle on a large platform. The winner was determined by which combatant survived by killing the other; that female and her group would be awarded the land. To this day, it was claimed that at midnight, when the moon was full, a ghost of the Indian maiden killed walked slowly over the water and "wept" words that described how much she wanted to come back and rejoin her family. Jack continued, "Let's wait 'til midnight and go down to the lake. We are lucky; there is a full moon tonight."

Everyone went to the lake and was told to be still. Midnight came and went, and nothing was seen. Zachary began to laugh to himself and turned to go back on the trail leading to his cabin. Strangely, for some reason he took one last look. The wind had picked up, and for just a moment—not more than a few seconds—he thought he heard a cry, a remorseful noise of some kind. Suddenly, he saw a silhouette dart across the water. He punched the guy next to him and told him to look and listen; the irritated kid said he heard and saw nothing, and that if Zachary hit him again, he would return the favor with a direct strike to the nose!

Arrowhead Lake was not as round as it was long, and there were many inlets, especially on its most outer boundaries. There was a large Girl Scout camp that could be seen from the boat docks, but its distance from the boys' camp was hard to estimate. From across the lake, the faces of the girl campers were not identifiable. Rather, the camp appeared to be inhabited by midgets running in many directions. If one used binoculars, discernment of human body size increased, but not appreciably, and faces were still hard to discern. If any camper was caught covetously observing the camp, that "lurid behavior" resulted in dinner being a long time in coming, if at all. That person would be compelled to stand up before his village and explain his misdeed, and how he planned to change such lustful behavior.

The direction of the long-awaited canoe race on Arrowhead Lake was from the camp's boat dock south, around two inlets, one of which was directly in back and to the side of the Girl Scout camp. Then the contest continued around the lake for about a quarter of a mile, u-turned, and came back to the starting point.

Two people were assigned to each canoe, both had paddles, and this time, safety first: tight-fitting life jackets. A time was recorded when the participants left the dock and returned; a trophy was given for the fastest time. Joe and Zachary had snuck down and practiced a few days before the race, a flagrant foul, but so what! Many campers started out and bragged about how they were going to win. Most of them had no idea what was ahead.

Although the rowing part looked easy, it did not take long for them to quickly find out they were in for a lot of work. The paddles became heavy, and it was difficult to work in sequence so the canoe moved quickly and consistently. Zachary and Joe started out close to the bank and worked toward the middle of the lake. Joe seemed to learn the paddling sequences, and he yelled encouragement to help Zachary get in rhythm. Joe enjoyed the competition and prided himself on their earlier practice and its helpfulness. They moved at a fast pace by the time they were in sight of the Girl Scout camp.

Then, things suddenly became weird. Several of the racers headed their canoes off course and started to go into one of the inlets where a few girls were playing. At least four campers jumped out of their canoes and started to swim toward the Girl Scouts, who had yelled un-discernable words, waved, and ran to the shoreline. The inlet was at a point where none of this action could be observed by the staff from Zachary's camp.

As Zachary and Joe moved closer to the camp, they noticed that some of the girls had taken off part of their swimsuits. Joe had an odd look on his face, but a wily smile; Zachary found it difficult to get his breath, a throat felt dry. Were these changes solely due to paddling the canoe? Attention waned. Stimulation was felt in a lower part of a body that he understood needed to be covered up quickly; this move, though, was a struggle and not totally successful.

For just a moment, they stopped and gazed over to the shore; more kids jumped out of their canoes and joined the girls. Then, there she was! A girl with long brown hair waved directly at Zachary and yelled something that sounded like, "Come here, handsome." Joe turned and said, "What are we going to do? Do you want to jump out and swim to that girl? We will lose the race. But I am feeling strange, excited, maybe it doesn't matter. Everybody else has gone completely nuts!"

They came closer to the bank, and the girl's voice became even clearer, "Hey there, come over here. We can swim together." She had kept her suit on, but now the bottom part began slipping. Zachary was poised to jump out of the canoe. He thought about praying to God for direction—maybe strength to avoid temptation, but that idea escaped quickly without further reflection. He voraciously yelled out, "Wait, I will swim toward you! My name is Zachary; I will be right over!"

Then, other canoes collided, and many of the boys lost any interest in the race. Temptation was indeed rampant. All Zachary could contemplate was that girl who waved to him.

Joe said, "Let's try to get back on course. There is nobody ahead of us, and we might just have a chance of winning the race. Isn't that more important than some girl you will never see after today?"

Zachary was conflicted. The girl waved and yelled more things he couldn't totally decipher, or maybe was afraid for what he might hear. Joe strenuously paddled again, and Zachary found himself doing the same. Temptation wailed, bucked, and exited, but vowed to return. Nothing more was said. Eyes became focused back on the lost time they needed to make up as they continued around the lake. They got back in the groove and eventually finished the race.

Most of the other competitors failed to complete the race, but instead became sidetracked across the lake. Counselors from the Girl Scout camp discovered what had happened and called the staff at Zachary's camp. A motorboat was quickly dispatched to investigate. Suddenly, many campers were paddling their boats straight back to the dock. Trouble was ahead for them. Fortunately for Joe and Zachary, they were free of such difficulty.

Both Zachary and David acknowledged they had done the right thing by continuing to paddle. But thoughts remained about what might have happened had they stopped and gone after those Girl Scouts. Zachary would not let go of a memory of a girl who smiled and waved at him. They had made eye contact with each other, and he wanted to learn more about her. Her beauty left him speechless—so much he truly wanted to say and do. But now, for him, she was lost to the ages.

When the results were posted, Joe and Zachary had the fastest time—not that surprising, since just about everybody else had quit before ever arriving at the finish line.

Back in the cabin, the rest of their group heard what had happened, and they had a good laugh. The counselors joked and said some kids had been caught up in the "Girl Scouts' Lair" from across the lake. None of the campers had the slightest idea what those words meant; again, a testimony to the oddness of camp counselors. Maybe it was something bad, not to be discussed with a family back home. But other thoughts and memories of a girl's smiling face found their way into Zachary's restless mind and caused a partially sleepless night. Oh, the beginnings of adolescence with its physical pleasures, but some pain too!

At breakfast, Joe smiled and said he thought they should feel good about their accomplishment. It was one of the few times Zachary had seen him express much emotion. Joe had learned that he could break out of his shell and be a winner. There had been a challenge, and he had shown focus and effort. Zachary and Joe never asked each other about feelings and thoughts when some of those Girl Scouts took off their swimsuits. Maybe it was just as well—silence this time seemed okay, maybe even precious.

The two boys had worked together as a team, and at the same time avoided the embarrassment which awaited those kids who had chosen to not complete the race. Those poor souls were paraded out in front of the entire camp, and names and hometowns announced. Later, calls were made to their parents, and most likely sore buttocks were to be in the making! Lust and more irresponsible action would never be tolerated by a Christian camp, and certainly not by an all-knowing God. Punishment would be the order of the day.

It was, though, a good feeling that Joe and Zachary had avoided trouble. There would be other days and other places, in the months and years to come, when Zachary could not brag about self-control, nor have the luxury of a friend who was more interested in winning a boat race than swimming in the nude with a bunch of Girl Scouts!

Carl Stewart wanted many things. But money, lots of it, was foremost in his mind. He dreamed of buying a new car and lots of clothes. It was his way of expressing to others how important he was going to be in life—famous, rich, and desirable to many. This thought stuck in his mind. Its attachment was poisonous, but he enjoyed its presence. It was good company to him.

Thirty minutes had been spent "casing" the grocery store, and this was not the first time. He knew when there were few customers and car traffic was not heavy. It reminded him of another store, one that he had successfully robbed in another lifetime. He had not been captured then, but there had been a disappointment. His dad had retrieved all assets earned. Plus, there had been a witness—a kid who lied a lot, but one who had never been trouble for Carl. This time, money earned would be money kept.

The sun had just risen over a grove of trees, which shaded the back of a grocery store in a small town seventy miles southwest of Elm City. A car was parked in the rear, and a dark shadow of a man very quickly gained entrance through a carelessly left-open door with rusted, creaky hinges. Then, a masked man made a quick run from behind the meat locker to the front of the store, where many varieties of groceries waited painstakingly for observation, handling and subsequent purchase. A gun was held in a right hand. Carl was now at his best!

The skinny grocer never had a chance to even think, much less act. "Place all of the money in this bag!" a voice commanded. "Don't shoot! I don't want to die. I just buried my wife last week," replied a second unstable voice from behind the counter. This distraction kept Carl from hearing the front door open, followed by two policemen on their way for coffee before their trip to town and work at the jail. A strong shout: "Put that gun down, now!"

Carl, in a reflexively executed move, turned around and inadvertently pointed his gun at one of the officers. Suddenly, there was noise and then pain immediately felt in Carl's left leg, followed by sudden darkness; retribution was now complete.

<hr>

The letter, in an unmarked manila envelope, came without warning. It was from Zachary's friend Bob. He had sent a copy of the *Elm City Courier* published two days earlier. On the back page, where all the local news was found, a short note reported about a guy who had previously lived in Elm City by the name of Carl Stewart. He had been involved in a lot of fights and "minor" crimes in and around town. Eventually he had left town and, most recently, became involved in an armed robbery just outside of Indianapolis. The guy had been shot during the armed robbery, and prison was now surely in his future.

Zachary looked at the picture and determined it was the same guy who had stalked and threatened him. Bob wrote, "Is this the guy you think robbed the store, Zachary?"

"Yes," Zachary said quietly to himself. "He is the one." A tremendous sense of relief overwhelmed. His emotions churned, and without warning, the tears came as if a huge floodgate had opened.

Suddenly, the emotional outbursts stopped, and reality set in with its questions. *What if he escapes from prison and returns to Elm City? Maybe I will never be free of him.* For now, he could only believe he would never see Carl Stewart again.

Luck or something else was with Zachary. Carl would later become involved in a fight with another inmate and die because of stab wounds that cut a major artery in his leg. Maybe Zachary never saw the connection of events from a previous nightmare, but he must have truly had a "guardian angel" who relayed hope to him around veiled dreams, shadows, and even whispers so often too faint to hear.

* * *

The campers picked up their things on Saturday morning, and a bus took them back to Elm City. Zachary and David said very little to each other; they had their secrets, and a strong handshake said enough. David told Zachary how thankful he was that he had been around for him during the time they both tried to be fishermen. Maybe they would meet again someday. Then David said an odd thing. "If not in this world, for sure in the next one to come, we will see each other. It will be more perfect and more merciful than this place."

Zachary smiled and thought: *What a strange thing to say. There must be something spiritual in all of that, maybe a calling out; I am not sure. I guess we are both searching for something, who knows whether we will ever find it!*

Joe and Zachary hoped to meet again. For Joe, there would be a journey back into a difficult life— one very different from Zachary. A canoe experience had been what was needed to give the two kids confidence, and Zachary agreed it felt good to be a winner and to also find such a good friend. They planned to write each other, although inwardly they knew that would never happen. They were both correct.

Zachary arrived back home, and all were anxious to see him. A banquet of meatloaf, mashed potatoes and a chocolate pie was prepared. Many questions were asked, and the kid did a good job of deflecting some, and maybe telling a few lies too. He had to make himself look good, didn't he?

Prayers had been offered up daily by Grandmother, who said she felt God watched over him. Perhaps it might be guessed that Zachary never realized, when he was young, just how much protection his grandmother's intersession with higher powers must have been with just a few angelic hosts!

He decided to keep his mouth shut about more of his "awakened feelings and emotions," including certain sexual mentation held during a canoe race. It was personal, and his mother and grandmother would never have understood. Would they have found it humorous? Most likely not!

Singing for God and Jesus, Boy Scouts, and YMCA camping were now all things of the past, swept up by travels that forged ahead with no time to rest. Now, Zachary Stevens was to learn about new battles that involved fist fighting and wrestling, telling of tall tales, bragging, sports, and allowing a gang of boys and their many personalities to leave indelible imprints on mind, body, and soul. For now, there was to be a new but also a continuation of a journey, another passage forward, ever learning, ever being surprised about the many unpredictable twists and turns, the vicissitudes of life.

Six:
Buddies for a Boy's Life

A gang of boys with hopes, cares, and dislikes,
Nine kids playing baseball, fighting, riding cheap bikes,
A gang of boys moving onto life's prime,
Nine kids forming friendships lasting a lifetime

A FRIGHTENED BOY'S HEART BEAT FAST; feelings of foolishness were rampant! Clothes had been taken off behind a bush, and he questioned: *What if someone sees me naked?* As he looked down at the lake, with the help of a slight breeze, the water produced miniature waves. It still appeared cold and forbidding. Thoughts crossed his mind: What if someone steals my clothes? *Worse yet, what if I drown in the lake?*

Zachary Stevens had started his first year in high school. For better or worse, he also made the decision to start a second journey beyond the academic—to join a group of boys from his neighborhood, the SMG. If he passed the initiation ritual, he would be accepted as a gang member. If he failed, he was still accepted, but nobody bothered to mention this insignificant fact.

Three things were needed to become a gang member. First, swim naked across Lake Elm City, rest for a few minutes behind a tree, shielded from everybody, and then swim back. The second ritual was to play a game of basketball, one on one, with an SMG member during the hottest part of the day. Breaks were taken, and any one member of the gang might substitute himself at any time and continue the competition against Zachary. The score didn't matter. The game was finished at 100. Third, he had to eat five hot dogs and four ice cream cones in sixty seconds. Gastric anomalies were of no matter. But complete cleansings were expected, almost demanded; or so all the gang members thought and hoped.

As he jumped in the lake, the cold water hit his face. The lake's bad smell caused gagging. A swim was a short distance to the other side, and not difficult because he had learned the basics of arm strokes and kicking earlier at Boy Scouts and subsequently reinforced at a summer camp. The biggest challenge was to keep the water out of his mouth and nose. Arrival to the shore was quick and non-eventful.

The lake bank was muddy and full of sharp pieces of wood, which cut into Zachary's cold feet. He ran and rested for the mandatory three minutes behind a large elm tree that provided cover from gawking eyes, as well as shielding him from the Elm City police who routinely patrolled the area.

Loud car honking and shrill voices, full of laughter, came next. A bunch of girls in a black convertible drove by and yelled at a helpless nude kid. Words were not understood; no doubt a good thing. Very slowly he slipped around to the other side of the tree. Out of the corner of his eye he saw the one thing he dreaded most, a police car that had turned and headed to the side of the lake where he was hiding. Much to his surprise and frustration, the policeman stopped his car just as Zachary peered from behind the tree. Was an arrest to be eminent? The headline in the *Elm City Courier* might read, "Local Boy Caught Swimming Nude in Lake Elm City."

The officer went behind some large bushes, about thirty yards from the tree, and took a nature break. He must have stood there for at least five minutes, doing something known only to him and his God.

He then got in his police car and drove away. Zachary quickly returned to the water, and he made it to the other side, quickly retrieving clothes. The raucous laughs and cheers of the other gang members were not entirely reassuring.

The second rite of passage was longer and more exhausting. It challenged Zachary to compete against kids, most likely more athletic than him, to the running sport of basketball.

The day had started hot and dry, but by noon, a miracle. Clouds appeared, and for the first thirty minutes, with a breeze in tow, he fought hard and won the first half by six points. However, during the second half, things imploded. He played against one kid he did not know, one who was a better rebounder and much faster. Then a second kid came and took the first kid's place. Before Zachary got a break, the score changed, and he eventually lost by eight points—100-92. No refs, no foul shots, no fights.

The third rite was the one Zachary most feared. A Dairy Belle store had opened on the corner of South Main and Michigan Avenue earlier in the year. They served up hot dogs that were soggy, tasteless, and not very appealing. Zachary began eating and stuffed them one by one in his mouth, accompanied by a lot of laughter from the SMG. He chewed very slowly, and his stomach agreed with the plan while the gang members more than slightly encouraged him to "pick it up."

Four large ice cream cones came next. The first one went down easy, as did the second one. The next one was eaten the slowest, and his stomach mounted a huge argument. Someone watched a wrist watch and yelled, "You have five seconds!" That was it! The food demons rallied and then went into action. Behind a tree, with no apologies, relief came quickly.

There had been failure in two respects. He had lost the basketball game, and he was unable to keep the food in his stomach; so he guessed that he would not be asked to join the gang. What did he care? Maybe he might try again; then he thought, *the hell with all of them! But then, a surprise!*

The boys came up to him and said, "Congratulations, you're a member of the SMG." Tired and sick, Zachary slid down the clean side of the tree and relaxed for a minute. He felt accepted, happy, and relieved while a slightly displaced stomach inventoried and found mind, brain, and other physical faculties intact and still working. Zachary was now ready for a new "soul trip," all directed to shape and fuse together bits and pieces of a questioning but developing personality.

The SMG was now his gang, and Zachary would remain close to this bunch of ragtag kids, eight of whom lived on South Main Street, for the next few years. One member resided a block away on a secondary road named Michigan Avenue. That kid was granted "honorary membership" because he hit baseballs, shot basketballs, and played tackle football so much better than anyone else; however, his crowning attributes were that he told the best jokes, had the funniest and maybe strangest laugh, and bragged he knew lots of girls, some of whom had "wild ideas" and "wild behaviors!" This last descriptor was mostly fantasy, but nobody much cared.

None of the SMG was a delinquent, weirdo, or snob. They were simply a clique of boys who maintained friendships and sanity. They did not fight with other gangs, never got in trouble with the law, never took drugs.

This was the 1950s and life was easy. Or, so they wanted to believe. Their sports competition was an ongoing activity, and many friendships developed; maybe a little jealousy, too. Girls were initially disliked and distrusted, or at least that was always the mantra when the gang got together. Several of these "strange female creatures" lived in the neighborhood. Thoughts about them—youthful lusting and untold dreams— were rampant, but they were never openly discussed and certainly not admitted to.

The youngest SMG non-full-fledged member was a "partial comrade" because he visited Elm City during the summer and some weekends throughout the year. He was only on the periphery of gang involvement, but that was okay, for he influenced many of the gang in ways he may never have realized.

His name was David Wright, and there was something unusual and special about his parents— they were both deaf and did not speak. David had learned sign language early in life, and there were many challenges, periods of shame and guilt, much sadness and tears. His thick head of black hair, a small body, and terrible muscle coordination made for an interesting mix. Football, basketball, and baseball were sports he needed to avoid but never did. His strong enthusiasm for the gang and for sports was an attempt to be just like everyone else, but that was the problem. He knew he wasn't just like everyone else. His parents were different; therefore, he must be different. Emotional pain was readied and available too much of the time.

He would sit and talk for hours with Zachary about his dreams—for a girlfriend; to not only play baseball but to be the best; and even travel to far-off places he had read about in adventure books. He spoke of the struggles with his parents, with whom feelings were in constant flux, often out of control.

How could his mom or dad be expected to understand his emotions when they were too encumbered with their own difficulties? Could they ever relate to a young, healthy boy speaking and hearing in a world that for them was so different, so quiet, maybe even without life? David was convinced his parents felt ashamed of their disabilities, maybe even punished, and retreated into their own worlds often to share their commonalities.

Zachary listened carefully to David ventilate, and a thought was given to organizing a plan to help this sad and confused friend with a missing part his life—socialization with the opposite sex!

Of course, what did Zachary know about such things? Absolutely nothing! Yes, in the past, there had been a lot of talk, stories, dreams, and even fantasies, but now why not come up with a plan to create a new and more pleasant reality for helping one's fellow man? Zachary vaguely remembered his church taught that Jesus emphasized doing things for others, creating a better world, one devoted to God. Zachary wasn't sure about higher powers being served, but he certainly yearned to better understand about males and females, including his own transient physical desires, which had been laid bare at summer camp. Zachary's new buddy might be an unwitting helpmate, a conduit to a new exercise, a voyeuristic journey never taken before. And at the same time, the plan would allow for David to reach down and learn about deep fragments of sexuality parceled into his own anxious mind and soul. But the real question was: whom would this scheme selfishly serve the most?

Two houses from where Zachary lived, an older couple welcomed a granddaughter during the summer. She came from Illinois and generally stayed for three months while her parents worked overseas doing missionary work. Barbara Whitlock was an inviting, attractive young girl who Zachary guessed was about David's age. Her eyes were a deep blue, blond hair, a smile that lit up a face exposing perfectly straight teeth, white beyond description. Dress was simple: colorful blouses, jeans or shorts. Zachary knew Barbara would be *the* ideal friend. Why? Simple craziness! She was nothing more than a tomboy who climbed maple trees, especially those in Zachary's backyard, and looked for anything and anybody. She had her own agendas and, as they would soon find out, was much smarter in gamesmanship than either of the boys. Within this crazy scenario, Zachary decided he must become a matchmaker.

During a holiday weekend visit, Zachary asked David if he would like to meet a neat girl who temporarily lived a couple of houses down the street. David's face came alive with lots of smiles and blushing.

Zachary invited Barbara to play in the backyard; it was summer, and a cheap sprinkler attached to a hose was used to cool off. He told her that a friend from Indianapolis was in town, and he wanted to meet her. A story was concocted that David was rich, smart, and looked like a movie star. Of course, no thought was given to the slight bending of truth. An explanation: Throughout Zachary's childhood, he and others seemed at times to downplay telling lies. They reasoned there were gradations of "little lies" okay to tell, because no one would get hurt, and those that were "big lies" had more dire consequences, especially if the law was involved. The one Zachary told fit into the former category; it was okay and passed all "conscience" inspections. The other, more serious lies remained carefully hidden inside Zachary's mind, working diligently toward and keeping denial most active.

The day of the "friendly encounter," David showed up in shorts, just as Barbara did. It was not long before she realized that Zachary was a good liar. After a lot of talking about nothing, punctuated with giggles and laughter, Zachary realized that the small amount of shyness of a missionary's daughter matched well with the awkward reticence of a kid with deaf parents.

The three of them ran around the water sprinkler a few times, and then Barbara said something and pointed; suddenly, she and David disappeared into a neighbor's yard, where there was a field that at one time had been used as a garden to grow vegetables. Now it was engulfed in tall weeds. Beyond the field was a small red shed where shovels, hoes, and other yard tools were stored. The place was an absolute mess—several broken windows, a door hanging from its hinges, and a wooden roof, partially collapsed—a less than inviting ambiance for a romantic interlude. But for two kids with a budding sexuality, what mattered? Who cared?

Barbara held David's hand tightly as she led him in the direction of the shed. They appeared to be lifelong friends who had participated in similar types of rendezvous and intrigue many times before. Which one was more nervous? Only a guess, but smart betting had to be on David!

Zachary observed them disappear, and he felt a twinge of excitement course through his body. He very much wanted to sneak out and take some peeks. But how could he? This "theatre show" was none of his business. Then he reflected and rationalized that David might need help. Zachary must go out and ensure they were protected against unwanted intruders. It would be the right thing to do—provide safety and privacy, while satisfying self-urges perhaps a little stronger than just curiosity.

He ran to the area where they had disappeared, and he slipped around the side of the shed and peered in through some cracks in the wooden wall— all done very quietly. A very faint light came from a window in the front. David and Barbara were giggling and talking in hushed tones to each other. Zachary saw what appeared to be Barbara's hands move around David's face, and he realized they were kissing each other on the lips. The exchange continued, and then they reclined in what appeared to be a bed of straw. Barbara appeared to be the director of this production, David the student. She placed his hand on her leg, and a scant smile was barely observable from her face. There were more movements, but Zachary could not fully see what they were doing; only weak whispers and intermittent muffled giggling could be heard. Then there were more movements and more laughter. Suddenly, there was a loud call from the grandparents' house: "Barbara Ann, time for dinner!" Zachary knew he needed to get away and back home without being seen.

A smiling warrior appeared at Zachary's back door a few minutes later. His clothes were ruffled up, but he was relaxed, and he had a big smile on his face.

Zachary inconspicuously asked where they had gone. David lied and said that Barbara had taken him to see a rather large garden pond her grandfather had built in their back yard. Details of the visit were sketchy. Zachary kept his mouth shut, and then very quickly, David changed the subject and inquired about when the next football game between gang members was to be played.

Later, Zachary relived the sordid details of the day. He remembered voices, two in number, and the pleasure and enjoyment that must have radiated around those broken walls of a red shed. Sleep that night for Zachary, student voyeur, was long in coming.

David would visit Elm City many more times, and he always asked about Barbara. Sometimes he relayed to Zachary very sketchy tales of things she had taught him—things Zachary had not heard before but feigned he did. More details of that first encounter were asked for, sorely needed, but David refused. He said he was held to secrecy by his new friend, the experienced young female who visited her

John Spencer

grandparents and serendipitously gave two boys a
side journey about life. Zachary was left to only
imagine what went on in that broken-down shack.
But that was okay too; fantasies now swirled through
a very open and layered mind, devoid of any purity,
where dreams were manufactured and enjoyed their
temporary resident status!

There was, though, a driving and inexplicable
need to rationalize some incompleteness in a growing
boy's life, a loss of not understanding more about
females and close encounters of a personal, prurient
kind.

David, his friend from summer camp, said that
his father had a disdain for the opposite sex, based
on their failure to obey commandments as reported
in the Bible. He guessed that Eve's downfall in
decision-making and temptation led to a downgrade
of status to simply a comforter and helpmate. Man,
though, was not much better. But this talk seemed
of little relevance. Zachary, quite honestly, felt that
girls spent their lives in an unreal world of make-
believe—dolls and playhouses, frivolity and
immaturity. They seemed secretive, plotting, and
manipulative. But he admitted to a desire for them,
a fostering of acquaintances and friendships that
might help change his mind and bias. Somewhere in
this frustration, a voice needed to take command
and tell him it would be best, for now, to ignore
tempting and foreboding whispers, especially from
those who climbed maple trees and led a somewhat
naïve boy to his doom in a broken-down red shed. .

Summers in Elm City were miserable. The sun
was always unforgivingly hot, the wind absent, and
the clouds totally obedient to allowing their removal
from the sky.

On one of these days, Jerry Little walked by
Zachary's house with a frown on his face and a
baseball glove in his left hand. Suddenly, a change;

he smiled and acknowledged a skinny kid with braces on his teeth and greeted, "Hello." His muscular body, brown eyes and brown hair slicked backed with just a dab of some strong-smelling, greasy oil that provided for not one strand of hair to be out of place. Zachary was impressed!

They went to Zachary's back yard, tossed a hardball around, and a temporary frown disappeared as if it had never been part of a face. Zachary suggested they cross the street and climb the fence to the hospital grounds, where they could hit and fetch baseballs and talk about nothing. "Heck no," Jerry replied. His dad had forbidden him to go near that place. If he was caught on the state hospital grounds, a good beating was assured.

So, they hit grounders, and Zachary noticed something about his new friend. He was a natural athlete, one who moved quickly to throw a baseball with force and speed. He swung the bat with precision, and Zachary was impressed with how Jerry's eyes carefully followed the speeding ball before quick hands propelled the bat at just the right time before finally and squarely connecting. This was a kid who would easily make school teams.

But he also never bragged. He spoke softly and was a good encourager. He taught ways to hit by using a broken broomstick and a small rubber ball for practice; how to use eyes to follow the ball as it was delivered from the pitcher's hand; how to time a swing with the arrival of the ball. He was patient with Zachary's mistakes, and he reminded Zachary of his own miscues during the many days he had practiced with his older brother.

The two of them took breaks and sat under two large maple trees, spun tales about dreams of them someday playing baseball for the St. Louis Cardinals. Jerry mentioned he missed friends from his former town in southern Indiana. His closest buddies called him "Cotton," because when he was younger, his hair was very light colored. Zachary thought, *"What an unbelievable story. Is he kidding me?"*

Jerry spoke about his family and described them as religious; they went to church somewhere on the outskirts of town several times a week. When he spoke about what went on at church, he appeared serious but also a little excited, engaged about what he called "spiritual things." There was one other notable observation Zachary made. Jerry carried around a small Bible he read from daily, and on more than one occasion offered to share some "important" verses. Zachary politely declined!

At one of their practices, Jerry mentioned that he worked weekends at a restaurant located further down South Main Street. He seemed to be proud of his first paying job and very eager to describe and share his experiences with the Southern café, a "renowned eatery" that had been in Elm City for years. He spoke of that well-known large neon sign that partially hid a brown-asphalt shingle siding attached to a one-story building. In the back was a pile of junk, garbage cans and empty carboard boxes, which previously held produce. Boards with nails sticking out and the rotting siding of mildewed sheet rock made up a large portion of the area. Construction of some type must have been tried, with a miserable job of clean-up.

The owners, Randy Jones and his wife Beatrice, lived in a small apartment adjacent to the restaurant. Randy was fat and smoked a big cigar. He always sat in the front booth of the restaurant with a mean face that always stared at all of the employees. His major complaint concerned the laziness of employees. Beatrice wore the same brown cotton dress every day, teetered in red high heels, wore much too much makeup and lipstick, but smiled a lot and was friendly. Their lives evolved around serving food with no rest, no vacations, and questionable profits.

Jerry's pay was fifty cents an hour, including one free meal eaten before work. The kitchen staff, according to Jerry, was friendly and his interaction with them the best part of the job. The waitresses were pleasant and friendly, as long as their tips given by customers were never stolen. Then, he surprised Zachary with the comment, "Think you might want to work there, Zachary? I have a new job at a grocery store down the street."

Zachary eventually got his mother's permission and began work as a busboy. He cleaned tables and carried dirty dishes back to the kitchen to a man called Lloyd, the "Dishwasher Man," who always yelled out, "Keep those dishes coming!"

The guy's hands were worn and sometime shook with fervor; his fingers were thick and nubby. When he walked, it was with a shuffle and a creaking sound—artificial legs put into play helped, but sometimes were noisy, while a facial grimace was always noticeable. He had a mixture of white and grey hair, combed straight back. When he spoke, a very slight stutter was detected. He monitored the busboy's work, and any laggard behavior was called out with no shame.

The biggest infraction committed was not stacking the dishes in an orderly way, so that Lloyd could place them in a rack to then go through the large dishwasher. It was hot near that loud machine, and Lloyd often dripped sweat onto the floor. A toxic and unpleasant smell surrounded the entire place.

At break time, Zachary often went back and sat on a tall stool and gabbed with his newfound friend. Lloyd's hurt and worn face initially made Zachary afraid, though he quickly discovered the old guy was lonely and longed for companionship.

The man's teenage life had been working in the wheat fields. A wheat reaper had accidentally rolled over him, and both legs had been immediately sawed off. He confessed that he struggled with intense pain every day and always used stationary objects for support. His sister drove him to work, and he was grateful for the two free meals he received each day. It was obvious he was not well-off financially, maybe close to poor.

Lloyd listened intently when told of Zachary's confusion about his own father, who had left the family and moved to Chicago, disgraced by a life of alcohol addiction. Zachary confessed that he was afraid he might end up doing the same thing. He smiled and said, "Don't worry; things will get better for you. Your mother will find answers to her many problems. Time always has a way of working things out. Remain patient, and understand that forgiveness always works wonders in your life. I understand that you are angry about what your father did. I had a dad who left my mom and me when I was only eight years old. Bad things happen, but I've finally learned that keeping the wrong kinds of feelings inside only hurt me and don't change nothing."

He encouraged Zachary to listen to songs sung by the head cook-chef, "Pappy Yordan," a big Negro man who wore a towering white cap on his head. The words had emotion: "troubles, nothing but troubles, but someday I know there will be no more troubles for nobody." Lloyd explained those words meant there was to be hope for the future, when God will make things right for everybody who loves him. There will be no pain, no discontent, everybody with God will be happy.

Zachary concentrated and felt something emotional inside—at least for a moment. Then it was back to reality after a waitress reminded him to get his ass back into the restaurant and bus dishes. Once, when Zachary had taken a break, he talked to Pappy about the words in his songs about troubles. "What do they mean?" Zachary inquired.

"Life is hard for some people, harder than it should be."

Zachary kept inquiring, "Why is that?"

"Some people just judge others by the color of their skin. I have friends who work at the Elm City Country Club, and they always have told me how lucky they are to have a job. Of course, none of these folks would ever be considered for a job on the square, and even if they had the money to join that club, they would never be allowed to because they ain't white. It is in some club rule book, Negroes ain't allowed. Why can't people be accepted for who they are and not if they is black or white or green? It is something evil and dark, deep in certain peoples' souls, and I don't think it will ever change until Jesus comes back to earth. Then we will all be just one people. I pray for that day all the time."

Zachary then replied, "I never thought like some of the other white folks here in Elm City, that people should be judged by the color of their skin. It just doesn't make any sense. And anyway, nobody cooks like you, Pappy, nobody. You should get a reward for that."

A big smile crossed Pappy's face, and he said, "Someday I will, yes, someday I will."

One afternoon, after a very busy time cleaning tables, Lloyd motioned for Zachary to come to the back of the kitchen. He gave Zachary a new baseball and a book about faith. "Read this book. It will change your life." A smile followed, and a hand still shook, but there was emotion—enough for both of them.

The baseball was well used over the next summer. The book stayed by his bedside and was never read. It contained a lot of religious things with which Zachary had struggled with earlier in life — things about a God and a Jesus and a new hope for the future. Memories of church and a reciting of a creed came back but for only a short visit. A mind tried to listen, but no personal connection was ever made to a boy's life. There were simply more tempting and tantalizing things to focus on— especially, and very secretively, girls! Foundations of behaviors were in the process of being set, soul habits acquired, ones so brittle at first, but deeply instilled and very unwilling to leave or become extinguished, and for that Zachary should have felt some privilege and some embarrassment. He felt neither.

Salary was paid in cash on Monday and placed in a brown envelope with each person's last name handwritten in pencil. All workers had been told that if anyone was caught taking tip money from the waitresses, they would be fired. Customers would routinely give quarters, dimes, or nickels, and this money must remain on the table, reserved and collected only by the serving staff.

Often, though, when cleaning the table, there was no one else around, so it was easy for Zachary to slip a few coins into his sweating palm. Then later, behind some well-shielded vegetable crates in the kitchen storeroom, the stash was transferred to a jeans pocket. It was done by others, so it must have been okay.

Somewhere deep in Zachary's brain, he knew stealing was wrong. Waitresses worked harder than everyone else (except maybe the kitchen people), and they were deserving of the money. After all, they were the ones who talked to, smiled at, and sometimes flirted with the customers eager for interaction and perhaps even a fantasy or two.

A chubby woman named Elaine once asked Zachary if he had ever stolen any of her tips. He thought how crazy she must have been to ask such a direct question. Would he ever simply say, "Yes," and then get fired? Zachary was not that dumb! He of course lied and told her that he had never done such a thing. Then she told a frightening story about boss man Randy and his whip, a long, ugly-looking thing, a well-worn leather strap used on anyone caught stealing from his waitresses. The police were then called, and the guilty person could possibly face a judge and reform school.

Initially, Zachary laughed and thought for sure Elaine was joking. Upon further reflection, he decided to take no more money and stop his criminal behavior. That was until three weeks later, when temptations and whispers from somewhere suggested, "what nonsense" and the vicious cycle of stealing restarted with only slight remorse. He was never caught. Did luck prevail? Did God watch or even care? Imponderable questions with no answers!

Buddy Logan had a limp and a partial gold tooth. The limp, a result of being hit by a coal truck, was most noticeable when he walked; it defined him. The doctors told him he had broken his leg and bruised his hip, while a tooth was partially knocked out of his mouth. He jokingly bragged about his wealth from just this one tooth and its contents. The broken leg eventually healed, and Zachary was sure the limp simply disappeared. This kid was one of Zachary's earliest neighborhood friends, even though they often fought over such trivial things as an argument about the winner of a stupid game of marbles or basketball, one on one. Size can have its advantages.

Zachary and Buddy were friends and stuck together in any encounter. At school, Zachary was sometimes bullied and picked on. Maybe it was because he was small and skinny, or maybe the kids were just jealous for some inane reason, but that can only be a guess. Most likely, there were no good reasons. The bullies were unquestionably just a bunch of cowards who reflected a lack of self-esteem issues and were probably abused by their parents or brothers at home.

Once, a bully ran after Zachary, caught him, and swung at his face. Jerry Little had previously taught Zachary how to use his feet defensively; so he kicked hard and selectively. The punk ran away, yelling in pain. Other friends of the bully were told, and plans then laid for a revenge match. When they realized who Zachary's best friend was, they reconsidered.

In one area of Zachary's backyard, Buddy, Jerry, and Zachary built a clubhouse behind a broken-down trellis of vines, weeds, and dead growth. There was a garden beyond the clubhouse where tomato plants and green beans grew and competed for attention.

The sides of the shed were composed of wooden forms taken from a torn-up turkey coop. The roof was made from tin, cut as a jagged edge, totally incorrect in size to cover the entire top. Concrete nails were used to attach the floorboards and separate side forms. A neighbor, Mr. Scott, supervised, and his patience was a virtue and important, as were his building skills. The clubhouse belonged to the boys and the gang. They owned it, and inside stories and jokes were shared that nobody else needed or most likely cared to hear. The entrance door was eventually painted with the words "Girls Not Allowed." It was important for boundaries to be set, but enforcement was another issue.

One evening, Zachary wandered out to admire his "new and special home," and he discovered his friend Jerry standing near the clubhouse. He appeared upset, so Zachary invited Jerry to sit down in front of the shack just as the sun was setting beyond a group of adjacent elm trees. A lone swing hung from one of their branches, and Jerry sat on it and twisted one way, and then another. His head remained low, and he stared at the ground.

"I am so angry at my brother for not taking me to church last night. He said that because I had been messing around with one of the girls who lived behind our house, I needed to cleanse myself of sin. What does he know about what I did? He just heard my parents complaining I had not done chores."

Zachary remained silent for a while, then ventured, "What kind of messing around was your brother talking about?"

"This girl and me are just friends. I don't do any stuff like I hear other kids do. We just like to imagine what it is going to be like when we grow up. Where will we go and live, how many kids will we have, and what kind of work we might do. She tells me that she wants to be a nurse. I told her that I want to preach.

"What?" Zachary was flabbergasted! "Why would you want to do that? I have had many conversations with our preacher at the Methodist Church, and he says things that are difficult for me to believe. Like this Jesus guy and His many miracles. Jesus seems like a nice enough man who wants to try to help people, but instead ends up dead. I still don't get the point."

Jerry reiterated that his pastor taught that God cared enough about all the people in the world, and that this Jesus came to care for the sick, help the poor, teach about God, and later would be all people's way to get to heaven. Most importantly, Jesus continues to help people out today.

"I know that story," said Zachary, "but He is not here now helping anybody. He certainly didn't help my parents out when they couldn't get along."

Jerry was quiet for a long time, and then said, "You know, Stevens, I can't explain a lot of the Bible, and I certainly don't understand it, but I always felt guilty when I was doing things I shouldn't. My thoughts are often bad, you know, like girls and sex, or envy I feel about a kid who lives across town by the name of Mike Scooter and what a great short stop he is—so much better than me. I must bury those feelings and be Scooter's friend. My dad tells me to just pray every time I get a bad thought in my head."

After hearing that comment, Zachary wondered out loud if prayers were ever answered. "I pray every night for God to watch over and protect me, but I don't know how safe I really am."

Jerry retorted, "You are still alive, aren't you?"

An awkward, quiet moment, then Jerry said that he wanted to tell Zachary something that should remain a secret between the two of them. A few months ago, he went to bed one night but had difficulty sleeping, so he got up and went out in his backyard to an old barn that was currently not used for anything. He sat and thought he heard a voice from one corner of the barn, which said, "Why not think about someday preaching in a church and saving lost souls?"

Jerry wondered, though, if it had not been the wind whistling and making sounds, but suddenly a light flashed. From that point on, Jerry was convinced an angel had visited him. This intercessory matter from "above" had to be kept quiet, nobody ever told. Otherwise, Jerry reasoned, he might be forced to spend time over at the Elm City State Hospital—not to play baseball with the gang, but to live there as a resident!

Zachary didn't say anything, but he certainly had his personal thoughts: *What nonsense! What an unbelievable story. I don't want to hurt his feelings and tell him that he must be crazy, but who really believes in angels? It will be best for me to keep my mouth shut because he is a friend and helpmate, even though he is odd about religious things. My friends are so different about what they believe, but I guess I should accept them as my best buddies, even though I don't understand a lot of things about them.*

Then with a disrupting commotion, Buddy Layhill plowed through the weeds and inquired, "What are you guys up to?" Both Zachary and Jerry remained quiet and, no doubt, felt embarrassed "We have been talking about God," one of the boys replied.

Buddy, with an awkward look on his face, said that he and Stevens heard about all that stuff when they were younger. Then he directly shouted out, "You had better not mention that stuff to some of the guys in the SMG."

"Why not?" inquired Zachary.

"Because they think that people who go around talking about God and religion act like they are better than other people. And besides, if you

two are religious, you can't have any fun. Nobody wants to be your friend."

Jerry wondered: *Am I going to be like that? I really want God, but I know that I have other feelings that are not what the Bible says I should have. What am I to do? Will those feelings stay around and be so strong forever?*

Over the weekends, the three boys often slept inside the shack and pretended they lived in the woods. If they heard noises, they jokingly asked if coyotes or bears were waiting to attack.

"You guys think we can stay here all night and survive?" Jerry would half-jokingly ask.

"Why not?" replied Buddy. "There is nothing around here that is going to hurt us."

But then Zachary reminded them of a story he had heard from neighbors who lived behind his house on East Street.

Years earlier, there had been two dogs living in an old house that had been built on a field adjacent to the clubhouse. The house and the occupants were now long gone. The dogs had been raised by an old man who lovingly cared for the animals. One of the dogs had a slightly deformed leg and sometimes appeared in pain. The man faithfully walked his canine friends around the neighborhood and was rarely seen without them. They shared an irrevocable partnership of love.

One day, though, the dogs were mysteriously found dead. Upon further examination, it was discovered they had both been poisoned. The old man was devastated and subsequently rarely left his house. He wept for his dogs, and in a just a few months he died, some suggested of a broken heart. People guessed and wanted to believe that now he was happy, reunited with his family of dogs.

But that was only part of the story. A few doors away lived a couple who always fought and yelled at each other. One of them was heard to say, at times, that because the dogs barked and made noise, it would be best if they were both dead. "Good riddance that the three of them are gone from this earth."

Other neighbors disagreed and insisted the dogs had always been quiet, and that the couple was just jealous of the old man's happiness with his two dogs. Who might have killed the dogs? Some had their suspicions. What was known, though, was that strange noises now could be heard outside the couple's window; sounds of barking, wailing, and sometimes laughter. It became so noisome at times that the police had to be called. Finally, the couple moved, and the neighbors reported that the day after the storage van departed, a fire destroyed the couple's house.

Buddy listened intently to this strange story, and then went outside and thought he heard barking sounds. Jerry reported hearing a man's voice say, "It is all right. Everything is just what it should be now."

Zachary said out loud and frustratingly, "All is quiet, shut up and go to sleep!" But the wind picked up, the tree branches waved back and forth, and there were non-perceptible noises and sounds of some kind all around the shack—a visitation from ghosts and demons? Certain boys who lived on South Main Street had their guesses.

In the years to come, the SMG's abode, a broken-down shack, would become a place where the insanity of school, adults who behaved badly, or troublesome kids might escape to, and replace with a more pleasant reality. It was a world where it was safe and okay to act in any way they wished. Here they truly could: *"Be fearless or be scared; be stupid; share an honest laugh, or maybe even a tear."*

He was the oldest member of the SMG, and his name was Gale Rodgers, anatomically the skinniest of the gang, one who wore braces on his teeth and glasses for his eyes. However, he had the unique ability to hit home runs in slow-pitch softball and produce melodious sounds from a clarinet. He practiced his music intently and was rewarded by eventually sitting first chair in the high school band. Eventually, local Elm City musicians recruited Gale to be part of a band that played at dances for patients who resided at the state hospital, located across the street from where the boys lived. The hope was that the music helped many forlorn and lost people smile, if only for a brief time.

Gale would become popular with one patient, a guy who had previously played in a jazz group. He taught Gale how to hold the clarinet for long periods of time and still allow his hands and fingers to feel comfortable. The two of them spent time talking about ways to read music, to listen to other instruments, and when to join in and play "when it just felt right." The teaching word used was "improvise."

Gale's musical talent helped him keep a narrow focus, and Zachary and Buddy guessed that Gale saw the uselessness of arguments and subsequent fighting for either survival or friendship. Most likely, however, an even better reason why Gale avoided such nonsense was that he had extremely skinny arms, no muscles, and would have been severely injured, most likely killed in any battle.

What Gale believed about more spiritual things, such as God, was difficult to discern. He and Zachary had tried at times to talk about religion, but the conversations seemed to fade away into confusion and ambiguity. An invitation was once given for Gale to attend the Methodist Church.

"No, I don't think so. I have tried to go to several churches in the past but have not enjoyed the experience. I don't like hearing about how rotten all of us are."

And then Zachary gave a rejoinder: "You might be able to play your clarinet in the church orchestra."

"Why would I do that? If I did go to church, I would have to behave, 'rightly and good' all the time. Who wants to be perfect? My dad says that the whole idea of religion is just too difficult to understand, so the best thing to do is simply ignore it and have a good time. Want to go out and hit some softballs?"

Two brothers, Dwight and Jim Allan, were early members of the SMG. Dwight joked around with the other gang members; he also had a fantastic memory for the batting statistics of the St. Louis Cardinals, something that was a unique possessed talent. But who cared? No one else paid any attention to his musings.

One additional fact about Dwight: He was not a kid to be picked on or bullied. He could very capably fend for himself. Kids from other parts of town learned quickly to keep their mouths quiet around Dwight, because if they didn't, they would soon be sent home with bloody noses and black eyes. His major sport was running, and running fast; he would eventually compete on the high-school track team, the only one of the SMG to do so.

Dwight's brother, Jim, was very different. He grew to over six feet four inches tall, remained skinny with lots of blond, curly hair and partially crooked teeth, always in need of a good brushing. He acted silly, seemed more like a clown, but certainly had the best sense of humor of any of the gang members. His sport was basketball, and he eventually made the junior high and high school teams, and even later played in college. While several of the kids had problems with their temper, Jim resisted the urge to lose control; instead he would smile, tell a joke, and then scream out,

"Long Live the SMG!"

Jim, in addition to sports, played the trumpet and was multi-social, so different than some of the other gang members, including Zachary Stevens. He performed in both the junior high and high school bands, but for reasons unknown only to him, he never spoke much about his interest in music. . Perhaps he just had too much else going on, including an alliance with several partially deaf patients who lived at the Elm City State Hospital.

How he became interested in these patients was never clear, but Zachary knew that Jim and David Wright had spent time together and must have discussed the life and difficulties of family deafness. Jim watched the patients speak in sign language, and became motivated to learn ways of communication of words and feelings. He commented that the patients' laughter seemed loud, but also sincere, and it made him feel happy, light inside, when the deaf patients smiled and thanked him for spending time with them. He probably didn't realize it, but he was beginning to develop a place in his heart for people with disabilities.

Dwight and Zachary, throughout the next four years, would become trusted friends and spent many hours in a broken-down clubhouse, sharing stories. There seemed to be an element of trust and sincerity between the two of them. Maybe it was likewise an appreciation of humor, or maybe it was just preordained. Years later, Zachary would go halfway around the world to see his boyhood friend and tell him of his strongest beliefs about Christ, only to find out that Dwight was waiting for him with a very similar witness.

Zachary struggled with so many thoughts concerning family marriage failures, and more recently a failure in conscience and just plain "guts" concerning a vicious grocery store robbery. Dwight likewise had things percolating in his mind, secrets from the past, but maybe of the more difficult kind, unknown and never told.

One day, the two of them sat outside the SMG shack, and Zachary said out loud, surprising Dwight and himself, "My father has been a total failure in life, but I still miss him and have a spot of love in my heart for him."

Zachary then went on to describe a visit he had a year ago with his dad while visiting an aunt in Chicago. What he saw was a very old man who had a chalky, heavily lined face, swollen enlarged feet, and a partial limp from sitting on the cold floor of a jail for a week. A few front teeth were missing, clothes were soiled, and although the kid bravely tried to form conversations, no meaningful communication occurred.

The dad reported a craving for alcohol that had never stopped, and as a "friendly" addition, strange recurring voices that resonated inside his head and kept him company. Their content was a mixture of accusatory, mean, and humorous thoughts; non-sensical and certainly unfriendly. Emotion, as if it had no place to go swelled inside Zachary.

What could this useless man say to his boy? In just a few short years, the alcohol abuse and life in jail had taken its toll. There had been state hospitals, homelessness, drug abuse, and just plain failure. Had the ol' man given up on life? Maybe one sign of hope—a close friend was a Catholic priest. Zachary returned home, discouraged. Later that year, he and his mother received news that the old man had been found dead in an alley.

Intently, Dwight listened and then mentioned that his own father had likewise left the family when Dwight had started the first grade. Nothing was explained. Then almost reflexively, Dwight commented, "Wow, Zachary, I never knew that your dad had such a messed-up life. I just thought that he had moved away and was doing okay. I remember seeing him a few years ago at your house, and he seemed fine. He had on a suit and a bowtie. You certainly hid things about him. But I guess all of us don't like to discuss hurt and failures very much, especially when it is personal."

Zachary found words to that remark hard in coming . . .

More silence, and a very gentle rain began. The tin roof of the shack recoiled with muffled pings, and in a couple of places, leaks brought moisture. Amid this, Zachary told Dwight he needed to excuse himself for a minute, go outside the shack, and walk around in a deserted garden patch to clear his head.

A sudden realization: Daniel Stevens was really a total unknown to everybody. The kid's honest refection of memories of interactions with the old man had brought back all kinds of intense feelings, ones he had pushed down and refused to let come back.

I never knew him. What did we really talk about? Nothing much, that is for sure. He seemed quiet and soft-spoken, almost shy, never willing to get into an argument about anything. Mother was the same way. The plan in our family was to either ignore, or refuse to discuss anything of importance. I hated and was ashamed to see him as a bum on the streets of Chicago. He must have felt embarrassed too. But for some strange reason, I don't feel awkward talking to Dwight about my old man's failures. My mother will never say or tell me anything about him. Sometimes I think she just slips off into a pretend world that allows her to think she was never married in the first place. I do remember my grandmother and her strong feelings about the failed marriage. My father once asked me if she still hated him or saw him as a bad person. Dad thought "Granny" was a major reason for divorce.

But I still wonder at times what kind of a father he would have been, had he not used alcohol and chased women. In my pretend world, he would have shown interest and concern for me and Mother, and maybe even himself; he would have cheered me on as a partial athlete and been there for so many discussions about school successes and failures, including feelings out of control.

My old man must have been unhappy. Mother told me that right after I was born, his younger and only brother, Tony, contracted pneumonia and died. After the funeral was over, my dad would go to his brother's closet and look at his clothes hanging there and cry. I was told later that my middle name, Anthony, was given in recognition of "Uncle Anthony."

Was this parental split my fault? What did either Mother or I do to cause him to want other women?

I tried to understand my father's behavior by enlisting others—the church pastor, but I never felt that he understood my hurt and disappointment. His focus was on Mother and me surviving. Maybe that is the way it should be. At least after my old man left, the phone calls from other women stopped.

I should tell Dwight about my encounter with Carl Stewart. Dwight may realize what a coward I am, but right now, I don't give a shit!

A quick return and rebound from a mental escape, a deeper breath taken. "Dwight, promise to keep a secret?"

"Yeah."

"Do you remember the grocery store that was robbed some time ago? Well, I saw who did it and know his name, but I never told nobody."

"Who was it?" Dwight asked.

"Carl Stewart," replied Zachary. Dwight looked surprised. "I know about him. He used to hang around the high school and try to pick up some of the girls. He was a big braggart, and mean as hell. I heard he was recently put in prison. I would not want that guy anywhere near me. I once heard he got into a fight with some guy in a bar and tried to stab him. He cut the guy bad. The police got involved, but a lawyer got him off because he claimed self-defense." Zachary then thought, *maybe I have said enough.*

190

As Zachary and Dwight grew older, they tried their best to understand and learn about some of the girls in Elm City. They shared many stories, rich with dreams and fantasy, and while some were humorous, the truth was that many of these girls had no interest in either kid, Zachary or Dwight, and honestly viewed them as a little strange. But the other girls, the ones who were not as pretty and not as popular, those young women formed a reality that replaced a lot of dreams or fantasies about love and romance. Rendezvous and encounters with these "idle creatures" were shared or discussed with very few, if any, of the other gang members, and for good reason: avoidance of teasing, fewer sharp comments or criticisms, and an absolute denial of learning and realizing they most likely were not the first young men in line for such dubious attention.

"Hey Zachary," Dwight said on day, "I have some concerns about your slow running of laps in high school gym class."

The Elm City High School had a requirement for graduation by all males, mandated by the State of Indiana, to run a mile in seven minutes or less, a boring run of 11 ½ times around an upper area of the local basketball gymnasium. But there was hope. The state hospital provided a practice venue; a single paved road went around the outer part of the center grounds. A car odometer was used as a best guess for distance.

Many days, rain or shine, two boys, Zachary and Dwight, could be found at the hospital grounds where Zachary would run, and run, and run some more until his mouth and lungs felt they were on fire, in need of water to quell dryness and heat, gasping for air. A second wind eventually came with practice, while a look of concern remained reflected on Dwight's face when Zachary came in and crossed the finish line. More work, more aches; there had to be a victory sometime. Zachary fought on. "I want and must graduate from high school."

Both the Allan brothers attended the Presbyterian Church across the street from Zachary's church. They went every Sunday because their parents demanded it; neither spoke much about the experience, and Zachary kept his mouth quiet and asked few questions. When he sometimes forgot and started talking about church or God, he was given looks by both brothers detailing what he needed to do—shut up. As with so many other experiences, the best reason for their attendance never involved an appreciation for God o much as it did for tempting interludes with certain "creatures," young girls, and dark corners of the church where different "focused educational exercises" might be expanded upon.

* * *

Steve Jackson lived on Michigan Avenue in a small white clapboard house. As a kid, he had physically grown much faster than the other boys, and by age twelve he was one of the tallest of the SMG. His hair, always in a flat-top, was accompanied by a ruddy face at minimum, inflamed beet red at maximum. He loved to play jokes on everyone. Baseball mitts might be hidden, or bicycle seats removed. A high-pitched laugh, some even thought slightly weird, could be heard across long distances—welcomed by some, made fun of by others, but never forgotten.

One hot summer day, just after Zachary joined the SMG, he and Steve learned about corn and beans grown within a misguided field of labor and love. The two boys had been hired to cut corn stalks out of a bean field. The pay was good, and they considered themselves lucky to have a job. But a hot sun rose in the east, and heat produced burned skins with secondary jabs to soul and spirit.

Up one row and back down another, they went with accompaniment of aches and pains. They walked, cut, hoed, and placed corn stalks in a burlap bag, which became heavier by the minute. A filled water jug and a small sack lunch disappeared before noon. Breaks were taken, songs sung, jokes told, and then serious questions asked concerning why they agreed to undergo this torture from such an unforgiving sun. At noon, Steve turned to Zachary and more than shouted out, "This is hell, let's quit!" A rejoinder from Zachary: "If we stay the day, we each will get about six dollars, and how would we get home, since the owner won't be back till evening?"

Arms burned and ached from hoeing and digging; throats were dry from thirst; a cold bath tub was only a dream, far from reality. Zachary thought for at least ten seconds and decided they should become "quitters," no apologies offered. Two hoes and two shovels were quickly propped up against a lone elm tree, and a proudly displayed written note said, "too hot; we quit; good luck ZS, SJ"

"We need to hope and maybe even pray that we will get a ride back to town," Zachary touted.

"Stevens," replied Steve, "why would God care if we ever get back to Elm City? At my church our pastor tells us to pray without ceasing. That it is our only hope. Church is boring. There are a lot of things I need, but after I pray, nothing much ever happens. Most of the time I just think about this good-looking girl in my Sunday school class who sits and smiles at me. I wish for a lot of things when I think of her, things God might not like me asking for. But I don't care; it is so much easier imaging her and me together, kissing and touching each other, than it is thinking about Jesus and all of his problems while on earth. Besides, doesn't the Bible say we should love our neighbors more than ourselves?"

The two boys walked, and then walked some more on a dusty road. Boredom and lots of it was everywhere, as were the beginnings of tired feet and hot, sweaty bodies in need of relief from the sun.

The road forked around a creek bed, and then it veered to the left and went over several small hills.

The sun had disappeared behind some clouds. As Zachary and Steve came over a small mound and proceeded through a thick grove of trees, they saw something unbelievable.

In the back of a parked vehicle were vaguely perceivable silhouettes of two people involved in some type of physical action. The two boys snuck up very quietly and hid behind a large bush that provided cover.

The squealing sounds were vocalized from the flatbed of a Ford truck and were loud, rhythmically repeated every few seconds. A girl appeared, pinned underneath a guy who wore a cowboy hat that partially covered his entire head and face. Zachary Stevens witnessed from afar and thought she was in danger. He was concerned for her welfare and voiced his worries to his gang member friend, Steve, who replied, "No, leave them alone, she is okay, they are just relaxing."

At that point, the cowboy and the girl heard the kids' voices, jumped up, and someone yelled out, "Who is there?" and then unstoppable cussing began. The guy adjusted his jeans, which appeared to be bulging in the front, while the girl yelled out some indecipherable words and readjusted her blouse. A shadow-like figure moved around toward the front of the dirty, rusty vehicle, where a gun rack with a rifle was mounted. Two young boys felt fear as hearts pounded; *was this to be the end of them?*

Perhaps gunshot-riddled bodies might rot in a cornfield for days, maybe even months before discovery. Then he noticed that the guy had opened the truck door and climbed inside. He started the truck and, after the girl jumped in, drove off quickly.

What did Steve mean by 'relaxing'? He told Zachary that some things would be explained later. They never were. It was doubtful Steve understood what was going on in the flatbed of that truck, but maybe he had some good guesses. He was, after all, one year ahead of Zachary in school. More thoughts bounced around in Zachary's head as he continued his trek with Steve back to town. A memory of a discussion he had with a kid from Ohio about certain facts of life popped up. Certainly, if Zachary could have been closer to the truck, he would have been able to see more and offer help.

For a long time, he had to admit to difficulty of forgetting that girl with the dark hair, the one who seemed to be in such a difficult situation with a guy who wore a big cowboy hat. He hoped she was going to be okay—maybe she might even find a new boyfriend, one who would treat her nicer and with more respect.

A few more miles traversed, and a second, even crazier experience came forth for dissection and evaluation. The boys had walked and found the state highway. Very few cars and trucks passed, but those that did refused to stop. Finally, a rather beat-up old green truck slowed down, and an elderly man with a toothless smile who chewed a lot of tobacco cried out, "My name is Jake, and I farm a lot of land around here! If both of you can fit in the front seat, I'll take you to Elm City." Two thankful kids climbed aboard.

At first the truck only veered into the other lane intermittently. Jake announced he had lost his glasses and was having trouble seeing the road. Zachary sat in the middle of the seat next to Jake and assisted by suddenly grabbing the steering wheel and turning it to the right, avoiding a tractor that had pulled onto the road.

"Thanks," was heard from somewhere, and a familiar smell was simultaneously detected. It was the same odor Zachary had remembered when his father came home late at night. He looked over at Steve and noticed he had slid down in the seat and refused to look at anyone. Zachary thought that Steve's mumbles were an attempt to summon angelic hosts, God, or somebody—and quickly.

It was obvious that Jake was impervious to everything, but he had the most pleasant smile on his face. Zachary asked for permission to guide the truck, and Jake agreed. A song that made little sense came next from Jake. A scared kid held tightly onto the wheel and watched Jake's right leg carefully to make sure it was not extended onto the gas pedal with too much force.

Steve then came back up from underneath the dashboard with a plan of action. Allow the old guy to drive slow, and just work the gas and brake pedal. Zachary would continue to hold the wheel; when they arrived at Elm City, Jake would be given a dollar for his good and responsible behavior. Of course, the plan was not without problems, because neither boy had any money. Jake agreed, and kept the speed at a fast pace of ten miles an hour. Steve remained silent, most likely not in prayer, but with thoughts not to be shared. If anyone might have viewed this trio of characters trying to remain alive against all odds, chuckling if not outright laughter would contribute to an otherwise pathetic situation.

They arrived at O'Brian's store, and the two boys jumped out. Jake said, "Thanks for the company, boys. I enjoyed having you with me." He continued down South Main. Neither kid looked to see how straight he drove; it was just good to be home. Their half-day work in a cornfield was over and never discussed again. But memories lingered and stayed around in restless and curious minds.

The SMG had one very smart member—one who got straight A's in school. Joe Gruneau was the "brain" of the gang. He excelled in school, and did so with an unbelievable memory of names of people from history, plus he had a unique ability to write cogent English theme papers; he also readily solved any math problem offered up in school. While others feared, dreaded, or complained about school homework, Joe never did. His schoolwork was always finished quickly, and he then eagerly went out and engaged in a game of basketball or softball. Schoolbooks that most kids took home for study at night were never a part of his after-school life. There was no need for them —he had memorized everything at school.

His body frame was a bit skinner than the rest of the kids, accompanied by a flat-top haircut, and traces of pimples which populated an oily face always covered up by an odorous cream. Glasses with partially broken frames were worn during school, but disappeared when it was time for sports.

During pick-up basketball games, if mistakes such as missing a simple lay-up were made, the anger demons took control. He yelled and cursed, and the afternoon air became heavy with much tension and turmoil. When he got knocked down, he wrenched in pain and became upset. Tears came, but then he picked himself up and played harder, most of the time with mixed results.

Joe fought battles at home, including one with an abusive stepfather who drank and often made Joe sleep in the garage at night, where there was no heat, no lights, and certainly no love. For Joe, at times, it must have been difficult to see much hope or civility in the world. He was a kid in need of friends because of an appalling home situation. On more than one occasion, he and SMG friend Jerry Little would talk.

"My stepfather is always on me for the least little thing I do wrong. If the dishes are not washed and dried and put away immediately after dinner, he explodes and often slaps me, and sends me to the garage for a few hours.

"I have thoughts to myself, thoughts I hope, Jerry, you never tell anyone. I would like to shoot the guy. Before my mom married him, things were different; we were happy, and then this guy showed up. I just wish he was dead."

"What do you mean Joe? You can't be serious," commented Jerry.

"I want him out of my life, period! He is not normal. I think there is something wrong in his head. I go to bed at night and think about ways to pay him back. I wish I could tell you about how he disciplines me, but I can't. You know why? He once told me that if I ever mentioned how he punishes me, he would send me away to an orphanage." Then Joe whispered, "He beats me with a whip. Tell no one"

"I bet if you talked to your mother she might be able to get your stepdad to be nicer to you," Jerry said encouragingly.

"I've tried everything. Mother just says that is the way Frank thinks and behaves, and I will have to accept it. She says to just work harder and stay out of his way."

When any of the gang talked about things such as love, church, God or Jesus, Joe's response was simple: "Avoid those thoughts at all costs! It's time to choose up sides for a baseball game."

Jerry knew that talking about Jesus and God would be of no use, so instead he tried to make another suggestion: "How about going with me and my family this weekend to Springdale to fish? You can plan to sleep over."

"I don't think so. Mom and me are going to some furniture sale while Frank stays at home and gets drunk. He has told me that I can't ever go and sleep at a friend's house, no matter what. I just wish he would get sick and die."

"Let's go over to Clancy's store," Jerry yelled out as the two started jogging. We'll get sodas, I am buying."

Life is never predictable; neither is it fair. But the unexpected shooting of Joe Gruneau by a handgun needs to be told.

Several streets behind Joe's house lived a couple of older high school boys who periodically bragged about the pistols and rifles they had, ones they used exclusively when they went hunting with their dad. Zachary and Joe had gone over one day to view this weaponry that included rifles, shotguns, pistols, and even a few grenades. There was little if any supervision, and little training—all elements in place for a risky and dangerous situation.

Initially, Zachary and Joe handled the weapons and pretended they were cowboys. That acting out was benign enough, but then things went to a more dangerous level. One of brothers aimed a pistol at Joe and said that he needed to raise his hands.

"Come on, Fred," Joe said, "put that gun down."

"Never, you must obey the command or face the consequences."

"I am going to run away from here if you don't put that gun down."

Fred thought that the gun was empty—isn't that what safety demands?

"Oh, no, you are not," Fred responded, and he pulled the trigger, simply as a ploy. A lone bullet discharged, striking Joe in the stomach.

A wounded kid, immediately startled and in great pain, fell down yelling and made speech sounds that were not discernible, while Fred ran into another room. Zachary helped Joe to a nearby bed. Panic and chaos blended together nicely as everybody began yelling and running all over the place. Medical personnel, parents, and neighbors were called, and arrived at varying times.

While confusion mounted, Zachary tried to make Joe feel as comfortable as possible and reassure him that things were going to be okay; he was, though, completely unaware they may not have been totally alone.

At first, Joe appeared to be losing and then regaining consciousness. He looked at Zachary and said: "I feel myself suddenly coming out of my body.

I can see things happening all around, as if I am looking down from someplace, but I feel no pain. I think I see some fast-moving bright lights and hear intense music, people singing; I feel total peace, and my heart is light and appears to want to jump out of my body. I thought I heard the lights say something like, 'put him back; put him back. It is not his time.' What is happening to me?"

Joe then went back to sleep while Zachary tried to convince himself that he had not heard the previous conversation; denial always worked best when things happened that are not explainable. But he had to admit that he was both confused and scared Joe was going to die.

Eventually, to everyone's relief, a wounded kid was taken to the hospital, operated on, and survived. A couple of kids were harshly disciplined by their father, while the police had more than just a few words with the owners of the guns.

But plain facts could not be ignored. Zachary's friend had just been shot. He was going to live, but it sounded as if Joe had partially left this world and gone somewhere for a moment. Zachary first reasoned that Joe was just scared, and that what he said had simply been misunderstood. But deep down, Zachary was troubled by a lot of questions and wanted to talk more with Joe when he came home from the hospital.

The opportunity to do so came a few weeks later when Joe, somewhat recovered but still sore, asked Zachary if he could speak with him alone. Zachary requested that Jerry Little might join in, and Joe made both boys swear to secrecy for as long as they lived in Elm City. The clubhouse seemed the most obvious place to meet. It was the most private abode in the world, at least to kids in need of intense conversations about seemingly separate worlds, far apart from each other.

"I feel much better now," Joe said, "but I still can't get that angel out of my mind."

"What are you talking about?" asked Jerry.

"When I was first shot, I felt like I was leaving my body and going somewhere, but I don't know where. I saw a lot of bright lights and, off to the side, there was a fire of some kind and people with faces distorted and strange. I am not sure they were people at all. I can't explain very well what I saw. Then this bright light came, and a voice said that I was going to live. A peace came over me like I had never experienced before. It was like I simply wanted to stay with that angel."

Jerry asked, "Do you think you were seeing parts of heaven or hell? I think you might have. In my church, the pastor reads from the Bible about places which sound like what you are describing."

Joe laughed, and then quieted. "Are you kidding me? Heaven! Never! But that being, whatever it was, I just can't get it out of my mind."

The final member of the SMG lived on a small farm located a mile out of town on an extension of South Main Street, now designated as a state highway. His father grew corn and worked the fields twelve or more hours a day, with much effort and little recoverable money. Willie Gray was the friendliest and most sociable of the gang. He was not as athletic as some of the other gang members, but he tried hard. His laugh began with a huge smile that covered a face that became redder by the minute, while the rest of his body did mini-contortions, followed by noises with loud guttural sounds. An added advantage to his membership in the gang was his dad's familiarity with the farmers in the county. One summer, Willie had found good paying jobs for the entire gang. Young, healthy kids were in demand because of strong backs and a willingness to endure hot work. Zachary had already graduated from part-time strawberry picking and cutting corn out of beans— he was eager to move up in farm-job importance and salary.

"Baling hay" was done by a machine that took loose-cut alfalfa hay, packaged it into rectangular-shaped bales, and wrapped it in wire. Then human labor stacked it onto a small flatbed trailer. Pay was two cents a bale. Later, it was restacked in a hot barn that felt like an oven from hell. The work was tiring, and the bales of hay became heavier as daylight proceeded to nightfall.

Lunch was the treat of the day. Large tables were set under tall elm trees. Fried chicken and mashed potatoes, iced tea, and pie were served. If the workers were lucky, fifteen minutes were given for a nap. Then it was back to work. By the end of the day, Zachary wondered if his arms would remain attached to his body. Money earned went for a prized new baseball mitt displayed in the window of Frank's Sporting Goods, located on the south side of the square.

Willie went to the Baptist church and took a small Bible with him, but he never admitted to what was either read or believed. There was a special girl he was attracted to, and Zachary often wondered if that wasn't the real reason Willie went so faithfully.

But he at least attended church, unlike some of the other SMG who chose to never go. It seemed that boyhood entrapped kids into so many distracting endeavors of work, play, school, and of course, girls.

There was one other kid who lived on South Main Street. He was an outsider, one who was odd and different and never asked to be part of the SMG.

Lawrence Tanner lived a few houses from the Allan boys, and his story was as strange as his personality. His house was lonely-looking, not well kept, but a place where Lawrence hid from a world perceived as too mean, too threating. He was shy, more within himself, and he wanted it to stay that way.

When he did go outside, he spent hours with imaginary wooden toy soldiers in a sandbox in his backyard. As an only child, like Zachary, he had few friends and must have been sad, discouraged, and in need of acceptance. Home life was terrible. He once told somebody he hated to face his mother, who always seemed upset. She, on many occasions, appeared at the back door and hollered, "Lawrence Tanner, get in here immediately!" There were never smiles, and both parents looked angry all the time. The gang guessed his father must have beaten him with a strap that hung outside the back of their house. Curtains were always drawn and doors shut tight, as if the place of residence was preparing for some type of an explosion or a rocketing into space.

Athletic abilities were nonexistent. When he ran, there was only awkwardness. Feet and legs refused to obey messages from the brain; they had their own agenda, with the result consisting of tripping over feet and falling on the ground, only to then get back up and start the whole clumsy process again.

On the basketball court, he was a disaster; no one included him in any plays or team actions. If he grabbed a rebound, those on his team cried out, "Pass it here, quickly!" Soon, he received the message of a reluctance of friendship, and his interactions with the gang lessened; no doubt some were thankful.

Previously and on a more personal level, Zachary had experienced a difficult encounter with Lawrence during an afternoon when the kids were in grade school. Lawrence had been bothersome; very unlike him, because he was mostly quiet. He began to make fun of the braces on Zachary's teeth. Put in SMG parlance, he became a complete asshole! Fists and muscles knew they were to be readied for action. "Those silver things on your teeth look ugly. No girl will ever kiss you."

Zachary remained silent for a long time and thought that if he just ignored Lawrence the needling would stop. He was feeling his heart begin to race faster, but his resolve was to not get into a fight with him.

"You should not come to school anymore. Those things make you look like some kind of monster. Look at me."

Lawrence then began to make faces and dangle his arms in strange positions. Zachary kept walking, looking ahead, and the other two boys with them began laughing and goading Zachary to act. Then Lawrence pushed Zachary, and that was the point where boxing bells went off in one kid's head.

The first swing caught the provocateur on the side of the eye. Stinging must have been harsh, but he ignored the pain and grabbed Zachary, and the two of them went to the ground. Fists hit faces and body positions changed by the second. During one set, Zachary was able to pin Lawrence down by placing his own knees on Lawrence's arms while sitting on a chest and stomach that was breathing rapidly.

"Get off me, you shit," Lawrence cried out.

Silence from the one on top, followed by a few slaps to a face, distorted and in pain.

"I said get off me, #%@&-face!"

"Not till you give up."

"That will never happen."

More rolling around on the ground as Zachary felt his arms tiring; Lawrence kicked at Zachary, missed and then fell.

The owner of the house, in whose yard this lightweight encounter was occurring, came out and pulled the combatants apart.

"Stop this nonsense immediately. Apologize!"

Two fighters shook off some blood and sweat, refused to look at each other, deftly touched hands, and then Lawrence ran away. The matter was never discussed again.

Some of the kids around where Lawrence lived continued to speak about questionable goings-on within his house, where it was reported that strange noises and shadows were purported to be seen and heard. Zachary wondered if there were not ghosts and other scary things up to no good.

Steve reported that one night, as he was passing through Lawrence's backyard, he thought he heard voices of people that came from a dark room in the back of the house. A curtain moved a bit, a light came on, and Steve was sure he saw a face that looked very old and wrinkled with a frown. It had very big, crooked yellow and black teeth. Steve ran home and made himself believe the whole thing was a bad dream. Later, when this account was given to the rest of the gang, most of them were not all that surprised, because the whole family was simply seen as different, weird, and maybe even evil.

But some type of social and educational redemption prevailed! This odd-ball kid grew to manhood and fooled everybody. He received a Ph.D. and became a college professor. Lawrence Tanner, a kid who might have had few social talents or abilities, knew little love, and may have lived in a house with ghosts, something the rest of the SMG could never brag about.

The boys often had meetings down in the Allan brothers' basement. When the gang was not working at various part-time jobs, other things became the order of the day: playing sports, arm wrestling, joking, and complaining. Sprinkled in was a lot of gossip, complete with rich lies and bragging. As they grew older, music was played from a 45-rpm record player. Ideas for things to do were suggested for the day, or the next day, or a weekend. The schedule was never followed, and the importance of anything planned was irrelevant.

One Saturday morning in the spring of some year, several of the gang members sat around staring into space. Boredom was rampant.

Gale spoke: "It is Saturday and there is a car show today downtown at the square. Old trucks and old cars are on display, and I'll bet we can sit in the autos. Hoods will be opened so we can look at and maybe even start the engines."

Steve, though, was not impressed with Gale's idea. "No, we should go down the street and play some tackle football over on the hospital grounds. We have enough to play, because several kids who live on East Street will join us. It's not that hot out, and I am ready for some good tackle ball. I have to be on the opposite team from Stevens, who outran me last week. I am going to be sure that never happens again. I want to see what he says this time when I stop him and take his legs out from underneath him. He won't have a chance."

Jim agreed, "Yeah, I like Jackson's idea. We haven't played football for some time. Maybe we can get two older kids who play on the varsity football team, Tony Scott and Billie Chatsworth, to coach because they know the best plays to call, and most of the time they don't get angry if we mess up. They could at least referee and teach us about passing and tackling. It will be good practice for us when we continue through high school and play other teams from Spring Dale and Mount Olive."

Buddy then chimed in. "I think we should get some of those kids from the rich end of town to come over and play us in a football game. I think they are nothing but a bunch of assholes. They are all rich and think they are better than everybody else."

Dwight nervously said, "I have some things to do here at home, so I think I will just hang around and clean my room."

The basement became saturated with non-stop whistles, and Steve's face became a bright red; he coughed uncontrollably with nonstop cachinnations and said to Dwight, "Why don't you tell us what you are really going to do? I know you want to see Connie Feller who lives on Michigan Avenue. I heard she likes you, and I bet the two of you are going to mess around."

Dwight became good and angry. "Shut the *%#* up, Steve. I know you are the one who has gone over there all the time and tried to kiss her. I heard you talked her into playing a game in which she rolled and folded her dress up seven times above her knees; isn't that game called Seven-Up?" More raucous laughter bounced off the walls. Things warmed up nicely.

"I don't have any idea what any of you are talking about," from a very inaudible voice.

Several more of the gang members laughed even harder, and perhaps hoped the two of them might start swinging wayward fists. The likelihood of that ever happening was quite small, since they were indoors, and parents were upstairs.

There had always been rumors about Connie and her availability and openness to entertaining naïve boys concerning "the facts of life." Put more bluntly, she lived for emotional encounters, sex in many forms, with just about anybody from any place. How and why she developed this way many, including the SMG, never understood or much cared about, but never complained and lived for the rich fantasies derived.

Zachary attempted to change the direction of the conversation. "I like Gale's idea because if the trucks and cars are not very good, we can all go to the movies. I think there is a good western starring Roy Rogers at the Times Theatre."

Then Joe became involved in a mixed-up conversation and made things more complicated. "I would rather play some baseball over at the state hospital softball field, if we can get some of the patients to be part of the teams."

Nobody said anything, so that idea went away quickly.

Willie Gray commented: "I am going to have to leave in a few minutes, because I must help my dad do some plowing in one of our cornfields. It is likely we will have to cut some beans out of the corn. Anybody want to help?"

Steve and Zachary looked at each other and laughed, but said nothing. The rest of the gang expected that kind of behavior from the two of them—they were simply two weird kids, at least some of the time. Secrets, however, remained as they should be—well-kept and deep inside sun-parched minds and souls.

Joe, Gale, and Zachary often spent time at Buddy's house where they played senseless games of checkers, crazy eights and poker. One night after an intense game of cards, Buddy slipped upstairs from the basement and got a couple of beers—a first attempt to be men. Now, with drinks in hand, they acted like they were big-time gamblers at a casino situated directly on South Main Street, right in the middle of Elm City.

Gale gave Zachary a few sips from his glass. It tasted horrible and had a rotten smell. The other kids laughed while the card playing continued. Somebody won thirty cents. All felt sick. One threw up. What was going on with these kids? Most likely they were just a group of hotshots with few cares in the world, ones who just mimicked what they saw their heroes—movie actors— do on the screen at the Times Theatre. The only difference was that these kids were never able to hold their liquor. At least for now!

Afterwards, they went outside. Joe said that he had been down at Joe Bruski's Pawn Shop on East State Street, and a guy named Tex had given him a book.

The boys gathered under a street light on Superior Avenue and took a quizzical look at it. Someone said it was called an "eight-page Bible." It certainly didn't look like any Bible Zachary had ever seen. Inside were drawings and cartoons of men and women in various positions. The characters were illustrated without clothes, and Joe said they were "screwing each other."

Buddy asked if it had anything to do with a tool he had in the basement called a screwdriver. Joe clarified that it was some kind of "love stuff" and babies resulted in mysterious ways. Other pictures revealed that there were men kissing men and women doing likewise. Cuss words were written in and used to further the entertainment. One picture showed a close-up detail of "private parts," to which everybody laughed. Zachary remembered a summer camp conversation and accompanying details. He tried to make a connection in his mind, but only confusion abounded.

When they finished with this unbelievable conversation, Gale commented, "Who wants to keep the 'Bible'?" There was no response, so they threw it down a gutter drain and went home to bed. Any further awakened emotions, thoughts, and memories about those pictures were never again discussed; maybe, though, fantasies and dreams not always shared with others were activated, including more intense feelings and behaviors lasting varying periods of time, either before or after prayers.

Four outdoor basketball courts, coated in asphalt, were located at South Elm City Grade School and welcomed the SMG, and anybody else for that matter. The backboards, with protruding heavy metal hoops, were supported by metal posts set in concrete. A small chain-link netting provided instant gratification when some lucky kid swished a shot from twenty feet. This was one of several "second homes" to the SMG.

Straws were drawn to decide who would pick each team's players. The taller kids, like Jim and Buddy, went first and then, because of their dribbling and speed, Jerry Little and Steve Jackson; and finally, the rest of the gang followed in varying, maybe even nonsensical order.

The games were never refereed, so there were drastically different points of view on fouls, double dribbles, and out-of-bounds balls. The games had no time limits and were played until someone needed a nature break. A large grove of trees, less than fifty yards from the courts, served a useful purpose.

In one game, Zachary scored sixty-five points, high for that day! Free throws were not allowed because fouls were never called.

Self-control was always the goal in any of the athletic games. But intensity and gamesmanship, and varying degrees of athletic ability, eventually lead to arguments, shoving, and fisticuffs. One example: Junior Winter, who lived close to the school, often joined in the games. He was fat and not well coordinated. One of the kids, Frank Martin, yelled out that Junior needed to stop knocking everybody on the ground; otherwise, there was going to be trouble. Play intensified while the players positioned for rebounds. Shoving was intense, sweat drowned the court, and Junior elbowed all. Frank rebounded a missed shot, and Junior proceeded to push him down. Frank got up, started cursing, and landed a direct hit to Junior's mouth. Blood gushed out, and there was one further observation—a missing front tooth! Junior yelled at the top of his voice, "Frank hit me in the mouth, and now I got no tooth!" At that point, only his fast-moving backside pointed in the direction of his home was observed.

Later, after the game, everyone sat down to re-evaluate. Junior had provoked, but Frank was guilty too, for not controlling anger. He was counseled accordingly. But according to him, all of this aftermath was simply bull. Frank went home, never to return. That was okay, because the SMG didn't like him anyway. But didn't tempers have to be simply an extant part of growing up? Maybe the bigger question was: *Did this emotion remain around for a lifetime?*

For some, self-control seemed to come easier than for others. Frank apparently took a long time to get control of his emotions. Several stints in reform school helped. Most likely out of embarrassment, Junior never asked to play again. That was a smart thing for him to do—at the very least, he kept the rest of his teeth.

* * *

On cool autumn days, mostly Saturdays and Sundays, the gang played football within the huge grounds of the hospital. The field was a section of seventy-five yards of open space, directly across the street from where several of the SMG lived.

Billie Chatsworth was a senior in high school and once commented that the high school football coach thought he was a poor defensive player. However, at one game, when substituted in with little expectation of success, he made sixteen unassisted tackles. His comment: "I made the coach feel like a complete asshole." His inclusion as a player was always welcomed!

One Saturday afternoon, the sky appeared a partially dull grey, and then it slowly darkened with storm clouds intermixing, eventually overtaking. A light snow began to fall, and the stage was set for a perfect football game. Flakes of different sizes and shapes came down furiously, stinging a group of kids' red faces; what didn't hit bodies exploded onto the ground, causing a blanket of white and very slippery conditions.

Zachary occupied the position of halfback on one team, and with "big Billie" in front blocking, he was successful in making much yardage. He just followed behind Billie, who took down players, which then allowed Zachary to scoot down the field for easy touchdowns. The players from the other team were not impressed. They yelled "unfair, unfair!" Zachary Stevens, though, was on a rampage and nothing stopped him. On one play, as Jerry Little ran around Billie and grabbed Zachary's ankles, the flashing halfback sped up, jumped to the side, and ran to Billie's left for a touchdown. Tempers flared all over the place; spit and sweat flowed freely; healthy and unhealthy smells abounded everywhere, while dreams became manufactured for a kid ready to turn professional and sign a contract with the Chicago Bears.

On another possession, Zachary started to run a play and was met by defenders Jerry Little, Joe Gruneau, and Jim Allan, all of whom carried a healthy mix of hatred and fortitude that blanketed huge portions of their faces. They were determined to stop him regardless. Jerry grabbed his waist and threw him down. His good friend took his fist and started to drive it into Zachary's waist. Zachary thought: *This should not be allowable. I am going to hit him in the face.* Then a still, small voice from vast reaches of a more rational mind recounted: "let it be, otherwise he will whip your ass good."

Play continued, and Billie came through again. With one arm he pushed Jerry back, and then he moved quickly to block both Joe and Jim from tackling Zachary, who continued straight down the sideline for another touchdown. By the end of the day, Zachary's team won forty-two to six.

Billie thanked everyone for a good workout and left. The opposing team glared at Zachary and said nothing as he climbed over the fence and ran home to his backyard, where he laughed and cheered for at least five minutes.

An important caveat: There would be other days not so kind to Zachary and to his sports dreams. He had, though, convinced himself that with a 200-pound lineman in front, he was invincible. The next time, in a game played without Billie, a price was paid: Zachary felt the pain of bruises to the arms, legs and chest, and the sting from a smack to a nose and cheek. Somehow his teeth stayed together, and the only other pain was the jeering by the opposing team, inquiring of him to describe how much he had enjoyed the game today!

Their voices sounded light, with much laughter. When the wind blew, there was a smell of perfume in the air. It was a Sunday afternoon, and Zachary had just finished catching and punting with several SMG members.

Across South Main Street, a group of about ten girls jogged on the sidewalk and waved to the gang. Gale called them over and they came. "Would all of you like to play some touch football?" he asked. He spoke loudly in the hope of drowning out some of the snickers from behind him, mercifully provided by a few gang members whose names will not be disclosed.

The girls climbed over the green wrought-iron fence as if they had done the exercise many times. They appeared to be the same age as the SMG, muscular, and in good physical shape. One girl caught Zachary's glances. She smiled broadly—things appeared hopeful. The ladies replied that they would not play football, but how about basketball? Steve commented, "Let's split two teams into half girls, half boys."

"No," came the reply loud and clear. The game would be girls against boys, with no further questions or comments.

An outdoor basketball court was located behind one of the women's residences at the hospital. Since it was the weekend, it was not in use and would be a perfect place for the contest between "sport savvy"

John Spencer

males and "feckless" females. The gang thought to themselves that they would not push the margin of victory too much—they wanted the girls to stay around for a while after the game to see what might develop; dreams and fantasies flew around uncontrollably. Some of the girls were Negro and quite attractive. The SMG always prided itself on never having even the smallest hint of racial discrimination!

The game started, and from the outset it was evident that something was very odd and very wrong. The girls had moves that none of the gang had seen before. Their quick reflexes slapped the ball out of frustrated hands. Then they performed a disappearing act as they flew down to the opposite basket and scored.

When the girls were on offense, they developed tricky plays in the center court and fed into the post for easy scores. Then there was an even quicker retrieval down the court for a rugged defense, which suffocated scoring attempts by any of the SMG gang members. If there was a miss of a basket, they were much better at positioning for rebounds. At half time, with no refs, they were ahead by fifteen points. Even with the best basketball players, which included Steve, Buddy, and Jerry, nothing seemed to prevent the girls from scoring.

Zachary felt frustrated and angry at the failed efforts. To make matters worse, a group of patients from the hospital showed up and cheered at how well the girls played, and how foolish the SMG looked.

Eventually, the game ended. The gang lost by twenty points. Conversations were attempted, but the girls said they needed to leave; a bus was waiting. One of the patients wondered if the girls had come from another planet. Everybody laughed, but the gang was more subdued with mumbles not entirely audible; that was probably a good thing. The girls climbed back over the fence and disappeared down the street.

The gang stood in disbelief. "Wow! What happened?" somebody commented.

"Nobody needs to know about the game just played. It was simply a dream," mumbled Willie Gray.

Gale was in absolute amazement. "I thought I was a good dribbler, but one of those girls took the ball from me so many times that I felt like a complete fool. How did they get to be so good?"

"Yeah, they were certainly the best basketball players I have ever seen. I thought I could outplay the girl that was guarding me most of the time, but Zachary kept getting in the way, and she beat me on most of the fast breaks," Steve said in a noticeably depressed voice.

Zachary disparagingly blew off, "I had to guard several of them at once just to keep the basketball away from the goal. The tallest girl on that team really jumped, and I could not get around her. They also seemed to have a lot of plays that they must have practiced a lot. I wonder if they were not from a special school team."

"One of the girls, I think her name was Alicia, elbowed me a lot in the stomach. I wanted to knock her down," Buddy mumbled as he kicked the dirt.

"I thought I was fast, but the girl I was guarding outran me, and had fakes that I have never seen before. Do you think they might come back and play us again? It would have been good to have Jim Allan to help rebound under the boards. I felt silly and mad at the same time, maybe a little excited too," Jerry said in a somewhat shaky voice.

Joe was more humorous. "I think we need to forget the whole thing. They were nothing more than a bunch of midgets from some circus; I am sure they were much older that us."

"Gruneau, you are crazy! Those girls were normal size, and they had high, squeaky voices. There were not midgets!" shouted Zachary.

Steve became pensive. "I don't know where they came from, but somebody has taught them a lot about playing basketball. Who knows, maybe the patients were right, and they did come from another planet." Lots of disconcerting laughter followed.

It was apparent the conversation had become nonsensical, so Joe suggested, "Let's go up to O'Brian's and get some soda. All this talk has made me feel angry. I am going to rack it up to a bad dream that I know will eventually go away."

Buddy wondered, "Are we going to have to play kids like that when we are older? I hope not. We will never win a game. I have to get on home and do some work in the backyard."

Still, somewhat restless, Jerry asked Zachary to stay and shoot some hoops, but Zachary was fixated on other things. "I want to find that girl that smiled at me and learn more about her." There was much laughter and jeering. "Who knows," Zachary continued, "maybe the two of us could play a game of H-O-R-S-E, or just a one-on-one scrimmage."

Gale then got back in the conversation. "Zachary, you are a dreamer. Those girls have no interest in us, and besides, they probably think we are a bunch of dumb farm hicks. I am going home to practice on my clarinet. I have to get ready for a concert at school next week."

"Zachary, let all of us know if you find that girl and her basketball team. Just don't try to kiss her; she and her friends might give you a black eye or a bloody nose," Buddy said as he ran off, laughing.

"I will remember that!" Zachary shouted as he ran in the opposite direction with new and potentially interesting plans in mind. The rest of the gang failed to stop laughing as they all dispersed for home and a rest to try to forget a rather embarrassing sporting moment in time, hopefully never to be relived.

Zachary jumped over the fence and followed the route the girls had taken on South Main to catch their bus. The best guess was that they might have turned right on Route 73. Just a block beyond, at the Elm City Motel, he saw a large bus parked out in front. The whole team had climbed aboard, and the engine started up. The bus whizzed past him and turned south toward Indianapolis. He took a chance, went to the motel, and asked the guy behind the desk about the group of girls who had just left. The man replied, "Oh that was a group of grammar school all-stars from somewhere in Kentucky, on their way back home after attending and playing in a girls' basketball tournament in Chicago."

Zachary slipped back home to tell everyone what he had learned. Then he realized the disappointment and embarrassment the SMG would feel, that a group of very athletically trained girls had whipped them in a simple game of basketball! Willie Gray was right. The whole incident needed to be disguised as a dream. The best thing to do was to say nothing. And for a long time, everyone felt foolish. Maybe, though, they all had learned something far more important; something they would need to take with them on their journeys through adolescence—the art of the acceptance of losing, and learning to sprinkle a little bit of humility into the mix.

Women's sports in public or private schools, and even professionally, was just a twinkle in the eye of many hopeful female sports enthusiasts growing up in Elm City and anywhere else during the '50s. But another time was coming. The wait would be championed by some, ignored or criticized by others, but anticipated and made real by future women athletes in many sports. Maybe, unknown to them at the time, the SMG played a small role in that development and for that they should have been most proud, but of course they weren't. Instead, memories were sent to dark places and held there unattended, never to be called back into such a denied and foolish consciousness. It was safer that way. Egos remained protected.

The SMG had been Zachary's first true introduction to the confidence he needed to socialize and be part of a network of true buddies. They provided the support for him to try many behaviors, to see how they fit for general wear or for more special occasions. The large grounds of the Elm City Hospital had been a perfect place to practice football or baseball skills. The SMG learned from each other how sensitivities and attitudes were to be tamed and dealt with—when to talk up and defend, and when to keep thoughts, ideas, and attitudes to oneself.

The gang, the SMG, had become a family; brothers Zachary never had. Jerry and Steve helped him become a better baseball player with more focus and more determination. Jim and Steve role-modeled humor. Dwight taught him the best ways to defend against bullies, including fight positions for the protection against swings to the face by raising and moving elbows; he more than encouraged Zachary to run fast and fight another day, when necessary.

And then there were the neighborhood girls, about whom no one ever spoke. Zachary learned from them too. The motto, their motto, "Long live the SMG," signified the boys' invincibility to themselves and each other, and to future days to come. The sense of trust and camaraderie was real, and life seemed full of potential.

The boys would need all the strength and mindset available to muster up positive energy for what was ahead of them in their passage of life. They were to learn about darkness of soul and mind. Lurking in the shadows of time and place was a pathology that would temporarily infect virgin minds and souls—expose and undress the frailty of the human psyche.

Weakness and deceit were placed on full display for a bunch of kids to try to understand. The outcome would leave indelible prints that would not wash away easily. The gang always assumed that insanity resided within the wall of the Elm City Mental Hospital. They were to soon find out otherwise.

Seven:
Old Sins Cast Long Shadows

He had yellow buck teeth and a soul in despair,
Strong lusts for young boys caught in his lair,
Innocent kids called him coach and learned about silence,
Play ball, ignore lies, and never show any defiance.

THE GUY WORE A SLIGHTLY FIENDISH SMILE and drove a large grey Packard Car. He carried a paunchy stomach that protruded out from a miscast body; huge teeth and vacant eyes disguised a dangerous and deceitful man. He was never a resident of the state hospital, but maybe should have been.

His name was Jeff Kitchen, and his pathology would infect the SMG. He worked as a salesman at some store on the square and his major goal, when not working, was to "scout out" potential victims— young, naïve boys. He told them he needed good athletes to play on his teenage boy's softball team. Things seemed innocent enough, because he taught ways to improve important aspects of play, hitting and fielding. But there were other, more sinister motives that boiled and festered inside this man, feelings and desires so uncommonly expressed by any healthy person, from any society.

Jeff's introduction to the SMG began one early June day over at the state hospital grounds. He watched a bunch of the kids play softball and said nothing, just gave a faint, duplicitous smile. After one game, the boys gathered around him, and Jeff volunteered to take them out to get something to eat. Nobody accepted. Jeff remained persistent. He had rehearsed well what to say and how to make offers attractive, most generally baiting part of his comments with his interest in the youth of Elm City and their athletic development; and about how he had inroads to the coaches at the high school, how he would put in a "good word" about each of them, especially those who wanted to someday play for the coveted school baseball team. Zachary heard the speech, and he along with several others eventually accepted Jeff's offer to go out and eat. Parents should have been informed about this man, intentions clarified; they never were.

The devious softball coach told the gang stories about the people he met on his sales trips. Some of the tales were funny, while others were just plain stupid. He said that if any boy made his softball team, sponsored by the Coca-Cola Bottling Company of Elm City, Indiana, that person would get to go to Indianapolis and stay in a nice hotel when the team played in tournaments. Everything seemed too neat and too good to be true. The sad fact: it was.

During one of the trips to the restaurant, a gang member told Jeff that he really wanted to play on his team. Jeff replied, "If you don't make the team, you can always be my batboy."

He then proceeded to grab the kid's leg just above the knee and squeezed. Everybody laughed. Jeff drove off with a villainous look on his face and no doubt unspeakable fantasies locked and loaded into a wrecked, perilous mind.

The gang thought that Jeff was more than just strange. What an odd thing to do, grab a kid's leg! Nobody made any further comments, but all certainly had their own perceptions and doubts about the kind of guy Jeff really seemed to be. Zachary felt sick to his stomach. The rest of the gang said they were going to have nothing more to do with him. But of course, that was simple bullshit, and perilous times were ahead. A new untested kid, a virgin of sorts, would soon be a temporary member of the gang. Naiveté was laid out in plain sight and eventually brought a group of kids to a closer realization about life, where untold desires were carried to a pathetic extreme.

⚬

Ken Matway came from Kansas, and during the summer months he spent time with his aunt, who lived next door to Gale Rogers. He was shorter than most of the other boys, had blond hair and an infectious smile. Of course, he was not a full-fledged member of the SMG, but rather a "visitor" who was appreciated and quickly accepted. The reason: the most important virtue to young boys growing up is to be a natural athlete and have a sense of humor. His moves were quick on a ball diamond, scooping up grounders and snagging line drives, and then easily throwing out even the fastest runners. At bat, he had a keen eye and hit baseballs to places in the outfield where players were not positioned. He was the only kid who really knew how to accurately bunt and get to first base quickly and safely. Everyone liked his sense of humor, it was not condescending; and his motivation to someday play professional baseball appeared obvious and sincere.

When the gang took a breather at their ball games, Ken and Zachary would spend time talking about many things. Ken's biggest embarrassment was he came from such a small town that you could drive through it in one minute. There was a drug store, a gas station, and a schoolhouse, plus a few houses, including the one where he lived. The town's people were all friendly and certainly dependable types, ones who supported and believed in God, country, and the American flag. "Not one sinful person in town," he commented with a wily smile.

"Stevens, let's go across the street and play catch at the softball field on the state hospital grounds."

"Okay, I will hit a few grounders for you to practice your throwbacks to me. I will show you how well I have learned to drop the bat and have my glove ready for the catch."

And so, two boys traversed a green wrought-iron fence and began a well-scripted exercise in drudgery, boredom, and aching muscles buttressed with gossip, jokes, and banality. They seemed to understand each other well, including the many times when either of them made some spectacular catch or clumsy error. There were never putdowns or stupid, jealous comments. Their play would last for hours with switches, and either Zachary took the field while Ken hit, or the reverse. When they tired, rest came, and they gave suggestions to each other concerning improving catching or throwing accuracy. Listening, trusting, judgments and advice was always of prime importance for these two boys. A friendship and bonding developed with no apologies.

"Ken, your play on that last fly ball was perfect. How did you know the exact distance to move backwards to catch the ball? And the throwback came in on one hop, directly bouncing where it should, right in my mitt; a good, powerful and accurate throw."

"Just a lot of practice, I guess. Try hitting me some line drives over my head. I need to learn to time my running backwards after I hear the ball make contact with the bat. I must remember to follow the arc of the ball while it is in the air, and ensure I don't go too far back and find I am out of position to make a catch. It seems that the transfer of the ball from mitt to throwing is becoming more natural as I practice."

With more hits and more throwbacks, both boys' arms became tired and legs became weary, while a sun refused to hide behind clouds.

"Stevens, let's stop for a while and take a water break."

"Good idea," from a voice and throat parched and in need of that very thing.

The hospital bandstand, with its cupola roof, sat on a hill and afforded a good view of the entire Elm City state hospital grounds. There were several benches for rest and, most importantly, a brownstone water fountain that was used to quench thirst, while a summer breeze whipped up and allowed for a drying out of perspiration.

"I really like coming back here, even if it is only for the summer. I am so lucky that you guys like to play sports. Back where I live, there are few kids my age. I wish I could live here with my aunt all the year. I do have friends back in Kansas, including a girl who likes me a lot, but I see more chances to play sports if I lived here in Elm City."

Zachary listened carefully and said nothing for a long time. Then he took a chance. "I know about a team you might try out for. The coach comes here to see us kids play baseball, and sometimes takes us out for hamburgers."

Immediately, though, alarm bells sounded; some further internal reflections. *Should I tell him about what some of the kids say about Jeff—the strange ways he looks at people? There is something about Jeff that is not right; I just can't put words to it. Maybe, though, it is just my imagination. The guy must be okay. But then, I am not sure . . .*

What ambivalence! What a mistake!

The plain truth was that Zachary found it hard to talk about unpleasant stuff. He had a family to thank for that. His parents had done similar things when their marriage fell apart. And when a punk kid decided to rob a store and slash a skull, Zachary pretended he saw and knew nothing; denial was the *modus operandi* to assuage an unrelenting conscience that had become alive, spewing guilt. But this situation was different, wasn't it? There was no evidence that Jeff was someone who hurt kids, just a lot of innuendoes and guesses about weird behavior that no one seemed to understand. Wasn't the guy generous about spending money on the boys and making them feel good? Best plan: keep a mouth shut. His dad would have agreed. Further, Ken's motivation and desire had to be admired, and maybe his confidence in himself must be an attribute. Why should Zachary try to ruin everything for a kid on his way to sports stardom? If he did tell Ken about the suspicions people had about Jeff, would it make any difference? Most likely Ken either would simply pass others' impressions off as wrong or not important, or he would simply not care. For sure, it was Zachary's guess that Ken was determined to play select softball, if he could make the team.

"I want to meet that guy and show him my skills. I just know that if I keep practicing, I will be able to compete against other kids my age and later make our high school team. I live in a very small town in Kansas, and the high school is in a place called Keef City where there are a lot of kids that are good athletes. But with a start here in Elm City, I just know I would learn a lot from the coach and be ready for tryouts when I go back home in late summer. Zachary, you have no idea how much I want to play sports. Do you think you might be able to introduce me to this coach?"

Internally there was the mumbling of something unintelligible; there were unpleasant feelings in a gut, as if an ongoing battle for control of spirit was at hand. An honest commentary: "I need to get home and do some work, but we will talk some more and later plan for you to meet him."

Jeff Kitchen's first meeting with Ken Matway came two weeks later. After Jeff watched Ken play a game in which he hit the ball well and made a couple of backhand catches, followed by perfect throws to first base for outs, he took Ken aside, and they talked for a long time.

Later, Zachary asked Ken what the two of them had discussed, and Ken just shrugged his shoulders and recounted, "He asked questions about my family."

"What do you mean?" asked Zachary.

"Oh, about what kind of job my dad had and how many brothers and sisters were in the family. Nothing much, but he seemed interested in me and said that there was a good possibility I might be able to play for his team. He just wanted to get to know me better."

Feelings percolated inside Zachary, and he felt uncomfortable again. Ken needed to be warned, but against what? That the coach was going to grab his leg? Zachary was sure that something about Jeff just wasn't quite right. But he also had to admit that, as far as he knew, Jeff had never to this point done anything that was crazy or illegal, but rather had just acted and given an impression about himself as strange. Warnings might have been guessed about, but never volunteered or acted upon.

The devious softball coach returned throughout the summer, and he appeared to take an interest in one kid—Ken. The coach just stood and watched Ken field and hit. A few times he yelled out advice and encouragement, and then they would go off and just sit and talk. On more than one occasion, Zachary asked Ken what they discussed.

"Oh, just ideas to improve my stance or get down lower when fielding the ball, learning signals for stealing bases, and being observant of the strength of the throwing arm and athleticism of the catcher on the opposing team."

One day after Jeff had watched the gang play a game of four-on-four, he asked if Ken would like to go riding in his car. The odd thing with this request was that none of the gang was asked to come along. Jeff and Ken left together. Although at the time it seemed innocuous, the boys noted that Jeff put his arm around Ken's shoulders for just a brief second, maybe a friendly "fatherly reassurance" connection, but its awkwardness could not be ignored. The two drove off while Zachary and others watched in silence. Left behind were nagging thoughts of concern, but it seemed unclear what worries really were of any relevance. This was a rare time when only one kid had gone alone with Jeff. Had a costly mistake been made?

The boys looked at each other and said very little. Maybe they were just envious of Ken getting some free food. One kid piped up and said he had heard rumors about Ken from some of the other kids who played on his softball team. He was too friendly with some of the boys, but when Zachary and others asked him what he meant, he confessed to not being able to explain anything, just a shrug of his shoulders. The kind of potential deviant behavior involving sex overtones seemed to be easier to laugh at rather than describe.

"I think one of us should have gone with Ken," Buddy said. "I don't know what it is about that guy, but he seems to always have a weird look in his eye. I never see him with other grown-ups, just kids."

"Naw, he's going to be okay. Ken is a big enough kid to take care of himself," Willie Grey retorted. "Jeff seems different from most people I know, but I don't think he would ever do anything to us kids."

"What do you mean?"

"I don't know, like do something to them."

"Like what?"

Silence.

Nighttime eventually approached, and Zachary jogged home from the baseball field—this time in a non-stop mode. He felt anxious and found himself running halfway downtown. When he had jitters, it helped to soothe his nervous mind to run fast, going nowhere in particular, continuing until exhaustion.

Later, he came back to his house and did a few chores. He was surprised that the nervousness had not gone away. Spurious thoughts: *Should he have divulged more to Ken about some of Jeff's strange ways? Is Ken okay? It is now too late to worry about things totally out of my control.* He was preparing for bed when suddenly the phone rang.

The call was from Gale. "Get up here right away! Ken is here with an unbelievable story."

The kid with the most ambitious sport dreams and partial naivete was noticeably upset! A surreal tale unfolded. Jeff had taken Ken to a hamburger place called Ranch Haven, and then proceeded to convince him to play for his softball team. Pure glee was felt, because now he would be able to showcase all his skills and begin competing against some athletically talented players that would force him to play even better. His dream of getting a college scholarship might be materializing. Life was too good, all too good.

They proceeded to drive around town for a while, and then Jeff went beyond the city limits, out to and behind some cornfields in a heavily wooded area, and parked the car. Ken felt a little strange and asked, "What are we doing here parked alone?" Suddenly, without warning, Jeff placed his arm around Ken's neck and moved closer to him. There was a hug, and for a minute Ken thought that Jeff was going to try to kiss him. But then things really turned crazy. Jeff had lowered his own pants! At that point, panic came in for a brief assist and allowed a frightened young baseball player to yell out, "Get away from me, you queer," while a shaking fist, lightly thrown, swung at Jeff's face and missed; then a quick exit from the car, followed by running and a disappearance into the dark.

"Come back here!" Jeff shouted. "I can explain everything. You need not be afraid of me. I want to be your friend."

And while this vocal action was being played out, a frightened call was only part of the narrative; other thoughts stabbed at Jeff's heart and conscience: *I must stop this kid. If he tells anyone, I will be in a lot of trouble, maybe with the law; I might be taken into custody and lose my job. Why am I having difficulty breathing? It is so f&%*(+@ dark out here, I can't see much. That kid must be found immediately.*

All of Jeff's ruminations had taken his attention away from stray objects on the ground, including a very small piece of wire connected to a broken fence. Now, outside his car, pants fully pulled up and buttoned, disorientation came next. He saw nothing and with just one step, a trip followed by a twisting of the foot, a sharp pain radiating up his leg from his ankle, and a body colliding with unmovable ground. He lay there for a minute and thought he might pass out. He must get his legs untangled from the wire and get back on his feet. Concerns about a bruised body were real, but the most important one, an ankle injury, was attended to first and determined to be only a slight sprain. For sure, there would be no search for Ken this night.

Meanwhile, a terrified and angry kid hid behind a tractor and tried to not breathe for fear of making noise as he quietly observed a mass of physical entanglement and vocal cussing, all from twenty yards away. As he peered out, he could partially see Jeff in some agony. His legs had become discombobulated, a shirt torn, while a face became frozen in pain, guilt-ridden with fear. A soul whimpered, but it was never heard; maybe of no matter.

The pathetic figure eventually limped back to his car. Broken and disheveled, he sent unpleasant, deep dark memories to the furthest corners of his mind, even though in the past they had always refused to stay there.

At the same time one deviant soul was in retreat, a young kid practiced patience, at least thirty minutes of quiet, before a dash for home with thoughts—angry thoughts. He wanted to take a knife or gun and shoot Jeff. *What did that son of a bitch think he was doing? What kind of a person was he? Did he think I was just a pervert like him? Who can I ever trust to tell this story to? I sure as hell will not be playing for any junior kid's softball team.*

In a perfect world, some might try to argue possible explanations for some of Jeff's behavior. But no one could or would accept the pathos demonstrated in the front seat of a grey Packard car one summer night, viewed by only bored cornstocks and perhaps the "spirits" of many persuasions. Jeff Kitchen's true and complete story, though, was one born from and locked into tragedy from another time and place.

Years ago, he and his family seemed to have it all; a self-employed business professional who sold stocks and bonds, a recent graduate from college and a good athlete who had played on a baseball team as a star pitcher. Family life was great, with a wife who had a conspicuous smile and a contagious laugh, and a one-and-only son with the curliest blond hair and eyes the color, someone said, of the Mediterranean Sea. The family appeared loving, so eagerly looking toward the future. Life could not have been better for Jeff Kitchen and his family—then, disaster.

The mother and her boy were driving home, rounding a curve, when they were hit head-on by a truck driven by some goof high on drugs. The boy was killed immediately, and the mother seriously injured. Her recovery came slow. Legs never worked well, and the limp was obvious. But it was the loss of their only son, with accompanying memories of his earlier growing up, that produced such pain. Alcohol was tried and abused, but it failed to help. Guilt hung around with a lot of amorphous blame. And there was more to the story . . .

Jeff Kitchen had another life. While he produced and enjoyed sexual relations with his wife, he also had other desires, ones that were too deep and shameful to admit to. They involved sexual fantasies and strong emotional lust for young boys. The habit had always been pervasive and embedded deep in mind and soul, for it had its history since he was youngster. He had perfected secrecy of these thoughts with a wife who never knew of his troubled and sick desires. Control of behavior was always an issue, and Jeff had many thoughts that were never acted upon. Guilt stayed around, though, in a conscience seared many times with temptations wrought with such profound abnormalities.

After the accident, as the years went by, Jeff and his wife never emotionally recuperated. No son, much emptiness, and a lot of misplaced guilt were the only things on life's menu. The boy had been their entire world, maybe too much so. Now there was just the two of them. Friends suggested starting a new family. They tried, but did not really exude much effort. They were caught in some type of web of despair and self-blame.

Eventually they drifted apart, and a marriage became totally ended and destroyed. The wife left for parts unknown, and Jeff took one job, then another, eventually ending up in Elm City.

As Jeff now sat alone in his apartment, after his failed sexual assault of Ken, he wondered: *I have so many conflicted feelings. I want to hold and love my son again. I miss him so! He is always on my mind. And I also have these other feelings that occupy so much of my life, the craving of young boys—to touch and love them. Everything is so mixed up. Why do I feel sexual stimulation when I am around young kids? Thoughts of twisted love are constantly with me.*

This guise of coaching boys to get close to them has now been exposed, and I have been revealed as a complete fraud. How am I ever to control this urge to physically love young boys? Is my soul so tortured that I can't rid myself of these demons of lost and unnatural love? I must leave town and not be found. There is no doubt; I would be better off dead.

❦

After hearing Ken's story, neither Zachary nor Gale knew what to say, but they reassured Ken that Jeff would never bother him again. They knew that parents must be told. Ken was frightened, and he begged them to tell no one. He was not going to mention anything to his parents, because he knew his father would explode if he were to find out his son had been in a stranger's car. Ken guessed that his father would go after Jeff and perhaps try to kill him

Zachary thought, and the questions came non-stop. *Why would Jeff do something like that to a young kid? Were any laws broken? What kind of trial would be held? If he was found guilty, would he go to jail? Maybe the townsfolk would hang him, or at least chase him out of town. When Zachary's friends talked about sex, it involved girls. How could anyone have sexual feelings for someone of the same sex? Nothing made any sense.*

He then remembered stories about a couple of girls in his grade school that had been caught kissing each other. He had asked Gale why people would be attracted to someone of their own sex. Gale feigned complete ignorance and tried to change the subject. Zachary remained puzzled, as he had about so many things—just more insanity, this time with an adult and misspent desires.

The gang never saw Jeff Kitchen again, but they heard he left town at the end of the summer. A sick man who preyed on an unsuspecting kid whose only failing was his love for softball. They thought that Ken had placed trust in a guy who should have been a hospital patient that needed to be locked up, rather than be a boys' softball coach. But there had been another part to a tragic story never heard. A personal side to deviancy not fully revealed, involving a loving family torn apart by a tragedy with disastrous consequences.

It seemed that the incident with Jeff Kitchen might have allowed for many things to be on display for the understanding of the insanity of human nature and behavior; however, the boys were never allowed much clarification. But who would have clarified anything? If parents had been told, the result might have been as much about recrimination as explanation, and teaching acceptable from unacceptable sexuality.

This type of deviancy during the '50s was poorly understood, certainly never talked about, and never considered. This was the decade to be quiet, silent, and not admit to such ignorance about any type of personal abnormalities. Boyhood and adolescence staggered along, and so too did a ragtag group of kids, the SMG, eager to learn and be successful in sports and life. But could the frailties of human interactions likewise be understood? That enlightenment would have to wait. Certainly, there was more to the story than just the tragedy of a man losing his only son. Why and how did sexual feelings become transposed, or maybe superimposed, with unnatural feelings toward children by an adult? This was a serious crime of sexual assault. But how could it best be handled?

A deranged man absconded with and destroyed a group of boys' virgin-idyllic view of life and its goodness. But kids are tough, and maybe less prone to judge; instead the SMG came together during this confusing time, and as a group helped by empathizing with each other, and then they moved on with life, even in its ugliest of moments.

Eight:
Other Voices, Other Places

Two days ago within the air,
Someone appeared who wasn't there,
Another question to be asked today,
Why won't it leave and just stay away.

SWEAT BEADED AND THEN DRIPPED from his wrinkled brow. Jack Lutz was hot and uncomfortable. When he moved around the hospital grounds, his hips and legs worked in opposition to each other. He ran, stumbled, regained his balance, and ran again. Laughter was loud and unpredictable, and perhaps disguised much deeper pain. But who noticed and who cared?

He may never have felt sensations on a face caressed by a strong wind, or missed any non-existent emotions, or possessed a mind that "listened" and came alive by thoughts or internal conversations. Did he see and react to people in the same way everyone else did? Maybe his whole life was just an illusion, with little purpose and little gain. Perhaps he was what people called crazy, nuts, or just insane.

A long and green wrought-iron fence surrounded the grounds of the Elm City State Hospital and identified its boundaries. During the '50s it was climbed and vaulted by a bunch of kids, the SMG, who tried on new behaviors and tested limits both within themselves and others. They listened, laughed, joked, and then argued, fought, competed, won, and lost at sports games; celebrated victory, and cried at defeat. Emotions were laid bare while attitudes and consciences were tested, refined and further developed. There was a character change for this gang of boys, a break from immaturity toward maturity, watched so closely by a group of people different from the boys and so many others.

The hospital had been built in the mid-1800s and was designed to be totally self-contained. The main entry point had no gates, because there was never a worry about escape. The mentally disturbed patients either didn't care about leaving, or they had no place to go. This was home for them now, maybe forever. For better or worse, they were insulated from a society that believed strange, odd, or "abnormal" behavior was never virtuous, never to be role modeled, and certainly never to be even slightly tolerated. And while the entrance to the hospital was clearly defined, marked by two limestone stanchions with round globes of light that provided illumination and direction into verdant grounds; regrettably, the darkness found in the patients' misspent lives, dreams, and ambitions hovered close and fought to squelch out any hope of happiness and survival.

Visible at the south end of the hospital grounds was a six-story administration building that was composed of yellow brick and stucco, and connected on either side to a four-story annex. Theses additions housed either male or female patients, and extended east and west from the administration building. Every window was covered with grey steel bars. Steps went up the front of the main building and connected to a screened-in porch where a few benches were located. On the front grounds, flowers had been planted. A small fountain gushed out a spray of water to cool hot summer air, if only for a minute, and maybe gave peace to restless minds. Behind the administration building was a gymnasium, along with smaller buildings where patients made crafts or sewed and cleaned clothes.

Set in one small corner, behind the main buildings, were fertile grounds for the farming and eventual canning of vegetables, including tomatoes, cabbages, carrots, beets, potatoes, corn, and green beans. The patients earned small amounts of money working in places like the laundry room, the farm grounds, and building maintenance. These experiences kept them occupied. The most important goal was to foster responsibility; at least, this was what the information flyer described.

A large power plant provided energy for utilities. Mounds of coal were piled below a tall smoke stack that disappeared into the sky. During the cold months, it belched heavy amounts of soot everywhere. At eight o'clock in the morning, there was always a fresh new start for the day when a large whistle blasted. The signal sounded again at eleven-thirty, noon, and five p.m. when the workday for the hospital and Elm City ended. The smoke, pollution, and likewise the time alerts become a part of the fabric, and a frame of reference for all of Elm City. The residual soot and dirt was tolerated, never boasted about. But on more than one occasion, the hospital whistle had been used as a signal to citizens of impending alerts for meetings on the square of dignitaries, or important events such as disaster drills previously announced in the evening paper.

Northward from the administration building was a full and commanding view of the hospital grounds. An asphalt drive circled the entire hospital and handled all traffic, foot and auto, which entered and exited. At the farthest point north, close to Route 73, and tucked into large bushes was a sign that read

"Elm City State Hospital." At night it was lit in a neon green hue, seen by anyone who traveled through town.

On the west side of the oval drive, a red brick building extended several blocks. The windows were covered with steel bars, and peering out were the vacant, broken-spirited faces of mentally disturbed patients. Voices, which were shrill at times, yelled words not entirely understandable. But the emotion was there—much pain, much hurt.

During hot days, many of these patients sat in front of the building, either on the ground or on benches, smoking and staring into space. They rarely smiled, but sometimes they might stand up and walk around, appearing sleepy or dazed, not particularly interested in much of anything. Maybe it was the drugs given to them to slow their minds down, or maybe they were in some communication with another world, caught between boredom and unhappiness.

Every morning, separate groups of fifteen to twenty males or females came out of the buildings, marching, but hardly in unison. The women wore cotton flowered dresses—some too snug, while others had coverings so large they appeared to be dressed in large sheets. Hairstyles were non-existent, and talk, laughter, and loud, discordant singing could be heard as lines of humanity weaved around the hospital grounds, surrounded by attendants who followed and spoke in hushed tones.

The male patients came in many different sizes, and so too did their clothes. Shirts and pants were homemade at the sewing shop. The colors of the clothes were a drab black or brown, and most of the shoes were sneakers of some type, often worn without laces. Some "maverick" patients removed their shoes and went barefoot, breaking rules and initiating rebukes from the attendants.

The journey of the patients took them past large elm or maple trees, flowering bushes, and a softball field. At several points on their travels, they could be observed by Elm City commuters as they drove down South Main Street on their way to work on the square. Maybe these folks might have tried to take some very small interest in these patients, the ones with lost souls, but work, debts, children, and marriages competed for and recaptured attentions and motivations.

As the patients walked, self-talk taken from within tortured minds was noticeable. They might point to the sky as if they saw something; maybe angels, maybe God. When they wandered out of line, the attendants eased them back into their group. The staff was well-trained and understood the frailty of these patients who, when out on their daily walks, tried hard to be well-behaved so privileges could be garnered that were not afforded to inmates who remained locked up all day. These other, less fortunate patients, especially if they were combative, might be restrained to beds in dingy old buildings. People in the know denied there were such living conditions, or that isolation and abuse even existed. What was the truth? Only God, the patients, and the employees at the Elm City Hospital knew for sure, and all refused to talk about such things.

A local softball team, the Elm City State Hospital Redlegs, provided opportunities for the patients and for the public to observe competitive sports. The team consisted mostly of former high school and college athletes from Elm City. In some cases, the players worked as state employees at the hospital. Jerry's brother, Earl, played left field.

During one intense game, a player from the opposing team ran into the Redlegs' catcher, which resulted in a collision with minor injuries. Many of the spectators gasped and hoped the player was okay. Raucous laughter could be heard from the patients watching the game. It appeared they were confused about what happened and failed to recognize that a potentially dangerous injury had occurred.

Some of the SMG had been at that game and observed the patients' laughter.

"Who is that guy in the strange hat, and why did he make such odd noises? There was nothing funny about that. I don't think a lot of the patients understand the game. Maybe he thought the team players were playing around," commented Jerry.

Zachary said that he felt kind of embarrassed for the patients, but also noted that they seemed to enjoy watching an injury occur. Gale conjectured, "I guess people who live over here at the hospital sometimes don't think like we do. They are different, not bad people, but why is that a surprise to anyone? Their injuries are in the head. It is not the same as a cut to the skin or a broken leg. It's invisible. I wonder if they will ever recover."

The softball field had a large backstop, twenty feet in height. There were no dugouts, just a couple of unpainted wooden benches strategically placed down each baseline for the support of tired legs and butts. An unpainted picket fence encircled the outfield; beyond were groves of huge elm and maple trees. Off to one side was a brown stone water fountain.

When the field was not in use by the softball team, it was a favorite of the SMG who, over three to four years, played many exciting games. They picked their teams with a common catcher and separate shortstops, first basemen, pitchers, and two outfielders. Patients attended, watched, and some even participated in the play.

Zachary quickly discovered his favorite positions were first base and outfield. Shortstop and third base were positions more difficult and challenging, because the ball had to be accurately thrown for put-outs. His wild throws, which often went over the first baseman's head, caused utterances of unrepeatable words screamed with much furor by teammates. Gale pitched, as did Jim Allan, and both at times were wild with their throws. Gale jokingly threatened to "reduce Jim's salary" if he didn't learn better control, shouting, "Settle down, we will never finish this game until next Sunday because the hitter can't even take a wild swing at the ball and hit it."

Jim then yelled back, "Bite the dust!" The gang liked that expression, remembered it way too long, and used it ad nauseum, much to the delight of hospital patients who had no idea what it meant; but neither did the SMG.

Behind home plate, on a slight hill, was a small band house with a cupola-style roof. On Sunday afternoon, musicians played recitals for the entertainment of everyone, including those whose minds sometimes bounced between reality and other worlds. When the music started, the patients would sing, generally off-key, songs that may or may not have been related to the music played. Some might dance around and laugh, while others stared and said nothing despite the hospital attendants' arduous attempts to encourage them to get more involved with the spirit of the music.

One gang member, Gale Rodgers, would eventually become involved with some of the musicians and patients. For him, the opportunity to play and learn music was priceless. Some of the other members of the gang took less than an active role in such entertainment, and used the interludes as rest to chat and think about nothing.

"What are you contemplating, Stevens?"

"I don't know, maybe why I still can't hit hardballs."

"Wanna go over and visit Ramona White? Maybe she will be in a good mood today."

"Nope, she is too boring. I just want to sit here and look at the sky."

The hospital gym was a large brick building adjacent to one entrance into the hospital. Movies were shown on Saturday night, and several members of the gang, including Zachary, snuck into the back of the auditorium and hoped they were not seen by the attendants. A chance at a free movie, plus a cartoon, could hardly be ignored.

Friday night was the dancing showpiece for the hospital. Male and female patients made efforts to hold each other and dance. A group of wide-eyed boys watched from open side doors, which allowed cooler outside air into a much warmer, non-air-conditioned building, sometimes to the dismay of nervous hospital attendants who disdained the "outside public" observing. Tunes from the orchestra sounded artful and rhythmic, while the same could not always be said about those executing collateral movements.

On display was perhaps a bit of awkward humor, paired with inner pain and turmoil that flowed from emotionally distant and contorted faces. These lost souls were encouraged to step out into a "new" world, if only for a few minutes. For some patients, this risky task was easier done than for others.

The band played while the patients wandered around the dance floor. Some of the luckier ones obtained partners, generally of the opposite sex, but not always. The smiles on their faces might have been a hopeful sign, but who knew for sure what was operating in their minds?

The women dressed up and appeared sociable. They were always the aggressors. The men sought to remain centered, protecting the very last vestiges of safety in a very unsure, most likely frightening environment.

Sometimes, though, there were welcomed changes. One Friday night, several gang members including Zachary went and observed a rare event—real professional dancing by a couple who may or may not have been patients. Who really cared?

A tall man with shiny hair that was very thick and greased with no doubt smelly tonic, tight-fitting pants, and a colorful shirt came out on the dance floor and signaled to a woman to join him. All other patients immediately vacated. The band played some very rhythmic music, and an older observant, Zachary's neighbor, told him the dancers were going to perform the "tango." When he asked her what that meant, she simply said, "Watch and keep your mouth quiet."

The two dancers moved quickly around the dance floor and seemed to glide back and forth to the music. They stared into each other's faces, no smiles, no emotion. They circled and twisted, and then it appeared to Zachary that the male dancer lowered his partner almost to the floor. He held onto her, and she amazingly came up again without changing posture or facial expression. They moved some more, and then he kicked his leg out at an angle, and so did the woman. The dance ended to the applause of all. One of the other girls with Zachary said, "Now, that is real dancing!" The couple walked around with each other for a minute, appeared to smile, and then they disappeared.

Suddenly, outside where groups of people had gathered to watch, there were streaks of lightning across the eastern sky, followed by a clap of thunder. The dance was over, and Zachary was at least ten minutes from home. The wind blew in every direction; dust and objects from the street sliced into faces and eyes; then moisture, sprinkles at first, were followed with heavier drops at a much faster pace. Such unpredictability! Ah, Midwestern summers!

Directly across the street from the state hospital was a grocery store owned by O'Brian & Kelley. It was a favorite place for the SMG to spend or waste time during the summer. Zachary read comic books, smelled packaged coffee, and was told not to bring his dog in the store because, "It might shit on the 'taters."

It was here, behind a green wrought-iron fence, that hospital patients sought to interact with a sane world. They wanted human recognition and yelled out a need to first be heard, and then to purchase supplies from the store. If the employees of the grocery did not answer the calls, Zachary Stevens and others did.

"Hey kid, hey kid, come over here for a minute. I have a list, and I will give you a tip." An arm and hand stretched out from the fence and shook ever so slightly, while a face looked sad, tense, and worried; a voice painfully whispered without much hope or much joy to someone, anyone.

Her clothes were simple faded jeans, a stained shirt, and hair thrown together in some odd-looking wrap. The request: chewing tobacco, cigarettes, candy, shampoo, and a special kind of soap, items necessary to make a life just a little more pleasant.

Cynthia was her name, and she seemed older in years than she probably was. Thick glasses covered a face, a face adorned with too much makeup, not neatly applied. A slight smile revealed yellow and crooked teeth. There was always just enough money to cover the cost, plus a nickel given as a tip for services rendered.

"Where do you come from?" Zachary asked.

The answer: "I can't remember." She thought it was a place called Bloomington.

Conversations continued: "The place where I work, the laundry room, is a place of hell. It is hot all the time, and only cooled down when the windows on the side and back of the building are opened for brief periods of time." Zachary was fascinated by her purchases of chewing tobacco, so he once asked her, "What does that stuff taste like?"

"It's kinda like leaves."

Red-Man Tobacco was her favorite, and the only brand requested, because coupons were redeemed for baseball cards that were later sold to other patients for much-needed cash.

When she was in a particularly good mood, she showed Zachary a collection of baseball cards. On one of them was the prized player Stan 'The Man' Musial. The cards had facts describing when and where Musial was born, and a small story about his playing days with the Cardinals. Zachary tried to convince her to give him the card for a nickel. She just smiled and asked his name. Did he have a girlfriend? He stammered, she laughed, and baseball cards were not mentioned again.

Later that summer, Zachary took a chance. He tasted some of her chewing tobacco. Maybe it would give him extra strength and stamina, and he would appear tough, like the guys in the big leagues. Most, if not all, of the opposing team would strike out, and he would be a hero to his teammates.

The chewing tobacco did not taste like leaves, however, but instead was bitter. He gagged and almost threw up. Willie Grey suggested spitting some of it out just before throwing the baseball. That turned out to be a terrible idea, because he then almost swallowed the whole wad. He felt light-headed and slightly dizzy. Everybody laughed, including Buddy who, on the next pitch, hit a long home run.

Cynthia was not crazy, but she was a lonely spirit; one without much hope, or so it seemed. She battled all kinds of emotions and things never understood by others, but she remained a friend, someone who crossed Zachary Stevens' path, interceded into his journey in life, albeit for a short time.

One day she stood behind the fence in front of O'Brian's store and motioned for Zachary to come over. She had saved coupons from the tobacco pouches, and someone had helped her redeem them for a St. Louis Cardinals baseball hat. She gave it to him and said that it was a gift for the times he had helped her get things from the store. Zachary felt a lump in his throat and thanked her. That baseball hat remained with him for many years. Maybe it was a reminder of the goodness and strength of the human soul and spirit, given with no expectations but to only teach about the insanities, the unfairness, and the total incompleteness for some that life too often captures and enslaves.

Frank talked nonstop. A lot of what he said was difficult to understand and made little sense. Descriptions of hot weather were followed by comments: "Damn, I think I just saw my aunt go by in that truck. No, I think it was my long-lost brother."

He wore clothes that were colorful and included pink shirts and green pants; his hair was always slicked down with some type of greasy, smelly hair cream. His face was scarred with pimples, and he had teeth missing. The pills, given to him every morning after breakfast, made his arms and legs shake so much that he often could not control himself. His grocery store order was always the same: a pack of cigarettes, Camels, that cost twenty cents, and a pack of gum for five cents.

After he gave money to Zachary, he watched carefully to see where the kid went and, no doubt, was relieved when Zachary ran directly into the store. He called the kid "Curly." Questions were nonstop: "Did he like school? Was the war in Korea going okay? And, what was it like to live in Elm City?"

Frank thought the hospital was a place where there were too many rules to remember, the food was never any good, life was boring, and the only thing he looked forward to was the picture show on Saturday night. He likely would spend the rest of his life here, because he had no family and no identity;

Frank, a man struggling to search for a friend in a world where for him there were few, if any.

"Honey bun, you come over here this minute!" A tall, skinny Negro lady named Louise waved and called Zachary to the fence. She wore a large black pair of glasses that rested gingerly on a large nose, held together by a dirty piece of tape. She stood and yelled out that she wanted a Coke and a pack of Lucky Strikes and asked how he was doing, and when he asked the same question back, the reply was always, "Problems, problems, nothing but problems. This hospital is no good, but I ain't got no place to go. It's my home, my home for life. It's noisy, full of people who talk to themselves all the time. The fighting between other patients never stops."

Emotions inside of Zachary became jumbled and rolled around in his mind. He needed to say something, but what? He became temporarily frozen, partially out of disbelief, partially out of simple ignorance and naiveté.

She seemed so young, with such a long life ahead. How could she ever survive in a place for crazy people? Maybe, just maybe, someone would come and rescue her and take her far away—just fly her over that old green wrought-iron fence.

He gathered enough courage and told her of his dream to be a baseball player, and that someday he hoped and believed she would get out of the hospital. Louise looked at him, smiled ever so gently, and then walked away. Maybe she needed to hear a word of encouragement from somebody that she was a person to be cared about, important enough to hear some small aspect of another person's life. Louise's face has remained embedded in Zachary's mind for a lifetime. Maybe a smile of so long ago was a slight sign of resurrected thoughts and feelings so sensitive, but also ones never to be discussed with a teenage boy.

Nathan Russell was skinny but well-built, with a smile that stretched across his face from ear to ear. Teeth were perfectly straight, and when he smiled, whiteness radiated from his mouth, or so it seemed. He came down from his hospital ward, watched the gang as they played baseball, and clapped if good plays were made. What caught Zachary's attention was the guy's intense stare as he studied each of the individual gang's movements. He listened to every word said, and he seemed content to sit very quietly, lest he disturb a thinking process embedded into a sensitive mind

Someone from the gang asked if he had played ball before. He replied, "A long time ago." All thought he might be a good addition to play baseball with the gang, so outfield became his position. He had no mitt; they loaned him one. He easily caught balls and threw them back to the infield; good hand and eye coordination with speed and tracking ability was readily apparent. He had a strong arm that threw the ball back to the infield quickly. But when he came to bat, he appeared reluctant to swing and failed to hit the ball. The gang said they just knew he was going to get better, and they made an attempt to encourage him.

After the first game, however, a look of failure covered his face. He left and went back to his ward. Nothing more was said except, "Nathan, we all know you will do much better tomorrow." He was gone for several days, but then he came back with a smile and asked if he could play. This time, when he came to bat, he smashed the ball over the left field fence. It traveled fast, hit some tree branches, then arched off, and by the time one of the gang members jumped over the picket fence to retrieve it, Nathan proudly run the bases. Laughter and cheering erupted. Today, he was a hero because the homerun had won the game for his team. The gang had found a new friend, one who could hit, run, and throw a baseball. He needed a group of guys to tell him how much he was appreciated, and how much they wanted him on their team. He heard their positive comments. Life was good.

As the summer moved toward autumn, Nathan and Zachary became the best of friends. He told of growing up close to the downtown area of Indianapolis and quitting school after the sixth grade. When asked his current age, he laughed and replied, "Sixty." His family was large, and as a child he had slept on a floor that had rats all over the place. There were three brothers and two sisters, all of whom he had few proud memories of, who were out of the house early in his life. The father left the family before Nathan started school; the mother worked several jobs.

When he was ten, Nathan and two other boys robbed a store. All were caught and sent to reform school, except Nathan. As a first-time offender, he was put on probation. With a somewhat remorseful voice, he said, "There was a lot of hurt in my house because everybody was angry with life."

He continued to drink a lot of booze and take a variety of bad pills. Some made him feel full of energy, while others caused sadness and depression. It was not unusual for him to drink at least five or six beers and a half-pint of whiskey every day. Nathan's family eventually rejected him, and he was kicked out of the house. After he left home, he was in and out of reform schools, jails, and he was eventually declared by a court of law to be insane. He was sent to the Elm City Hospital and medical pills were given, although he did not know the names of the drugs. He felt better, thought the medicine helped, because he reported feeling less nervous and depressed.

But the pill treatment may have also caused certain problems. Zachary wondered why Nathan's hands and arms shook. "I gots used to a lot of the shakes; it is worse after I take my medication. But at least I was never 'experimented' on, my brain cut in some way to make me behave good. Other patients told me about some hospitals doing them kinds of things."

Zachary was astounded by this bit of information and asked Nathan to tell him more, like, "Did the surgery help?"

"I don't know, because I only heard stories. One patient who sleeps a couple of beds from me said he knew a guy in another hospital who had the top part of his brain operated on, and he never acted angry or fought with the attendants. But there was another guy who after the surgery never talked, or seemed do much of anything. Kinda like in was in some kind of 'zombie' state."

"Once a guy came back to the ward and said he had been 'brain shocked.' The staff had put a belt around him to keep him tied down. Some little buttons were stuck on his head, and then electricity was delivered through them to his brain. He reported strong tingling of some type in the top part of his head. A stick was placed in his mouth, so he would not swallow his tongue while his body twitched; the guy reported feeling sick to his stomach. Later, he reported a hard time talking; it was like he could think of what to say, but had trouble speaking it out. I guess by changing the brain in some way, the doctors thought they could make them voices go away. I don't know, it seems more like torture to me."

One hot summer evening, Zachary and Nathan sat under a large maple tree on the grounds of the state hospital. It was very quiet, and Nathan looked at Zachary for a long time without saying anything. Then he asked if Zachary could keep a secret.

"Of course."

He described that once after he drank heavily, passed out, and then woke up, he thought he heard a voice inside his head ask, "Do you feel tight? Other voices laughed, and one said: "You are no good and should jump off a rooftop."

As Nathan spoke to Zachary about these voices, it became apparent emotions had been triggered from inside. His face changed to sad and withdrawn, a face filled with perspiration. He then seemed to move around a lot, and it was obvious to Zachary that Nathan was upset.

For a long time, they said nothing, and then he quietly asked Zachary, "Do you believe me? Are you okay with what I just told you?" Zachary said, "Sure," but recounted that he had never heard voices in his head. Maybe he wasn't old enough. Nathan said that many people he knew, both from his home in Indianapolis and the state hospital, told him they had heard voices inside their heads—loud noises from unknown people who acted like they wanted to control everything the person thought, planned, or did.

When certain medication was taken, the voices he heard in his head left—perhaps they took a vacation—but they remained "on call" and came back, especially when he forgot his pills for any reason, or he got stressed out. Nathan confessed that he believed the devil was inside his body, and most likely demons as well; he felt helpless and possessed by evil.

"Many of the patients at the Elm City Hospital have been in the hospital for a long time, perhaps thirty years. Some of them have been put in the hospital when they were young, and simply left to live out their lives. Families were no longer able or interested in returning and visiting. Maybe they were too ashamed. When the patient died, the remains were placed in a small grave in a cemetery on one side of the hospital, and now God and his angels was in charge."

Zachary asked if Nathan missed his family.

Nathan appeared dazed for a minute. "My family don't want me, and I guess I don't want them. I have been in this hospital for about three years, and I guess it seems to be more like home than any place I've been. The food is no good, but I get to come out of my room and walk around the grounds and see people. I get to go to the dances on Friday night, and I got a girlfriend I like a lot. We always dance together, and she is real friendly. She lived in Gary before she came here. I really like seeing all of you guys playing baseball and talking about things. It makes me feel good inside, like somebody wants to talk and listen to me. It is lonely at times and hot inside where my bed is. I got nothing, so I don't expect nothing."

"Kinda like a prison," Zachary commented.

"We is grouped by age. It smells a lot, because many of the patients pee on themselves. Sometimes the attendant gets mad and starts shouting and cussing at all of us patients, but we can't help ourselves. I don't think we know if we is doing right or wrong. Maybe all them pills we take, or the shock treatment, is the reason. The beds are lined up against the wall in a great big room. I can shower and shit. In the morning we cleans the floors, and they make us throw this type of soap on the floor that smells and burns your nose, but I guess it keeps the place clean. I don't argue with nobody, cuz if you do, they will not let you go outside. One time they hit a guy in the mouth for talking back. I don't want no trouble."

More silence, and then Zachary decided the levity of conversation needed to lighten up a bit more. Talk might be directed about sports—how the gang really wanted to reassure Nathan that they wanted him to play ball with them every time there was a game. He had the talent, and they could see he was a guy who played to win. The SMG liked to see him smile and be happy, hear an all-familiar laugh.

"Everybody wants you to just be yourself."

At that stupid comment, the old guy's face broke out into a broad and genuine grin. "I like being with

you guys a lot. You all make me feel I am important.
I really want to do my best. Where I grew up, nobody
much cared about nothing except getting in trouble.
I never had no friends who would say nice things to
me. You have made me feel like I can plays with you
all. I have learned how to hit better, and I feel good
inside when we all laugh about each other, even
when we make mistakes. Sometimes I want to play
all day and wish the day would not go away. You all
are my best friends, and I trust you. I don't thinks I
will ever forget you."

Zachary felt emotion, something he could not
describe, certainly not understand. But what the
hell, it was all good, all for real.

A risk needed to be taken. He spoke very quietly
to Nathan and asked if a secret might be kept,
something personal.

"Sure."

Zachary awkwardly admitted that when he was
at bat, he was afraid of being hit in the head by a fast
pitch. To combat this emotion, as the pitch came
toward him, he would step back and quite often the
result was an untimely late swing that missed the
ball by inches. He was ashamed of this habit and
asked if Nathan might give him some tips.

Baseballs were first thrown slowly, hitting was
easy; and then velocity increased. The ball came in
and often struck Zachary's lower body or shoulders.
Some pain resulted, and Zachary would return to his
old habit and jump back on the next pitch.

A comment from the pitching mound: "You gots
to get hit a few times to lose your fear. Get down in
your stance and watch the hand that has the ball in
it. Don't take your eyes off the ball; follow it when it
leaves my hand. If you see the ball coming, keep your
eyes on it as it comes to the plate."

The two of them would stay until it was so dark,
they could hardly see each other. But there was good
news; hitting increased and fears decreased.
Sometimes, though, Zachary would swing and never

connect with the ball. He would become frustrated and yell out that he was going to quit and give up. Nathan smiled, and then told Zachary to "time out" and take some deep breaths. Baseballs were thrown again, but a little slower; improvement came.

When they took baseball breaks, conversations became scattered. Once, Nathan asked Zachary about his dad. A familiar story followed describing drinking and the confusion that he and his mother felt so many nights, especially when the old man disappeared with other women.

Nathan listened intently and said, "No matter how much other people hurt you or are mean to you, don't be like them, cuz it only makes you feel worse inside and then you might get in trouble. I know, because it has happened to me. Zachary, you got a long life ahead of you. I bet your mother wished that things would have worked out better for your family. Nobody likes to hear about a father who has disappeared or failed in life. I know I sure didn't about my old man. You can do better. You can learn not to do what your dad did. Don't give up on life! Never! Never! You are the kind who will survive in this tough world. I wish I believed in myself as much as I believe in you making it. Somebody told me a long time ago that I should never take my eyes off God. He will never fail you. I just wish the devil in me would leave and never come back."

One day in late October, one of the patients told Zachary that Nathan had been discharged from the hospital and sent back to Indianapolis. Zachary would never see or talk to Nathan again. He missed their talks, and a friend who had taken the time to help him understand life. For Nathan, that same fight for survival would always be much more difficult.

Zachary received a letter postmarked Indianapolis a few months after Nathan left the hospital. His baseball friend wrote about his loneliness. Most of his friends and family had failed him. They did not like to have a former crazy person living with them. He understood, and said to Zachary in his letter, "I will never forget how good all of you made me feel. You guys accepted me and understood me better than any of them dumb doctors, or even my own family. Maybe someday you will get an award in heaven for all the love and patience you showed me. I miss you, and I believe we will see each other again someday in a far-off place that will be so much better than where we are now. Your friend, Nathan."

Did the friendship with Nathan leave much of a legacy? Certainly, there were friendships and acceptance of disabilities. But there was more . . .

The summer of 1955 was one for the ages, at least in Zachary's mind. The time Nathan spent coaching the kid paid off, because a better baseball player developed, and his gang, the SMG, showed respect for his abilities.

Tryouts took place for the Elm City Pony-League baseball teams. During the player selections, Zachary hit a home run, and one of the coaches saw his hitting skills and running speed. He spent almost all his "draft money" for Zachary to be on his team. This over-paid financial draft allotment was to be a rather stupid mistake, because the amount of "money" left only bought younger players who were not very adept at fast pitch hardball.

The team on which Zachary played never won a game. It did, however, afford him the opportunity to play every position except catcher, to bat clean-up, and post a high batting average. During one game, he caught a line drive hit that began to arch over his head, and as he ran with his back to the infield, he jumped up and caught the ball bare-handed. Most likely all the stars in heaven were correctly aligned that night! More realistically, and others agreed, he could never have repeated that catch again. They were probably correct. But that never diminished the glow felt in heart and mind the night he made a catch of a lifetime. He held onto the memory and enjoyed it way too long; but then again, it was his and no one else's—one never to be taken away.

Later in the summer, the best players were chosen to play on an all-star team that represented Elm City at a district tournament in Fort Wayne. Zachary was chosen for the team, and for one of the starting nine that played its first game against a group from Kokomo.

The contest was played in a minor-league baseball park with a picket fence used to provide a demarcation for the smaller field for teenage boys. Zachary played left field and during the game got two hits. They won the game 8-4 and moved on to the quarter-finals.

Their next opponent, a team from Indianapolis, had strong hitters, and Elm City subsequently lost 6-2. Zachary got another hit and made no errors in the outfield. His mother came to the game and yelled out from the stands, "Come on, Stevens, hit a home run!" He wanted to disappear over the outfield fence, but because everybody laughed, he was persuaded to find some humor in the remark.

The "baseball star" had dreams, which started and ended with a most unlikely coach —one who showed interest in a kid who had no idea of the possible latent abilities he might have. "Coach Nathan," a man described by some as crazy, came into Zachary's world, touched it gently with good and real memories. If only a degree of self-confidence might have stayed around longer. It didn't. Zachary failed to continue to practice, and soon any hint of serious baseball skills slipped out the back door. Other interests took over, and Zachary Stevens' hope for baseball or any sports stardom was lost forever.

Nelson Manning was a muscular man who chewed tobacco—lots of it. He watched the gang play softball, but he never asked to join in. When the gang

needed additional players in the outfield, they pleaded with him to play, but he refused.

The gang remained persistent and kept asking; finally, he agreed. Most of the time he seemed confused, and he wandered around with a blank stare on his face. He was not good at catching or batting, plus he ran terribly slow. But he was an extra body, added extra forced merit.

One hot Sunday afternoon, Nelson came to bat with men on second and third base. The score was 2-1 in favor of the team fielding. Gale Rogers pitched, and there was a count of two strikes; a third strike and the game would be over. Gale delivered a fast ball right across the plate, and Nelson swung and surprisingly made contact. The ball soared high and into fair territory behind first base. Buddy Logan ran backwards to catch it, but he misjudged the ball's trajectory, and it fell out of his reach. Both runners scored, and Nelson's team won.

Game over.

Not quite.

Nelson ran around all the bases and went into home plate standing up. He collided with Jim Allan, the catcher, who wondered what the hell Nelson was doing! Buddy ran over and told Nelson that his hit had won the game, and that it was now time for everybody to go home. Suddenly, for no apparent reason, Nelson swung at Buddy, who then grabbed him around the shoulders. Cussing and swearing ensued, and Nelson threw Buddy to the ground.

The two were eventually separated. Buddy had a cut above his eye where Nelson had struck a blow. Gale tried unsuccessfully to get Nelson and Buddy to shake hands, but Nelson refused, continued cussing, and then he ran off.

The gang went home and stayed away for several days. They were worried of the ramifications if Nelson told a staff hospital person that he had been in a fight with some young kids at the softball field.

Nelson apparently kept his mouth shut; a good thing that the gang appreciated.

About a week later another baseball game was scheduled, and to their surprise, Nelson showed up. "I got angry the other day. I guess I thought everybody was laughing at me. I went back to my bed and took a rest. I want to play now."

It was apparent that Buddy still had feelings over the matter and felt a bit awkward, but tried his best to cover things up. "You hit me hard, and my eye hurt; but I am okay now."

Both might have wanted to apologize, but neither said anything, and a softball game started—neither looked at the other during the game. Afterwards, Zachary went over and spoke with Nelson.

"Are you still mad at Buddy?"

"Naw, not really," Nelson said. "I know he made me real mad, and I swung at him. I guess when he yelled at me, I thought he didn't like me. I didn't mean to hurt him. Is he okay? Does he want to fight some more? I felt bad and did not sleep for a couple of days. I remembered that I got in trouble when I was growing up; some guy said that I was stupid, and I became so mad that all I wanted to do was rip his head off, beat his face in with my fists. I started for him and suddenly his friends grabbed me and started hitting, kicking, and throwing me down on the ground. One guy kicked me in my side, and I could not breathe for a minute. They called me some names, and then they left. I got up and ran home. My dad was mad about what happened. He said it was my fault, and he took his belt out, and he beat me till I could not walk no more."

"I think Buddy wants to forget about what happened the other day," Zachary replied.

"Hey Nelson, how do you like living here in the hospital?" somebody asked.

"I don't like it here. I want to go back home to Evansville. I worked in the coal mines before I had my accident," Nelson replied.

"Accident?" Zachary inquisitively asked.

Nelson's face became remorseful and sad. "Before I came here, I fell down a mine shaft, knocked myself out, and went to sleep or something like that. When I woke up, I had trouble hearing, and I felt real sad inside. My parents did not know what to do with me. I was only eighteen. Some doctors checked me out, and they said I had mental problems and needed to go to the hospital to get rest. I came here fifteen years ago. My parents are both dead now, and I got no family. I sure wish I could go back home and work the mines."

"Do you think you will ever get out of this place? How do people who live at the hospital ever get well?" Zachary wondered.

Nelson then proceeded to tell an all-too-familiar story the boys had heard from other patients. "I should get out of here, because there is nothing wrong with me. A lot of people are crazy and belong here. I still feel sad, but not like I did a long time ago. I eat good and don't cause no trouble. I think there is something wrong with this place. They just like to keep people here, even if they want to go home. I sometimes feel angry and want to hurt somebody, but I think that would get me in more trouble, and then I would never get out."

Steve, for a change, had been quiet, but then he spoke up. "You seem okay to us. If you left the hospital, your great clutch hitting would be missed." Of course, that statement was a lie, but who cared? "I think it is wrong that the hospital wants to keep patients and never let them out. Why would they do that?"

Gale added, "You don't seem sad to me. You did hit the ball well the other day."

For a long time, nobody said anything. Then Nelson commented, "Yes, for all my life I have been alone, but you have made me feel like I belong and am part of a group of friends. That is more than I have when I go back to my room."

Buddy eventually mustered up enough courage to go and tell Nelson he was sorry he yelled at him. He congratulated Nelson on hitting the ball that won the game. Zachary never forgot the look on Nelson's face, and it made Zachary wonder if anyone had been a friend to Nelson. Buddy became that friend, and a group of kids bet it made a difference to both.

But not all the gang felt comfortable. Willie Grey and Dwight Allan said they were not sure they wanted to come back and play with these patients.

"They are too unpredictable. I am afraid that one of these guys will go nuts on us and really do some damage. Some of them appear strange, and their eyes look angry," Jim commented.

"Yeah, I am not sure that we should stay here and talk to these people. What if they go up and tell lies about us to the guards on their wards?" Dwight railed.

Steve then said, "The thing with Nelson won't happen again, and what he said today makes me think that he has his shit together."

Laughter at that remark moseyed up to the surface of consciousness, the nervous type, and certainly not unanimous in agreement for mixed softball games with mental hospital patients. But the kids decided to go forth, be risk takers, and learn more about life, even when some of it might reflect varying degrees of sanity mixed with insanity at numerous and complex levels of understanding.

Female patients might show up and watch the SMG play a meaningless game of hitting and catching a ball on a field of dirt and clay. Late one afternoon, Zachary had cleaned up the infield and run lines of white chalk that marked foul lines down to and past first and third base. The men's select softball team had a game at 7:00 PM. After he finished, a rather slender woman came up and sat next to the backstop and stared at him. She wore a plain red cotton dress with flowers printed all over, complemented by a large bow in her hair. A smile and, "Hello, my name is Karen."

Zachary noticed she had some missing teeth and large scars on the side of her legs. One of her feet appeared shriveled up, causing a noticeable limp.

"You come here often?" Zachary asked.

"I have been here in the hospital for a year. I come from Scottsburg. Do you know where that is?" Karen replied.

Zachary was somewhat caught off guard and stammered, "No, I really have not learned all of the towns in Indiana. I bet it is north of here, maybe close to Lake Michigan."

An incorrect guess. "No, it is south of Indianapolis, not too far from the Kentucky state line. I have lived there all my life. I came here when my parents died in a fire."

"A fire?" Zachary replied. Now she had his attention.

Her face looked sad, eyes noticeably red. A voice trembled. Emotion was apparent. Karen continued: "Yes, a few years ago fire broke out in a small stove we had in the back of our house. It was old, and part of the bottom came off. We did not know that it was broken until smoke came into the room. By then the whole house started to burn. My dad tried to stop the fire, but part of the roof came down on top of him. My mother passed out, and I didn't know what to do, so I ran out of the house and over to my neighbor's place. I was scared.

"The policeman came, and a lot of people asked questions. Before all of this happened, I had gone to school, but the teachers said I was not real smart and I should stay at home and get my parents to teach me. So, I did. I was fourteen. My parents died in the fire. After they were buried, I went to see a man who was dressed in a black robe who sat behind a large desk. He said that I could go to a special place where I would be happy again and learn to read. So, they sent me here. But I don't like this place; it is full of women who scream and cry at night. It smells, and at times I see things that scare me."

"Like, what do you mean? What scares you?" asked Zachary.

Karen smiled just a little and said, "I see people staring at me, and sometimes it is like they are laughing at everything I do. I can hear them making fun of me, and saying things like, 'She is dumb.'

The doctors say that if I take some pills, I won't see these people anymore. When I take the pills, I just get dizzy and my mouth feels funny, like I can't talk; and I just shake all over. I wish these people that say that I am dumb would just go away and leave me alone."

Willie Grey inquired, "Do you have any friends that ever come here to see you?"

"I had a neighbor who came to see me about a year ago. She was a lot older, and she had someone drive her to the hospital. She told me that I was looking old and worn and was worried about my health. But I think I am going to be okay, if I could just get back home."

Gale asked if she did any work at the hospital.

"I work in the cleaners. It is real hot there, and the other ladies are sometimes mean and make fun of me. The boss yells, and I don't get much money. Once a couple of ladies began to argue over some money, and one of them took a hot iron and tried to burn the other lady's hand. Then some of the women started fighting, and the boss lady had to call the police people to come and get everybody calmed down. I heard someone say they had a dungeon for bad people, and they would go there if they misbehaved. I don't feel that this is a good place for me. I want out."

She stood alone with a cigarette in her mouth and leaned against the side of a building next to the gym.

Zachary noticed her one night, and decided he wanted to talk with her.

The lady was pretty, even without any makeup; jet black hair and taut, tan skin with very few wrinkles. Jewelry adorned her neck and hands and appeared to sparkle, at least to a kid with no knowledge of such accoutrements. A smile, ever so slight, revealed perfectly straight teeth with the reddest of red lipstick. Rich-smelling perfume aided romantic fantasies for the kid. Might one guess that a couple of sensual demons were on assignment to destroy Zachary's virginity? Help! Were there any Godly angels around? Spiritual testing was in the air! Surely, God would come to the rescue.

Kay related that home was Indianapolis. Her husband worked at a bank near an area called "the Circle." They had one child and a very unhappy marriage, often punctuated with lots of arguments. The plain truth was that the husband eventually got tired of the turmoil and wanted to throw Kay out of the house. Lawyers were employed to get her committed to the state hospital in Elm City for an evaluation. The husband's scheme did not work, because the attorneys were not able to persuade the judge that she was potentially insane, so no evaluation was ordered.

One night, however, the couple had a scuffle, and she stabbed him in the arm. This time the husband got his wish, and she was sent to the Elm City State Hospital for mental testing. That was three months ago. She had only recently been allowed off the ward to socialize with other patients.

"Most of the movies they show here are not good. They are old ones that I saw years ago. But I like to get out and just feel life beyond the walls of my ward." She sounded despondent.

Zachary asked her, "What is the hospital like?"

"I live on a ward in an old section of the hospital that must have been built a hundred years ago. There are large rooms with many beds, but some patients have separate rooms. Where I reside, there are many beds crammed into a small space. It is hot, and it smells, and there are all kinds of patients with many different problems. Some of them laugh or cry all day. Others just sit and stare and say nothing. Some seem to shake and twitch their hands and legs all the time. Many of the patients have saliva dripping from their mouths. Every morning, for a few minutes, I go out for a walk, and then go work in the bakery.

"Nobody tells me much of anything. I have taken tests and answered questions about myself and explained why I stabbed my husband. It is noisy all the time, and the food is awful. I do like the vegetables. I think they are grown on some farm around here. You know something? I will tell you a secret. I don't want to go back home.

"My husband wants me to become a Jew. How can I do that, when I don't even believe in God? If there is a God, how could He allow a place like the Elm City Hospital to exist? Maybe I am wrong. Maybe there is a God, and this place protects people who are crazy or in some way hurting. I don't know. Where I grew up, my parents told me not to believe in anything like a God. They told me that there may have been a God in the beginning, but now He has become angry with all the people and because of the complete mess this world is in. So, He has gone to some other place and started a new world where people are kind to each other, and there are no voices in people's heads. I feel I don't have a home anywhere."

"If the attendants weren't looking, would you run away?" Zachary asked half-jokingly.

Kay answered immediately, "No, because I have no place to go; and if I got caught, I would just be sent back here. I think I am in worse shape after being here for three months than I was before I came in. My biggest fear is that I will never be set free—I will never get out."

263

Zachary then asked, "What would you do if you got out?"

"I would move to Chicago; yes, to Chicago, and get a job somewhere. I went to La Cone University for three years before I got married. I wanted to be an accountant. Maybe I might find a part-time job and go to night school. Other people start over with their lives. Maybe, I will someday find out about God. I guess anything is possible. I wish I didn't have to go back to the ward tonight. It is going to be hot, and the woman next to me laughs all night."

She then began to cry very softly, and Zachary did not notice how she was partially studying him very intently. He had become distracted now, dealing with a moderate amount of pain in a sexual part of his body.

The kid knew he was out of his league; perhaps out of his mind with uncontrollable sexual urges. He must console Kay, but he didn't know how she might respond. So, more rich fantasies and dreams entered for presentation and temptation purposes:

He would causally walk over and look directly into her eyes as he put his arms around her. She would respond by taking her hand and arm and placing it around his neck while pulling his face to hers; maybe, she might gently pull him to the ground, and they would then be hidden by a ten-foot thicket of bushes. Nothing would be said, but she would show with her hands and teach fundamentals. He would learn quickly and respond. Two lonely people would find an emotional closeness which had been missing in both of their lives; for a young kid, the beginning of a new education about life, sex, and passion; for a scorned woman, the validation of still-present emotional needs and sanity, support, and acceptance.

A lot of noise and people came out of the gym after seeing a stupid movie of little consequence. Kay and Zachary stood awkwardly and looked at each other very quietly. A group of ladies appeared, inane conversations about nothing flew around like hot air, and a then a grand disappearance act by all patients, including Kay

Zachary was left with a preserved reputation and a lot of uncomfortable physical feelings. He must see her again. Things had ended too abruptly. It would never happen. Kay got her wish sooner than expected—a discharge, and the start of a new life in Chicago.

———◇———

Dwight Allan ran home one evening after a softball game, eyes focused straight ahead as if he was in a race for his life. He often felt this way, but if you were to ask him about his thoughts, he would be clueless. Then a patient appeared juggling small bowling pins.

"Hey buddy, come here for just a minute. I have some tricks to show you," shouted a tall guy with a lot of red hair.

Dwight, somewhat reluctantly, ran over and said, "Let's see what you got."

The guy, dressed rather shabbily in old faded jeans and a ragged t-shirt, proceeded to take some cards out of his pocket and ask Dwight to pick one. He did, and then he placed it back in the deck as requested.

"Do you remember the card?" asked the guy.

"Yes," replied Dwight.

Then the cards were shuffled, and suddenly the guy pulled out a five of diamonds.

"That was the card," affirmed Dwight. "How did you do that?"

The guy said nothing, smiled, and then pulled out the bowling pins and again began juggling them.

"Why are you a patient here?" asked Dwight. The guy just ignored the question and kept juggling. He eventually stopped and said that he had some small coins, and then without further ado rapidly moved them through the fingers of his right hand, crossed his left hand over the right, placed them out palms up and displayed no coins; then he reached behind Dwight's left ear and presented him with a shiny quarter.

"Show me how you did that trick?"

"Nope, it's a secret, and besides you would never understand about the invisible forces of magic."

Dwight again asked, "Why are you here at the hospital?"

The guy looked at Dwight for a long time, and his face took on a mournful appearance.

"You have no idea what pain is like. How lucky for you to never care about anything but a good time. I hurt inside and see little hope that anything will ever change for me."

He then jumped up, face now rapidly changing to anger, and he gave Dwight the finger and ran away, shouting something unintelligible. Dwight, caught off guard, thought for a minute and wondered more about the mysterious magician. What was his story . . . ?

Five years earlier:

The noise from the carnival rides, plus the rich smells of oil and exhaust from non-stop pumping machines, overwhelming to mouth, eyes, nose, and ears, was all good. A kid, tall for his age and with his father, walked slowly around grounds, carefully studying all the excitement.

"Dad, there is so much energy here. The smell of cooking food and people yelling out to other folks. I wish I could stay here and work, be part of this community. I have done what you and Mom asked and finished high school. I hated every minute of it, the teaching, the 'blab, blab, and blab.' I could never concentrate and study. All I ever wanted was to get out on my own. Let me join this carnival!"

Sadness slowly worked its way up from heart and soul to the reticent brain of an older, wiser man, one who knew honesty so well.

"When I was your age, I felt the same way. A circus came to town, and I ran away and hitched myself to its passing train's flat car while a couple of workers helped me get on. I became a part of that circus for many years, a clown and a magic entertainer. You have learned all the tricks I ever knew, plus some of your own improvisations. I will miss you, and I know if your mom was still alive she would also, but now run and be part of what will make you happy. Call, write, and come back when you can; peace, my son, to you always."

And so, this lanky red-headed kid started a new life. He fared well for awhile, loved entertaining kids who watched in wonderment at his magic, making things appear and then disappear. Then, trouble—at first the money he stole was small, change here and there from the clothes of unsuspecting comrades working like him for such a small salary. Food was sparse and costly. He needed to survive. But then the habit began to overwhelm him, and he found it relatively easy to not only take small amounts of money from the clothes of fellow employees, but also from customers careless with how they placed wallets in their back pockets as they innocently stood gawking at rides and people, not paying any attention to their surroundings. Hands were quick and light. It was not unusual to make fifty to seventy-five dollars on a weekend. Life was now more than just good; it was fantastic. Then a drastic turn for the worse . . .

The red headed kid dressed in street clothes quickly removed a billfold from some fat guy with farmer-like overalls, an easy pick. Suddenly, a strong hand grabbed his wrist and refused to let go. The kid then did something exceedingly stupid. He drew a knife and stabbed the guy in the arm, resulting in a superficial cut. Commotion, fighting, and pushing ensued, with finally the owner of the carnival called. He arrived and separated all parties, apologized, and then said, "I'll handle the problem."

Two disparate souls, one leading, the other following, appearing in some pain, sought refuge in a broken-down trailer, the carnival's administrative headquarters.

"What the f%^#$ were you thinking, you idiot?"

Silence

"I am going to have to call the police. You are through working here. Do you understand?"

Response: Only head movements.

"If I tell them what you did, you will first go before a judge, and more than likely you will get jail time at Stateville, where the prisoners are hungry for kids like you. But I am going to do you a favor. When the police come, I will lie for you and tell them I think you are crazy and not responsible. You were told to take that billfold by the devil."

"Do you understand?"

"Yes."

"Can you act like a crazy person"?

"Yes."

"We are close to Elm City, where there is a mental hospital. I know some people there that might help out. Tell the doctors you heard voices in your head that told you to stab the guy to protect yourself. The criminal system must be avoided at all costs."

And so, this surreal scene was played out well by two carnival participants—a sometime magician, sometime thief; and a boss man. Both played their parts well, and an insane asylum got an "insane" magician. Confinement was easy; grounds privileges were given and punishment in the dungeon avoided; a young kid became careful and obedient. He would eventually get out of the hospital and disappear into society. For now, patience must be a virtue.

As Dwight continued his walk home, an awakened, honest feeling and thought appeared for digestion: *he really wanted to see that guy again. But why?* Maybe he would encourage him to do his tricks and give the guy a friendly smile. Tell him how good he was at entertaining and making people feel good. But maybe it didn't matter; weren't they just patients anyway? Who cared?

Dwight's mother, who worked at the clothing shop within Elm City State Hospital, had previously spoken about the elderly lady patients who were assigned to spend their days stitching and sorting clothes. "They seemed normal, some just a little forgetful at times. Yes, some of them might have been in other worlds and said strange things but most were no different than my own mother, who is sweet, gentle, and always interested in friendships." Mrs. Allan often wondered aloud if many of these patients had been assigned to hospital wards for reasons other than a diagnosis of insanity; maybe old age and no place to live, or people, "just not a good fit for our society, people who had families that didn't want them anymore." Could it be that within this mix of humanity was a red-headed kid who dreamed of an exciting life, and maybe got more than he ever bargained for?

Mr. Barton, a local businessman in Elm City, played trumpet and led the dance band at the hospital. How he became involved in such leadership endeavors was never revealed and most likely of little importance. People had nicknamed him Kickers, a title which never made any sense. The guy was slightly pudgy, rarely shaved, had a robust laugh, and most importantly had a gentle way with people. Clothes worn included a slightly dirty shirt, a pair of wrinkled dress pants, and socks that often did not match. He was a true musician.

Gale Rodgers took a chance one night and asked Kickers some musical questions, and if he might sometime be allowed to play in the band. Efforts were appreciated, and encouragement was given to a young boy by allowing him to at first hang around the dance band.

Since Gale played clarinet, he was paired with a tall, slender guy described as playing a mean horn. Gale had no idea what that descriptor meant, but what did it matter? One other fact of little relevance: The guy's name was Charles, and he was currently a patient at the hospital who suffered from a disease of highs and lows. That was okay with Gale, because he was more interested in learning how to play notes and read sheet music than think about mental behavior.

These two musicians would arrive before dance concerts and review sheet music. Gale listened as Charles played additional notes to sort of "jazz up" musical pieces. He was good artist, an encourager for Gale—a friendship in the making.

"Did you practice the notes I showed you the other day?" asked Charles

"Sure did, and I like the way you rewrote some of those notes. But I still can't move through certain sections of music and hit all of those higher ones."

"Keep practicing. It's all in the movement, you gotta feel the movement. Let me show you an easier way to hold your clarinet by shifting part of your shoulder as you move around in your seat; it takes some of the stress off your whole body."

Charles told Gale that he needed to learn to not be so uptight and nervous. "Relax and enjoy yourself, and just feel the music all around you, kinda like it's gathering you in."

One day, however, after first meeting to practice, something appeared puzzling to Gale. At first Charles began joking around, clapping his hands and talking non-stop. Gale initially just ignored the behavior, but when the director arrived, Charles was asked not to participate that night.

Some angry words were then exchanged, and Gale noticed a look in Charles' eyes that he had not seen before, one of intense anger. Charles started swearing and became more agitated. He screamed out that people were all against him, and then he threw a chair out onto the dance area. Several attendants "helped" Charles back to his hospital room. Gale was frightened and felt somewhat relieved when Kicker explained that some new medicine had been tried on Charles, and it was apparently not working.

Of course, Gale really didn't understand any of this talk about medicine and strange behavior, but he was glad that Charles had been relieved of his duties for that night. He continued playing solo, not daring to try any improvisation, and was complimented on a job well done, even though some confusion about prior events remained as an unwelcome guest.

Later, when Gale went home and told his dad about what had happened, further music activities with the patients were ordered stopped. A dejected Gale asked Kicker to come over to his house one evening and persuade the family to let Gale rejoin the band. Persuasions and arguments were in vain.

Charles was eventually seen around the hospital grounds from time to time, but never acknowledged or spoke to Gale again. A sad commentary in which Gale lost the opportunity to learn any more music from Charles, but maybe even worse was the loss of a friendship.

There was one positive memory that occurred several years later at a high school football game. Gale had played in the band one night, and a couple who worked at the State Hospital came up and asked him if he had not once played for a jazz band. Gale said he had, and they reminded him of how much they enjoyed his music, especially when he was backed by some skinny guy who played like Benny Goodman. Gale smiled, and just so briefly with emotion remembered a teacher and a student in such a different time and place. He thought about Charles and wondered what might have happened to him. Zachary had heard rumors about the patient, but had the good sense to keep his mouth shut. Perhaps, for Gale, it was a good thing he never learned of Charles' suicide by hanging.

Years later, Zachary, now as an adult, would remember that rumor of suicide and realize that like the history and narrative of sexual deviant behavior, at least during the '50s, people rarely talked about or understood such complicated issues. Why would anyone take their own life? Would not God be mad and refuse entrance into heaven? How could a person ever become so discouraged that he or she would give up on the many challenges afforded them from and in such a unique, but also unexplained and unpredictable cosmos? The internal pain these individuals must have felt had to be unbearable to contemplate such an act. Zachary recalled that after his parents divorced, once and only once, he got the idea that his sadness would go away if he tried to hang himself or jump from a tree. The idea, however, quickly went away.

Suddenly, a trace memory popped up, and Zachary remembered something from long ago about one patient at the Elm City State Hospital for the Insane. The whispers were faint, but hauntingly real.

The woman's name was lost to the ages, but her face came back into Zachary's mind. He remembered that she had long hair, and eyes that were beyond just sad. She cried easily and spoke words filled with sincerity, but containing little hope or care for survival. Happiness was never part of her life, and she never fit in with any part of a family or friends. Bouts of thick sadness surrounded her all the time, leading to tears that refused to dry up and stop wetting a fearful face. But why did she feel this complex and hopeless way? She said she had no idea. Counselors and other mental health professionals were claimed to have been involved, but to no avail.

The woman talked at length about being "consumed" with thoughts of finding a way to end her misery. Perhaps she might try hanging, or overdosing on pills, or a gunshot to the head, the quickest way. But she settled on placing her head in an oven and experiencing sleep and then complete freedom.

She had made several attempts and discovered that just thinking about killing herself seemed to give her more motivation to complete the task. There were times when she thought she heard voices, or at least got ideas from deep within herself that seemed to be directing, encouraging, and even deriding her hesitancy to "get on with it." She prided herself on her selection of method— quiet, painless, and easy.

Once, she stuck her head way back in the oven close to the gas jets, and the smell of gas at first seemed pleasant enough. But then she became sick to her stomach, and her nose burned; feelings of lightheadedness, a ringing in her ears, and then pictures in her mind of her parents calling to her, motioning her to come to them. She took her head out of the oven, only to discover that her mother had been observing from afar. More mental health evaluations were done, and then a mandated order to admit her to the Elm City Hospital.

The stay at the hospital was beneficial. There was found a slight bit of hope for life, not giving up or into internal thoughts. A support for her was a friend she met at the hospital, a lady who had similar problems and challenges. The two talked and comforted each other.

Zachary thought about this sad, troubled, and lost woman; and he had questions now, even at adulthood, about that lady of long ago and if she ever made it through life and its many difficulties. There were doubts, but just maybe a trickle of hope too.

Joe Gruneau, the gang member with so much brain power, ran so fast that he almost tripped on a broken branch from an elm tree. Jerry, Buddy, and Bob Allan were ready to go home after playing fungoes. Joe shouted out, "I have some news!"

He told them about a patient he just met who was neat—a stock car driver from somewhere around the city of Terre Haute. Apparently, the guy had been in an accident and had been knocked unconscious. He had lost some of his memory but was now in recovery. The strange part, according to Joe, was the guy described that right after the accident, a black-looking spirit with many eyes and many wings flew around and above his head. When he mentioned this to the staff at the local hospital, he was immediately transferred to the Elm City Hospital, where medicine was started to keep the unwelcomed guest away.

The patient's family brought their son pictures of things from his house, so that he could relearn the names of objects. There were illustrations and drawings of tools, both simple and complicated; types of instruments, many of which he had difficulty naming. Even when they brought the actual tool, and he handled it, he had problems saying its name, but interestingly, he smiled as he touched the items.

Most of his words either made no sense or were not clearly enunciated. Sometimes when he became excited or frustrated, his speech was reduced to stuttering, emotions apparent. Joe was told that the part of the patient's brain that helped him speak was "not working well, at least not yet." Joe and Jim Allan helped the guy learn to say the names of things written on the back of the pictures. From that interaction, a friendship developed—a friendship Joe had told no one about, until now.

The patient's dad came up from Indianapolis, and he had arranged for the two of them to take short trips to a local garage to work on engines and racing cars. Elm City had a small track on the west side of town. Joe was asked to come along, and he agreed.

The smile on Joe's face said a lot; he had a new friend who needed a "jump start," or a new lease on life. Joe also learned about racing stock cars, and over time how to work on flathead engines in the pit using tools with strange names. Joe found a friend, an attachment, and maybe a small purpose and confidence in a growing boy's life.

For him, the dividends paid were priceless.

And then there were other patients—very different ones—some who caused embarrassment, and others who stirred curiosity.

Grandpa was an old guy. He came down and watched the gang play baseball; he often chewed tobacco and spit it everywhere. He talked to himself, and then suddenly would drop his pants and pee. On more than one occasion he would motion to one of the gang members to go into the bathroom with him. At first everyone tried not to laugh, and instead simply ignore him.

"We need to do something about Grandpa. It does not seem that any of the attendants even care what he is doing down here," Gale frustratingly said one day.

Zachary agreed, "Yeah, I know. I have tried to talk to him, but he just keeps spitting tobacco, and he has never listened to me."

"Do you think if we all tried to talk to him, he might pay attention?" Jerry asked hesitantly.

Then Buddy had an idea. "Maybe what we could do is grab his hand when he starts to lower his pants and make him pull them back up."

Zachary had doubts. "I don't think that would work, and we might get in trouble for being too close to a patient."

Steve came up with another, more novel move. "Let's make a circle around him and yell out together real loud, 'No!' the next time he starts to lower his pants."

Jim warned, "We should not laugh at him. This plan may take several times to work."

Joe and Dwight were extremely skeptical. "The whole thing sounds stupid to me. I want no part of it. You guys are full of it."

The rest of the gang, however, was determined to try Steve's plan. "The heck with Joe, let's give it a try," some weak voice responded from the periphery.

The next day Grandpa showed up and wandered around the water fountain. The kids had been practicing bunting slow-pitched baseballs, when suddenly Grandpa dropped his pants. The gang ran around him and cried out in very loud voices, "No, No, No!"

Grandpa pulled his pants up and mumbled something no one could understand. The gang then played an intense game of hardball. When they finished, Grandpa was gone. He never came back.

"Tinker" was slender and skinny like a rail, a middle-aged man who truly resembled a piece of a tinker toy. Sometimes he ran and stopped, and then he made odd facial grimaces, ran again, stopped for a long time, and then watched the SMG play. He talked very fast, and none of his conversation made any sense. The gang tried not to giggle, but it was difficult, if not impossible. They knew it was wrong to make fun of him, but they were also sure he had no idea what was going on, or that he much cared.

"That guy is really different. He can't stop talking. He moves a mile a minute; I don't mean to laugh at him, and I feel bad that he is like that," Joe admitted with some embarrassment.

Zachary agreed. "We all do. How can we stop laughing at him?"

"Maybe we should thank God that we are not like him. Then I bet we would not laugh," Jerry volunteered.

Steve disagreed. "I don't think it will work. What is God going to do for us, a bunch of kids just trying to grow up and stay out of trouble?"

Jerry defended, "Somebody in the church I go to told all of us that there are people not lucky in life, and things we can't explain happen. We should be considerate of him, and then maybe we will stop laughing." It was then suggested by Gale that the whole gang try to get to know Tinker better when he came back to watch them play again. Zachary inquired, "Are we going to do it?" The whole gang then replied, "Yeah, at least we should try."

Tinker did not come around for several days, and then one day, as if by accident, he appeared while sides were being chosen for a softball game. He ran around, up and down the right or left field lines, and he made an odd sound and motioned as if he had an engine attached to his back. The gang looked at each other, went over, and with no laughter asked if he would play catch with them. His face became sad, and Zachary thought he saw a tear in his eye. For just a minute, it appeared that he might come and play. Then for some unknown reason, he stretched his arms out as if he was an airplane, made another, even stranger sound, and ran off through a grove of trees and disappeared. Like Grandpa, he too never returned.

One patient the whole gang fell in love with was a young girl named Lois. She was very pretty, and all the gang fantasized about catching her attention. They hoped she would come down every time they played softball.

Zachary and Bob tried to talk to her and impress her. She smiled and said nothing. One day she told all of them that she was in the hospital for an evaluation because of her addiction to prostitution. Gale joined the gang later that day, and the gang asked him what that word meant. He replied that she would agree to have sex with a person if they paid her money. Buddy asked, "What does that have to do with mental problems? Why would someone pay for sex? I thought it was free, especially after you got married, but before too." Not clear, certainly no rational answers were forthcoming.

Lois, like so many of the patients, simply disappeared one day. But the stubborn dreams about her stayed around with much intensity. Fantasies, it seemed, refused to leave, because they were just too satisfied to remain in fertile young minds that welcomed them and enjoyed their presence. Certainly, one SMG member named Zachary Stevens understood and appreciated that sentiment!

The sun had finished its job for the day and had completely disappeared behind the red brick buildings at the Elm City State Hospital. Evenings came earlier now than when school let out in May. It was still hot with little rain, but Zachary knew that autumn would soon arrive. The leaves from the maple trees did not look as green, as alive, as they had in the spring. Their colors were mixed, and some had a faded tint of green with just a hint of yellow. There would be a gallant fight as colors changed, but yellow and orange would be predominant, maybe a fitting victory for the leaves before they dried up and disappeared with the cold of winter.

This long summer, Zachary learned a lot about human nature—the need all people have for acceptance, to be loved, and to be appreciated. Patients from the state hospital, Nathan, Nelson, Cynthia, and Kay had become his friends.

But there were also others who lived in the massive buildings—patients who yelled out from their bar windows and cried and said things Zachary failed to understand, and certainly never mentioned to anyone. He sensed their pain, and he felt ashamed. How could he or anybody really help people so out of luck with life?

Many years later, Zachary relieved some of those feelings when he read a book entitled *God Knows His Name* (1), and heard a song, *John Doe Number 24* (2).

(1) Bakke, Dave, (2000), "God Knows His Name" Southern Illinois University Press, Carbondale, Illinois.

(2) Mary Chapin Carpenter, (1994), "Stones in the Road," Columbia Records, New York, NY.

Both book and song reminded him of other places he had spent his early life, growing up as an innocent and immature kid learning about life through the eyes of the patients from Elm City State Hospital.

The book told the story of a deaf Negro man committed to state hospitals, and although ignored, he lived to survive a harshness and hell for forty-eight years until his death. The song's lyrics were never accurately remembered, but the haunting melody penetrated both mind and soul, while words told about the hard times of a Negro boy with no hearing and no sight, and maybe very little mind; certainly, he was motherless, fatherless, and homeless, with a restless and wild spirit taken to many ports of call. He had been captured and placed in many different mental hospitals, where lots of questions were asked but never answered, and while others looked on with pity and not much else, this man with the name of "John Doe" exemplified the mystery of life and its unfairness and unforgiving nature. He truly was like "an old and worn orphaned glove from the lost and found, always missing its mate."

But here comes a victory: John Doe made a valiant attempt to survive in a world he never understood, and only a few understood him. He made friends, learned humor, communicated in some fashion, and even worked for many years within cold hospital walls. John lived out one of life's important truths—finding and developing an inner strength that was powerful enough to refine both a spirit and soul that remained together, compliant and satisfied.

There were many "John Does" at the Elm City Hospital. Zachary and his gang met them and learned of their struggles to find a new day, and a new hope. Zachary remembered what someone long ago told him. "We are here for such a short time on this earth that we must make each day count."

The SMG travelled on sidewalks, through open hospital gates, and climbed over green, wrought-iron fences into an insane world. They played sports, had fun, and then took those same sidewalks back out into a world that John Doe and so many others never knew, never found. What did Zachary and the SMG take from these patients' worlds of lost people, people who might have been closer to the gang emotionally and spiritually than they might want to admit? Many questions and a lot fewer answers; but maybe gratitude, hope, and forgiveness lightly danced around the borders and edges of the sanity and insanity the boys observed, and rarely did these "dancing partners" ever give more than a slight whisper to be observed and felt.

But even the most precious and oddest of experiences had to end, move on, and change heart and spirit. As Zachary and his buddies began their last years of high school, they saw less and less of each other. Girls became more popular and stole away a lot of hearts, minds, and souls. Some of the gang procured jobs after school as carhops, or sold cheap clothes at Woolworths and John Green, while others played out their last great baseball or track fantasies on the Elm City Crimsons school team.

The gang could not wait to get out of the hick town of Elm City and discover themselves. Some planned for college, others for the Marines, Navy or Air Force. There was little time now for hospital patients, softball, or secret talks in a largely ignored, weed-infested clubhouse. Young men were on their way to make their mark on a big and, at least to them, a very unproven world.

In a far-away place, angelic commentaries . . .

"Those SMG kids have wasted their youth talking and interacting with crazy people; But at least they stayed away from the heavenly realm, the belonging to God and Jesus and becoming 'born again.' What nonsense!" That Jerry kid, though, managed to avoid our attempts at tantalizing his soul. But we are still working on him. A whole life is still to come, and the entire bunch of kids is a rich target," said several angry and sullen evil spirits. "We will have many opportunities to continue to work and implant OUR OWN design in each of them."

But then a counter-argument is made by a few good angels expressing their own observations of the SMG.

"Human beings are frustratingly complicated and unpredictable in much of their behavior. They are disadvantaged at birth, because both good and evil are contained within the same body. When they are children, they act foolish. Their major redemption is a capacity, as they grow older, to learn and change beliefs about themselves and others. Through this maturing, a more complete meaning of forgiveness, mercy and grace allows a coming out for God and more spiritual things. They will always remember much about their boyhood and keep positive memories of being 'help-mates' and expressing support and caring for others, the patients at the Elm City Hospital. The South Main Gang was more than lucky for their growing experiences, never lost but rather slowly savored, honored, and made relevant. We have hope for them . . . but still, we are at times bothered by seemingly facetious behavior. Why won't or why can't that Zachary kid hear God loudly pounding on the veil separating human from spiritual mindsets? If only he would learn to listen!"

Nine:
The South Main Gang Shall Rise Again

Memories of a boyhood become increasingly alive and real,
Hearts, minds and souls on display, totally unsealed;
A gang of kids has grown up and gone so many ways,
While never forgetting the good old days.

ZACHARY'S BOYHOOD GANG, his friends, and their adventures are now gone, exited stage left. They taught him much—the way to listen, to joke, and even when to keep a mouth shut. The memories, some good and some not so good, still hang around and expect to be acknowledged, made to feel important, maybe even when they are not.

The years have chased by with no apologies. Now, at adulthood, he thinks more than he would like to admit about the SMG and his innocent childhood in Elm City, Indiana. Life is now drawing down—a curtain slowly closing. Those "buddies for life" were his first memories of his own existence—they were more than just temporary friends, but "forever friends." Trust and acceptance came easy during childhood, when there were no facades and no hidden agendas to deal with, the kind so maliciously present at adulthood with its complexities and falsehoods. The events of Zachary's childhood are seared into a mind and soul, never to leave, but instead to be there on call for tender and warm memories.

Yes, it is true, the little boys from Elm City have grown up. They have become husbands, fathers, working professionals; some have been successful in marriage, some less so. They are no longer kids who once argued if a baseball pitch was a strike, or wondered if Ramona White honestly wanted their love in a distant and hidden patch of weeds; humorous considerations, yes; and totally unimportant, yes too. Or maybe not!

Certainly, growth and maturity are noble achievements, even when most success in life is likely made up of stupid luck and good genes. But why can't there be some reward for those rare individuals who hold on to innocence and keep a childish spirit, allow a small trace of humor to remain about life and not take it so seriously? Maybe it is hyperbole to imagine living in a bubble where there is only one pleasant memory, and you live it forever. But it is equally senseless to live in a cage of hurts, failures and disappointments, where life is just a field of depression, one stroke from incapacitation from everything.

These boys, the SMG, saw many things as they moved through childhood. People came in and out of their lives with a cacophony of feelings, twisted minds, and untold demons, none of which the gang could have ever *truly* understood; what they did hear or see were ever so slight whispers and shadows as they moved from the *insanity* of observable behaviors to the *sanity* of a more "inner respect," the caring and acknowledgement of imperfections everyone is crowned with, like or agree with it or not.

David Wright, Zachary's neighbor, friend, and partial SMG member, eventually stopped his visits to Elm City. His reasons for not returning were unknown. Maybe he just grew older and found more friends in his hometown. But within the winds of time, there was the excitement of a first sexual experience ever so quietly and confidentially written across the pages of time. It could be debated, but for Zachary, that experience David had in a red shed "grew" a needy kid in many ways, especially social competence. And more—there was the demonstration of character development when David modeled for others the acceptance of the disabilities of his two deaf parents. Jim Allan saw something in David that must have influenced a coming of his own career. A small light still shines through a corner of Zachary's mind, detailing a friend with the blackest of hair, a smile and laugh that was sincere and honest, still heard at the most unexpected of times.

⁂

Jerry Little became a preacher at a small church in Dale City. He heard a spiritual voice early in his boyhood that the rest of the gang either never heard, or failed to pay much attention to. He once told Zachary that the hospital patients made him feel more complete, more forgiving, although when pressed to explain, he often whimpered. Jerry had many questions about those patient-reported voices emanating from within their own heads. It likely was of consequence when patients such as Nathan spoke of things that few understood. An unexplained dichotomy existed between what Jerry witnessed— struggling human beings with mixed-up brains — and the spiritual possibilities of evil demons responding to unimaginable commands from the Devil himself. Jerry, as a developing Christian preacher, might well have recognized and appreciated the good and evil forces at battle. Few others, though, may have shared such insights!

When Nathan hit that home run over the left field fence, Jerry believed something more than a softball was smashed; something came out of its cocoon—a butterfly flew over an old picket fence. Confidence was gained by someone who needed it, and Jerry witnessed and felt that change. Hope was alive for several people that hot, dusty day, and for Jerry, it spurred an interest in and recognition of something more than just spurious, but rather a demonstration of the strength of the human spirit. Most important was the greater need for attention and companionship, including witnessing reflections emanating from a wrinkled Negro face that echoed thanks from a caring friend. Jerry saw firsthand how important it was to connect and demonstrate empathy. That would be something he would learn and do more completely as a pastor over a lifetime. Was Jerry perfect? *No.* Did he make foolish mistakes? *Yes,* probably more than he would like to remember and admit to. But the SMG was just a little insane, certainly naïve, but faithfully growing, too!

Buddy Logan graduated from Wolcott College and worked in Terre Haute, selling stocks and bonds. He learned much from the hospital patients, especially forgiveness from one who never stopped running around a softball diamond until he found a friend who accepted him. For the two of them, human emotions were laid bare, now encapsulated in time but also providing lasting memories—good ones.

The kid with the slightest of limp, the biggest and tallest member of the SMG, always remained optimistic about the future. He and Zachary spent many Sundays in Elm City at church, hearing about God, singing more than just a little off-key, songs of praise and hope. The choir histories are long gone, but perhaps a foundation for reverence to spiritual things was laid down in a Sunday school. As kids, the anxiety of standing in front of grownups and first memorizing, and then reciting religious statements now seems of small relevance. But the importance of that church experience was the learning of a "creed for life" that must have been at some level forged into an early and complicated, amorphous belief system that for Zachary, and no doubt others too, patiently waited for just the right and best time to come alive—adulthood.

Buddy always wondered about the unexplainable gross and illegal behavior of a softball coach. For the longest time, he tried to find some rational explanation for what happened to Ken Matway. He never did. It seemed crazy and out of place in a supposed ordered universe. But that might have been the point. The universe, as constructed, is perfect; humans are not. His caring and concern about Ken's hurt and anger and his prolonged involvement with a kid with a broken spirit revealed a growing and maturing adult.

Gale Rogers moved to Kokomo and became a barber. Over the years, he listened to the joys and sorrows of his clients as he cut hair and shaved faces. He continued to play the clarinet in a local jazz band and was never to forget a group of musicians from around Elm City who taught him more than just the collective reading of sheet music and instrumental operations. He and that dance band helped a group of lonely people at the state hospital connect, shuffle around an outside dance pavilion, and maybe for just one moment, feel some happiness. The little talks and smiles the band gave forth helped form a small reality for people so much in need of human connections. Gale later became a steady and strong member in his local church, where he played in the orchestra. Did this change in attitude have anything to do with his experiences growing up with a gang of boys in such a one-horse town? Maybe the best answer is that the small imprints of caring for others did engender a soul and

conscience, and become a major part of Gale's
character.

Dwight Allan made a career in the Air Force and
Navy, and served as a patriot all over the world. He
and Zachary formed a close bond with many shared
secrets; so many girlfriends and so many funny
stores never to be forgotten, while there was a
forming of identity for the two of them. They have
kept in touch for over sixty years and have traded
information and advice to each other. Confidence
and respect as boyhood friends never left. How could
it? It was cemented together early on the grounds of
a basketball court and an oval track which extended
around a state mental asylum grounds, where they
learned about both the *insanity* and *sanity* of life
and, most importantly, themselves.

Jim Allan graduated from college, taught, and
later became an administrator at a large school for
the hearing impaired out West. He saw hurt and
disabilities from a group of mental patients when he
was growing up, insanity in the raw, which later may
have led to a career of helping others who
communicate from silent worlds.

He spent time with David Wright and learned
about sign language. The two of them became
friends, and Jim realized how David struggled with
life and parents who were never able to
communicate, except through signing. He admired
David's focus and resilience, and through many
opportunities taught David about being strong in the
face of interpersonal difficulties, especially when
some thoughtless boys from around town made fun
of a kid with deaf parents who they referred to as
'deaf and dumb.'

Armed with much humor, Jim was always a
favorite among the gang, and while he was quiet
about his spiritual beliefs, on more than one

occasion, his eyes filled with tears when others spoke of their walk with God. Jim searched and had questions and doubts about a "higher power." Did he find answers? Only he knows for sure.

———◇———

Steve Jackson was the one gang member to return to Elm City after college. He raised his family and became an important part of the community. His choice of careers was easy—a continuation of the family business of selling insurance. His lighthearted way with others, and his ability to organize so many SMG athletic games, was put to good use as he became involved in local city government, where he learned the art of strong negotiation. He may have long forgotten about his work in a cornfield one summer, but his work buddy, Zachary Stevens, never did.

That poor, wretched girl in the back of a truck— did she ever survive such abuse? Voices are locked in time. But strong betting might be that Steve heard more than just brief muses of noises in the wind as he drove around Elm City for so many years, selling life insurance and catching a glimpse or two of activity on the old state hospital grounds.

———◇———

Joe Gruneau dealt with many challenges growing up. He became restless and eventually joined the U.S. Navy. Things, unknown to others, happened in his boyhood home that may have contributed to his eagerness to leave Elm City, including an uncompromising stepfather who was abusive to a kid just trying to grow up. But Joe survived, even after receiving a careless bullet to the stomach and finding himself in some other place of serenity, albeit for too short a time. One might only guess what spiritual things were laid down in heart, mind and soul. He eventually married a young girl from a faraway place out West and became the first of the

SMG to become a father. He later went into law enforcement.

Zachary believes that Joe never forgot the hospital patients, especially one who took an interest in him and taught him about stock cars and the unwiring of a human brain. Yes, he saw and witnessed a lot of strange things, but the most important feelings he spoke of many times were the good ones; ones that came from helping others. Other memories, such as of a stepfather, were gathered as dust and thrown to blowing winds.

Willie Gray joined the U.S. Army and then came back for a short time and worked in a local bar. His humor remained, as did the memories of his many practice miniature golf sessions on the state hospital grounds; and time spent interacting with others, including people who smiled at the wrong times and asked so many strange questions. His dream to become a golf professional never materialized. Sometime in his early twenties, Willie left town and was never heard from again. A more complete story waits to be told.

Zachary Stevens and his journeys were both similar to and different from the rest of his gang. He struggled with immaturity and kept the inner child hidden inside, and not very well, only to have it reappear without notice. It became an internal shield of protection at times to a seemingly hostile world. He remembered the insanity of a vicious robbery, and how he cowardly took no responsibility for helping law enforcement catch a brutal man. A later encounter with a thief and a knife partly revealed his personal beliefs about himself—gutless.

Yes, Zachary let an old friend down; one who had taken blows to the head and never fully recovered. Many internal conversations have been held between mind and spirit. Honesty and maturity always fought to be more active in a personality, but slippages occurred. He tried, sometimes more successfully than not, to make excuses, to use denial, or finally just to accept his blunders, even when others counseled, "You were just young and didn't know better." Advice from others, though, never took the scars from the biting reality of an all and permanent incomplete perfection within each one of us, until death.

Arrival at adulthood—in one piece or many—was a drama of mistakes, misjudgments, and covered-up feelings. Zachary needed to get away from his town, to grow and experience life without the excess baggage of memories and failures strapped on a back.

After high school, he left Elm City and joined the Navy. He worked as a medic, became serious about school, and after the military went on to college and eventually trained as a mental health worker. His choice of career was predictable. The influence of the state hospital, and its broad reach and call, was strong and very real. By learning and feeling and searching through others' lives, Zachary found small facets of his own existence.

His life was both happy and challenging at times, but during one difficult period, he would remember a verse from the Bible learned many years ago during a sweaty day in a small Sunday school room. The narrative asked for forgiveness and an acknowledgement of God's love and Jesus's saving power. Words came alive, and a prayer was prayed with sincerity and humbleness.

When he now comes back to Elm City, he finds himself returning to the old state hospital grounds, looking for something—but what? Maybe it is a lost part of a self.

He sees a guy sitting on a bench, just staring, not talking. Could it be his old friend Nathan? No, it is someone else. And that kid playing baseball with his dad on the old softball field; his throws reminds

Zachary of another boy from years gone by, someone who was such a good athlete, a friend and confidant who shared his personal stories of God. Would it be all right to just yell out, "Hey, Jerry! It's Zachary. I think I can still hit a small ball with a broomstick, for I have not forgotten what you taught me about keeping my eyes open and ready."

Out of the corner of one of Zachary's eyes, he sees another man, one that is running around the grounds. Or was it just a car that whizzed by? Then he remembers about a hospital friend of long ago named "Champ." They had become friends for a brief time. Champ would do whatever command was given him: "Run, Champ;" "Hop, Champ;" "Skip, Champ;" "Jump, Champ." Some of the kids laughed at him, but not Zachary. The two of them formed a friendship, and they communicated through the pitch and catch of an old baseball. *Someday that big old guy will learn his real name, and no doubt a lot more too,* Zachary quietly mumbles to himself. He closes his eyes and fantasizes what Champ's face and his smile might look like on that blessed day.

Across the street from the state hospital, Zachary can still view the house where he grew up—the one with such a long front porch and a swing, ensconced and still hanging alone, waiting for someone. Zachary remembers a mother who tried her best to raise a young boy after a dad fell off the radar screen of life, while his son tried to reach high enough to hold onto a very small piece of a Pop's latent love. Yes, his parents failed at marriage and a hole was created in a boy's heart, but he never stopped loving them.

But there also remains a vacuum of sadness. The last time he was with his mother, years ago, the two of them had an argument over some petty issue. Nothing was resolved. She would unexpectedly develop a brain aneurism and depart this world. He feels a tear well up and trickle down the side of his face as he wishes for that "just one more conversation of closure and forgiveness" for the hurtful things he must have said that day.

The gang had reunions. Some adults attended, others didn't. All laughed and remembered the fun, and some of the tragedies as well. With passing years, the gatherings became fewer, but telephones, mail, and the internet helped keep connections.

At one of the early reunions, someone asked about Ken Matway. He never came back to Elm City after his incident with Jeff Kitchen. Pain and emotional hurt must have stayed around for a long time. The SMG found it awkward talking about what had happened to Ken. Jerry, now Pastor Little, said, "I wish I had tried to say more to Ken when that incident with Jeff happened. I did want to encourage Ken, but maybe I was too young to be of much help. I bet he would have many things to tell me now."

When Jerry finished, the room suddenly became silent. There was a time of uneasiness, and perhaps a snicker or two. Steve Jackson changed the subject and said that he had enjoyed college, but he complained about the effort required to pass some of the courses. "I have always looked forward to the time when I would be working at a real job."

Dwight Allan asked about Nathan Russell: "What a change in that guy after he got that first hit. I have never seen a face become so bright and happy. I sure hope he is doing okay. I remember that guy and his laugh. I still hear it sometimes. It made me feel good inside."

One of the SMG, Zachary can't remember who, recounted that he accepted Jesus as a savior one lonely night somewhere, in some other place, perhaps on-board a ship far from Elm City.

"The stars never seemed so bright, and my heart felt such relief. I don't know why or where any of those feelings and thoughts came from, but someone must have been praying hard for me. I never got

much spiritual or religious stuff when I went to any
of the 'Four Corner Churches' in Elm City. I must
have been asleep a lot when personal accountability
and salvation were mentioned."

A few of the SMG looked at the person speaking
and wondered if he had gone crazy, while Jerry Little
said nothing, but just smiled. Maybe he knew
something and wasn't sharing, but then again . . .

Gale came to one of the group meetings,
recounted that he was doing well, and now had a
family. He often thought about some of the patients
and what might have happened to them. He noted
that the many differences he had observed in
patients from the state hospital had helped prepare
him for adulthood, and he was glad for the
experience.

The clients he serviced in his barbershop also
had many personalities, and even prejudice. He
smiled and said that once a guy in his barbershop
began talking about a neighbor who was "crazy as a
loon." The guy talked about hearing voices. "Those
nuts need to be put to sleep, or at least kept locked
up and away from society; they do no one no good."

The reserved barber said little while the client
rambled on. Inwardly, though, Gale felt silent tears
slurp around in a winsome mind and heart. He
finished cutting the guy's hair, and said, "May I have
five minutes of your time? I would like to tell you a
story about my boyhood."

All of the SMG listened intently as Gale recounted
this story, the silence penetrating. Emotions each
grown gang member felt at that moment were private
and understood, so very real.

Jim Allan spoke, and said how he always wanted
to be a strong champion of the underserved. He
hated the word "disabled." He saw and heard so
much of that as a young kid. The mental patients
were his friends, and their suffering "burned a big
hole into my heart and soul that never left. I just

knew that someday I would work with people who did not have all of the advantages I had.

"The work I did as a student basketball coach at the deaf school taught me many things, but mostly that I needed to accept people with no pretense and help them grow, and not allow them to feel sorry for themselves. Happiness and success must be measured in many ways. Acceptance has to be a start."

Then Joe surprised everyone. He recounted that he still wrote and kept in touch with the man who had sustained a head injury and had been a patient at the hospital. The guy recovered well, but never forgot how much help Joe had been to him.

When Joe came back to Elm City, he made a special point of driving to see this ex-patient friend from childhood—a man who claimed to once hear voices from strange places, voices that long ago departed for good. What remained was a friendship that never went away, but instead stayed around and became a true blessing for two very needy people.

Joe never spoke of any great spiritual transformation, but Zachary and Jerry remembered "an unusual trip" Joe had taken many years ago after a terrible accident. Jerry had told Joe that maybe he confronted angels and was very close to God; however, Joe was never able to reach high enough to grasp what Jerry was trying to explain— that at times, heaven was closer than we think, even within our personal grasp.

The gang kidded Jerry about now being such a "religious man," for they knew him in another lifetime when spiritual things seemed farthest removed from any sphere of influence he ever operated within. Joe then spoke up and acknowledged that he understood the battles of conscience that Jerry experienced, and that before he left the reunion, he wanted to talk about God and hoped that Pastor Little might be able to clarify some things for him.

Jerry smiled and said, "For sure."

The two men, still buddies and forever friends for life, then took a long walk into the night.

Epilogue

THERE HAS ALWAYS BEEN BUT ONE unescapable fact about life; everyone wants to live forever. The topic of death and eternity has never been fully understood, but rather feared, with the knowledge that it will surely happen. We all live under the shadow of death and seek not to talk about it. Zachary Stevens and his gang always hoped to escape the dreaded experience—they will not.

An uncompromising "Dr. Death" continually scouts and finds recruits and gingerly handles their souls, while remaining surprised at the inherent motivation for both good and evil acts that are simultaneously found in each human being. But this dreaded being, feared by all humanity, comes so quietly and unannounced, patiently waiting for the final, ultimate decision of action to be given . . .

Now, over sixty years later, for a scrawny kid from Elm City, Indiana, there are still memories: of a short, stocky, and lisping church pastor who first introduced him to a God and a spiritual life that allowed for a seed of hope to be laid down, then brought to fruition so many years later; of forgiveness to a militaristic scoutmaster who matured and taught a kid about sore butts and responsibility while turning out countless numbers of Eagle Scouts; of some lost camp in Kentucky where a little reality, a little humor, and honesty showed up to be recognized; of a gang of boys who forever were friends, always supporting each other; and finally that girl from high school, his first love, the one with the thickest and longest yellow hair and a smile that ignited such deep passions. Unfortunately, he was so unkind to her. Where did she end up? He bets she married early and had lots of kids. There were other people throughout a lifetime, some of whom he recalled less than fondly, but they all blend together with passing years, and past unpleasant incidents become of no relevance.

Death circles, pawing, and lusting at a soul, still unable to pluck it away; stubbornly, Zachary continues to try and hold onto a life and keep that most important *dream of a new day*, one designed to be beautiful and so close to heart and mind. The sky will be a brilliant azure blue, accompanied with tinges of red and gold extending in varied directions. The place he will be in, reside in, cannot be totally describable. There will be a strong sense of well-being, a fluttering of physical lightness, a feeling of laughter inside a heart and mind while any dimension of time, fast or slow, is no longer of any certainty, not even partially comprehended.

And now, reality: *'Pass on, good soul, you've fought a fair fight, find your final passage and peace, welcome home . . . '*

Quite by accident, it appears, Zachary comes upon a dusty ball field where a group of boys and grown-ups toss what appears to be a baseball. He wonders if he is not in some other "body cover." The place where he finds himself is certainly not where he has ever resided before.

He joins the boys and is surprised to recognize so many friends from his youth—his gang, and patients from a state mental hospital lost in time. He locates his mother and father smiling, reunited as they stand afar. And isn't that David Wright *speaking* and laughing with his parents, no hands or fingers necessary for communication? Nobody reports hurt or pain, sorrow or discontent. There is no mention of voices inside peoples' heads, strange behaviors, or lost old men and women without names and without hope; no dark shadows to cast ugliness. Instead, there is a serene peace.

Wait! A recognizable voice comes forth from someone he thinks he might know. This is no whisper, but a sound that cries out loudly as it cracks and shudders across time, space, and memory so clearly: "Play ball! Bite the dust! Watch out for wild pitches! We are together again and maybe, just maybe, we may play here if only for a short time, and then again tomorrow, and many more tomorrows, God willing!"

"But let me reveal to you a wonderful secret. We will not all die, but we will all be transformed. It will happen in a moment, in a blink of an eye, when the last trumpet is blown. For when the trumpet sounds, those who have died will be raised to live forever. And we who are living will also be transformed into bodies that will never die; our mortal bodies must be transformed into immortal bodies."

—*1st Corinthians 15:50-53* (The NIV Study Bible, New International Version, Zondervan, 1985)

www.ingramcontent.com/pod-product-compliance
Lightning Source LLC
Chambersburg PA
CBHW070918260626
47162CB00007B/2719